Wisconsin WEDDINGS

Wisconsin WEDDINGS

Three Brides Can Never Say Never
to Love Again

ANDREA BOESHAAR

BARBOUR
PUBLISHING

Always a Bridesmaid © 2006 by Andrea Boeshaar
The Long Ride Home © 2004 by Andrea Boeshaar
The Summer Girl © 2003 by Andrea Boeshaar

ISBN 978-1-59789-631-3

Scripture quotations are taken from the HOLY BIBLE, NEW INTERNATIONAL VERSION®. NIV®. Copyright © 1973, 1978, 1984 by International Bible Society. Used by permission of Zondervan. All rights reserved.

Scripture quotations are taken from the King James Version of the Bible.

This book is a work of fiction. Names, characters, places, and incidents are either products of the author's imagination or used fictitiously. Any similarity to actual people, organizations, and/or events is purely coincidental.

Cover photography: Joseph Sohm/Corbis Images

Published by Barbour Publishing, Inc., P.O. Box 719, Uhrichsville, Ohio 44683, www.barbourbooks.com

Our mission is to publish and distribute inspirational products offering exceptional value and biblical encouragement to the masses.

ecpa Member of the
Evangelical Christian
Publishers Association

Printed in the United States of America.

Dear Reader,

    I'm a Wisconsin woman, born and raised, and what I find incredible about this fine state is its four seasons. Each is a rich display of God's mastery, from the snow-covered farm fields in winter to the budding tulips and apple blossoms in spring, from the hot sandy beaches and cool—make that cold—waters of Lake Michigan in summer to the crunchy brown, gold, and magenta colored leaves in autumn.

    Fall is my favorite time of year. There's nothing more breathtaking and inspiring for me than to look out over a valley of flaming treetops.

    There's much more I could say about Wisconsin's many landscapes, and I tried to incorporate a touch of some or all of them in the stories you're about to read. I hope I'm able to whisk you away to Wisconsin for a brief mental and spiritual retreat. Afterward, I pray you'll feel refreshed and encouraged.

    So clear your mind of its worries and troubles and escape to Wisconsin for a bit of romance and, of course, a few weddings!

Wishing you God's best,
Andrea Boeshaar
www.andreaboeshaar.com

Always a Bridesmaid

Dedication

To Sally, Nancy, Jeri, Christine, and Tamela—
my Red Pen Club buddies.
Thanks for your comments and suggestions. . .
and especially for cheering me on as I wrote this book!

Chapter 1

The news of her younger sister's engagement hit Melody Cartwright like a thick slab of icing off the side of an expensive wedding cake.

"Y—you're getting married?" She could hardly make the words form on her tongue.

Bonnie nodded while sheer delight heightened her lovely pale features. "Isn't it great?"

"But you just met the guy."

"Two months ago," Bonnie countered. "I wouldn't say I 'just' met him."

Mel considered her half sister. Even with her blond hair tousled and wearing an oversized red and white baseball jersey, Bonnie made a fetching sight. From her huge blue eyes and pert little nose to her slender tanned legs and polished toenails—any man with eyes in his head could see she was a cute little package. No big surprise that Bonnie had gotten herself engaged.

But to whom? Mel shook her head. They knew nothing about this guy!

"A wedding to plan," their mother, Ellen Stenson, said on a dreamy note. She clasped her hands together. "This will be so much fun."

"Oh, won't it, though?"

Mel took in the gleeful expressions on Bonnie's and Mom's faces. They were so alike. Mom was Hollywood gorgeous, too, and typically became absorbed in Bonnie's pie-in-the-sky ideas.

"Aren't we jumpin' the gun a little bit here?" Dad asked. He sat in one of the matching armchairs on this sunny Saturday morning, attempting to read his newspaper.

"You're right, Bill. First things first." Slipping her hand around Bonnie's elbow, Mom guided her to the red, beige, and blue plaid sofa where they both sat down. "Tell us how you two met."

"I met him at work. He's a med student." She blushed. "Actually, I helped push through his application and he got accepted. He'll start this fall. Meanwhile, he's working part-time as a nursing assistant."

"Nursing is women's work, isn't it?" Dad remarked, peeking over the top of the sports section.

The ignorance of his remark caused Mel to grin; she knew he meant no insult. She knew her stepfather well. After all, he was the only dad she'd ever known. Her biological father had been killed during a routine Air Force training

9

maneuver shortly after Mel's birth. Within a year, Mom had met and married Bill Stenson, a steely construction worker with a cushy heart. Eighteen months later, Bonnie was born.

However, this current scenario seemed a tad unfair to Melody. How could it be that her younger sister would get married before she would? That was Mel's dream—to be loved, honored, and cherished. But lately, with all her friends making their way to the altar, Mel was a bridesmaid over and over again, never the bride.

And now Bonnie. . .

Lord, please quell this envy in my soul!

"Dad, being a nursing assistant isn't 'women's work,' " Bonnie argued. "It's hard work and preparation for becoming a *doctor*."

"Humph." Dad raised his newspaper a little higher so that only the bald patch on his head was visible from Mel's vantage point.

"We have lunch together every day," Bonnie said, beaming. "We meet in the cafeteria."

"How—romantic." Mom pushed out a smile.

Mel folded her arms, wondering who paid. After all, a part-time nursing assistant wouldn't earn a lot of income. Melody worked a full-time job as a dental receptionist who, at times, assisted the hygienists. She didn't earn a whole lot of money and felt grateful her parents allowed her to live with them until she finished college via the Internet courses she took—or until she got married, the latter being Mel's preference. But if she weren't living at home, she didn't know how she'd afford rent, car payments, gasoline, her cell phone, utilities, ongoing college expenses, plus her student loans—and romantic cafeteria lunches.

"He's so wonderful," Bonnie gushed. "He's handsome and kind and—"

"Let's see your ring," Mel said, determined to shake off her misgivings and be happy for her sister.

"Oh. Well—I don't have a ring yet." Bonnie wiggled her bare left ring finger. "I have to pick it out at the jeweler's."

"Hmm. Well, did he give you something else, like a locket or a bracelet?"

"When did you get so materialistic?" Bonnie charged. "No, he didn't give me anything, but I love *him*, not inanimate objects."

"No offense intended, Bon-Bon," Mel said, using her little sister's nickname. "I just thought maybe he gave you. . ." Melody looked from Mom to Dad and realized they wanted to hear the answer to this question, too. "I just thought he'd given you a token of his love and commitment."

"It's coming." Bonnie relaxed as a wistful smile curved her pink lips. "I'm so in love."

Mel didn't like the sound of this already. It seemed too fly-by-night. Too fast. Choosing one's spouse needed to be done with great care. Melody had learned that fact the hard way.

She'd known a guy in college who was bound for medical school. Scott Ramsay. She'd never forget him. Back then, Mel had thought he was Mr. Right, but he'd turned out to be Mr. All-Wrong! While she'd fallen in love with him, Scott had been dating half the female population on campus. That experience—while it took place more than three years ago—had been devastating. What's more, it had taught Melody to be very wary of whirlwind relationships where the opposite sex and her heart were concerned.

The big sister in her wanted to spare Bonnie the same anguish.

"Did it—um—ever occur to you that this guy might be using you, Bon-Bon? He could be an opportunist looking forward to you putting him through med school."

"Good point," Dad said.

Melody found the gumption to continue. "Bonnie, think about it. You work at the medical college as the dean's administrative assistant, which means you've got connections. You already got him accepted—"

"No! That's not how it is." Bonnie stood, and her sapphire eyes flashed with anger. "Why can't anyone be happy for me? Why is everyone being so negative?"

Dad lowered his newspaper to his lap. It lay there in a wrinkled heap. "Oh, now, don't start crying, Bonnie. I can't stand it when you girls cry."

Mom stood. "Bonnie, we're all—happy for you. It's just—well, such a shock. You haven't mentioned this young man before this morning." Mom's forehead wrinkled in a frown. "He is *young*, isn't he?"

"Of course he is!" Bonnie stamped her foot. "Do you think I'd marry some old geezer?"

"Watch it there, girly," Dad warned with a teasing gleam in his hazel eyes. "You're treading on thin ice."

Melody laughed, and the atmosphere in the room changed at once.

Wearing a hint of a smile, Bonnie sat back down on the sofa. Mom did the same. Then, as Bonnie began babbling away about her fiancé, Mel walked to the kitchen and poured a cup of coffee. All the while she half listened to the conversation taking place in the living room.

"You didn't even tell us you were dating," Mom said. "Now suddenly you're—engaged?"

"Well, I didn't really know I was dating, either. But then. . . It just happened. We knew we were. . ." She paused dramatically. ". . .*in love.*"

Mel sipped her coffee as her father strode into the kitchen. Reaching around her, he grabbed a mug from the cupboard.

"This is like a bad soap opera," he groused.

"For sure." Melody grinned. She'd always appreciated her dad's sense of humor—even during the tough times.

11

"And just wait until I get my hands on this guy. Imagine asking my daughter to marry him when he doesn't even talk to me first! I mean—I haven't even met him."

"Right. And I'm sure you'd want to meet his folks, too. What if he was raised by an ax murderer or something?"

Deep creases appeared on Dad's brow. "Oh no; I never thought of that!"

"Dad, I'm kidding." Mel laughed before taking a drink of coffee. She loved to tease her stepfather—and he teased her right back. "I'm sure this guy's parents are nice people."

"We'll see, won't we?" He shook his balding head. "And what about his faith? I just hope he's a believer!"

A moment later, Mom appeared in the doorway of the sunny yellow kitchen. Her eyes were wide, and a tight smile tugged at her lips. The expression on her face said she'd overheard their conversation. "According to Bonnie, he's a believer. And guess what, Bill? God's granted your wish. Your youngest daughter's beloved will be here in less than an hour!"

"What!" Dad set down his coffee mug with a pronounced *thunk* before moaning his displeasure. "Saturday mornings are for leisure, family-only time!"

"I know, I know." Mom stepped into the kitchen, her hands raised palms up as if to quell further argument. "But we have to meet him sooner or later. And as serious as Bonnie is about this man, I'd say the sooner the better!" She paused before adding, "Besides, weddings take a long time to plan."

Mel deposited her coffee mug on the counter beside Dad's. She had to shower and dress; she still wore her cotton pink and white pajamas.

Mom sighed. "Good thing I cleaned the house yesterday." She tossed a glance at Mel. "I get first dibs on the bathroom."

"Go for it." Mel smiled in spite of the profound sense of foreboding gnawing at the pit of her stomach.

∽

Some ninety minutes later, Melody stood in the large upstairs bedroom she shared with Bonnie. Her family lived in a typical Milwaukee, Wisconsin, bungalow; it had two bedrooms downstairs along with the living room, dining room, kitchen, and one bathroom. Mel and Bonnie's bedroom had once been a walk-up attic until Dad refinished it and the adjoining stairwell. Now the sisters shared a feminine peach-colored suite that included two half-wall partitions that gave them a semblance of privacy. However, Dad hadn't had the foresight to build another bathroom.

After dressing in blue jeans and a short-sleeved yellow cotton shirt, Mel stood in front of the closet mirror and brushed out her short, light brown hair that was just long enough on the sides to tuck behind her ears. She could hear voices wafting up from downstairs: Bonnie's laugh and Dad's baritone as he spoke to Bonnie's intended.

I can't believe Mom and Dad are going to allow Bonnie to marry someone they've never met until now and Bonnie has only casually dated—if you can call meeting in the cafeteria for lunch "dating."

The situation brought a sigh to Mel's lips. Weddings. She'd be a bridesmaid for the umpteenth time in June when her friends Darla and Max got married. Mel had grown up with Max, but Darla had only recently moved to the area; however, they were all a part of the career group at church.

And then Bonnie's wedding, whenever that date would be—Mel would most likely stand up at her younger sister's special ceremony.

Always a bridesmaid and never a bride. Lord, it just doesn't seem fair!

Melody crossed the room and stepped out onto the railed wooden platform. The city had required that another exit route be built for the attic bedroom, so Dad complied and added on this small porch overlooking the backyard.

She gazed upward. The sun warmed her face and neck. Temperatures were unseasonably warm for late April, and after last week's rain, the clear azure skies were a welcome reprieve.

Lord, please take away my jealousy over Bonnie getting married. Mel gazed heavenward, then closed her eyes. *Please help me to be happy for her. I would want her to be happy for me if I were getting married. And on that subject, Lord, I just wondered—*

"Hi, Melody!"

Her prayers interrupted, she looked down and saw Luke Berringer lift his hand in a quick wave.

She waved back. Luke had been her next-door neighbor ever since Mel could remember. They'd gone through elementary school and high school together and attended the same church. Luke was as familiar a fixture in Melody's life as the chestnut tree in her backyard—and she gave Luke just about as much thought.

"Are you going bowling this afternoon with the career group? We're going out to eat afterward."

"No. Can't go." Mel had actually forgotten all about the outing. "We're having company. In fact, I think he's arrived. I need to get myself downstairs. See ya later."

She waved again, and before Luke could say another thing, she reentered the bedroom. After giving her hair another good brushing and a shot of hair spray, she prayerfully descended the steps into the back hallway just off the kitchen and headed for the living room to meet her younger sister's fiancé.

∽

That woman is really bad for my ego, Luke thought as he resumed raking his yard.

He blew out a frustrated breath. He'd been infatuated with Melody Cartwright since the fourth grade, but she barely knew he existed. During high school he'd been too shy to ask her out, not that his parents would have allowed it. His folks, both now in heaven with Jesus, believed dating was a prelude to marriage and not the "sport" society made it out to be. Luke had adhered to their wishes. He didn't date in high school, but in the years that followed, he dated here and there, although he hadn't found a woman who captured his full range of emotions like Melody did. He admired her tenacity, her wit, her lovely smile—and *wow*, could that woman sing! She lived up to her name, that's for sure, except he hadn't heard her sing in a long while. She'd dropped out of the choir at church when she came home from college a few years ago. Nevertheless, Luke sensed her deep faith. As for looks, Melody was about the prettiest girl he knew, but pretty in a wholesome way—one his mother had approved of. Mom had always adored "Mellie," and now Luke would sure like to date her—and in his parents' sense of the word. He was no longer a shy and reclusive boy, and at twenty-six years old, he'd already forged out a successful career for himself as a real estate agent. He'd purchased the house he'd been raised in, and he couldn't help thinking about a wife and family as he roamed around the large rooms.

Luke raked out a pile of muck from underneath the evergreen bushes. They grew along the chain-link fence separating the Stensons' yard from his. So how could he get Melody to take notice of him? Luke hadn't a clue. He'd tried just about everything except a bullhorn. Even Dan Rebholtz, the pastor overseeing the career group at church, had commented on Luke's interest in Melody. Several of his friends knew about it, too. Why was it obvious to others but not her?

Well, maybe it wasn't meant to be. Luke tried to keep an open mind. He wanted God's will for his life, after all.

He just wanted Melody to be a part of it.

Chapter 2

M el, come on!"

"I'm coming." She strode across the dining room's hardwood floor and smiled at her sister's enthusiasm.

Bonnie took several impatient steps toward her, looped her arm around Melody's, and propelled her into the living room.

Seconds later, Melody came face-to-face with her sister's heartthrob.

Disbelief rocked her as she took in the man's reddish-brown hair, teal green eyes, roguelike grin, and broad shoulders.

No, it can't be!

"Mel, I want you to meet Scott Ramsay," Bonnie said in a girlish tone. "Scott, this is my sister, Melody Cartwright."

Recognition flashed in his eyes, but he didn't acknowledge it. "Nice to meet you."

He extended his right hand, although Mel didn't take it. Hurt, anger, betrayal, envy—practically every emotion known to humankind pumped through her veins. Her face flamed with all she felt inside.

"Actually, we've already met." Melody's tone was sharper than she intended, so she made a concerted effort to soften it. "Yeah," she said, ignoring Scott's look of chagrin, "we met at college, the University of Madison. We were part of SFC, Students for Christ." Melody tipped her head, surprised and hurt by the blank expression on Scott's face.

"Um—yeah, I participated in SFC, but. . ." He narrowed his gaze as though struggling to remember her. "What's your name again?"

Mel figured his question was intended to maim—and it did. It gouged open a three-and-a-half-year-old wound.

Years ago, Scott had said he loved her on more than one occasion. He'd whispered her name in the most intimate of ways. How could he forget?

Then again, he'd had a virtual harem on campus. Scott put King Solomon to shame—before he vanished, that is.

Mel had searched high and low for him, fearing something terrible had happened. But what she found were other women looking for Scott, too—and one was pregnant. Ginger Atavack. Feeling helpless and alone, the young woman chose to have an abortion in spite of Melody's attempts to talk her out of it.

"Mel and I are half sisters," Bonnie said. She'd obviously sensed that Melody was at a loss for words. "Her last name is different because she's the only Cartwright grandchild and Mom promised Mel's grandmother she wouldn't change it. My last name is. . . Well, you know—my last name." Bonnie giggled, evidently embarrassed by her uncharacteristic babbling.

Scott tore his gaze from Mel and bestowed a handsome smile on her younger sister. It was a smile she remembered well.

Melody felt sick.

"Well, it's great that you've met Scott already, sweetie pie," Mom said, wearing an odd expression.

Glancing at her mother, Melody sensed she'd have some explaining to do later. But for now, she'd have to hide behind a polite facade.

"Well, let's all sit down and eat." Dad held out his hand, indicating the dining room table. "Don't know about all of you, but I'm starved."

Mel took a seat across the table from Bonnie and Scott. Throughout their lunch, which consisted of hard rolls and deli-sliced cold cuts and cheese, Melody kept her gaze as far from Scott as possible. It was a good thing she liked to eat when she felt stressed, or she might have seemed rude and called further attention to herself. She didn't want her family to think she was jealous of Bonnie—even though she was, to a degree—and she'd never told her parents about Scott, although she'd meant to. But between classes, homework, her involvement in SFC, and making time to see him, she'd never gotten the chance. She had dreamed of bringing him home during spring break. However, by then, Scott had disappeared.

With their meal finished, Melody jumped up and offered to clear the table and wash dishes.

"Well, thanks, honey." Mom smiled. "Now I can spend time getting to know Scott."

A grateful gleam shone in Bonnie's blue eyes.

"Hey, no problem." Melody carried plates into the kitchen. Little did her family know that she wouldn't have sat in the living room and chatted with Scott Ramsay if her life depended on it. The more she remembered about him, the more she felt hatred worming its way into her heart.

Lord, help me. I'm feeling anything but Christlike at the moment.

Mel battled her emotions and focused on the tasks at hand: putting away leftovers and loading the dishwasher. She wondered what she should do about Scott. How would she tell her parents? And what about Bonnie? Melody knew her sister was crazy about the guy.

So was I—once.

At the sound of a man clearing his throat, Mel whirled around and found the object of her tumultuous thoughts standing in the kitchen's entrance.

"What can I do for you, Scott? Want another cola?"

Shaking his head, he stepped forward, and Mel willed herself to stay calm.

"I remember you. It's coming back to me now. We were friends, but I can tell you don't feel that way about me anymore. In fact, I'd say you dislike me."

"Friends?" Melody blinked. "Is that what you call it?"

"Sure." Scott paused, and then a look of pity crossed his features. "Oh, I get it. You thought our relationship was something more, huh? That's too bad."

Melody clamped her jaw shut and glanced away from Scott's condescending stare.

"Look, I know I said and did some things in Madison that I shouldn't have. Those were wild days for me, but I'm a changed man."

"Yeah, that has yet to be determined."

He raised his hands in a helpless gesture.

"Scott?"

At the sound of Bonnie's voice, he pivoted, and Melody glanced at the doorway. Bonnie was dressed in a denim skirt and pink V-neck sweater that heightened her rosy complexion; it wasn't hard to see why Scott or any other man would be attracted to her.

And Melody felt it was her duty to protect her sister. She had a feeling Scott Ramsay hadn't changed all that much. But how did she sound the warning without appearing like a jealous green monster?

"I've been waiting for you, Scott." Bonnie sent him an uncertain smile. "Thought you got lost."

"Well, he does have a knack for disappearing," Melody mumbled under her breath.

Scott laughed it off. "Melody and I were reminiscing about our college days. We sure had some fun times in Madison, didn't we?" He nudged her with his elbow.

Melody wanted to sock him. How dare he make light of the worst time in her life! Because of Scott's "wild" days on the UWM campus, Melody's life would never be the same.

Neither would the lives of several other young women.

"So—um—did you end up graduating?" Scott ventured casually. His gaze rested on Melody.

She shook her head, deciding she'd rather die before admitting that he was the reason she didn't return to school.

"But she's taking correspondence courses," Bonnie offered. "She's close to earning her degree in English, right, Mel?"

"Right."

"I thought you were a music major."

"You remember that much, do you?" Mel slid her gaze to Scott.

A look of chagrin crossed his ruddy features. "Yep, it's all coming back to me."

"Mel decided she can do more with an English degree," Bonnie said. Confusion puckered her winged brows as she gazed from Scott to Mel.

Melody smiled at her sister. Bonnie had earned her degree in professional communication and business management in less than four years. Melody always found it amazing that for a woman with little to no common sense, Bonnie was really quite brilliant.

"What do you say we rejoin Mom and Dad in the living room?" Bonnie held out her hand to Scott. "I know they want to hear more about you."

Scott took it and the two strolled toward the doorway.

Bonnie glanced over her shoulder. "Coming, Mel?"

"No, I—um—I've got to go—somewhere."

"Oh yeah, today's the bowling outing with the career group."

Before Melody could answer, Bonnie had disappeared with Scott into the next room.

Mel sagged against the sink. She felt emotionally bruised from her exchange with Scott and feared more of the same would occur in the future. She had to do something. But what?

Deciding a drive would clear her head and get her out of the house, Mel ran upstairs, grabbed her purse, and then made her way outside and across the backyard to the carport. In this particular neighborhood, there were no driveways in front of or alongside the homes; instead, the garages were built just off the alleyway running parallel to the rear property line. The Stensons were fortunate to have a two-car garage, and Dad had built the carport for Mel's and Bonnie's vehicles. Both of their cars fit inside the open-ended structure, but with little room to spare. Still, it lent some protection against the harsh Wisconsin winters.

Climbing into her yellow Cavalier coupe, Melody stuck the key into the ignition and fired up the engine. She considered the career group outing, but she didn't feel like bowling, and she certainly didn't want to answer questions about Bonnie's new beau! Before Scott arrived, Bonnie had telephoned at least a dozen of her friends and announced she was getting married.

Lord, why is this happening?

Putting the car into gear, Mel backed out of the carport into the alley, concentrating on keeping enough distance between her vehicle and Bonnie's little red SRT; however, in doing so, Mel failed to look behind her—

Until it was too late.

Chapter 3

"Melody, are you hurt?"

Dazed, she blinked before staring up at the man holding open her car door. His light brown eyes were wide with concern; then the rest of his features came into focus.

"Luke!"

"I couldn't stop in time. I'm sorry. Are you all right?"

Melody shifted the lever into park, wiggled her toes, flexed her fingers, and did a few neck rolls. "I think I'm fine. Just a little shaken."

Luke extended his hand and helped Melody from the car. "Doesn't seem to be any damage to my vehicle, but your rear quarter panel got pretty smashed."

Melody gaped at the huge dent in the left side of her car. Although Luke couldn't have been going more than fifteen miles per hour, the collision had swung her vehicle forty-five degrees. Her Cavalier now faced one end of the alley and Luke's black Durango faced the other.

"Like I said, I couldn't stop in time."

"I–it was my fault," she stammered. "I should have looked before backing into the alley. But I was so worried about scratching Bonnie's car that I forgot to check for oncoming traffic."

Luke didn't reply but bent at the waist to give the damage to her car a closer inspection. Next he rechecked his SUV.

Melody thought about how she'd have to call her insurance agent on Monday. She had a five-hundred-dollar deductible, which meant she'd be forced to dip into her savings. Her goal was to have twenty thousand dollars in the bank by the time she got married so she could have the wedding she always wanted. She'd already selected her wedding gown and her colors—deep blue and gold—and she knew exactly where she'd hold her reception. All she needed was the groom and about fifteen thousand more dollars. Mel stared at her car. Another setback. Another dagger—tearing her dreams to shreds.

Unfortunately, in her imaginings about her wedding day, Melody had always pictured a man who looked very much like Scott Ramsay—Mr. All-Wrong—at her side. It was a disconcerting image.

Then she recalled all his empty promises to her and other women years ago, and now his adoring looks at Bonnie this afternoon.

What a jerk!

"Melody?"

She snapped from her musings and wiped an errant tear off her cheek. She hoped Luke hadn't seen the gesture.

"I think your whole back bumper is going to have to be replaced," he told her, wearing an expression of remorse. "Your Cavalier was no match for my Durango, I'm afraid." He paused. "Hey, are you all right?"

Melody couldn't contain the onslaught of emotion. It had already been a trying day, and this ill-fated fender bender just topped it off. Thankfully, it hadn't been a noisy accident. The last thing she needed was her family and Scott out here, gawking and asking questions.

Luke stepped closer, and Melody got a whiff of his spicy, woodsy cologne. "Don't cry. Do you have car insurance?"

She nodded.

He set his hand on her shoulder. "Tell you what—I'll pay half of your deductible. Will that help?"

"That's not necessary," she murmured. Oddly, his benevolence only made her tears flow all the more. "It's just been a bad day."

"Want me to get your dad?"

"No!"

At Luke's wide-eyed gaze, Melody felt the need to explain her exclamatory reply. Besides, Luke would probably hear about Bonnie's engagement soon enough.

"My parents have company. You see. . ." Melody sniffed. "This morning Bonnie announced she's getting married."

"No kidding!" Luke brought his chin back. "To whom?"

"No one you know. Bonnie met the guy at work. Except, here's the thing—I knew him in college."

"At UWM? In Madison?"

Mel bobbed her head, feeling a little surprised that Luke remembered which university she'd attended. "His name is Scott, and—well, I sort of dated him," she added, brushing the last of her tears away. A renewed burst of resentment caused her to clench her fists before she shoved them into the pockets of her jeans. "And now he's marrying Bonnie."

Melody gazed at her dented automobile while she spoke. But when Luke didn't reply, she glanced back at him. He looked as if someone had just punched him in the gut.

Melody blinked. "What's wrong?"

Luke seemed to shake himself. "Um—nothing."

He shifted, appearing uncomfortable, and Mel wondered what she'd said to put him at such unease.

"Well—um—if you're okay, I guess I'll be going."

"Oh, right. The career group outing." She waved her hand at him. "I'm fine. Sorry to have held you up this long."

Luke replied with a slight nod and then climbed into his SUV, leaving Melody with the distinct impression that she'd offended him.

As she slipped into the driver's seat of her car, she mentally went over everything she told Luke and couldn't fathom that any of her words would cause the slightest offense.

Unless Luke was interested in Bonnie.

Mel considered the notion as she started her engine and backed up. A sharp scraping noise caused her to slam on the brakes and grimace. Apparently, she wasn't driving anywhere now.

Moments later, Luke's SUV reappeared. Melody realized he'd gone around the block and driven back into the alley. He passed his driveway, pulled up beside her, and stopped. He rolled down his window, and Mel did the same.

"Let's go have a cup of coffee."

"What?" Mel found it a strange offer.

"You're obviously upset, and—well, I'm a friend. We've known each other forever. I—I just want to be there for you."

Melody was touched by his kindness. "That's nice, Luke." She even managed a smile. "But—"

"I don't feel like bowling anyhow."

Mel looked at her steering wheel and thought it over. "I have to get my car back into the carport until my dad can look at it."

"I'll help you. You drive, I'll push."

Melody opened her mouth to protest, but before she could utter a single sound, Luke pulled forward and parked. Then he hopped out of his SUV.

Melody relented; it didn't appear he'd take no for an answer anyway. Besides, having coffee with Luke would kill some time, and it sure beat hanging around the house with Scott Ramsay all afternoon.

∞

Luke willed his heart to stop hammering as he pushed Melody's vehicle into the carport. Was it jealousy or anxiety pumping through his veins?

Melody parked and killed the engine. Luke walked back to his Durango and slid behind the wheel. He hadn't meant to come off as pushy, but as a real estate agent, he'd learned how to propel people toward making decisions—especially when they wavered, as Melody had done moments ago. Had he left it up to her, she wouldn't be climbing into his SUV right now. But he couldn't let this opportunity escape him. This was his chance to be her hero—the moment he'd been waiting for since grade school!

Lord, help me not to react negatively to anything she might tell me about that guy she dated in Madison.

Luke clenched his jaw but then forced himself to relax. What did he expect? Melody was a lovely young lady with a matching personality. Of course she'd date. But what did that word really signify? Dinner at the pizza parlor a few times or something much more?

Luke sensed it was the latter or Melody wouldn't be so upset that the guy was marrying Bonnie.

He shook off his troubled thoughts and waited until Melody strapped on her seat belt before he drove to the end of the alley and made a right.

"It's a nice day. Want to go to that new coffeehouse on the east side, by the lake?"

"The farther away the better." There was an edge to her voice.

"I take it you're not pleased that Bonnie's marrying this guy. What did you say his name is? Scott?" Luke cleared his throat. "Is it because you still have feelings for him?"

"Which question do you want answered first?"

Luke raised his brows, feeling a tad insulted by her tone. But in the next moment, she apologized.

"I'm sorry, Luke. I don't mean to take it out on you. I'm just really upset and angry. I thought I was over Scott. I thought I didn't feel anything for him anymore, but then seeing him today brought back all the hurt I felt when he dumped me. Actually, I think it's more about the humiliation I still feel than anything else. And he was so arrogant today. Not a single word of remorse or regret. He's just a complete jerk, and I can't believe Bonnie's going to marry him!"

Luke felt that maybe he'd gotten in over his head. He sent up a quick prayer for wisdom. He didn't have much experience with "upset and angry" females. They scared him to death.

But this was different. Melody was a sister in Christ, his next-door neighbor, and the girl of his dreams. The way Luke saw it, no pain, no gain.

"So—um—how'd you meet Scott?"

"We met at one of the on-campus meetings for Students for Christ. Ooh, was I stupid. I didn't recognize a danger sign when it stared me in the face. I mean, talk about a wolf in sheep's clothing!"

The dam broke, and as he drove the next fifteen miles, Luke listened to Melody pour out her heart. In a way, Luke felt privileged to be her confidant, but he also had to force himself to watch the road and pretend that none of what she said hurt his feelings.

"So as far as I was concerned," she prattled on, "we were in love. But then Scott disappeared off the face of the earth. That's when I discovered he'd been dating half the women on campus—and one woman was carrying his child, but she terminated her pregnancy. I tried to counsel her, but it didn't help. It was a very traumatic time in my life. I felt like such a failure both emotionally and spiritually."

"I can imagine," Luke said, parking his vehicle in the coffeehouse's crowded parking lot.

"Then this morning, Scott shows up in our family's living room, engaged to Bonnie!" Melody released her seat belt. "What's more, he corners me in the kitchen to tell me he's a changed man. But he never apologized for anything. He just made excuses. He referred to his experience in Madison as his 'wild days,' and he termed our relationship as 'just friends.'" Melody expelled an audible, exasperated breath. "Oooooh! What a rat!"

Luke felt as if he had twenty daggers protruding from his chest as he walked alongside Melody to the coffeehouse. But he reminded himself the pain would be worth it if he could get closer to Melody.

∽

Melody was awed by her surroundings as they entered the Cream City brick building. Milwaukee was famous not only for its beer manufacturing in the late 1800s, but for a certain type of clay found along the shores of Lake Michigan that, after being fired, turned a buttery color, earning the name "Cream City brick." The coffeehouse, originally a pumping station, had been constructed of the strong brick and recently underwent a face-lift after the coffee company purchased it from the city. Melody had heard about this place, driven past it, and even read about it in the newspaper after it opened, but she hadn't actually been inside. What impressed her most about the coffeehouse/deli was that, although renovated, much of the structure's charm still remained, from the lofted ceiling with its brightly painted piping to the unpainted brick walls and plank floor. Mel was something of a history buff with a penchant for old buildings, and this one certainly filled her senses.

But at the moment, the coffeehouse was packed, so after purchasing flavored brews, Melody and Luke decided on a walk along the lakefront. The breeze off Lake Michigan felt cool, but the sun was warm.

"Did that ever happen to you?" Mel prompted.

Luke glanced at her before sipping his coffee. "Did what ever happen?"

"You know, falling for someone only to find out she didn't feel the same about you—or she cheated on you."

"Well, not in that way, but—um—yeah, I guess it has happened to me." Luke paused and seemed to collect his thoughts. "I'm crazy about someone who barely knows I exist."

Mel found the information fascinating. "You are?"

Luke nodded. "Uh-huh."

"Who is she?"

"I'd rather not say." A sheepish expression crossed his face. "I'd feel kinda stupid if the news got out."

"But that's just it, Luke. You have to let the news out. How else is this person supposed to know you're interested in her?"

He shrugged and sipped his coffee. "I'd like the Holy Spirit to let her know."

"Yeah, I guess you're right." Melody thought God's way was always the best, and she chided herself for being so impatient. And curious. "So do I know her?"

"Yep, you sure do."

Melody knew at once who this mystery girl was: Bonnie! *So my hunch was right!*

They walked awhile longer, then sat down on a park bench that faced the lagoon. In the distance, the Milwaukee Art Museum's modern structure, created by Santiago Calatrava, spread its wings toward Lake Michigan.

Melody pulled one leg up so her left foot rested on the bench and then wrapped her arm around her knee. In the other hand, she held her coffee. She didn't say a word and neither did Luke, and Melody was amazed at the amicable silence that settled quite naturally between them.

Except the silence made her wonder what Luke was thinking. She'd mentioned Ginger and the abortion. . . .

"Luke, just for the record," she began, "I never slept with Scott."

The poor guy almost choked on his last gulp of coffee.

Melody laughed at his reaction, clapping his back between his shoulder blades.

Hunched over and wiping dribbles of coffee from his chin, he glanced at her. "The thought never entered my head."

"I'm glad." Relief washed over her. "But I felt I had to say something and put all doubts to rest here and now. I mean, you and I attend the same church, and we're part of the same career group—I don't want you to think I'm a hypocrite."

"You know what, Melody? I've always been amazed at your ability to say what's on your mind."

She lifted her shoulders. "Bad habit."

Luke grinned, sat back, and extended his arm along the bench's backrest. "Look, *just for the record*," he said, quoting her, "I'd never think the worst about you. I only think the best of you."

His words stirred Melody in an odd way, and she noted it was the second tender thing he'd told her today.

Then suddenly Mel looked at him—*really* looked at him. Perhaps for the first time in years. Luke Berringer had always been that shy, dorky boy next door. But today he seemed anything *but* dorky. His short, straight, dark brown hair was combed back in a style that was longer on top and shorter around the sides and back. Dark, rectangular wire-framed glasses complemented his honey-colored eyes. A handsome guy, according to Mel's appraisal. When had that happened?

Her gaze traveled downward, and she noticed Luke possessed a strong jawline, a muscular neck—a telltale sign that he habitually worked out, maybe lifted weights. His broad shoulders strained against the fabric of his mossy-green polo shirt.

Melody quickly glanced away. What did she think she was doing, gawking at Luke that way! What was her problem?

She stared out over the lagoon where ducks swam atop its murky depths. But it soon became apparent that Luke might become just the friend she needed right now—the one who'd be able to relate to what she was going through. After all, if he had planned to pursue Bonnie, he'd had his dreams dashed today, too.

"Luke, I think we have a lot in common," she muttered before taking a sip of coffee.

"I think you're right."

Melody turned and regarded him once more. She noted the hint of a grin that tugged at his mouth.

She smiled. "Guess I'm glad I *ran into you* today."

At that, they both laughed.

Chapter 4

Melody couldn't say for sure how it happened, but at suppertime, she found herself at a restaurant with Luke and the rest of the career group from church. Maybe it was the fact that Luke was driving combined with the reality that Melody didn't want to go home for fear Scott Ramsay was still there. But whatever the case, Mel decided to relax and have a good time with her friends. She'd taken Luke's advice, and when asked about Bonnie's sudden engagement, she merely stated it wasn't for her to discuss; they'd have to talk with Bonnie about it.

"Oh, come on," Wendy Tomlinson prodded. Her green eyes were lit with curiosity and her long, light brown hair hung in curls around her sweet round face. "You can at least toss us a morsel. Is he nice? Good-looking?"

With all eyes on her now, Melody didn't know how to reply. Of course Scott was handsome, not to mention charming. And Mel recalled how years ago he could make her knees weak with a simple glance in her direction.

But nice? Hardly! A rogue and a scoundrel? Definitely! Of course, Mel couldn't give such a description of her younger sister's fiancé.

"Scott's okay," she finally replied. She hoped she sounded flip and disinterested. "But we have better-looking guys right here in this career group."

The men at the table cheered as if they were at a basketball game, turning heads all around the restaurant, and Melody laughed. Beside her, Luke chuckled, and soon the topic changed, much to Melody's relief.

"Hey, Luke, how's the home-selling business going?" Mike Johnson asked. He leaned forward, and the light above him gave his blond crew cut a funky golden hue. Mike had joined up with the National Guard right after high school, so he'd been dubbed Military Mike. "Now that interest rates have gone up, no one's buying, eh?"

"On the contrary, I sold two—possibly three—houses this week." Luke grinned. "Great week for me."

"Sounds like it," Mike replied with a smirk. "But no one's buying electronics. Maybe I should get into real estate."

"I've only been telling you that for the last five years."

Everyone chuckled at the comeback, and for the second time that day, Melody scrutinized Luke Berringer. His dark hair had fallen into a casual, off-center part, and he reminded her of the lead actor in a movie her sociology class had been required to watch years ago.

So if he's Hollywood handsome, why isn't he married—or at least spoken for?

But then, Melody reasoned, if Luke had his heart set on Bonnie, he probably hadn't made himself available.

Melody mulled over the situation and wondered if she could somehow make Bonnie see that Luke was the better catch. Maybe then Scott would slither back under whatever rock he came from and leave her family alone.

With dinner long finished, members of the career group left one by one. Finally, Melody and Luke were the only ones at the table.

"I don't feel like going home," she admitted, "but I don't want to keep you out if you need to be on your way." She sipped the cup of lukewarm decaf she'd been nursing for the past half hour.

Luke shook his head. "I don't have any pressing engagements."

"Thanks."

He grinned. "Sure."

Melody returned his smile. "So tell me, do you like working in real estate? I sort of forgot that's what you did for a living."

Luke sat back in his chair. "Yeah, I enjoy it. I'm basically my own boss." He tipped his head. "Do you like working as a dental receptionist?"

Melody blinked in surprise. She couldn't believe he remembered her occupation. She figured he must have one of those incredible memories. "Actually, I hate my job, but I love the people I work with, so that makes going to work every day tolerable."

"Why do you hate your job?" A frown pulled at Luke's dark brows.

Mel stared into her coffee. "Well, it was only supposed to be a temporary position. I had hoped to get married and have kids, but—"

"But things didn't work out with Scott Ramsay."

Melody tried to discern the edge in Luke's voice and finally attributed it to losing Bonnie to the creep.

"Just for the record, it 'didn't work out with Scott' long before I was hired at Dr. Leonard's dental office."

With a pitcher in each hand, the waitress paused at their table and refilled Melody's coffee and Luke's ice water. Then she scurried away.

"Actually, I have a lot of respect for domestic engineers," Luke said. "It's a noble profession. My sister—you remember Amber, right?"

"Of course." As Mel recalled, Amber was four years older than she and Luke.

"Well, Amber and her husband, Karl, have four children, and whenever I visit them I'm reminded of what an awesome responsibility parenting is."

Mel agreed. "But I think it's a big turnoff for guys—you know, a woman who wants to be a stay-at-home mom. Men these days want a career wife, someone who can ease their financial responsibilities. At least that's been my experience."

"Do you date a lot?" Luke asked, lifting his glass and sucking an ice cube into his mouth.

"What's 'a lot'? I think I've had three dates in the past year. None went any further than a second date, and I met all three guys at my friends' weddings."

"Hmm. You've got a better track record than I do. I'll bet I've had three dates in the last five years."

Mel shook her head. "What's up with that? You're a terrific guy. I'm surprised some woman hasn't snatched you up by now."

He shrugged, and a sheepish expression spread across his face. "I must be dating all the career women."

Mel found the remark amusing. But then her smile faded, and she looked at him thoughtfully. Curiosity gnawed at her. "Is the real truth because you had your heart set on—on that woman you told me you're crazy about, only she barely knows you're alive?"

"Naw, I don't think so. I'm somewhat of an opportunist, and if the chance comes along to go out to dinner with a pretty lady who happens to be a Christian, I'll take it." Luke leaned closer to her. "In other words, I know better than to sit at home alone and pine away for someone." Sitting back, Luke took a deep breath. "But you know, things are looking up."

"They are?" Mel couldn't help feeling a little conspiratorial. "You mean with this woman you're crazy about?"

Luke nodded.

"Was she here tonight?"

"Yep." The wry grin on his face grew into an embarrassed smile.

"She was!" *So it's not Bonnie after all.*

Melody thought about the women at the table. Wendy Tomlinson, Marlene Dorsche, Sarah Canterfield, Jamie Becker, and Alicia Sims. "Well, that narrows it down," she said smugly before pointing a finger at him. "I'm going to guess who this mystery girl is, Luke."

He laughed and pushed his chair back. "You do that." He stood and extended his hand, helping Melody to her feet. "This place is getting crowded and noisy. Let's get out of here."

∽

Since the night was still young, Luke pulled out his cell phone and called his buddy Tom Wheeler. He asked if he and Melody could stop by. Tom replied with an emphatic "yes" that Mel could hear from where she sat in the passenger seat of Luke's SUV.

"You'll like Tom and his wife, Emily," Luke told her as he drove to the Wheelers' home. "I've worked with Tom for years. He and Em are believers, and they were a big help to me after my parents died."

Mel digested the information. "It was tragic that you lost both your mom and dad so close to each other." She only vaguely recalled that time; she'd been away at school in Madison.

"Yeah, it was tough. Mom died of breast cancer, and Dad had a stroke shortly after. He went downhill from there."

Melody thought back on her childhood, remembering Mr. and Mrs. Berringer. "I always liked your folks."

Luke shot her a grin. "They liked you, too." He chuckled. "You amused them for hours with your pet rabbit in the backyard when you were a little girl. My parents talked about it years later."

"I was always trying to train my rabbit—I must have been eight or nine years old." Mel grinned at the memory. "All my life I've wanted a puppy, but my parents never let me have one because my mom has a lot of allergies. So I had to make do with Snowy the rabbit—and Snowy was never allowed in the house. During the wintertime, my third grade teacher kept Snowy in our classroom."

"Oh sure, I remember Snowy and her glass-sided cage with its metal screen top sitting in the back of the classroom." Luke chuckled.

Melody expelled a dramatic sigh. "Yeah, well, I never did get her to bark. She certainly wasn't the puppy I always wanted."

Luke laughed again, and Mel decided she enjoyed making him smile. She always remembered Luke as being a reticent kid. In his teens he was a geeky bookworm. But now he appeared every bit the handsome gentleman—but maybe still shy, if he didn't want to tell the woman whom he was "crazy about" of his feelings.

Maybe I can help him along.

At last they arrived at the Wheelers' ranch-style house. The couple lived in the village of Brown Deer, not too far from the urban neighborhood in which Luke and Mel resided.

"Please come in," Emily Wheeler said as they reached the front door.

They entered the living room, and Mel noticed the modest furnishings. She also sensed the warmth and hominess of the place. Framed needlework graced the white walls, and an autumn-colored knitted afghan covered the back of a beige, three-cushioned sofa.

Luke made the introductions.

"Nice to meet you," Emily said.

"Same here." Mel gave her a smile while taking in the other woman's appearance. She was tall and slender, and Mel thought of her as plain at first. Her ash blond hair hung straight nearly to her waist, although the top section had been secured in the back with a barrette. But moments later, Mel saw the sweetness in Emily's countenance and decided the woman was actually quite lovely.

"Have a seat," she urged.

At that moment, Tom entered the living room and pumped Luke's hand with enthusiasm. "Luke, buddy, I'm glad you dropped in."

Once more, Luke introduced Melody, and Tom shook her hand with an equal amount of exuberance.

"Are you two up for a game of Trivial Pursuit?" Tom cast an eager glance at Luke, then Melody.

Luke leaned over and muttered, "Tom's a TP nut."

"So am I!" Mel couldn't believe her good fortune. "What versions do you have?"

"All of them." Tom's grin lit up the living room. His height matched his wife's, but instead of being slender, he possessed a stocky frame. "What's your pleasure?"

"How 'bout the Know-It-All edition?"

"You got it! What do you say we play guys against girls?"

"Well," Melody said with a wry grin, "only if Luke wants to lose."

Luke chuckled.

"Lose? Ha!" Tom lifted his chin. "I'm the champion at Trivial Pursuit."

"I don't know about that," Mel countered. "You may have just met your match."

"Oooooh," Luke said, feigning an ominous tone.

Mel elbowed him in the arm for the retort.

Emily laughed softly and lowered herself into a nearby armchair. Meanwhile, Tom left the room to get the board game, and Luke took a seat on the couch. Melody plopped down next to him.

"Hey, Em? Maybe you ought to put on a pot of coffee."

Emily's smile grew, and she nodded. "I was thinking along the same lines, Luke. Between Tom and Melody going at it, this could prove to be a long night."

Chapter 5

I can't believe he's still here!"

Melody gazed out the passenger-side window as Luke pulled up to the curb in front of his house instead of driving into the alley out back where the garages were. Luke killed the engine and said he'd decided to keep his SUV on the street tonight. Parked just ahead of them, in front of her parents' house, sat Scott Ramsay's sleek silver Pontiac Trans Am. Mel guessed, with little effort, that the sports car belonged to Scott because its license plate read "RAMSAM."

"So how does a part-time nursing assistant afford a Trans Am?"

"His great-aunt bought it for him?"

"What?" Mel turned and peered at Luke's shadowy figure.

He laughed, and she realized he was teasing.

"Well, whatever. It's after midnight," she lamented. "It's time for that man to *go home!*"

"If you want to forestall the inevitable some more, I suppose we could go get some ice cream or order a pizza."

Mel frowned and placed a hand over her stomach. "After all the munchies I ate at the Wheelers' tonight, I don't think I could swallow another crumb."

"Okay, just remember I offered."

Luke's quiet chuckle reached her ears, but before she could retort, he was out of the SUV. Walking around the vehicle, he opened her door and helped her out.

"I had a fun time today, Luke."

"Me, too. I especially enjoyed watching you and Tom spar over that Trivial Pursuit game."

Melody laughed. "Em and I let you guys win. You know that, right?"

"Right." There wasn't much conviction in Luke's tone.

"Well, thanks for everything."

"You're welcome."

"Good night."

"Not yet." Luke walked beside Mel as she ambled to the front steps.

She glanced at him, surprised.

"I'm afraid the curiosity will keep me awake all night if I don't meet this guy—Scott."

"Really?"

31

They reached the door, and under the soft glow of the porch light, Mel saw him nod.

"Good, then I won't have to walk in alone."

She stuck her key into the lock, turned the knob, and gave the heavy wooden door a bump with her hip. The door opened and Melody led Luke inside. They found her family—and Mr. All-Wrong—seated in the dining room. Paper and magazines were scattered across the table's polished surface.

"Oh, hi, Mel!" Bonnie extended her arm in a large wave. "How was bowling? Hi, Luke!"

He inclined his head. "Bonnie."

"We didn't go bowling," Mel said, setting her purse on the buffet. "But we met up with the career group for dinner."

"Oh, that's nice," her sister replied with a distracted grin.

Realizing they had another guest, both Mom and Dad rose and greeted Luke. "How've you been? I haven't seen you in half of forever."

Mel smiled as she watched her mother give Luke a hug.

"Luke, come over here and meet my fiancé," Bonnie interjected. "Honey, I want you to meet Luke Berringer. He's our next-door neighbor."

Honey? Mel tried to choke down her cynicism as the two men clasped hands. She decided it'd be interesting to hear Luke's first impressions. But in the next moment, she recognized the disarray on the table.

"Hey," she said, pointing to the open magazines.

"Oh, I borrowed all your bridal magazines and catalogs," Bonnie explained. "I figured you wouldn't mind since I'll need them before you do."

Mel clamped her jaw shut.

"And look! I've already selected my colors. Navy blue and gold."

"What?" Melody felt as though she'd been slapped.

"Navy blue and gold," Bonnie repeated, slower this time.

But those are my colors! Mel wanted to shout.

She compressed her jaw even tighter.

"The kids decided on a date," Mom informed both Melody and Luke. A gleam of anticipation deepened the hue of her cobalt eyes. "Next April. That'll give us a year to plan."

"And a year for Bonnie and Scott to make sure this union is God's will," Dad added.

"Oh, Daddy. We *are* sure."

Bill Stenson sent his youngest daughter a look saying the topic wasn't open for discussion. Mel knew that expression well.

Does Dad have his doubts?

"Bonnie, next April will come soon enough. The months will zoom right by. You'll see."

"Your mom's right," Scott said, stretching an arm around Bonnie's slender shoulders.

Watching the scene, Melody felt a headache coming on. "I think I'll turn in." She massaged her right temple where it had begun to throb.

"Yeah, I'd best get home, too," Luke said. "Nice meeting you." He sent a single nod in Scott's direction before smiling a good-bye at all three of the Stensons. "Great to see you folks again."

"I'll walk you out, Luke." Mel turned. "Night, everyone."

Amid the calls of "Good night" and "Sweet dreams," Melody distinctly heard Scott say, "G'night, Mellow."

She missed a step and suddenly felt as though she might be physically ill.

Mellow! Scott called her *Mellow*!

Dazed, she trailed Luke through the kitchen and out into the dimly lit back hall where the handle on her tightly reined emotions slipped.

"Luke," she whispered, grabbing the front of his shirt, "did you hear what he just called me? Did you hear that?"

"Melody—" There was a note of alarm in his voice as he caught her wrists.

"He called me 'Mellow.' How dare he! That's what he used to call me when— when we. . ."

The words jammed in her throat, and tears clouded her vision. She yanked her hands free from Luke's grasp and buried her face in them.

Then the sobs started.

❧

Luke stood by, feeling as helpless as a boy while Melody cried her eyes out. He fought the urge to march back into the dining room and sock Ramsay a good one for hurting Melody like he had.

"Shh. Don't cry," he whispered.

She sagged against him, and Luke enfolded her in the most proper embrace he could manage.

Oh Lord, please don't let Bill Stenson find us here in the back hall like this. I'll have a lot of explaining to do.

A heartbeat later, Luke shook off his trepidation. Melody was hurting. She needed a hug. She needed a hero—and here was just one more chance for Luke to fulfill that coveted role.

"Shh, Melody, don't cry," he said again, resting his cheek on the top of her head. Strands of her short hair tickled his lips.

He tightened his hold on her, and the realization hit: After spending the day with him, Melody Cartwright was in his arms! A dream come true—well, sort of. He would have preferred she wasn't spilling tears all over him because of another guy.

"I really l–loved him." Melody sniffed. "I was so s–stupid."

33

"We've all done stupid things." Luke grimaced; he hadn't meant to agree. "I mean, we all make mistakes, and it's the lesson God taught you that's important."

He felt her nod, heard another sloppy sniff, and with one hand reached into the back pocket of his jeans, hoping he still had a tissue or two. He sighed with relief when he found a couple still folded there.

"Here." Luke set them into Melody's palm.

She moved backward and dabbed her eyes, then blew her nose.

"Sorry, Luke. That was rude of me."

"Thar she blows," he teased.

Melody smiled, and Luke felt that his mission had been accomplished. But seconds later, her sadness returned. She sniffed again.

"How am I going to survive this next year?" Her voice was barely audible. "Scott will be here all the time, as a constant reminder of my stupid naïveté. This is so humiliating."

"I'll help you through it, Melody—me and all your other friends. And you've got the most important Friend of all on your side: Jesus Christ."

She didn't reply.

"It might sound trite because you're hurting right now, but Jesus really is the One you've got to hang on to through all this."

"You're right. Thanks, Luke." She leaned against him again, this time in an awkward show of gratitude.

"Better now?"

"Yeah. Better. Thanks."

"Anytime."

With that, Luke leaned forward and placed a kiss on Melody's cheek. He took his time about it, relishing the feel of his lips against her petal-soft skin. He wished he could kiss away all the angst she felt inside. But that privilege didn't belong to him—not yet anyway.

As he wished her good night and walked around the yard to his place, Luke felt more determined than ever to win Melody's heart.

Chapter 6

On Sunday morning Melody sat between her friends Sarah Canterfield and Jamie Becker, while on the other side of the sanctuary, a small crowd gathered around the Stensons. Eager friends stood in line to meet Scott.

Sarah gawked. "Is that Bonnie's fiancé?"

"Where?" Jamie, sitting on Mel's right, squinted her eyes. "Oh, there. Yeah, he's gorgeous, huh? I met him during Bible study this morning."

Melody's heart sank. It seemed nobody saw through to the real Scott. But she felt forced to go along with crowd. "He's okay."

"Just 'okay'?" Jamie nudged her as if to say, *Are you blind?*

"Well, you know what I mean." Turning, she noticed her friend's brown eyes sparked with curiosity. "Beauty, or in this case handsomeness, is in the eye of the beholder."

"Whatever." Jamie folded her long, skinny arms. "I think Bonnie ordered that guy off the cover of a macho-man magazine."

Mel flung a gaze toward the arched ceiling.

"Aren't you happy for Bonnie?" Sarah asked. "She's your sister."

"Of course I'm happy." Melody's conscience wouldn't allow her to finish the sentence. Happy? No, her heart ached, and she feared for her younger sister's future with a man like Scott Ramsay. She opened her Bible and stared at it, unseeing.

"Oh, I get it." Jamie's naturally deep voice was now laden with sarcasm. "You're jealous, and your apathy is just a cover."

Mel clapped her Bible shut. "I'm hardly apathetic." She was surprised by her own harsh tone.

Her friends exchanged curious glances, and Mel regretted getting drawn into this juvenile banter.

Melody reopened her Bible and leafed through its delicate pages. She considered her two friends, whom she'd known for years. She'd heard people say Jamie wasn't pretty, that she was too skinny and plain. The words were unkind, however true, but Jamie's outward appearance didn't bother Melody. She tried to see the best in people—to see their inner beauty. After all, she'd learned the hard way with Scott that a handsome face often didn't reach beyond the cheekbones. But now with Jamie, Mel saw it wasn't anything physical that caused her friend to seem unattractive; it was Jamie's cynicism.

"I feel a lot of things about Bonnie's engagement," Mel said, trying to explain herself. She felt the need to make peace with her terse emotions before the service began, and she promised herself she'd sort out all her feelings later, once she was alone.

"Are you just a little jealous of Bonnie?" Sarah asked. "I mean, it wouldn't be normal if you weren't. I'd be green with envy if my younger sister snagged the handsome prince and left me looking like the old maid."

"Old maid? Thanks a lot."

"Oh, you know what I mean." Sarah laughed and tucked strands of her sienna-colored hair behind one ear. The silver earrings she wore swung from her lobes.

"So are you jealous or not?" Jamie persisted.

"No, I am *not* jealous." Mel felt she spoke the truth, too. Sure, she'd felt the pangs of envy when she first learned that Bonnie would be getting married, but had her sister become engaged to any other guy, that initial resentment would have worn off by now.

What Melody felt inside were feelings she didn't want to describe—and they were all directed at Scott. That man had stolen her heart and stomped all over it, and he wasn't even sorry! Worse, he was now engaged to her little sister.

"I think you're jealous," Sarah said in a singsong voice. She leaned into Mel, and something between amusement and intrigue glimmered in her emerald-colored eyes.

"Thanks for giving me the benefit of the doubt, *girlfriend*." Melody collected her purse and Bible, stood, and stepped over Sarah's white stocking–clad legs. "Now I know how Job felt."

"Oh, get a grip," came Jamie's insensitive reply.

Melody ignored it and strode down the side aisle just as the lights dimmed and the choir began to sing. She spoke to no one as she walked through the foyer and exited the front doors.

The April sunshine peeked through fluffy clouds and warmed Mel's face and arms. She had every intention of hopping in her car and driving off to Anywhere, USA. Her fight-or-flight response had kicked in and flight had won out; however, she suddenly remembered her car was at home. Dad had taken one look at it this morning and decided it would have to be towed to the mechanic's tomorrow. So Melody had come to church with her parents.

An expletive made it as far as Melody's lips before she choked it back down. Where had that awful word come from? She didn't talk like that. And why did she feel so hateful and angry?

There in the parking lot, she lowered her head. *Lord, forgive me. I'm a mess. Why is this happening?*

She gazed at the blue sky above, and her heart seemed to say she needed to hear the pastor's message. She spun around and walked back into the church building.

The lobby was now bustling as choir members made their way from the front to their seats. Mel wrapped her arms around her Bible, holding it close, and just stared through the narrow windows of the sanctuary's doors. She wasn't sure if she should go in and find a place to sit or stay in the foyer for the service.

∽

Luke sang with the choir as he did every Sunday morning. As he was making his way through the lobby, he spotted Melody across the way. She wore one of those wrinkly skirts, the kind his sister said were twisted around a broomstick or some such thing. It was beige with a navy print, and with it she wore a silky dark blue blouse. A crinkly shawl that matched her skirt was slung over her shoulders.

Luke's appreciative gaze moved upward still until it rested on Melody's face. Judging by her forlorn expression, she felt miserable. Luke stepped forward, and before he really had the chance to think things through, he found himself at her side.

"Good morning." He tried to sound his cheery best.

She gave him a quick glance. "Oh, hi, Luke."

"Are you going in?" He nodded toward the sanctuary.

"I'm thinking about it. I—I just don't know."

Luke guessed she didn't want to sit with her family because of Ramsay.

Melody turned and faced him. Her indigo eyes were filled with unshed tears. "You know what? You're the only one who understands what I'm going through. My friends don't understand, and my family won't, either."

Luke wasn't about to debate the latter, although he knew the Stensons were reasonable people. But his heart ached for Melody. "Want to sit with me?"

She replied with an almost indiscernible nod.

He placed his hand at the small of her back and led her to the main doors of the sanctuary, then down the middle aisle where he found two seats on the right-hand side. He allowed Melody to slip into the row of cushioned seats first before claiming the chair on the end. The congregation had just finished singing the classic hymn "Make Me a Channel of Blessing."

Melody leaned into him. "Thanks, Luke. You've been a blessing to me." Her voice was but a whisper.

"Anytime." Luke's spirit soared.

∽

Melody spent Sunday afternoon holed up in her bedroom. Bonnie and Scott went to lunch with a half dozen of Bonnie's friends. Melody and Luke had been invited, but he had a house showing this afternoon and Melody refused to be in Scott Ramsay's company any longer than necessary. So she rode home with her parents, and now, while Mom and Dad tinkered around downstairs, Mel checked her e-mail and worked on her online assignments for the college courses in which she'd enrolled. She tried to keep her mind busy, but those haunting thoughts seemed to prevail.

Bonnie's getting married—I should be the one getting married. I'm the oldest!

She chose my colors for her wedding—my colors!

My dream is becoming Bonnie's reality—it's totally not fair!

Mel powered down her computer and decided to read. She went downstairs and pulled out sections from the Sunday newspaper and retreated back upstairs to her side of the room. Sitting cross-legged on her bed, she pored over the news, hoping to find an article about someone whose life's crisis was a whole lot worse than hers.

To her shame, she found several.

Around suppertime, Bonnie and Mom entered the room. Bonnie carried a pizza box.

"I bought dinner," she announced.

"I have the cola," Mom mimicked.

Mel looked up from the newspaper.

"We decided it's girl-talk time," Mom said, positioning herself on the end of Melody's bed.

"Sure." Girl-talk time was a habitual thing around here. She always figured their discussions kept them a close family.

Collecting the newspaper, Mel tossed it on the floor beside her bed. She felt starved. She hadn't eaten much lunch.

"Thanks, Bon-Bon. This smells delicious!"

"It's your favorite," Bonnie said as she handed out thick napkins.

The cynical side of Melody emerged. "My favorite pizza? What's the catch?"

Mom laughed and took a slice of the stuffed-crust, garden veggie delight. "You'll see."

"Well," her sister began, picking off all the black olives on her piece of pizza, "I want you to be my maid of honor, so I thought I'd bribe you with food."

Mel was touched. "You don't have to bribe me. Of course I'll be your maid of honor!"

"*Now* you tell me," Bonnie quipped, "after I spent fourteen bucks on this pizza."

All three women shared a laugh.

They ate and Bonnie talked about her lineup. Mel would be maid of honor, and Susan, their cousin, would be a bridesmaid along with their friends Terri, Sonya, Amy, and Debbie.

Those would have been my choices. Mel set down her second slice of pizza. Suddenly she'd lost her appetite.

Her mother seemed to sense Mel's mood change. "There is something else we need to discuss."

"What's that?" Mel glanced at the now somber expressions on her mother's and Bonnie's faces.

"It's Scott," Bonnie blurted. "He told me that the two of you dated in Madison."

"He told you that?" Mel felt wary. She would have liked to hear Scott's version of "dating." Mel had little doubt his terminology differed vastly from hers.

"Of course. Scott and I have no secrets between us."

Whatever, Mel thought, her heart like stone.

"Scott said you mistook the casual dating, you know, two friends going out for a hamburger, as something more serious," Bonnie relayed. "He feels like you hate him now."

"I do hate him." Mel caught herself. "Well, I mean—hatred is a sin, I know that. But I—um—dislike Scott greatly. How's that?"

"That's not acceptable," Mom said. "Scott is going to be part of this family, and you need to love him, first as a brother in Christ and next as your brother-in-law."

"I'm working on it," Mel replied, picking at her pizza. "It's just that—it was just a shock to see him yesterday."

"Why didn't you tell your father and me about Scott if you were dating him?" A stern parental spark entered Mom's blue eyes. "And if you felt serious about him?"

"I had planned to bring Scott home over spring break, but he'd disappeared by then." Melody looked at Bonnie. "Did he tell you that he just up and left, leaving a lot of broken hearts behind?"

"Scott ran out of money," Bonnie explained. "The university forced him to drop out. He moved back to Iowa and lived with his dad for a while before returning to Wisconsin. He finished his bachelor's at UW-Oshkosh. He graduated with honors." Bonnie beamed. "Now he lives in one of the apartment buildings his mom owns. He manages the building for her as well as working at the hospital."

Melody bit back a retort.

"Scott's parents are divorced," Mom said.

"Yeah, I seem to recall that was the case."

"He feels bad that you took your relationship with him more seriously than he ever did," Bonnie said.

"Oh, how considerate of him to feel bad," Mel all but spat before the whole ugly truth poured out. "For your information, our relationship was more than just 'two friends going out for a hamburger.' Scott said he loved me, Bonnie. He said he wanted to spend the rest of his life with me." Mel ignored the way her sister seemed to pale. "I was naïve, I'll admit it. I believed every word he said. What's more. . ." Melody gulped down her shame. "I allowed Scott some privileges that I shouldn't have."

"Like what?" Mom appeared appalled—and Mel figured she had the right to be.

"Like kissing, inappropriate touching." Melody felt her face flame with disgrace. "I've asked for God's forgiveness. It wasn't right. You brought me up better than that." She looked back at her mother. "I was just so in love with Scott. He knew it and took advantage of me."

"Did you—and Scott. . ." Bonnie looked as if she might cry. "Did you?"

Melody instinctively knew what her sister wanted to know. "No, we didn't go that far."

Relief flooded Bonnie's features, and her slender shoulders sagged.

"Why didn't you say something when you came home from college, Mel?"

She turned her gaze on Mom again. "I was embarrassed, and I knew I'd done wrong." Mel drew in a deep breath. "There were other women, too." She looked at Bonnie. "He didn't just tell me he loved me. He told lots of girls he loved them. We all found each other after Scott disappeared because. . . Well, we were all searching for him. We were worried about him, initially. After that, we all wanted to lynch him."

"I—I need to check this out." Bonnie rose from the side of the bed, grabbed her cell phone from off her desk, and strode out to the back porch.

Melody felt somewhat insulted that Bonnie hadn't taken her word for it.

"You wouldn't make this up, Mel, would you?"

Mel's eyes widened at the implication. "Mom, how can you ask me that? I'm not a liar."

"But if you're hurt, you might want to drive a wedge between Bonnie and Scott."

"No, but I'd like to drive a wedge through Scott's heart—make that a stake."

"Melody, how can you spout such evil?"

A grin slipped out. "Well, I was mostly joking."

"It wasn't funny."

All mirth disappeared. "But that's how I feel." She closed her eyes, despising the hatefulness inside of her. "Mom, I'm still hurt. Yes, that part is true. But I'd never be manipulative and lie—and I'd never want to hurt Bonnie."

Mom seemed satisfied with the answer and finished her piece of pizza.

Minutes later, Bonnie reentered the bedroom, closing the patio door with a decisive slam. "Scott said what you told us is pure fabrication."

"What?" Mel brought her chin back in surprise. She'd expected Scott to deny it, but she didn't think Bonnie would take his word over hers.

"You're lying, Melody, because you want to break up Scott and me."

"I have no intentions of coming between you and Scott." Mel stood. "And

I'm not the liar, Bonnie. He is. I can give you names, and you can personally ask the women he hurt. One even carried Scott's child, and she had an abortion!"

A gasp escaped from Mom's lips.

"No! That's not true." Bonnie's face turned an angry shade of scarlet. "Scott said he dated you and maybe one other girl from SFC. He said he always made it clear you were just friends because he knew he had to go on to med school."

"He's a liar, Bonnie." Mel held her ground.

"No, he's not!"

Mom stood. "All right. That's enough. I don't know how we'll resolve this, but for now, this discussion is over."

Bonnie stomped toward the bedroom's entryway. "I'm retracting my offer," she told Melody, her hand on the doorknob. "I don't want you to be my maid of honor."

Mel suddenly felt as though she'd had a stake driven through *her* heart. She glanced at her mother. "You believe me, don't you?"

"I want to be fair to the both of you." She pushed her blond hair from her forehead. "I don't know what to believe anymore."

"You think I'm lying?" Tears gathered in Melody's eyes, and her throat constricted. She felt accused—convicted without a fair trial.

"Like I said, this discussion is over until I speak with your father."

With that, Mom left the room, and Mel felt as if her heart had been smashed to bits.

For a second time.

Chapter 7

Luke parked his SUV, then killed the engine. Leaning toward the passenger seat, he grabbed his suit coat, along with the bag containing the foot-long submarine sandwich he'd purchased on his way home. He climbed out of his vehicle, locked it, and headed for the house. After this afternoon's showing, he'd gone back to church for the evening service. He didn't see Melody there, but he hadn't expected to; the Stensons weren't a family that habitually attended church on Sunday nights.

Darkness had descended and the neighborhood was quiet as Luke ambled up the narrow sidewalk toward his two-story home. He glanced up at Melody's bedroom window. The light was on, but the back porch door was closed. Sometimes when the evening air was mild, like tonight, Luke caught glimpses of Melody sitting on the adjoining porch. He always said hello and she replied in a neighborly way, but the exchange never developed into conversation, much to Luke's disappointment. However, after yesterday and this morning, he felt hopeful—hopeful but cautious. He didn't want to make a pest of himself, and he couldn't shake the gnawing fear that one of these times when he approached her, Melody would flat out refuse him.

Luke reached his side door and flipped through his key ring for his house key. It was at that moment he heard something. Something odd. A cat? No. He listened, then decided what he heard were guttural, unadulterated sobs.

He frowned. Melody?

Pivoting, he glanced up at her bedroom window again, then decided the sound was much closer. Had he missed her sitting on the upper porch?

Luke stepped back a few paces but couldn't see anyone on the small wooden balcony. His gaze traveled downward and across the Stensons' backyard.

He finally spotted her. She sat on the ground, just behind the tree, her back against the garage, and she was most definitely crying.

Helplessness enveloped him. What should he do? Go over and try to comfort her? What if she told him to mind his own business?

Luke had an older sister, so he was familiar with those female hysteria jags. Sometimes they were a result of the most illogical circumstances; however, in this case, Luke knew Melody was struggling with her feelings for Scott Ramsay. And Luke would like nothing better than to rid her thoughts of that guy.

But if I go over there, will I be her hero or her number one nuisance?

A few more seconds passed, and Luke decided to brave it. It pained him to hear Melody cry.

Leaving his suit coat and bagged sandwich in between the doors, he traipsed down the walkway, praying for the words to comfort Melody—and praying she'd allow him to comfort her. As he walked up her yard's sidewalk, Luke prayed for calm.

He reached Melody and slowly hunkered down beside her. She hadn't noticed him yet. He touched her shoulder, knowing he'd likely startle her one way or another.

He did.

She jumped. "Luke! You scared me half to death!"

"I'm sorry. Are you okay? I—I saw you from my yard."

She didn't reply right away but choked out another sob. "No, I'm not okay," she said at last. "M—my whole family hates me. I t—told my mom and B—Bonnie about dating Scott. I told them the whole truth, but S—Scott denied it. They believe him over m—me! Then Mom told Dad, and now my d—dad's angry with me because three years ago when I dated S—Scott. . ." Melody sniffed and gulped, and Luke began searching his pockets for a tissue. "I should have called and asked his permission. My dad says he's so disappointed in me, and Bonnie said I can't be her maid of honor."

Her arms wrapped around her knees, Melody lowered her head and let out another round of gut-wrenching sobs.

"Shh, Melody." He rubbed his palm across her shoulder blades. That powerless feeling crept over him again. "Oh no. I don't even have any tissues."

He'd muttered the latter, not really intending for her to hear, but she did. In reply, she held up the tissue box hiding under her denim-clad legs.

"This was a planned sob session," she informed him with a hiccup.

That she was weeping at all moved Luke to compassion. "Aw, Mellie." Speechless, he just continued to give her a back rub.

"You know, I don't think anyone has called me Mellie since I was in grade school."

"Did that bother you? I'm sorry."

"No, it didn't bother me." Beneath the slight glow radiating from a neighboring yard light, Luke saw a little smile break through her tear-streaked face.

"Want some company, or should I leave you alone?"

Melody regarded him while resting the side of her head on her knee. "I don't know."

"Here. Scoot over."

She complied and Luke positioned himself beside her. He soon realized they sat on the slab that usually supported the Stensons' tall plastic garbage bins. Since tomorrow was trash day, he assumed the bins were in the alley. He'd been so preoccupied that he'd likely strolled right past them.

He also discovered there wasn't a lot of room on this cement platform. He and Melody sat hip to hip.

For several long minutes neither spoke. Luke wished he knew just the right thing to say, but at the present, words failed him.

Melody dabbed her eyes and blew her nose. She seemed to have calmed down. "You smell nice, Luke."

"What?" He wasn't sure he'd heard her correctly.

"Your cologne or aftershave—whatever it is—it smells good."

"Thanks." He felt embarrassment warm his face. "I'm surprised you can even smell after your—um—*sob session*."

He heard her soft laugh as she leaned her arms on her knees, then placed her head on her arms.

Several more moments went by.

"You know? You showed up just when I needed you," Melody said in a broken little voice. "I was thinking about packing up my stuff and taking off in my car. But then I remembered my car's not drivable."

Luke sensed more tears were on the way. He put his arm around her. "Don't cry anymore, Melody, all right?"

She moved her head to his shoulder, and Luke suddenly felt like the luckiest guy in the world. For the second time in twenty-four hours, he held the girl of his dreams in his arms.

Then, much to his utter chagrin, his stomach moaned in hunger.

"Was that you?"

"Um—yeah. I didn't get any supper tonight."

"You're hungry!"

"Obviously." He laughed and thought of his foot-long sub. "Hey, want to split my sandwich with me? I bought it at a sub shop on the way home. Nice and fresh. . ."

Melody sat up on her haunches. "Can I cook something for you instead? I love to cook, and it'll get my mind off my troubles."

"Are you kidding? You can cook for me anytime you want." A vision of Melody moving about his kitchen amid mouthwatering aromas flitted through Luke's mind. It was a notion he didn't dare entertain. Could this really be a dream come true? "I—um—don't cook much."

"I don't know many single guys who do." She stood.

Luke did the same and took a mental inventory of his cupboards and refrigerator. He tamped down his sudden disappointment. "There's just one problem."

"And that is?"

"I don't think I have any food in the house to cook."

Melody actually giggled. "Luke, you *bachelor*."

"Is that a dirty word?" He grinned.

"In our career group it is."

Luke chuckled. He knew Mel referred to the overabundance of single women who joined the career group at church in order to snag a spouse. Sometimes they were successful; other times they weren't. But he never sensed Melody was husband hunting. Of course, if she'd been harboring feelings for Ramsay, that could explain it.

"Well, what about tomorrow night?" Melody asked, drawing Luke from his thoughts. "Can I cook for you then? You've been so sweet this weekend, and I'd like a chance to repay you for all your kindness." She sniffed again then bent to fetch the tissue box, which she tucked under one arm. "You said you wanted to be there for me, and you have been."

"Tomorrow's fine." Could this be happening? Luke wanted to pinch himself to make sure he wasn't hallucinating.

"I get off at four thirty, and I'll stop at the store. . . ." Melody paused in mid-sentence. "Oh, Luke, I forgot! I'll be without wheels for a while. My dad's having my car towed to his mechanic in the morning."

"I'll pick you up, and we can stop at the store afterward." The offer flew out of Luke's mouth before he had a chance to consider it. Well, he could adjust his schedule.

"Really? You'll pick me up from work?"

"Sure. Want me to drive you there in the morning, too?" Luke felt close to giddy. He took Melody's hand and bowed over it. "Your wish is my command, milady."

To his dismay, his antics were rewarded with more tears.

Placing his hands on Melody's shoulders, he leaned slightly forward, trying to glimpse her face. "What's wrong? I was kidding around."

"You're so n—nice and I don't deserve it. I feel s—so hateful."

"Will you stop it?"

The next moment, she was in his arms again, and Luke thought he could get used to holding her this way. A heartbeat later, he chastened himself for such thoughts. This woman was distraught, and here he was thinking of his own selfish desires.

"Mellie, don't cry." He stroked the back of her hair, marveling at how thick and soft it felt against his fingers. "Give yourself a break. You're going through a tough time."

She didn't reply, and Luke didn't move—until a disconcerting thought whirled through his brain.

"Say, Melody? If your dad comes out. . . I mean, I wouldn't want him to catch us like this. It might not look so great, especially since he's already unhappy about—"

Before he could finish, she took a quick step backward.

"You're absolutely right. I didn't think—it was so innocent, you know?"

"I know."

Luke felt a twinge of regret in voicing his concern since it meant loosing his hold on Melody. However, not thirty seconds later, the bright yard light went on, and Bill Stenson's voice boomed through the backyard.

"Melody? Mel, where are you?"

"I'm here, Dad."

He appeared on the walk and squinted in their direction. "How long does it take to roll the garbage carts into the alley?"

"I'm—talking with Luke." She turned and gave Luke a grateful stare.

He let out a breath of relief and sent up a prayer of thanks. He would have hated to get Melody in worse trouble with her folks. What's more, Bill Stenson's trust was important to Luke. He'd hate to do something foolish and lose it forever.

"Well, hurry it up, will you?" Bill said, sounding gruff. "I want to lock up for the night. If I have to get you to work by eight and then—"

"Luke says he'll drive me."

A pause. "Naw, we're not bothering the neighbors."

"No bother, Mr. Stenson," Luke put in. "I offered."

The older man stood arms akimbo while mulling it over. "Okay, fine. That'll work. Thanks."

"My pleasure."

Mr. Stenson strode back into the house.

Melody looked up at Luke and gave him a tenuous smile. Under the beaming yard light, he could see the sadness in her eyes and her tearstained face. He wished he could kiss away all her sorrow.

"My dad's angry with me."

"He'll get over it. He loves you. Besides, you told the truth, something you had to do even though it was difficult. That took courage."

In spite of her nod, Melody's bottom lip quivered. She lowered her chin and gazed at the white leather athletic shoes she wore on her feet.

"So what time do you want to leave in the morning?"

She looked back up at him. "Is seven thirty all right?"

Luke nodded. "I'll pull out front."

"Thanks."

He tipped his head, considering her circumspectly. "Are you still going to cook for me tomorrow night?"

"You bet." She sent him a determined grin before turning around and jogging toward the house.

∞

Melody saw Luke's Durango from the living room window. She snatched her purse off the coffee table and headed for the front door.

"I'm leaving," she called before slamming the door on any reply.

She bristled as she walked to the waiting SUV. No one was talking to anyone else unless it proved absolutely necessary, although Bonnie wasn't speaking to Melody at all.

She opened the door and climbed up into the passenger seat.

"Good morning." Luke sent her a sunny smile, a stark contrast to the gloomy skies overhead.

"Are you always this happy?" Mel teased, strapping on her seat belt.

"Only when I'm in good company." Luke headed the SUV down the street.

"Well, you can't be referring to me. I'm so angry. Scott Ramsay is tearing my family apart." She gritted her teeth before adding, "I've just got to do something about it—about him."

"You know, Melody, I've been thinking and praying about this situation, and I'm wondering if—well, the anger you feel. . ." Luke stopped for a red light and looked over at her. "Do you think you're still in love with Scott?"

"No. I hashed this all out in my head last night. I've concluded that if Scott would have apologized to me instead of pretending he didn't remember me, I probably could have forgiven him. It's just that seeing him again made all that old hurt come back, and then he added insult to injury."

"I understand." The light changed and Luke accelerated through the intersection. "So it's a forgiveness issue, then?"

"Yeah, I guess it is," Melody admitted. "And I know what I have to do—in fact, I've done it. I couldn't sleep all night, so very early this morning I knelt beside my bed and poured my heart out to God." Tears welled in her eyes, but Mel blinked them back. "I asked Him to help me forgive Scott, but I have to tell you, Luke, revenge is so much more appealing."

He laughed and pulled into a trendy coffee shop's parking lot. "We've got a few minutes, and I need some coffee. Want a cup?"

"Sure." Melody smiled.

"Cream? Sugar?"

"Heavy on both."

"Got it."

Luke hopped out of the SUV and disappeared into the building. Watching him go, Mel decided he sure was a special guy—a special friend. She wondered again who he was "crazy" about. If Luke displayed as much caring and kindness to that woman as he had to Mel this past weekend, then Mystery Girl would definitely be aware that he existed.

She'd probably even fall in love with him.

Chapter 8

Dinner will be ready in about an hour and a half." Mel stood over Luke's stove, browning the ground beef in preparation for making her famous belly-busting lasagna. At first, she had considered grilling outdoors since the spring weather had been unseasonably warm for April. But the morning clouds never departed, and this afternoon, the wind shifted. The temperature plummeted. Local weather channels reported a thunderstorm was on its way, so Mel decided to create her specialty for Luke. "I hope seven o'clock isn't too late for you to eat."

"Seven is perfect," Luke replied. He stood several feet away, leaning against the wall with his arms folded, watching her cook. "I had a late lunch today."

Melody peered over her shoulder at him. He still wore his navy suit and lavender shirt, minus the jacket and tie. "I hope you'll like my lasagna. My family nags me to make it for them all the time."

"I'm sure I'll enjoy it. I love Italian food."

"Just to forewarn you, I don't know how authentic my version is." She grinned. "I sort of improvised on a recipe I found in a magazine, and it turned out really well. I've been making lasagna this way ever since." She glanced at him again, then moved to the chopping block, where she diced an onion. "Was your mom a good cook?"

Luke shrugged and unfurled his arms before sauntering over to the kitchen table. Pulling out one of the Windsor chairs, he sat down. "Mom didn't cook a whole lot, but when she did meals were always tasty, as I recall."

"Why didn't she cook much? Didn't she enjoy it?"

"Oh, I don't know if it was so much that. Mom was just always preoccupied with whatever article she was writing. But as kids, we thought potpies and TV dinners were great."

Mel's smile grew as she imagined the Berringers' family life. Luke's dad had been a truck driver, and his mother had worked for the *Milwaukee Sentinel*, a daily morning newspaper that had since merged with the *Milwaukee Journal*. She remembered Luke's folks as kindhearted, churchgoing people.

But the house itself looked quite different from what she recalled. Melody had been inside this place a number of times, since she and Luke's sister, Amber, had occasionally played together in spite of their age difference. And if Mel's memory served her correctly, this kitchen was once paneled in a red brick and had a coppery-colored linoleum on the floor. Now, however, everything was white—from the walls to the window blinds, countertops, cupboards, appliances, and ceramic flooring. Much too sterile for Mel's tastes, but it would be fun to decorate it and give it some color.

"When did you remodel the kitchen?"

"After my folks died. I sort of went into a remodeling mode, thinking Amber and I would sell the house. But then I liked the changes. It felt like it was a whole different place when I finished, so I bought out Amber's half and decided to stay."

"I'm glad you did." She gave him a smile before turning to deposit the onions into the browning meat. "But don't you ever feel lonely, living here all by yourself?"

"Sometimes, but I keep busy."

Melody returned to the chopping block, where a plump green pepper awaited its turn under the knife. She grinned at Luke. "You could ask your mystery girl over for dinner one night. I'll even cook for the two of you."

He laughed. "I knew something like that was coming." He chuckled again. "I think I'll let God take care of my 'mystery girl,' all right?"

"All right. I'll mind my own business." Mel started to slice the pepper.

Their conversation lagged.

"Listen, Melody, I appreciate your offer. I really do."

"Oh, I'm not insulted or anything. I was just trying to help."

"I know, and I appreciate it."

"And you're right about leaving the matter in God's hands. I wish I would have done that with Scott. I was so crazy about him that I practically threw myself at the man." She arched a brow. "Of course, he didn't seem to mind at the time."

She chopped up the green pepper with more force than necessary before scraping the tiny pieces into the meat mixture. Next, she prepared a white sauce, which she used instead of ricotta cheese.

"I've been looking forward to your cooking all day."

Melody smiled, feeling pleased by his remark and the change of subject.

With the meat browned and the added vegetables sautéed, she preheated the oven. Lifting the jar of sauce, she tried to open its lid, but the thing wouldn't budge.

She handed the jar to Luke, who twisted the cap off with little effort.

"Show-off."

He chuckled, and Mel reclaimed the jar.

"Now, if I were a *real* chef," she told him, "I'd make my sauce from scratch. But this stuff's pretty good."

She poured the tomato sauce over the meat and then stirred it. In the meantime, the water for her noodles had come to a boil. After parboiling the pasta, she placed the first layer in the bottom of a greased rectangular ceramic baking dish.

Layer by layer, Mel assembled her creation. Noodles, meat sauce, white sauce, mozzarella cheese. Noodles, meat sauce, white sauce, mozzarella cheese. When she'd filled the entire pan, Mel topped it off with a generous sprinkling of Parmesan cheese.

"Okay, now lift this baby, Luke." She laughed.

He stood, crossed the room, and did as she bid him. "Whoa, that's one serious lasagna!"

"Want to put it in the oven for me—since you're such a he-man?"

Luke replied with a smirk and slid the pan into the oven. Then he rubbed his palms together. "Let's catch the news while dinner's cooking."

"Okay, sure."

Melody followed him into the living room. Luke sat on the leather couch, and she situated herself in one of the matching armchairs. Remote in hand, Luke flipped on his wide-screen TV and tuned in to one of the cable news channels known for its conservative views. Meanwhile, thunder rumbled in the distance.

"I hope we have a good thunderstorm tonight."

Luke regarded her with a grin. "You like storms?"

She nodded. "I especially like to curl up on the couch with a quilt and read a good mystery. But if it's too suspenseful, I get freaked out and turn on every light in the house, which causes my dad to have a fit because he pays the electric bill."

Luke chuckled.

"Do you read a lot?"

"Not as much as I used to."

"As I recall, you were sort of a bookworm." She laughed as another memory surfaced. "Hey, do you remember how you got into trouble for spying on Bonnie and me through our bedroom window with that telescope of yours?"

Luke's guffaw filled the room. "I can't believe you still remember that!"

"I do—and whew! Your dad was really mad."

"I was probably acting out the latest adventure novel I'd read. But I never saw anything scandalous, you have my word."

"Back then there wasn't much to see, Luke," she teased.

"Regardless, I got a lickin' and I deserved it. You can't let little boys turn into Peeping Toms."

Melody laughed. So Luke had been a typical little boy after all. It had always seemed to her that he was the teacher's perfect pet. It used to annoy Mel to no end.

The hour flew by, and when the lasagna finished cooking, Mel removed it from the oven. While it cooled, she threw together a salad, and Luke set the dining room table.

Then, just as she and Luke were about to dish up their meal, Bonnie and Scott showed up at the side door.

"Dad sent us over to tell you there's a severe thunderstorm warning," Bonnie said after Luke asked the couple in. "He'd like you home before it hits."

Melody heard the terseness in her sister's voice and wondered if their dad had sent Bonnie over to try to coax along the reconciliation process. "I'll be home soon. Luke and I are just about to eat."

Scott spotted the pan of lasagna. "Wow, that looks terrific, and I'm starved."

"We just had dinner." Bonnie gave him a frown.

"I know, but all those vegetables you served—they were good and everything, except they don't stick with a guy very long."

He winked at Melody, and she turned away, unimpressed by his attempted charm. She busied herself by carrying the salad plates into the dining room, praying Luke wouldn't invite Bonnie and Scott to share their supper.

"So is this like a romantic dinner for two or something?" Scott asked when Mel returned to the kitchen.

"You've got half of it right," Mel quipped. "It's for *two*."

Luke wiped his palm across his mouth in an obvious effort to hide his smirk.

"I don't think I've ever seen lasagna look that good."

What a beggar, Mel thought.

Bonnie hooked her arm around Scott's. "Let's go home, and I'll make you something to eat there."

"But they've got plenty here," he argued. Dressed in a plaid shirt that hung over his baggy blue jeans, he not only looked like a seventeen-year-old punk, but Mel thought he behaved like one, too. "That pan would feed eight people."

He turned to Luke. "Come on, buddy, what do you say? Can Bonnie and I join you two?"

Luke flicked his brown-eyed gaze in Mel's direction, and she could almost *feel* the battle warring within him. Scott had put Luke's back to the wall, and Luke was far too polite to tell Scott to buzz off. Melody, on the other hand, might have the nerve to say it, but this wasn't her house.

She turned and pulled two more plates from the cupboard. Again Luke glanced her way. She gave him a single nod, then walked into the dining room, where she heard Luke say, "Sure. You two are welcome to stay for dinner."

∞

Two days later, on Wednesday afternoon, Luke stared out his kitchen window. Melody had just pulled up and parked in the carport. He felt a tad disappointed that her vehicle was now repaired. He'd enjoyed driving Melody to and from work the last couple of days.

But now she didn't need him anymore—at least not as her chauffeur.

He wished and prayed that he could still be her hero if things remained difficult between Melody and her family. From what she'd told him this morning, tensions still ran high in the Stenson home—even after Monday night's dinner. Luke had hoped sharing a meal would help patch things up between the sisters, but the unpleasant nuance at the table that night was unmistakable. Bonnie's anger and resentment. . . Melody's deep sense of hurt and betrayal. . . The only one who'd enjoyed himself was Scott.

Afterward, Luke privately apologized for caving in to Ramsay's request. But Melody understood his predicament. In the days following, Luke must have told her a dozen times that she could cook for him whenever she needed a stress reliever, and Melody said she'd take him up on the offer.

But would she really?

She needs a reason to spend time with me. I need time to win her heart.

Luke watched as Melody, attired in the light blue scrubs and white T-shirt she wore to work, ambled up the walkway to her house. Her dad had fetched her this afternoon, then drove her to the mechanic's shop. Luke thought the guy had worked fast, but apparently he'd just fixed Melody's car so it was drivable until all the parts for the bodywork arrived.

A pity, Luke mused. He would have liked to continue driving Melody to work and back, especially since she'd decided to forgo the expense of a rental.

At that moment, Bill Stenson's blue truck proceeded up the alley and turned into the garage. It'd be just like Mr. Stenson to follow his daughter home to ensure she arrived safely, seeing as how she'd just had her car fixed.

Luke moved away from the window and made his way through the dining room and living room, then rounded the corner and climbed the steps of the open stairway. Once on the second floor, he walked down the hallway to the smallest of the four bedrooms, which he'd converted into a home office. He checked his answering machine messages and returned a few phone calls. With those tasks out of the way, he reclined in his black leather desk chair and stared unseeing at his neatly arranged bulletin board. His thoughts came back around to Melody.

What do I do now, Lord? Luke supposed he could just ask her out on a date like any normal single male; however, he sensed it wasn't the way to go about endearing Melody to him. From what she'd told him, Melody had "been there, done that." She didn't need another date. She needed a—*a hero.*

Well, I've been patient this long, Luke decided, reaching for his handheld daily planner. *I can certainly wait some more.*

∽

Melody arrived home from work on Friday afternoon and discovered Bonnie in the kitchen. They didn't speak; Bonnie hadn't said more than three words to Melody in the past couple of days.

Mel flipped through the mail, and then unable to ignore the clanging of pans, she glanced at her sister. "Are you cooking supper tonight?"

"Mmm-hmm."

"Is Scott coming over?"

Bonnie banged a mixing bowl on the counter. "What's it to you?"

Okay, we're up to seven words, eight if I count "Mmm-hmm."

Mel gazed into Bonnie's fuming countenance, deciding she'd never seen her sister so mad. "I didn't mean anything by it. I asked because if you're cooking for Scott, I'll find something else to do and leave you two alone."

"Mom and Dad will be here. We'll hardly be *alone*."

"Fine." Melody dropped the stack of envelopes back onto the kitchen table. "Just don't count on me being here tonight for dinner."

"Fine," Bonnie repeated in a huff.

Mel left the kitchen and proceeded upstairs. She wished her parents would intervene in this ugliness between her and Bonnie. But it seemed Scott had Mom charmed and Dad confused.

Entering her bedroom, Mel told herself she didn't care anymore—she just wished she really felt that way.

Once she'd changed into blue jeans and a sweater, she pulled her cell phone from her purse and walked out onto the back porch. The sun felt warm, but the temperature had only reached the midforties. However, a lifetime of living in Wisconsin had thickened Mel's blood, and the brisk late afternoon air didn't bother her.

She sat down on one of the two lawn chairs, kicked up her feet, and dialed several friends' numbers. Two had dates, one had the flu, and a couple of others weren't home.

Great. Nowhere to run and nothing to do.

At that moment, Mel saw Luke's SUV turn into the alley. She wondered if he had plans—oh, of course he did! He probably had a date. Maybe he had asked Mystery Girl out to dinner.

No, on second thought, he probably hadn't.

Melody lifted her feet off the railing and leaned forward. Luke was a puzzle. He was a special guy. Handsome. Caring. She couldn't understand why he didn't let Mystery Girl know of his interest—unless Mystery Girl had a steady boyfriend.

Mel snapped her fingers. *Then it's got to be Alicia Sims.*

Luke emerged from the side door of his garage. He wore dark slacks, a light blue shirt, and a coordinating tie. Over one shoulder he carried a large leather attaché, and over the other, he'd flung his suit jacket. As he made his way up the walkway, he flicked his gaze toward the porch. Seeing Melody sitting there, he stopped.

"Hi," he said.

Melody smiled. "Hi, Luke."

"I haven't seen you in a few days. How're you doing?"

"Okay, I guess. How 'bout yourself?"

"Terrific."

Maybe he does have a date after all.

"Got any plans for tonight?"

Luke tipped his dark head. "Nothing concrete. What about you?"

"No." Melody stared at her cell phone. "I'm actually looking for something to do."

"How does dinner and a Brewers baseball game sound?"

Melody smiled and looked back at Luke. "Great. Who's all going?"

"Um. . ." He shifted his stance. "Just you and me at the moment. That idea was—um—just off the top of my head. But I know the Brewers are in town and playing tonight."

Melody felt a twinge of discomfort. Dinner and a baseball game alone with Luke sounded an awful lot like a date. Then again, it sure beat sitting around here all night and listening to Bonnie and Mom make wedding plans while Scott and Dad did the male bonding thing in front of the television.

"Sure. It sounds fun. What time?"

"Really?"

"Sure, why not?" Mel wondered why he looked so shocked.

Luke glanced at his watch. "Give me a half hour."

"You got it."

She watched him walk the rest of the way to his house, pull out his keys, and let himself inside. That odd feeling came over her again. *A date with Luke Berringer. . . What if someone from church sees us, and it gets around?*

It was then that Mel put two and two together. Luke probably hoped the word would spread because then Alicia would hear about it, and if she had any feelings for him at all, they'd surface one way or another.

Yes sirree, that Luke was a crafty guy. *Those quiet types usually are.*

Mel stood and reentered her bedroom. She wasn't thrilled about it, but she'd play along because she had grown fond of her neighbor. He'd been a good friend to her last weekend.

Besides, if he and Alicia got together, maybe she'd end up a bridesmaid in their wedding, too!

Chapter 9

"I think it's shameful how you're using Luke!"

"What?" Melody whirled around and faced her sister. She had been about to climb into bed when Bonnie spouted off that ridiculous remark. "I'm not 'using' Luke. What are you talking about?"

Bonnie raised her chin. "It's obvious you're jealous, and you're using Luke to try to get what Scott and I have together."

Mel rolled her eyes. "Whatever! For your information, Luke and I are just friends, and *he* asked me out Friday night. He's also the one who asked me to that wedding yesterday. Some guy he works with got married, and Luke didn't want to go by himself."

Bonnie put her hands on her slender hips. "And what about this morning?"

"What about it? I sat with Luke in church. So?"

Melody climbed into bed, trying to tamp down the bitterness she felt. How could Bonnie accuse her of using Luke in such a manipulative and selfish way?

"Sarah said she thinks you're jealous of me. I'm your little sister, and you're mad because I'm getting married first."

"Sarah needs to get a life."

Bonnie shrugged out of her clothes, then pulled on an oversized shirt. "Most women our age want to get married. But what's soured our situation is that I'm younger than you, and you had a crush on my fiancé."

Melody felt her emotional wounds rip open all the wider. Her friends and sister had obviously been discussing this matter behind her back.

"It wasn't a crush, Bonnie. I really believed I loved Scott." She propped herself up on an elbow, hoping her sister would finally come to understand her side of this. "I'll admit to feeling envious of you at first, but that's worn off. I want to be happy for you. It's just that I'm still hurt that you believe Scott's lies instead of me."

"He never lied."

"Yes, he did."

"No, he didn't!" Bonnie raised her voice. "But Sarah and Jamie told me—"

"What?" Melody's hold on her emotions snapped. She flung herself out of bed, battle ready. "You, Sarah, and Jamie should be praying for me instead of gossiping about me and thinking the worst!"

"Don't lay sin at our door and turn this all around on us." Bonnie's face flamed with anger. "You're the one who's at fault here."

"And how's that?"

"You're jealous and now you're using Luke."

"I am not! You're delusional!"

Bonnie jabbed a finger in Mel's direction. "Jamie said she wouldn't put it past you to try to break up Scott and me."

"No way. I've decided you two *deserve* each other!"

Bonnie tipped her head. "And just what is that supposed to mean?"

"It means. . ."

A knock sounded, and without waiting for an answer, their mother opened the bedroom door and walked in. "What is going on up here? The windows are open, and the whole neighborhood can hear you girls arguing like you're ten years old!"

Bonnie sent Mom a little pout before she whirled around and climbed into her bed on the other side of the room. She left Mel to do the explaining.

Typical, she thought, sending a glare in her sister's direction.

"Melody, I want to know what you two are bickering about." Mom folded her arms, awaiting the explanation.

"Ask Bonnie." Mel found her jeans, then pulled a T-shirt from her dresser drawer. *I am out of here!* "I'm sure you won't believe anything I have to say."

"That's not true."

Oh yes, it is, Mel thought as she dressed. But she didn't say another word.

༄

Luke sat out on his back deck. He felt so worked up he couldn't fall asleep if someone paid him. Not only had he spent a lot of time with Melody again this past weekend, but he'd also sold a house this afternoon.

Lord, I'm rejoicing. . . .

And if he was crazy about Melody before, he was in love with her now. They'd had fun on Friday night and a good time at Bob and Sue's wedding yesterday. Even though she didn't know anyone but Luke at the reception, Melody was pleasant and chatty, and everyone she met liked her at once.

Strains of her voice wafted down to Luke's ears. He stood and walked to the edge of the wooden deck and peered up at Melody's bedroom window. The light shone through the blinds and the window was partially open. He heard Melody say something more, then Bonnie.

They're arguing.

Luke retreated to his padded lawn chair. None of his business. What's more, he'd heard enough catfights coming from the Stenson home over the years, having grown up right next door. But he really hadn't heard many disputes since the girls entered adulthood. He was apt to hear more giggling.

Well, siblings tended to have their spats. Luke couldn't even begin to count the numerous scrapes he'd had with his sister. But what troubled Luke now was that he could only guess why Melody and Bonnie were quarreling—make that *who* they were quarreling about: Scott Ramsay.

Lord, this shouldn't happen, but I know things have been brewing for over a week. . . .

He mulled it over some more. It seemed to him that Bill and Ellen Stenson were still so shell-shocked from Bonnie's announcement about marrying Scott that they failed to see Melody sinking into despair. Of course, Luke knew there were two sides to every story. Nonetheless, Melody and Bonnie had always enjoyed a close relationship. Perhaps the women would hash it out and put the matter to rest once and for all. But was that possible with Ramsay in the mix?

Only by God's grace. . .

The seconds ticked by, and Luke tried to tune out the bickering next door, but the sisters' voices grew louder, until all at once things quieted. Then the back porch door closed with a loud bang.

He grimaced. Silence. He began to relax. But not ten minutes later Luke saw Melody running for the carport. He stood, but before he could call out to her, Bill Stenson's voice rumbled like thunder across the backyard after her.

"Melody, come back here! Don't you leave this way!"

She didn't heed the command, and moments later her car took off out of the alley with tires squealing.

Luke's gut contracted with fear. *Oh Lord, protect her—and everyone in her path.*

❧

Melody stepped on the accelerator and headed for the freeway. She considered seeking refuge at Grandmother Cartwright's house in Genesee Depot. Grammy enjoyed pampering and spoiling Mel, as she was the only Cartwright grandchild.

She looked at the clock on the dash and realized that at this late hour, Grammy would be fast asleep.

Melody decided to just drive and see where she ended up. She pulled her car onto I-43 and headed north, ignoring the lively computerized tune her cell phone produced with incoming calls. It occurred to her that maybe she really wasn't part of the Stenson family. Maybe she'd always been the odd duck out.

Lord, I feel so alone. Life seems so unfair!

She fussed and fumed all the way to Manitowoc, then cried the rest of the distance to Green Bay. In the wee hours of the morning, she stopped for gas and found an all-night restaurant right off the interstate. She ate breakfast while reading John 15 in her Bible.

"*As the Father has loved me, so have I loved you. Now remain in my love. . . . I have told you this so that my joy may be in you and that your joy may be complete.*'"

Melody stopped reading and sipped her coffee, wondering when the last time was that she experienced true joy. Not mere happiness, but pure, unadulterated joy.

Lord Jesus, what's wrong with me?

" 'Greater love has no one than this, that he lay down his life for his friends. . . . You did not choose me, but I chose you. . . . This is my command: Love each other .' "

Those last words gave Melody pause. Love each other? She realized then that she'd been harboring a lot of hatred—hatred spawned by Scott's lies and rejection. How could the love of God penetrate through all those destructive emotions?

As she drove back to Milwaukee, she wept some more—but not tears of self-despair; they were tears of sorrow.

God, forgive me for hating Scott Ramsay. She prayed like David did in Psalm 51. *"Create in me a pure heart, O God, and renew a steadfast spirit within me."*

Her cell phone rang again. This time she answered it.

"Mel, where are you?"

Her dad didn't sound angry, just insistent. "I'm okay. I'll be home in a little while."

"That's not what I asked."

Melody expelled a weary sigh. "I'm just driving by the Port Washington exits."

"What are you doing out that way?"

"I drove around all night. I had a lot of thinking to do—thinking and conversing with God."

"Well, I'm glad for the 'conversing with God' part, but I lost a night's sleep over your *driving around*."

"You did? Why?"

"Because you're my daughter, that's why. What kind of stupid question is that?"

Mel felt her throat constrict with emotion. "It's just that—I feel like everyone's against me. It hurts so bad that you all believe Scott over me, and you think I'm a liar."

"We believe you, Mel. But your mom and I are trying to be fair to both you and Bonnie while giving Scott the benefit of the doubt."

She tossed a glance heavenward. "I hope you know you sound like a politician."

Dad didn't respond to her tart reply. "Look, I've gotta go to work, but you and I will talk tonight. Got it?"

She relented. "Got it."

"I love you, Mel."

She believed him. "Love you, too."

Bleary-eyed, Melody ended the call, and she couldn't help feeling a bit hopeful. Maybe Dad was on her side after all. Perhaps Mom would come around, too. Then Bonnie. . .

Once at home, Mel showered and changed into the light blue scrubs she wore to work. Everyone had left for their jobs, and Mel had already phoned her employer to say she'd be late. She dried her short hair, touched it up with the curling iron, and then applied a small amount of cosmetics, making sure she hid those dark circles emerging beneath her eyes.

On the way downstairs, the back doorbell rang. Mel stood on tiptoes and peered through the half-moon window.

Luke.

She opened the door, noticing his crisp white dress shirt, multicolored striped tie, and gray trousers. "Hi. What are you doing here?" She waved him inside.

"I was worried about you." He stepped into the back hall.

Mel caught a whiff of the masculine scent he wore—an oriental, woodsy blend. "Luke, you have got to be the best-smelling real estate agent in town."

He chuckled. "Thanks."

"I have time for a quick cup of coffee. Do you?"

"Sure."

She led him into the kitchen. Luke sat down at the table.

"I was on my deck last night when I saw you take off in your car," he said. "I got really worried, especially since you didn't come home all night."

Mel turned from the coffeepot and frowned. "How do you know I didn't come home all night?"

Embarrassment crossed his features. "I kept checking your carport from my office window. Like I said, I was worried about you."

"Oh." The intense light in his eyes gave her pause. But in spite of his scrutiny, she managed to fill two mugs with coffee from the thermal pot. She set one in front of Luke and brought out the cream and sugar. "If you were on your deck, I suppose you heard Bonnie and me arguing."

"I couldn't hear what was being said, but yeah, I heard you two."

Melody felt ashamed for her part in the squabble. From now on, she'd take the high road. She wouldn't let her emotions rule her actions.

She sipped her coffee. "I'm sorry you overheard, and I'm even more sorry for worrying you, Luke."

"I'm just glad to find you safe and sound."

"Well, I don't know about the 'sound' part." She grinned and told Luke how she'd driven up to Green Bay and back. He seemed to give great thought to her every word.

"You know," he said at last, "that's how women disappear." His voice sounded composed, although the hint of warning was unmistakable. "They take off alone, go someplace that nobody imagines they'll go, and they're never seen alive again."

"Stop it, Luke." Mel didn't appreciate the scare tactic—or whatever it was supposed to be.

He reached across the table and placed his hand on hers. "Promise me you won't take off like that again."

Mel retracted her hand. "I'm not a child, so don't treat me like one." Irked, she stood, knocking her mug. Coffee sloshed over its edge. She grabbed a napkin and sopped it up, realizing her temper had already gotten the best of her once more.

"Melody, don't be angry." Luke rose from his chair. He stepped in close to her and touched her shoulder. "I meant no offense. I just—I care about you."

Melody wondered if it was her imagination or if she'd heard tenderness in his voice as he'd spoken those last four words. Either way, her aggravation vanished.

Last night she'd felt as though nobody cared, but this morning God showed her that both her folks and Luke had fretted over her welfare.

She pushed out a smile. "Thanks, Luke. I care about you, too."

A pleased-looking grin tugged at the corners of his mouth. "Then will you promise? Next time you feel like escaping for a while, you'll call me first? Doesn't matter what time of day or night it is."

Her smile grew, and she concluded Luke Berringer had to be the sweetest guy on the planet. What's more, she really believed him when he said he cared about her. He meant every word; she could tell by the expression on his face.

"All right, I promise."

Chapter 10

D o you promise?"

Melody rolled her eyes. "Yes, Dad, I promise. And if it's any consolation, Luke made me promise him the same thing. No more 'dashing off to nowhere,' as you put it."

"Good." He leaned back in the armchair and narrowed his gaze. "Luke, huh? You two have been spending a lot of time together."

From her place on the sofa in the living room, Mel shrugged and staved off a yawn. "We're just friends."

"I've been hearing that word *friend* a lot around here lately."

"Yes, well, if you're referring to my so-called *friendship* with Scott, I'll have you know he led me to believe it was something much more."

"I know, I know." Dad lifted a hand, palm side out. "I believe you, Mel." He raked his fingers through the small thatch of hair he had left on his scalp. "I don't know why Scott would lie, or fail to remember, or whatever his problem is, but I do believe you."

"Thanks." Immediate tears flooded her eyes, a consequence of no sleep in the last twenty-four hours and a long day at work.

"Now don't cry. You know I can't stand it when you girls cry."

"Sorry. I'm overtired."

"All right. Now, about Luke."

"What about him?" Mel dabbed the corners of her eyes and wondered if Bonnie shared her opinion with their parents. "I'm not using him, if that's what you're wondering."

"Using him?" A deep frown furrowed her father's bushy, gray-streaked brows. "Why would I think that?"

Melody told him the particulars of the argument she'd had with Bonnie last night.

Dad shook his head and tossed a glance upward. "This nonsense has to stop."

"I agree, but how?"

"Well," he drawled, "I might have an answer." He sent her a dubious glance. "I did have all night to think and pray on the subject."

Melody shifted uncomfortably on the couch cushion. "I'm sorry I kept you up, Dad."

"Let's forget it. Okay, here's my idea. I say we call a truce. Whatever happened between you and Scott years ago is dead and done with. You told me you repented for any wrongdoing."

Mel nodded.

"Then God has forgiven you. 'If we confess our sins, he is faithful and just and will forgive us our sins and purify us from all unrighteousness.'"

"First John 1:9," Melody said, recognizing the passage of scripture her dad just recited.

"But now *you* have to forgive Scott."

"I'm working on it." She picked at a thread on her scrub pants.

"No, honey, the act of forgiveness is a decision. It's immediate, like deciding to turn on the TV. You just do it."

"I did, but memories come back to haunt me, and when new incidents occur, I'm hurt all over again."

"Then it's seventy times seven, just like Christ said."

Melody knew her stepfather was right. But it seemed so much easier to talk about forgiveness than to put it into practice. Nevertheless, she bobbed her head in reply.

"Good. Next, Bonnie has to quit acting so insecure. I'll talk to her. And Scott. That guy better watch his p's and q's, or he's going to feel the sting of this father's wrath—and don't smile about that, Mel."

She pressed her lips together.

"Forgiveness. Remember?"

"Yes."

"Now back to Luke."

Once more, Mel gave her father a quizzical stare.

"Why are you just friends?"

"Why?" Melody didn't get it.

"You want to get married. Luke is as eligible as bachelors come. He's a nice, decent Christian man, and—"

Melody shook off the notion. The last thing she wanted to do was fall in love with a guy who thought they were "just friends"—like Scott. Except, unlike Luke, Scott had professed his undying love for her. And she'd been too naïve to see the man for what he was.

What a liar.

"Melody?"

I have to forgive Scott.

She looked at her father, amazed at how her mind had wandered. "Um— Luke is actually interested in someone else. I guess that's why we're not anything more than friends."

"Ahh. Well, that explains it. Who is she?"

Mel shrugged. "Mystery Girl. Luke won't tell me. He said he'll feel stupid if his feelings for this person get around." Mel lifted her hands in a helpless gesture. "I've told him that women can't read minds. He's got to let his feelings be known."

Dad pursed his lips. "What'd he say to that?"

"Nothing specific except that he'd rather leave that up to the Holy Spirit. I've been trying to figure out who Mystery Girl is, and I've concluded she must already be seeing somebody and that's why Luke doesn't want to ask her out. He asks me out instead." Mel laughed and babbled on. "I told Luke that people are going to think we're dating, but apparently he doesn't care. I think it's because he wants to make his mystery girl jealous, but. . ." Mel frowned, rethinking her hypothesis. "No, on second thought, that's not Luke's style. He's really sweet and honest—a very compassionate person. I've told him about all this stuff I'm going through since Bonnie's engagement, and Luke's been so supportive. He cares for me. He's said so, and it really shows. He's a good friend."

"Melody?" Dad sat forward and clasped his wide, calloused hands. A speculative frown creased his brows. "Let's think about this for a minute."

"Sure." Did he have an idea who Mystery Girl was? Melody perked up, poised and ready to hear it.

Then, much to her disappointment, Dad shook his head. "Never mind. I'm not getting involved, at least not at this point. I have enough trouble on my plate with Bonnie and Scott." He stood and stretched before a chuckle escaped. "I'm sure the truth will sink into *Mystery Girl's* thick head one of these days."

Dad winked and strode through the dining room, toward the kitchen.

"What*ever*." Melody should have known her father wouldn't participate in any kind of guessing game. Trivial Pursuit was a favorite pastime of hers, but Dad never enjoyed such things.

"Just remember what I said." He paused under the dining room's archway and sent her a stern look. "Forgiveness."

Melody nodded. "Right. Forgiveness."

It was the third promise she had made that day.

∽

Luke pulled into the asphalt lot of the supermarket and parked. Grocery list and coupons in hand, he exited his SUV, locked it, and ambled in the direction of the store's entrance.

He couldn't remember the last time he went food shopping on a Saturday morning. Usually he stopped at the nearest convenience store and grabbed necessities on his way home from the office or while on the road to or from an open house. But he realized this morning, as he stared at the meager contents in his refrigerator and equally sparse cupboards, that if he wanted Melody to continue to cook for him, he'd better stock up on at least the basics. Thursday night had been a complete embarrassment. Melody offered to create a pot of spaghetti with meat sauce but had to run to the store first. She had laughed off the incident, but Luke didn't think it was so funny. He wanted everything in his house to suit her—to be perfect for her. In short, nothing would please him more than if she loved his home—and him!

Melody. That girl didn't stray far from his thoughts these days. Last night she'd actually asked him if he wanted to go out for a fish fry. Bonnie had decided to impress her fiancé with her culinary skills again, so Melody wanted an escape. Luke had been more than happy to provide it, although it troubled him that Melody still felt such derision toward Ramsay. She announced she'd forgiven him, but Luke still sensed an undercurrent of hurt and resentment. The day Melody felt nothing for the guy would be the day, in Luke's mind, that she was really over him.

"Hey, mister, wanna buy a puppy?"

Luke ground to a halt, having nearly collided with the boy sitting in a red wagon with four squirming bundles of black and beige fur. He glanced at the lady sitting in a lawn chair two feet away and guessed she was the boy's mother.

"Ah, no thanks."

"They make good pets." The towheaded youngster held up one of the animals. The boy's blue eyes were wide with eagerness. "And they don't cost a lot."

Luke grinned. The kid was a salesman in the making. "What kind are they?"

"We're not exactly sure," the woman replied before drawing deeply on a cigarette. She was noticeably thin and wore a purple shirt and blue jeans. She'd pulled back her straight blond hair into a ponytail. "They're half golden retriever and half something else. Might be a Lab and German shepherd mix. We're not sure."

"Hmm." Luke nodded his understanding.

"Only fifty bucks," the boy said, holding up a puppy. Then he quickly tried to subdue the others before they escaped from the high-sided wagon.

Luke scratched the animal behind its soft, floppy ears.

"We're trying to sell them," the woman added. "If we don't, they'll go to the Humane Society tomorrow. I've had it. My entire house smells like puppies."

"If they go to the Humane Society, they might hafta get put to sleep," the kid added, wearing a look of remorse. "They got too many dogs there."

Luke didn't think that was true, but he admired the sales pitch. "I'm sure these little guys will sell. But I'm not interested. Thanks anyhow." He smiled and walked away.

However, as he pushed his shopping cart down the produce aisle, he thought back to what Melody had said about always wanting a puppy. What if he bought her one? She could keep it at his house since her mom had allergies.

Luke quelled the grin twitching his lips. That'd be one way to lure Melody over to his house. Of course, he'd never want to appear manipulative or, worse, deceptive. On the other hand, he'd considered buying a dog on more than one occasion. He'd just never gotten around to actually doing it.

Yeah, I need a puppy like I need a hole in my head, Luke thought as he selected several tomatoes. But as he strolled up and down the food aisles, the idea gained merit. A dog would mean companionship. A dog would also be a means of protection for his property when he wasn't around. On the other hand, having a pet might infringe on his freedom. But if it didn't work out, Luke felt sure his sister Amber would take the dog. She and her husband and four kids lived in a rural area, and they loved animals.

What could he lose?

Luke found the dog food aisle and heaved a bag formulated for puppies into his grocery cart.

I must be nuts, he thought as he checked out.

With his items bought and bagged, Luke wheeled them out to his SUV. He loaded them into the back of the vehicle and returned the cart before approaching the boy selling the puppies.

"I changed my mind. I'll buy one."

The kid looked delighted to make the sale.

"If you don't have a preference," the blond woman with the cigarette said, "I'd suggest a female. I think they're easier to train."

Luke shrugged. "Okay."

"But there's only one girl left." The youngster found her and handed the puppy to Luke.

He inspected the roly-poly, wiggling pup. Her dark eyes shone with intelligence and spunk. Her floppy ears framed a black face with caramel-colored markings that was greeting-card cute.

A mental image of Melody at eight years old trying to teach her rabbit to bark flashed through Luke's mind. He had a feeling she'd fall in love with this dog in a minute, the lucky mutt.

Luke smiled. "Sold."

Chapter 11

Luke somehow made it home from the grocery store with a squirming, scared, ten-week-old puppy in his lap. When he pulled into the alley, he noticed the Stensons' opened garage door. As he pulled alongside his own garage and parked, he spotted Melody and her dad. With the puppy tucked under his arm, he walked next door.

"Hey, look what I got." Luke laughed when he saw Melody's eyes light up.

"Oh, how cute!" She hopped off the ladder on which she'd been perched. "Where'd you get him—or her?"

"Her, and I just bought her from a kid selling puppies at the grocery store."

"She's adorable."

Luke allowed Melody to take the puppy, and she enfolded the animal in her arms.

"You are so sweet," she murmured to the dog. The puppy responded by chewing on the collar of her short-sleeved forest green polo shirt.

Luke noticed Bill Stenson watching them intently.

"I've been thinking of getting a dog," Luke began in a lame way, "but now that I actually purchased one, I'm doubting my sanity."

Melody grinned. "I'll help you train her. When I was a kid, I read countless books on how to train dogs. I wanted a puppy so badly. . . ."

Bill rolled his eyes and returned to sanding the four-drawer dresser he'd been working on. The thing had been painted a gaudy red, and Luke guessed Mel's dad planned to refurbish the piece.

Luke returned his focus to Melody. "In all honesty, I hoped you'd say you'd help me."

"Oh, I will." She nuzzled the puppy.

"I figure if it doesn't work out, Amber will take the dog. I'm planning to spend July Fourth with my sister and her family anyhow."

"No, Luke, you can't get rid of her. Look how lovable she is!" Melody kissed the top of the dog's head. "She'll be a good girl, won't you, sweetheart?"

Bill stopped sanding long enough to send Luke a skeptical glance.

"Can I show my mom and Bonnie?"

Luke turned back to Melody. "Sure."

She headed for the side door of the garage.

"Hey." Bill halted her in midstride. "Don't take that dog in the house, or your mother will be in the emergency room all afternoon."

"I won't."

"And you'll have to keep your clothes separate from ours and do your own wash if you're going to be training that puppy."

"I wash my own clothes anyway. But yes, Dad, I'll be careful. And I'll just show Mom and Bonnie the puppy through the screen door." Melody turned back to Luke. "What's her name?"

"I haven't named her yet."

"Oh." She glanced at the puppy, then back at Luke. "Can I help you name her, too?"

Luke couldn't see why not. He nodded. "Yeah."

"Cool. You're awesome." After giving him a smile that took his breath away, she left the garage.

Luke's heart swelled in his chest, threatening to burst.

Bill stopped rubbing the sandpaper over the painted wood. "I'm thinking Mel's going to be spending a lot of time over at your place, what with helping you train that new dog."

Luke walked over to where Bill Stenson stood. "Is that all right with you?"

Bill replied with a single incline of his head. "But I trust you to be a gentleman at all times, Luke."

"Yes, sir. I wouldn't dream of being anything less."

"Good." Bill plugged in his electric sander while eyeing Luke. "I get the impression that you're romantically interested in Mel. Am I right?"

Luke was momentarily thrown off guard by the blunt question. "Mr. Stenson, I think I've loved Melody since we were in fourth grade."

He chuckled. "Well, I know Mel thinks highly of you. She told me she cares for you. Guess that's a good start."

Luke already knew that; Melody had said as much, but he wanted so much more. "Honestly, Mr. Stenson—"

"Call me Bill. It's not like you're just a neighbor kid anymore."

"Okay. *Bill.*" Luke grinned and shifted his stance. He cleared his throat. "I'm praying for two things. One, that Jesus will be Melody's first love, and two, that I'll be her second." He paused. "Make that three things I'm praying for." He paused, weighing his words with care. "I'm praying Melody will get Scott Ramsay out of her system once and for all."

Bill nodded, and his expression said he understood. "Your third request is well on its way to being answered. We had a family meeting and Scott was in on it. We talked about forgiving and forgetting and moving on."

"Glad to hear it." Luke, however, wasn't convinced Melody's emotions were so neatly packaged and ready to be stowed.

"We're one big happy family again, much to my relief." Bill sighed.

Luke offered a perfunctory smile.

"And Mel's made up with her girlfriends."

"Yes, I did hear about that."

"But. . ." Bill cocked a brow. "Mel thinks you're interested in someone else. Some *mystery girl*."

Luke hooted and shook his head. "Okay, I'll admit it. I've got a ways to go before I get the message through to her. But at least she's now aware I exist."

"Who's now aware you exist?" Melody asked, reentering the garage. She carried the puppy in the crook of her arm like a baby.

"None of your beeswax," Bill retorted while Luke stood by feeling somewhat mortified. He'd never intended for Melody to overhear their conversation. He should have been more careful. "This is man talk," Bill continued, "and not for your tender, female ears."

"Oh, Dad. . ." Melody threw an annoyed glance upward, but her gaze came back to rest on Luke. He saw the questions gathering like storm clouds in her sky blue eyes.

No way around it, he'd have some explaining to do later.

❧

Melody felt her face warm with an indignant flame. How could Luke share his secret with Dad but not her? Did Luke think she was a blabbermouth? Well, she wasn't!

Seconds later, reason returned, and Mel wondered if her father had been the one to broach that topic. After all, Mel had told Dad about Luke's mystery girl. Perhaps he had pressed Luke on the subject.

"I—um—have to pick up supplies for the dog," Luke said, and Mel heard the hesitancy in his voice. "I also have groceries to unpack."

She arched her brows. "You bought groceries?"

"Yeah." Luke smiled, and Mel thought he looked relieved. "So will you—um—come to the pet store with me?"

She cast aside the feeling that she'd been slighted and made a mental note to ask Luke about Mystery Girl later. "Sure, I'll come along. We can bring Lexus with us. I hear they allow dogs in the store."

"Lexus?" Now it was Luke's turn to raise his brows.

Melody felt herself blush. "Do you think that name suits her?" She glanced down at the now sleeping puppy in her arms. "Think of a sleek black car with tan leather upholstery—that's what this puppy's coloring reminds me of."

"I think of a Mercedes Benz." Dad's guffaw filled the garage.

Melody rolled her eyes. "You can't holler 'Mercedes' out the back door." She turned to Luke. "But you could call 'Lexi,' short for Lexus."

Luke pursed his lips and mulled it over. "Lexi's a cute name."

Melody smiled.

They left the garage and headed to Luke's house. He carried in the grocery bags, and Melody helped him unpack the food. The puppy awoke and nosed her way in between Mel's ankles.

"I can't believe you bought all this stuff," she said, eyeing the bags of flour, sugar, brown sugar, bottles of various spices, and packs of ground beef, chicken, and pork chops. He'd even purchased a gallon of milk, nondairy creamer, and sticks of butter. "It's about time."

Luke chuckled. "Yeah, I guess every couple of years I need to stock up."

"Every *couple of years*?" Mel laughed, deciding Luke needed a wife in the worst way.

Well, at least he had a puppy now. She supposed that was a start.

Chapter 12

Melody didn't have any other plans on this gorgeous last day of April, so accompanying Luke to the pet store gave her something to do. She held Lexi in her lap as they drove the distance in Luke's SUV. The store was animal-friendly, so taking a pet inside wasn't an issue. Then, while he purchased a dog crate and other supplies, Mel spoke with the store manager and learned several new things about housebreaking and training a puppy.

On the way back home, Luke muttered that dogs were expensive.

Melody laughed and cuddled Lexi. Minutes later, he turned into the alley and parked in his garage. Mel grabbed one of the many shopping bags. As she walked toward his house, her father hailed her from the other side of the fence.

"How 'bout you two plan to eat with us tonight? Bonnie's not cooking." Dad grinned. "I'm getting tired of eating that gourmet slop that she's been trying to impress Scott with, so I'm grilling burgers."

"Yum." Mel set Lexi on the grass.

"Sounds good to me, too." Luke's voice resounded from behind her, and Melody peered over her shoulder at him. His arms were full of pet equipment, so she stepped off the sidewalk and let him pass.

"Will it be just the four of us?" Mel asked.

Her father shook his balding head. "No, Bonnie and Scott will be here. So we'll be six altogether."

Melody felt a heavy frown settle over her features. She couldn't pinpoint it, but there was something troubling about Scott Ramsay—something that caused Mel to doubt his sincerity and even his faith.

Her dad narrowed his gaze as if he divined her thoughts. "Forgiveness, remember?"

"Yeah, yeah, yeah."

Dad gave her one of his hard stares before inclining his head. "That puppy is escaping, Mel."

She sucked in a breath of alarm before running after Lexi. Mel caught her before she disappeared around the far side of Luke's garage.

"Some babysitter you are," her dad teased.

Melody sent him a dismissive wave and walked into Luke's house. She found him sitting on the kitchen floor assembling Lexi's new crate. It was a cream-colored, hard plastic model with plenty of air vents and a sturdy grated metal door that clicked soundly into place.

"Doggy jail," Luke said with a laugh, pushing the thing under his kitchen table.

"No, it's her *bed*." Melody shook her head at him. "If you get me some old linens, I'll make a nice, soft place for Lexi to sleep."

Luke stood, left the kitchen, and minutes later returned with some well-worn towels and mismatched sheets that had obviously seen better days.

"Perfect." Melody arranged the bedding, then set the puppy in the crate and closed the door. "Nap time."

Luke chuckled and offered Melody his hand. She took it and he helped her up off the floor.

At that very moment, Bonnie and Scott burst in through the side door unannounced.

"Okay, what are you guys doing?" Bonnie set her hands on her slender hips. A smile tugged at her watermelon-pink mouth. "Dad sent us over here to spy."

Melody laughed and withdrew her hand from Luke's. "Yeah, sure he did. He probably wanted to get rid of the two of you for a while."

"You know, Mellow, I think you're right about that one." Scott flashed her one of his movie star smiles before sauntering over to Luke.

The men shook hands in greeting.

Melody stifled a grimace. Every time Scott called her "Mellow," she wanted to smack him.

"Actually," Bonnie said, "Scott and I have business to discuss with Luke."

"Want me to leave?" Mel suddenly relished the idea.

"No, stay. It's all right." Bonnie's blue-eyed gaze settled on Luke. "Can we sit down and talk?"

He nodded. "Let's move into the living room."

Mel followed her sister and the two men through the dining area and into Luke's comfortable living room. In the past couple of weeks, she'd learned about the extensive remodeling Luke had done on this place after his folks died. It made her appreciate everything from the paint and varnish to the expanded living room. What's more, since she'd started hanging out over here, Mel had begun to feel right at home, even though Luke's leather furniture was too "bachelor" for her tastes.

She plopped down on one end of the couch and folded her legs beneath her. To her shock and horror, Scott seated himself right beside her. He put an arm around her and hugged her shoulders.

"So how's my little sis on this fine Saturday afternoon?"

Melody gave in to her instincts and elbowed him in the ribs, but not quite as hard as she would have liked. Even so, Scott fell over onto the empty side of the sofa, feigning injury.

He's trying to be funny, Mel told herself. However, Scott's antics only caused her to dislike him all the more.

And this wasn't the first time he'd done something stupid, either. The night of their family meeting, Scott had sneaked up on Melody as she loaded the dishwasher. Placing his hands at her waist, he'd tickled her. Mel's parents and sister were still sitting at the dining room table and had, of course, heard the shriek that followed. Scott just laughed and announced that Melody "spooked easily." But it was Melody who'd received the cold stare from Bonnie and the look of reproof from her folks. Scott had a way of making her appear the guilty one, the instigator.

After discussing the matter at great length with Luke, Melody concluded she'd lost her parents' trust when they learned she hadn't told them about dating Scott. It hadn't been like her, hadn't been in her character, to keep anything from them. Now Mom and Dad probably felt as if they didn't really know her. Perhaps they wondered what else she hadn't told them, and Melody could visualize her mother wondering if maybe Bonnie's accusations had merit.

Melody glanced at her sister now. From her place in the overstuffed, tan leather armchair, Bonnie wore a tight, polite little grin. But when Melody glanced across the way at Luke, he replied with an assuring wink as if to let her know he was on her side.

She smiled at him. What would she ever do without a friend like Luke?

"I'm going to make some coffee." Mel stood and headed for the kitchen. She backtracked, eyeing Luke. "Did you buy coffee this morning?"

He scrunched up his face. "No, I forgot."

Melody laughed. "Okay, I'll run next door and get some."

She took her time about it and even stayed in Luke's pristine kitchen while the coffee brewed. Lexi slept, curled up, in the corner of her crate.

Once the coffeemaker finished its gurgling and sputtering, Melody pulled four mugs from the cupboard. Next, she fished out a black lacquer tray that Luke kept in the lower cabinet; Mel had seen it there along with his pots and pans. Dishcloth in hand, she wiped off the thin layer of dust and swallowed a giggle, wondering when the tray was last used. Placing the coffeepot and mugs on its shining surface, she opened the fridge and found the nondairy creamer. Luke's sugar bowl was in use again, too, ever since he returned from the store this morning. Mel set the condiments on the tray as well. Then she strode back into the living room.

Luke saw her coming and made room for her on the love seat. Bonnie still sat in the armchair, but Scott had stretched out on the sofa. His leather penny loafers dangled over the armrest.

"Just make yourself at home, Scott. Don't be shy." Mel couldn't resist the quip as she sat down and began pouring coffee.

Scott chuckled.

Bonnie cleared her throat. "As I was saying—"

"Sure, I'd be happy to show you and Scott the house," Luke injected.

Melody looked at her sister, then at Luke. "What house?"

"The old Thornton place." Luke sipped his coffee.

Mel fought the urge to gape. "The Thorntons' place?" The reply really hadn't warranted repeating, but Mel was battling shock.

"Scott and I are interested in buying it," Bonnie explained as she crossed the room and helped herself to a cup of java. She added a splash of creamer. "Scott and I saw the FOR SALE sign out in front and just fell in love with it."

But I've loved that old Victorian home ever since I can remember! Melody fought to control her envy.

"Like I said. . ." Luke sat back in the settee. "The property needs a lot of work."

"Oh, but it'll be fun to fix it up." Bonnie walked back to the armchair, looking Scott's way. "Right, honey?"

"Anything you say, babe."

Honey? Babe? Melody wanted to gag. But instead she pretended to be unaffected by this latest turn of events. She fixed her coffee, then scooted back on the love seat, folding one leg beneath her. She forced herself to act friendly and impervious in spite of her heart screaming, *It's just not fair!*

The Thorntons' house. It was located two blocks away and stood in regal splendor overlooking the northwest Milwaukee neighborhood. Melody figured it must have been one of the first homes built in this section of the city, and it had always been her dream to live in it someday.

But now her sister would live in it.

The last precious piece of her dream shattered.

Melody felt like sobbing. Everything she had always dreamed of and longed for in life, a beautiful wedding, a handsome groom, her dream home, was being handed to Bonnie.

Lord, this is so not fair!

∽

Later that afternoon, Melody kept silent throughout dinner. But the stress of the situation overcame her, and she polished off two hamburgers, a lumberjack-sized portion of her mother's potato salad, and a homemade fudge brownie. She figured at this rate she'd weigh five hundred pounds by the time Bonnie and Scott's wedding day rolled around.

When the meal ended, Mom and Bonnie strolled into the kitchen and talked bridal gowns while they washed dishes. Dad and Scott ambled into the den, but Luke declined the offer to sit with the guys and surf the cable channels.

"Maybe we should check on Lexi," Mel suggested. She suddenly yearned for a reason to escape the matrimony chatter, and she wasn't about to sit in the den with her dad and Scott.

"Great idea."

Melody called a farewell to her folks before following Luke to his place.

"I'm so–o–o full," she complained as he let them in through his side entrance.

He chuckled. "I was just going to ask: What's eating you? No pun intended."

Lexi whined in her crate, and Melody snapped to attention. She rushed to the crate and carried the dog outside, where Lexi did her business.

"Success!"

When she returned to the kitchen, Luke grinned at the small victory. He folded his arms across the periwinkle golf shirt he wore. "Now back to my question." He narrowed his gaze. "What's up?"

Melody shrugged. She knew what Luke meant. He evidently had sensed her inner turmoil during dinner. But where did she begin?

She sighed. "Same old stuff."

"It upsets you when Scott's around?"

Again she lifted her shoulders in uncertainty.

"Maybe you do have feelings for him after all."

"Oh, I have feelings for him, all right." Mel couldn't keep the cynicism out of her voice. "Irritation, aggravation, and annoyance are the top three."

Luke laughed. "Did you want to think about that for a minute?"

Melody smiled at the comeback and sat on the cool tiled floor. She pulled Lexi into her arms. "I think it's obvious how I feel about Scott. I dislike him. I have absolutely no respect for him." She exhaled audibly. "I'm not a person who can hide her emotions."

"So I've discovered."

"Then why did you ask if I still have feelings for him—and I assume you meant romantic feelings?"

"Just making sure, I guess." Luke sat down on the floor across from Mel. The puppy wiggled out of her grasp and bounded over to her new owner. She jumped into his lap, biting his hands and anything else she could sink her teeth into. Luke reached for one of the chew toys he'd purchased earlier that day and distracted Lexi, who obviously wanted to play. "I could tell something's been bothering you all afternoon."

"You're right."

"So what is it?"

Melody gave in, sensing Luke wouldn't be satisfied until she bared her soul—as she often did of late. "Luke, ever since I was a little girl, I've fantasized about living in the Thorntons' house. I imagined myself a sort of urban princess, serving tea in the parlor to my guests. I didn't even know the place was for sale, not that I could afford to buy it or anything. But the fact that Bonnie wants it, and will most likely get it, is like another knife in my heart."

Luke pursed his lips, mulling it over. "Have you ever walked through the Thorntons' house?"

Mel shook her head.

"Hmm. Well, as you know, the Thorntons were an elderly couple—"

"Ancient, you mean. They were 'elderly' when we were kids."

Luke chuckled. "Well, yeah, I guess that's true. Anyway, as they aged, Mr. and Mrs. Thornton refused to relocate, even after they required assisted living arrangements. So a nephew moved in and took care of them, although I cringe when I imagine what kind of care they received. Ron Pittman is the relative who inherited the house. He contacted our office, and I did a market analysis for him. When I did my initial walk-through, I was appalled by filth. The guy's a total slob."

Melody wrinkled her nose, imagining the sight.

"The place is a lot better now. Pittman moved out and hired a company to clean it up. But it's still in rough shape." Luke set the puppy on the floor, then stood. He held out his hand to Mel. "Come on. I'll give you your own private tour." He smiled before adding, "*Princess Melody*."

Chapter 13

Luke punched in the pass code on the lock fitted over the knob, and the back door opened. A musty, rotten odor assailed Mel's senses as she entered the spacious hallway. She noticed the cracks on the plastered walls that were painted a drab green color.

Luke grabbed a black flashlight hooked on a nail to his right and flipped on its switch.

"We'll start in the basement. Come on."

He led the way to the winding stairs.

"Watch your step."

He offered Mel his hand and she took it, thinking that each time her fingers met his palm, she enjoyed the sensation more and more.

"There's no electricity down here, and if you'll notice, there's a dirt floor and stone foundation."

"Is it crumbling?" Mel strained to see. It was dusk outside, but dark as pitch down in the basement.

"I think someone tried to plaster over the stone, and that's what's coming off now."

"Oh." She glanced around, then wove her fingers between Luke's and decided not to let him too far out of her reach. "It's creepy down here."

In the glow of the flashlight, she saw him grin at her. "You're not the kind of female who screams at the sight of spiders, are you?"

"No."

"Didn't think so."

"Just snakes. Big snakes, like the ones they show on the Discovery Channel or Animal Planet."

Luke laughed. "We're not likely to run into any of those down here."

He showed her the fruit and wine cellars, where the water heater and the monstrosity of a furnace were located.

"The furnace needs to be replaced." Luke stated the obvious. "I wouldn't be surprised if it was the original."

"Can we get out of here? I think I've seen enough of this dungeon."

Luke chuckled but shined the beam of light toward the stairwell. Melody ran up the steps and waited for him in the hallway. She watched as Luke flicked several switches at the top of the basement stairs and overhead lights went on.

"I'll show you the kitchen now."

Melody followed him up another short flight of stairs. He opened shuttered doors to reveal a washer and dryer.

"The utility room," he said.

"I'd say it's more like a closet with appliances shoved inside."

"Yeah, that's about it." Luke closed the door and turned on the kitchen lights.

Melody gaped at her primitive surroundings. Pea green rubber tile covered the floor. A white enamel-coated cast-iron sink from the 1940s occupied most of the far wall. A relic of a range stood against another, its oven door askew. There were no cupboards and no counters, no dishwasher, and the space where a refrigerator should have stood appeared useless. No refrigerator on the market today would fit in there.

"How did Mrs. Thornton prepare any meals?"

"Probably used her kitchen table like you'd use counter space."

"Mmm."

"My suggestion to prospective buyers is that they knock out this wall here." He led Melody around to the pantry where four wide, long shelves ran the length of the wall with cabinets underneath them. "This would enlarge the kitchen and then cupboards could be installed."

"Yeah, I guess that would work."

The tour continued, and Luke walked her through the large dining room. Despite its gaudy red and gold wallpaper, it showed promise. But the living room or "parlor" was smaller than the average bedroom. However, across the hardwood floor in the foyer there was another "sitting room" of equal size.

"Tell me what you think so far."

Melody turned and faced him. "This house is proof that looks are deceiving. From the outside this place seems like it would be a charming Victorian home. But the inside is so—so awful, it'll send the best do-it-yourselfer screaming into the night."

Luke appeared amused by her assessment. "Let's go upstairs."

Mel trailed him to the winding staircase. At first glance, it looked like a mahogany grandeur, but it creaked eerily with each step they took.

"This staircase is safe, isn't it?" Mel grasped the intricately carved but rickety railing. No help there.

"The inspector said it was safe."

Mel heard the grin in Luke's voice. "Are you laughing at me?"

"A little." Luke's tone grew serious. "Melody, I'd never lead you into harm's way. Don't you know better than that?"

"Well, yeah, but it never hurts to ask." The wood moaned in protest beneath her foot, and she hesitated to go farther.

Luke turned back and offered his hand. Mel took it; his grip felt strong and sure, unlike the wobbly railing.

"You're perfectly safe," he assured her.

Mel believed him, and her misgivings seemed to evaporate.

They reached the second floor, and Mel discovered it had four bedrooms and one good-sized bathroom. The only trouble was, none of the bedrooms had closets, and the plumbing in the bathroom appeared to be as old and outdated as the ancient furnace.

As they rode back to Luke's place, Melody retreated into contemplative silence. Luke, too, seemed consumed with his thoughts.

"You know what?" she said sometime later as they sat outside on Luke's back deck. "The Thornton place is sort of like my infatuation was with Scott years ago. On the outside it looked romantic and wonderful, like a dream come true. I mean, I sure thought so. But I never looked inside, at the real relationship, where the problems were hidden. That would be kind of like buying that old wreck without seeing the inside, naïvely believing I was getting my dream house."

"Spoken like a true English major."

She grinned and kicked up her heels, placing her feet on the wooden rail. "I suppose that's a weird analogy, but it sort of goes along with my girlish dreams."

Melody glanced at Luke. His puppy slept on his chest and with one hand he methodically stroked the animal's soft fur. Just watching him made Mel tired.

She stifled a yawn.

"I'm sorry you've had your dreams dashed."

She heard the note of compassion in his voice, and it made her wish she were Lexi, being held close to Luke's heart.

"But just remember—where dreams end, hope begins."

Melody thought it over and smiled. "That's really nice, Luke. 'Where dreams end, hope begins.' I'm impressed. That's rather poetic."

He chuckled.

She lazed back in the cushioned chair and studied his profile. She could see it clearly, thanks to the yard light and the glow of the streetlamps in the alley. His shadowy jawline, the contour of his cheek, the way his walnut-colored hair was neatly trimmed around his ear. . . His slightly crooked nose with its bump at the bridge—due to a kickball game injury in the seventh grade. . . Melody still recalled the buzz around school when Luke Berringer broke his nose.

Then suddenly his gaze met hers and Melody looked away. She felt embarrassed to have been caught staring at him. She couldn't imagine what was wrong with her tonight. Her thoughts were all askew. She and Luke were friends. Just friends.

"Hey, Melody, can I ask you something personal?"

She swallowed her sudden discomfort. "Sure."

"How come you don't sing anymore—you know, solo in church, rejoin the choir? You have such a pretty singing voice."

"Thanks." She had to laugh. "It's funny you ask me that. My dad and I were discussing this very topic right before you showed up to introduce your new puppy."

Luke wore a little smile along with an expectant expression.

"Why don't I sing like I used to?" She gazed out over Luke's backyard. "I guess it goes along with the whole forgiveness thing."

What Melody didn't add was that she used to sing to Scott. Her love for him had put the song of joy in her heart. When he dumped her, she felt as if something died inside. "I don't know. Maybe God took my gift away."

"Hmm." Luke seemed to mull it over. "I heard you sing last week when I sat next you in church, and your gift sounded pretty good to me."

Mel smiled at the compliment, and it occurred to her then that in grade school and high school, the object of her song was Jesus. Somehow in college, the show of affection had gotten transferred to Scott.

"Listen, you can sing in my ear anytime."

Melody laughed but felt flattered all the same. "Thanks, Luke. You have a way of encouraging me. Maybe I'll—I'll think about joining choir again."

"Good." He sent her a grin before glancing at his gold-tone wristwatch. Then he stood. "Ten o'clock news is on. Want to come in and watch it with me?"

"I suppose. . ." Melody lifted her heels off the rail, then pushed to her feet. "You're a news junkie, you know that? You watch cable news, local news, news magazine shows—"

"I know it." He heaved a dramatic sigh. "It's an incurable habit, I'm afraid."

"Well, there is hope," Melody said, entering the house while Luke held the door for her. "I did catch you watching a sports channel the other night."

He chuckled, and they made their way to the kitchen. Luke set the puppy in her crate and closed the door before walking the rest of the way into the living room. He collapsed into the far side of the love seat and lifted the remote, turning on his wide-screen television.

Melody ambled in behind him, and without giving it much thought, plopped down next to him. She'd left plenty of room between them, but it still felt too cozy for *just friends*.

Suddenly Melody was very much aware of Luke Berringer—and not as the shy, geeky guy she'd known most of her life, but as a handsome, *single* man.

Lord, my mind is going haywire here. What's the matter with me?

A commercial aired on TV, and Luke picked up the remote and pressed the MUTE button.

Luke cleared his throat. "Hey, listen. I've—um—wanted to explain about this morning. And it just never seemed like the right time—until now."

In an instant Mel knew what he meant. "About sharing your secret with my dad?" She shook her head and gave the topic a dismissive wave. "Don't worry about it. I told my father that you're in love with some mystery girl, and—"

"Melody, I'm not *in love* with anyone else," Luke said, cupping her chin, urging her gaze to his.

"I—I guess I didn't mean love, exactly." Melody felt oddly uncomfortable at the moment. "I meant—*interested.*"

Luke rolled his eyes and sat back on the love seat.

And then it dawned on Melody.

"You're embarrassed! Is that why you won't tell me who this woman is?"

He grinned and flicked his gaze in her direction. "Let's just drop it, okay?"

That's it. Melody concealed a smug smile. She still had a hunch that Alicia Sims was aka Mystery Girl.

As they sat there in silence, a weird kind of sadness coiled its way around Mel's insides. Mystery Girl didn't know how lucky she was!

Luke crossed his leg, ankle to knee, and unmuted the television. Melody felt as though he had somehow inflated his existence, because not quite an inch remained between them.

She stared at the TV, paying little to no attention to what the anchorman reported. All she could think about was how much she'd enjoy scooting a bit closer to Luke.

And that's a great way to ruin a perfect relationship—fall in love with a friend.

Melody stood. "I'd better go home. I have things to do before church tomorrow."

"Like what?" Luke wore a mischievous expression.

"Like laundry," Mel quipped.

He chuckled and rose from the love seat. "I'll walk you out."

"Don't bother."

"I insist."

Melody gave a careless shrug, but she failed to hide her grin as they walked to the kitchen.

"Wait a sec. I want to give you something."

Luke crossed the room and opened a drawer. He extracted a brass-colored key connected to a large round ring and tossed it to her. Mel caught it with little effort.

"What's this?"

"The key to my heart."

"Honestly, Luke." Mel laughed at his feeble jest, wondering how he could spout such nonsense with a straight face.

"Actually," Luke informed her, "it's the key to my house. Might come in handy if I'm not home and Lexi has to go out." He paused and regarded her for a moment. "You're still willing to help me train her, aren't you?"

"Of course." Mel slipped the key ring onto her wrist like a bracelet. "In fact, I was going to ask if you wanted me to come by and let her out on my lunch breaks. I get a whole hour, and I work just minutes away."

"That would be great. Thanks, Melody."

She gave him a smile. "No problem. What are friends for?"

But as she left Luke's place and made her way home, she had to admit her last comment belied the feelings in her heart.

Friends. She wouldn't mind if their relationship became much more. However, the realization was frightening. It couldn't happen again, falling for a guy who didn't love her in return.

Determination replaced the disappointment and trepidation mounting inside her. Melody wouldn't let it happen!

Opening the side door of the house, she let herself in and tried to mentally rewire her short-circuiting brain.

We're friends. Luke and I are just friends.

Chapter 14

For the next ten days, Melody did her best to avoid Luke. She decided putting some distance between them wouldn't be a bad idea. But it didn't work, and she found herself wondering if Luke had built-in radar. Mel scheduled her lunch hour at different times, but he always managed to show up while she let Lexi outside, and he often brought lunch for both of them. On some days Mel dawdled home after work, hoping Luke would get to the puppy first so she wouldn't have to go over and let her out. He didn't. Other afternoons she rushed home so she'd finish caring for Lexi before he arrived, but Luke always managed to be home when she got there.

Her plans failed on all accounts. Worse, Mel couldn't seem to get herself to turn down Luke's offers for dinner or a walk with the puppy or even a chat on his back deck. Her parents were fond of him. In fact, they had always liked and respected Luke, but now that he and Mel were good friends, they encouraged him to come around. Dad even invited him to spend Mother's Day with the family, which Luke did, and Mom blushed to her blond hairline when Luke brought her flowers and candy. Mel felt proud that he outdid Scott, whose name only appeared on the card and gift that Bonnie purchased for their mother. Moreover, with Luke nearby, the holiday was tolerable—actually pleasurable for Melody.

But in a word, she felt *doomed*. The more time she spent with Luke, the more time she wanted to spend with him.

Mel was only too glad when Darla and Max's wedding day neared. As one of the bridesmaids, Mel was soon caught up in final dress fittings, bridal showers, and last-minute preparations. She was forced to take a sabbatical from puppy training; however, Luke's friends, the Wheelers, promised to help him out.

"Hey, Mel, I need a huge favor."

She looked up from the bouquet she'd put together from gift bows, a memento for Darla from today's shower that the ladies at church had organized.

Melody stood and smiled at her friend, the bride to be. She'd seemed so happy today, so in love with Max. But now a heavy frown marred Darla's strawberry blond brows. "Sure, what's up?"

"I just found out that my cousin and her husband—you know, the two who agreed to sing the duet at my wedding. . ."

Melody nodded in spite of the immediate feeling of impending disaster clenching her stomach.

"Both have strep throat and laryngitis. They can't talk, let alone sing, and my wedding is two weeks away!"

"Oh, they'll be fine by then."

Darla shook her head, and then her hazel eyes filled with tears. "They canceled on me."

"Two weeks is a long time." Melody sensed what was coming, and she fought down the panic. "Laryngitis doesn't last that long."

"But what if it does? My cousin is right. We can't take chances. I have to find two more singers—"

"No! No! No!" Mel wagged her head. "I won't do it. I can't. I just can't sing anymore."

"Yes, you can." Darla looked stricken. "I called Max, and he phoned Luke, who said he'd sing the duet if you would."

Mel raised her brows. "Asking me was Luke's idea?"

"No, it was mine. I thought of the two of you right away, and Luke's already agreed to it."

Melody studied her friend's expression and decided she wasn't fibbing. But in the next moment, she wanted to laugh at the irony. "No, I am *not* singing a love song with Luke Berringer, okay?" Melody felt sure if she did, it would be the end of her heart.

"I thought you liked Luke."

"I do, but—"

"Pleeeeease," Darla begged. "You're the best soprano I can think of on such short notice. And Luke's a good baritone. You'll sound terrific together."

Mel rolled her eyes, and before she could refuse yet again, Darla shoved a score into her hands.

"Just try it. Will you?" she pleaded. "My cousin wrote this song for Max and me. This is our special day, and—"

"All right. All right. You guilted me into it." Melody sighed. "I'll try out the song and see what happens, but I'm not promising anything." She sent her friend a stern glare.

"You're awesome."

"No, actually, I'm pretty rusty. I might just croak like a frog, and then what?"

"What are you talking about? You sing like an angel." A grin spread across Darla's freckled peaches-and-cream face. "Thanks."

Mel handed her the ribbons-and-bows bouquet in reply, and her friend's smile grew. Then she hugged Mel before strolling off to chat with a group of ladies. Watching her go, Melody felt the proverbial noose tightening around her neck.

⁓

Downstairs in the fellowship hall of the church, Luke did his best to plunk out the tune on the piano. The Sunday morning service had ended, and he persuaded

Melody to do an initial run-through of the duet for Darla and Max's wedding.

"I'm not happy about this," she groused. She sat on the bench beside him, her arms folded tightly in front of her.

"Yeah, I can tell." He smiled and spotted a hint of a grin tugging at her pretty rose-colored mouth.

She relaxed her arms. "Luke, I can't do this. I just can't. I mean, have you read these lyrics? They're sappy. Can't Darla and Max play a tape or something?"

Luke mulled over her complaint. He didn't think the lyrics were "sappy," but he sensed Mel still wrestled with whatever roadblock held her back from singing. *Lord, tear down these strongholds. . . .*

He lifted his fingers off the piano keys and tried to reassure her. "Hey, listen, it's just the two of us down here. No one's going to hear us if we hit any sour notes. Let's just go over the song once and see what happens."

She pursed her lips but didn't reply.

"Close your eyes," Luke urged her, "and imagine Darla and Max at the altar. They've just spoken their vows. . . ."

Luke started to play again. The composer indicated the male voice went first, so he sang:

"Come now, my love, and take my hand,
"As we stand,
"Together as one."

The female part was next. Melody peered at the sheet music, cleared her throat, then sang:

"To you I pledge my heart, my life,
"Man and wife,
"Forever as one."

Every note was perfectly pitched.

Luke paused to tease her. "See, was that so painful?"

"Excruciating." Her azure eyes twinkled.

With a chuckle, he proceeded through the song. When they reached the chorus, Melody sang descant, and the blended harmony touched Luke's soul. He thought he could listen to Melody sing all day long. Even when she was sight-reading, her voice rang out like a professional's. The only unpleasant notes came from Luke's poor piano playing.

After they sang the last word, Luke looked over at her. "What do you think?"

"It's. . ." She faltered and ran her fingertips over the piano's ivory keys. "It's really a lovely piece, *I suppose.*"

He laughed and gave her a playful nudge with his elbow. "So what's the verdict? Do we sing the duet?"

He held his breath.

She hesitated but then nodded. "Yeah, we'll sing the duet."

Luke rejoiced, sensing this was no small victory!

~

It was the middle of June, and Darla and Max's wedding day had arrived. Melody dressed with the bride and the other bridesmaids in the spacious library of the church. Darla's white dress was an exquisite creation of pearls and lace, and the bridesmaids' tea-length gowns were a lovely magenta.

Brushing out her hair, Melody calmed her nerves by silently reciting one of her favorite Bible passages from Jeremiah: "*'For I know the plans I have for you. . . plans to prosper you and not to harm you, plans to give you hope and a future.'*"

God had a plan for her life. She could trust Him—even when she couldn't trust herself and her own wayward emotions.

Melody had rehearsed the duet with Luke enough times now that it no longer felt agonizingly uncomfortable. She made up her mind not to think about him standing next to her, singing words of love. Instead, she focused on the Lord Jesus and glorifying Him, praying the duet would be a blessing to Darla and Max.

However, last night at the dress rehearsal, her determination had almost crumbled. As they sang the refrain about undying love, Luke placed his hand on the small of her back. The inflection in his voice was unmistakable, and Melody had felt her knees weaken. She almost believed he was singing to her.

But, of course, he wasn't. Luke obviously gave the song his all because of his friendship with Max. Melody longed to do the same out of her love for Darla, and now she fought to get her derailed thoughts back on track before she had to sing with Luke again.

"For I know the plans I have for you. . .plans to prosper you and not to harm you, plans to give you hope and a future."

"You can do this," she murmured to her reflection. "With God all things are possible."

Once the bridal party was ready, the ladies gathered in the foyer of the church. The choir director, Ken Bartlet, sat at the organ. He had agreed to accompany Melody and Luke on the piano when it came time for their duet. The number would be memorable; Mel had no doubt.

The wedding procession began. Melody walked up the aisle with Max's younger brother, then took her place in line at the altar. Pastor Dan Rebholtz, who knew the couple well, gave them a short challenge and read from the scriptures. Next vows were said and rings exchanged. Mel felt herself grow teary-eyed as Darla and Max promised to love, honor, and cherish. Finally, the pastor asked all heads to bow as he prayed for the newly married couple.

This was Melody's cue. Just as they rehearsed last evening, she silently stepped down from the altar and walked to the far aisle where Luke already waited, poised and ready to sing. Melody thought he looked terrific in his black tux, and she gave him a smile as she moved in beside him.

But that's when she noticed it. Only one microphone. Yesterday there were two!

She turned to Luke with wide eyes, and he realized the problem. He calmly adjusted the mike in its stand to accommodate both of them, which would probably work fine, Mel decided, since her voice carried adequately without amplification. However, that was the least of her concerns. One shared microphone meant she'd have to stand closer to Luke.

Lord, I think those plans You have for me just ran amok.

Luke took a half step back and indicated that she should scoot in closer to the mike. He slipped his right arm around her waist in what seemed a polite gesture, as it eliminated the awkwardness of their close proximity. Mel had to admit, it was better this way than battling elbows. Unfortunately for her, she suddenly feared she might melt into one giant heap of magenta chiffon.

The choir director took his seat at the piano and began to play. Mel prayed her voice wouldn't betray her.

Think of Jesus. You're singing for His glory.

Luke started off the duet; Melody joined in at the appropriate time. They reached all the right notes and not a beat was missed. As they sang, the bride and groom lit the unity candle, symbolizing their oneness in marriage.

Several minutes later, the song ended, and Melody made her way back up to the altar and took her place among the rest of the bridesmaids.

Triumph soared within Melody. She felt like cheering. She'd done it! She'd sung in public. God hadn't taken away her gift; it had merely been in hibernation.

Chapter 15

D o you two sing at weddings often?"

Melody grinned and looked over at Luke. People had been asking them that question all afternoon. Now as they stood in the elegant lobby of the hotel before dinner, several more guests approached them.

"Actually, this is our first wedding," Luke replied to the elderly woman standing in front of him.

"Well, I'd say you both are on the brink of a new career. That song was just beautiful. Why, I never heard voices blend so exceptionally well!"

"Thank you," Melody said, feeling her cheeks warm with embarrassment.

She and Luke smiled at each other.

The white-haired woman took a step with her walker.

"Would you like some assistance getting seated in the banquet hall?" Luke asked her.

Melody grinned, thinking Luke was about as gallant as they came.

"Oh no, young man, I'll be fine. My great-niece is waiting for me near the door. See her? There she is!"

A girl about twelve years old waved, and the older woman shuffled off in her direction.

Then Bonnie hailed them. "Hey, you guys!"

Melody glanced to her right in time to see her sister approach. Scott trailed a few steps behind her. He seemed distracted, and Mel wondered if he felt bored.

"You sounded great at the ceremony," Bonnie gushed, smiling first at Luke, then at Melody. Next she hooked her arm around Scott's elbow and pulled him right up beside her. "We want you to sing at our wedding. Will you?"

Mel tensed. The duet might have gone well today by God's grace, but she wasn't sure she wanted to chance it again in a year. What if Luke and Alicia were engaged by then? How would it feel to sing with Luke under those circumstances?

She sent him a tentative glance.

"I'm willing," he said with a shrug and a chuckle. He turned his honey-colored gaze on Melody. "What do you think?"

"Um. . ." Lost in his stare, she almost forgot the question. "I—I don't know. . . ."

"Plenty of time to think about it," Luke said. "Besides, by the time Bonnie and Scott get married, you'll be an old pro, Melody."

She snapped to reality. "Oh yeah? How's that?"

"You'll have a year of singing with the church choir under your belt."

"You're joining choir again, Mel?" Bonnie's blue eyes widened with surprise. "Dad'll be happy to hear that."

"I'm *thinking* about it." Melody tossed a look of mock annoyance at Luke. He laughed.

Bonnie grinned and gazed around the lobby. "This is a nice place, and I hear the Terrace Room, where we'll have dinner, is gorgeous."

"Oh, it is. There are two magnificent crystal chandeliers hanging from the sculptured ceiling, and the ivory wallpaper is trimmed with gold velvet. I helped decorate last night. We placed vases filled with white roses in the center of each table. They added just the right touch." Mel tipped her head and regarded her sister. "Are you thinking of having your reception here, too?"

"Maybe. But what I really want is to rent the Mitchell Park Pavilion."

"At the Domes?" Mel clenched her jaw and willed away her envy. The Mitchell Park Horticultural Conservatory Domes, often called the Domes, was where she always dreamed about holding her wedding reception. The Domes were three glass beehive-shaped buildings that encompassed a colorful, eye-pleasing array of gardens, from desert blooms to jungle blossoms. Melody could well imagine her reception there and all her wedding pictures taken in the facility also.

Had Bonnie read her personal diary or something? Everything Melody dreamed of, her younger sister obtained for herself.

But then Melody cast a glance at Luke and decided she didn't care. If Luke fell in love with her and proposed, she'd marry him *anywhere*, and she wouldn't mind where they held the wedding reception.

The very idea took her breath away.

"Well, I suppose we'd better get seated," Bonnie said. She looked over her shoulder for Scott. He'd strolled off and now stood examining the framed artwork. "Come on, honey."

Melody rolled her eyes at the endearment, then happened to catch Scott cast a long, appreciative gaze at a shapely woman in a low-cut gown striding past him. Mel sucked in a breath and told herself she shouldn't be surprised. She never thought Scott had changed all that much from their college days.

But did she dare tell Bonnie?

Scott noticed her watching him, and Mel snapped her gaze away. He fortunately said nothing as he stepped in beside Bonnie. She took his hand before they proceeded toward the banquet room.

What a hypocrite.

Mel turned to Luke. "Did you see that?"

Luke arched his dark brown brows. "Scott's roving eye?" He nodded. "I've seen it a number of times."

Melody felt her jaw drop. "Why didn't you say something? We have to warn Bonnie."

Luke took her hand and tucked it around his elbow. "And how many times have you sounded the alarm already, Princess Melody?"

Hearing his nickname for her, a grin pulled at her mouth. "All right. Point taken." Mel knew she'd only be the bad guy in this situation once more. "You're right. We'll just have to pray God shows her and my parents the truth somehow."

Luke nodded in agreement as they walked across the plush gold and maroon carpet and entered the Terrace Room. Melody disengaged her hand and took a step toward the head table. Her place was with the bridal party.

He tipped his head slightly. "See you later."

She smiled at the promise before heading for the other side of the room. The bridesmaids sat on one side and the groomsmen on the other.

"Did you hear the sad news?" Wendy Tomlinson asked as Mel sat down and arranged the frilly skirt of her gown.

"Alicia and Jeremy broke up. Happened last night."

"You're kidding!" Melody tried to hide her sudden trepidation. Then guilt set in. She should feel bad for Alicia instead of worrying about herself. But try as she might to suppress them, those niggling doubts spilled into her consciousness. If Alicia Sims had broken up with her boyfriend, she was *available.*

"Yeah, Alicia's mom was just diagnosed with breast cancer," Wendy said, "and Jeremy is a rather high-maintenance guy. He wants Alicia's undivided attention, and right now she can't give that to him because her mother's ill."

"Understandable." Mel took a sip from the goblet of ice water in front of her. She hoped to swallow down her flustered feelings. On one hand, she was sad to hear about Mrs. Sims, but on the other, she felt scared of losing Luke.

It was then Melody realized that in spite of her best efforts, she'd fallen in love with her next-door neighbor.

"Oh, look," Wendy said, leaning over closer to Mel. "Alicia is sitting next to Luke."

Melody forced herself to glance out over the banquet room. Unmistakable dread grew inside of her when she spotted him at one of the round, white linen-covered tables, conversing with the lovely blond whose thick, straight hair hung to her shoulders in perfection. Melody then noticed Alicia's striking silver-trimmed red dress that hugged her slim frame.

Lord, help me. I don't want to live with this jealousy and envy.

"That'll be perfect," Wendy prattled on. She gave her French twist a pat as if to be sure every bobby pin was still in place. "Luke took care of both his parents before they died, so he'll know how to encourage Alicia."

Mel supposed that much was true. She recalled the in-depth discussion she and Luke had had about his parents, their illnesses, and deaths. As Luke had unburdened his heart that evening as they sat on his back deck with Lexi, Melody got the impression it was a therapeutic event for him. Later Luke said he'd never confided in anyone like he did in Melody.

"Alicia, that poor thing. She's really going through it."

And Luke is certainly in the habit of rescuing damsels in distress, Melody thought as her heart took a plunge.

All she had to do was think back on the last couple of months and all the times he'd shown up at the precise moment she needed him most. How foolish she'd been to take him for granted all these years.

Was it too late now to change things?

~

Melody wrestled with her emotions as the formal dinner progressed—tossed salad followed by the most incredible veal cordon bleu Melody had ever tasted. By the time slices of wedding cake were served, she'd asked God to help her cast aside all doubts, insecurities, and fears. Tonight's celebration was in honor of Max and Darla's union, after all. It wasn't about Melody Cartwright.

As she prayed through the tumult, a sense of calm settled over her, and Mel decided to just be herself and have fun. When the meal was over, she milled about the Terrace Room, talking and laughing with her friends. From time to time her gaze met Luke's, and he'd send her a smile from across the way.

Then the slide show began. One of Max's friends was a computer whiz and had put together pictures spanning the newlyweds' lives thus far. First babies, next toddlers, through elementary school and high school. Melody laughed when she glimpsed herself in a few snapshots. She'd been a gangly kid, somewhat of a tomboy who loved animals and climbed trees. But she also had a feminine side of her that enjoyed playing house and mothering her baby dolls.

Mel had to chuckle again when a photo flashed up on the screen of all the guys playing basketball. Mel guessed they were about seventeen, and what a goofy-looking bunch! Max had always been the tallest, so he stood in the back row. Luke was beside him, thin as a reed, wearing those midnineties teardrop glasses that took up most of his face.

"Praise God we don't stay teenagers forever."

Melody heard Luke's voice right behind her. "Amen!" she agreed with another laugh.

When the viewing ended, Mel was called away for another set of pictures with Darla and Max and the entire bridal party. Later she wandered out onto the veranda and sat down next to Jamie Becker on a cushioned settee. Her toes felt pinched in the strappy high heels she'd worn all day. In two discreet moves, she kicked them off and folded her legs under her skirt.

A small circle of six friends surrounded her in padded chairs. Tim, Military Mike, Bob, and Keith were at their obnoxious worst. They teased each other about the earlier slide show and laughed as they remembered humorous things about each other. Mel found them amusing and egged them on, tossing in a few of her own memories.

"And then, of course, there was the time that Bob was practicing before a baseball game," she said, "and he accidentally threw the bat through the sanctuary's stained glass window."

Everyone hooted, although it hadn't been funny when it occurred.

"Must you encourage them?" Jamie asked with a sidelong glance at Melody.

Mel didn't see any harm in the banter but gulped back the retort on her tongue. Jamie had attended a different high school, and Melody sometimes wondered if she felt left out.

But then, including her in their walk down memory lane, Keith began teasing Jamie about the time the youth group went to Chicago at Christmastime and she got lost in an upscale department store. The youth pastor's wife found her in the lingerie department.

"I wasn't *shopping* there," Jamie said, but everyone else was laughing too loudly to hear her defense. Finally, she stood and stomped off.

"Now you did it." Mel flicked her gaze upward.

"Aw, she'll forgive us," Mike said, straightening the jacket of his formal military blues.

"Yeah, she always does," Bob added, clasping his beefy hands.

Keith spouted off a goofy comeback and the rowdy laughter started all over again. Melody found herself giggling just because they were chuckling so hard.

"This seat taken?"

Mel glanced up and saw Luke standing beside the settee. She managed a straight face long enough to tell him the spot was vacant.

Luke filled it. But Melody soon realized he took up a lot more space than Jamie's skinny frame. They knocked elbows as Luke made himself comfortable, and Mel thought he still looked dapper in spite of the fact he'd shed his jacket. The night air was balmy, and she felt warm in her sleeveless dress, so she imagined how hot and uncomfortable a black wool tuxedo jacket would feel.

"Okay, boys, settle down," Bob said. "Luke's here, so we have to act sophisticated." He had a slight lisp, and perspiration trickled down the side of his pudgy face. "Luke thinks we're professionals like him, so we have to uphold our image."

"Yeah, whatever, you guys." Luke grinned and stretched his arm out across the back of the settee. He crossed his legs, the calf of his left resting on the knee of his right. "I grew up with all of you, remember? I know who you *really* are."

More chuckles and wise remarks emanated from the group, and Wendy piped up, giving the boys something else to howl at.

At this point, however, Mel wasn't paying any attention to the verbal volleying. Her thoughts were consumed with how pleasurable it felt to sit next to Luke this way. She had to fight the urge to rest her head on his shoulder.

Then he leaned over and whispered close to her ear, and it suddenly felt much warmer on the long, wide cement porch. "Darla's cousin asked if we'd sing at her wedding in the fall. She said she'll pay us."

She turned and regarded him, thinking his honey-brown eyes appeared like polished topaz under the soft glow of the outdoor lights.

"What do you think?" she hedged.

Luke shrugged and pursed his lips in momentary thought. "My schedule is pretty much my own, so I can plan around showings if I know about something in advance. How about you? How do you feel about singing at another ceremony— that's not your sister's?"

"I guess." She shrugged. "I wouldn't mind, but. . ." She considered Alicia and tried to imagine where Luke's relationship would be with her by then, assuming all went according to his hopes and plans.

And then it occurred to Mel that her present close proximity to Luke wasn't going to help him capture Alicia's affections. Didn't he realize that? Sure, they'd known each other forever, but had they become such good friends that Luke felt, perhaps, too comfortable around Melody now?

"Give the matter some prayer time," Luke said with a gentle smile that quickened her pulse. "We can let her know at a later date."

Mel nodded a silent reply.

"You two make such a cute couple," Wendy said.

Melody caught the enthusiastic spark in her girlfriend's eyes.

"Better make sure you catch the bridal bouquet, Mel," Bob told her with a conspiratorial wink. "That'll mean you're getting married next."

"Hold her back, Luke," Mike said. His indigo eyes widened as he feigned an alarmed expression. "Hold her back, or you're a marked man."

Melody laughed off the implications. She expected Luke to refute the misunderstanding anytime now, although she refrained from giving their friends any explanation. The deepest, most vulnerable part of her wished she and Luke were a "cute couple." However, the fact was they weren't even dating!

But to Melody's absolute astonishment, Luke chuckled and said nothing to the contrary.

Chapter 16

I have to set Luke straight, Mel decided on the drive back home once the reception ended. She'd stayed well past midnight to help collect personal items and tidy up the banquet hall with the other bridesmaids. Meanwhile, Darla and Max left to spend their first night together at a hotel near the airport. Mel glanced at the digital clock on her dashboard that read 2:00 and realized in just a matter of hours, her dear friends would be on their way to Hawaii for their honeymoon.

Melody hoped she'd have the opportunity to marry and experience a romantic honeymoon. Somewhere deep within her being she felt a longing to be loved, honored, and cherished—and to say "I do."

But it didn't appear her dreams would come true anytime soon.

Now what to do about Luke. . .

Melody pulled in next to Bonnie's compact SRT and parked beneath the carport. She collected her purse and duffel bag containing her bridesmaid's dress, shoes, stockings, and the cosmetics she'd used before the wedding. Once everyone had left the reception, Melody had changed back into her blue jeans and a T-shirt to help with the cleanup.

She made her way to the house and couldn't help casting a glance at Luke's place. All lights were off, and she thought of Lexi, her "baby." Mel couldn't wait to play with her again, and she was grateful to Tom and Emily Wheeler who'd agreed to puppy-sit so Luke could enjoy the reception tonight.

Somehow I have to tell him that our friendship crossed the boundaries, at least where I'm concerned. And what about our friends? They all think we're the next Darla and Max.

Melody unlocked the side door and walked in. *Luke is never going to get Alicia the way he's going!*

More than once tonight, Melody had entertained ideas of how she might steal Luke's heart. After all, it wasn't as though Alicia would find out what she did and feel hurt. Alicia had no clue of Luke's interest. But Melody recalled Luke saying he wanted God to orchestrate the match between him and the woman with whom he'd spend the rest of his life. If Mel set out to manipulate the situation, she sensed that she would end up with another broken heart, and she didn't think she could bear two in the same lifetime.

But could she suffer through losing Luke's friendship?

The next morning at church Melody had every intention of being cordial to Luke but aloof at the same time. She planned to discuss the particulars of their relationship with him as soon as time permitted. She wanted to explain her feelings—if she could, by God's grace, articulate them. But as she stood in the doorway of the sanctuary, looking around for a place to sit, her gaze immediately connected with Luke's. It was almost as if no one else existed.

He smiled and pointed to the blue padded chair beside him, and Melody nodded. Before she knew it, she'd seated herself next to him.

"Good morning."

"Morning." Melody felt the fingers of chagrin working their way up her neck and into her cheeks. She'd done exactly what she promised herself she wouldn't do. But somehow she couldn't seem to help it. "How come you're not in choir?"

He leaned into her shoulder. "Tom and Em stayed overnight, so I missed practice to have breakfast with them."

"That's nice—I mean, not that you missed practice, but that you ate breakfast with the Wheelers." Mel could have smacked herself. Now she'd lost her ability to communicate altogether.

"I knew what you meant." Luke chuckled and straightened in his chair.

She gave him an appreciative stare. As always, he was impeccably dressed. He wore a black suit, a French blue shirt, and a printed tie that complemented the ensemble.

"They say hello."

"What? Who?" Mel forced her attention back to the conversation.

"Tom and Em."

"Oh, of course."

She didn't have to see her reflection to know her face flushed crimson, but the choir's opening number saved her from further humiliation.

After a soul-stirring rendition of "Be Thou My Vision," the congregation was asked to stand and sing. Minutes later, the Wisbreck family played their woodwind instruments while the offering plates were passed.

Then Pastor Miller took the pulpit. Tall, blond, and in his seventies, he had a smooth-as-whipped-vanilla-pudding voice, and he resembled a gentle father figure to those under thirty. The older members of the church considered him a faithful friend and man of God. His message this morning caused Melody's spirit to take flight and helped her put things back into proper perspective.

"Loneliness," the pastor said as he adjusted his bifocals, "overtakes us only when our joy is dependent on someone or something else."

He went on to emphasize that a person can feel lonely even with crowds of people surrounding him. A woman might feel lonely in spite of the fact she's married. Same with a husband.

"Therefore, the answer to loneliness is the love of Christ. He has to fill that hole in your being before another person can."

Melody jotted notes in her wire-bound journal as the pastor spoke.

"Jesus is the Friend who will never leave or disappoint us. Just look at this promise recorded in the book of Isaiah. 'Then will you call, and the Lord will answer; you will cry for help, and he will say: Here I am. . . .'"

Love for her Savior swelled in Mel's heart as those words echoed in her mind. *"Here I am. . . ."*

Thank You for this reminder, Lord. I'll never be lonely with You in my heart—even if I'm always a bridesmaid.

She expelled a disappointed sigh, not intended for anyone's ears but God's. However, Luke somehow heard it.

"You okay?" he whispered.

"Yeah," Melody whispered back. "Just fine."

However, that "hole in her being," as the pastor termed it, felt like it was gaping. *Lord, You're going to have to help me. I love Luke.* She closed her eyes. Had she set herself up for yet another failed relationship? The fiasco with Scott had been more than she thought she could bear.

After the service, Melody stood and collected her purse and Bible. Luke tucked his large black leather-bound copy of God's Word under his arm, and they walked out of the sanctuary together.

"Are you busy this afternoon?" Melody still wanted to talk.

"Yeah, I have to show a house. You know I try not to schedule these things on the Lord's Day, but—"

"Yeah, I know." She'd learned months ago that a free Sunday in the real estate business was a rarity.

Luke glanced at his wristwatch. "I'm going to be late. Would you mind letting Lexi out?"

"Not at all."

"Great. Thanks." He gave her a grateful grin. "I'll see you when I get home."

"Sure."

She watched him exit the front doors of the building and jog through the parking lot.

And then it dawned on her that their parting conversation just now sounded far too familiar for "just friends." Passersby who didn't know better would likely think she and Luke were married. *"I'll see you when I get home."*

Melody made a mental note, adding this latest concern to her list of discussion topics.

⁓

As it happened, Mel never did get her chance to speak with Luke on Sunday. Business kept him at the office until the evening worship service. Melody met him at church, and while they sat together again, there wasn't any time for a meaningful conversation. Afterward, Luke apologized before dashing back to the office. He had to catch up on several issues, so Melody returned to his place and took care of Lexi. But by ten o'clock, she felt exhausted and couldn't wait for Luke another minute. She traipsed home, changed into her pajamas, and crawled into bed.

And then Monday morning arrived.

Melody stayed busy at the dental office, checking in patients, updating their accounts, and billing various insurance companies for last month's visits, but she managed to make it to Luke's at lunchtime. She let the puppy outside and played with her for a while before setting Lexi back into the crate. She thought it was odd that Luke didn't show up, since he usually did. Mel had been half hoping he'd bring her some lunch, but since that wasn't the case, she purchased a cheeseburger and chocolate shake on the way to work.

That evening, it was much the same scenario. Mel stopped at Luke's house around five, let Lexi out, and played with her in the backyard before crating her again. Mel ate supper at home, which meant enduring Scott's shenanigans. He always managed to do something obnoxious, and tonight was no exception. When the meal was finished, Melody carried a stack of plates into the kitchen. Scott was on his way back from the bathroom and purposely walked into her as they passed. The load in her arms teetered, and Melody thought for sure her mother's treasured dinnerware was about to crash to the floor. Fortunately, Mel regained her balance—and without any help from Scott. Then, as if bumping into her wasn't enough to fuel her agitation, he followed up his dubious act by saying, "Hey, Mellow, watch where you're going, will ya?"

Mom, Dad, and Bonnie all turned in their seats at the dining room table to see what was going on, and of course, Scott appeared the innocent one, while Mel looked like her sister's traitor.

She fumed as she scrubbed the roasting pan with more vigor than necessary, and she prayed her parents and Bonnie wouldn't make a big deal out of the incident.

With the kitchen cleaned, Mel decided to escape to Luke's place. *Wait until he hears about Scott's latest antics.* She hoped he'd arrived home by now so she could tell him.

The night air felt humid and uncomfortable as Mel made her way next door. It was impossible to see into Luke's garage, so she couldn't tell if his SUV was parked or not.

She reached his side door, unlocked it, and let herself in. When she reached the kitchen, Lexi pranced in from the living room to greet her, so Mel knew Luke was home.

"Luke?" She bent to give the puppy several affectionate strokes before heading through the dining area. "Hey, Luke, you're not going to believe what happened—"

Melody halted in midsentence, seeing Alicia Sims and Pastor Miller seated comfortably in the living room. Luke sat in an armchair and twisted around to smile a greeting at her.

Mel returned the gesture. "Sorry, I didn't know you had company."

"That's okay. Come on in and join us."

She stepped forward, about to take Luke up on his offer, but then out of the corner of her eye, Mel spied Pastor Miller's colorfully bound eight- by twelve-inch booklet that he'd put together on the topic of courtship. She'd seen it enough times; the homemade publication was available for free at church. It sat front and center at the welcome booth, and Melody even owned a copy.

Her heart lurched. "Um—I just remembered I have to do something." She backtracked. "Sorry to have interrupted."

"You're not interrupting," Alicia said with a pleasant smile. "Come sit down."

Mel shook her head. She wasn't about to sit in on the planning stages of Luke and Alicia's courtship. She'd likely lose her supper. "I have to go."

She fought to keep her voice light and friendly. She'd promised the Lord, after all. She'd never be lonely with Jesus in her heart. "But it's good to see you both again." She sent the pastor her best grin before spinning on her heel and striding toward the door. She tried not to run.

On the way out, she glanced at her house and realized her choices were next to nil. She could hole up in her stuffy room or listen to Bonnie and Mom make wedding plans. It seemed Cupid's arrows were flying everywhere, and Melody felt caught in the crossfire.

Keys in hand, she decided on a drive. She strode to her Cavalier, climbed in, and started the engine. She took a deep breath and prayed for calm as she backed out of the carport.

It was only after she'd driven several blocks that she realized she'd left her purse and cell phone at home. She blew out a breath, pondered the matter, and then decided it wouldn't matter. She wasn't planning to stay out for long.

Chapter 17

Luke sat back in the black leather executive's chair and put his feet up on the corner of his cherry-finished desk. He stared at the photograph of himself and Melody, and his heart twisted. The photo had been taken at a wedding they attended this last spring. His buddy at work had given him the picture, so Luke framed it and kept it next to his computer up here in his home office. The snapshot served as a reminder to pray for his future with Mellie, although things didn't look so great at the moment.

Monday night she broke her promise to him and took off in that sassy yellow coupe of hers. He tried to reach her on her mobile phone, but she didn't answer his call. He felt so worried about her that he ended up telling Pastor Miller and Alicia Sims everything. Neither was surprised. His feelings for Melody were quite obvious—to everyone except Melody.

After he shared his heart, the three of them asked God to protect Melody and prayed for His perfect will to be done. Luke had to admit the time of prayer with Pastor Miller and Alicia stilled the tumult inside of him. What's more, he sensed it helped Alicia, too. She was full of questions about her mother's upcoming surgery and chemotherapy. She also loved Jeremy, and it appeared the two would get back together soon.

At the wedding reception this past Saturday, Alicia had asked Luke if she could stop by and continue their dinner discussion about her mother's illness. Luke agreed and invited Pastor Miller over for extra advice and spiritual support. It would have been an added blessing had Melody joined them that night, but instead she'd acted as if they all had the plague.

Lord, what is it with this woman?

Luke lifted the picture and cradled its silver frame in his hands. He stared at Melody's smiling face and thought over the events that occurred yesterday. Luke had a hunch she'd gone out of her way to avoid him.

Well, she wasn't going to get away with that nonsense today. Luke set down the picture and glanced at his wristwatch. He had an appointment at two thirty, but he planned to be home when Melody came over after work to let Lexi outside.

◦⌀◦

The sun shone down, bright and hot, from a cloudless blue sky as Melody parked her car. She was glad the carport provided her vehicle with some shade. The temperature had soared into the nineties, and the air was thick and muggy, so after entering the house and climbing the stairs to her bedroom, she changed out of her scrubs into a lightweight cotton dress that she could wear to church this evening.

She opened the porch door and eyed Luke's house, deciding he wasn't home, which meant the puppy needed attention. But as she made her way next door, she hoped it was one of those days when Luke had appointments all the way up until the time the midweek worship service began. Melody just wanted to stay out of his way for now. Once the Lord healed her heart, she'd be able to feel happy for him and Alicia.

Mel unlocked the side door and let herself into Luke's house. He hadn't turned on his air conditioning since the weather had been cooler yesterday and last night. But now his home was beginning to heat up.

Mel opened the crate, and the puppy, now four months old, bounded out with her tail wagging. Mel stroked her soft fur. "How's my baby this afternoon?"

As if in reply, Lexi bolted for the living room.

"Hey, come back here!"

The rambunctious dog ran through the house, circling the kitchen, dining room, and living room. Melody laughed as she watched the puppy doing laps.

Picking up Lexi's leash, Mel decided it was time to go outside. She whistled for the puppy, who continued tearing through the house.

Then Lexi took off up the steps.

Melody groaned and started after her. In all the months she'd been hanging out at Luke's place, Mel never had cause to go upstairs; however, she knew from his telling her about all the remodeling he had done that four bedrooms and Luke's office were up there.

Along with one very hyper puppy running to and fro, up and down the hallway.

"Lexi, come."

Mel tried to chase her down, but it was no use. The dog ran from one room to the next. However, it did give Melody a chance to check out the second floor of Luke's home.

At one end of the hallway was a guest room with beige carpeting and a multicolored quilt covering the full-size mattress. Across the hall was obviously Luke's weight room, as a large home gym contraption loomed in the center of the hardwood floor. Melody imagined him working out and felt oddly impressed.

In the middle of the hallway was a large bathroom. It had white ceramic tile on the floor and a newer-looking sink, vanity, and bathtub. Through the glass shower doors, she noticed the molded plastic tub surround—and the general neatness of the blue and white room. Luke might be a bachelor who hated to grocery shop, but he certainly was no slob.

At the other end of the tan carpeted hall were Luke's bedroom and his office. Melody didn't enter his room, feeling as though she'd be trespassing on sacred ground if she did, although she allowed herself a quick peek. Masculine cherry furniture occupied the wall space, and his bed was neatly made, covered with a black, white, and teal patterned spread.

Lexi suddenly ran past her and scooped up one of Luke's leather shoes from off the floor.

"Hey, put that down!" Melody tried to sound firm, but she couldn't contain her giggles. She made a grab for Lexi's collar, but the dog bolted past her. Then she paused at the top of the stairs and dropped the shoe. It tumbled down with several decisive thuds. Next, the pooch scampered into Luke's office.

"Lexi, no!"

Melody grimaced when she heard something hit the floor. She followed the puppy into the office and found the plastic trash bin on its side. Paper had spilled out onto the floor. The puppy lifted a crumpled wad with her jaws and took off again.

Oooooh, that dog is going to get it.

Melody righted the plastic wastebasket and picked up the discarded paper. The puppy stood at the doorway, wagging her tail and panting.

"Don't you laugh at me, you naughty thing."

Lexi scurried off again.

Melody began to feel irritated. It was way too hot for a game of chase. Her hands on her hips, she listened for the dog, hoping Lexi would come back if she didn't run after her this time.

At that very moment, Mel blinked and her line of vision came into focus. She saw a silver-framed photograph perched beside Luke's computer. *That's us!*

She crossed the room and lifted the sturdy frame. She examined the picture and realized it had been taken at the wedding she'd attended with Luke a couple of months ago.

"Now, why would he have something like. . ."

Before she finished her spoken thought, the answer hit her like a two-ton brick. Her mind rewound time, then played back incident after incident.

She recalled their tender encounters, like the many times he'd taken her hand in his—a gesture of mere kindness, or so Mel had led herself to believe. They were just friends, right? But what about those instances when he placed his arm around her waist or stretched it across the back of the love seat on which they sat?

He faithfully phoned her every day, asking if she had plans for the evening. She seldom did, so Luke always came up with an appealing idea. A walk by the lakefront. A Brewers baseball game at Miller Park. Sitting out on his back deck and talking. He treated her to lunch and took her out to dinner at upscale restaurants, always refusing Melody's offers to pay. Didn't friends take turns picking up the tab? Luke wouldn't hear of it. And if she even hinted at a need, he was there to meet it.

Luke wasn't just a friend, although he certainly had become the best friend she'd ever had. No, he had been *pursuing her*.

And all the while she had been falling in love with him.

Oh, duh!

By now, Lexi had returned and sat beside Mel, licking her ankle. Mel glanced down at the puppy. "Stop that!"

Mel wiped the slobber off her leg with one hand and returned the framed snapshot to its place on Luke's desk with the other. Then she clipped the leash onto Lexi's collar.

"Well, I guess I know who Mystery Girl is," she told the mischievous but lovable mutt. "It's me."

Even as she spoke the words, a sense of disbelief engulfed her. But it had to be—and suddenly everything fell into place like pieces of a jigsaw puzzle. The total picture filled Melody with awe and happiness.

The sound of a door closing downstairs jolted her back to reality. Luke was home, and it wouldn't be cool if he found her in his office.

Her fist around the leash, Mel led the dog to the stairway. She got about halfway down when Luke appeared. He wore tan trousers and a short-sleeved navy blue polo shirt, and as he peered up the stairwell at her, he finger-combed his nut-brown hair off his forehead.

"Hi."

"Hi." Melody grinned, watching him retrieve his shoe off the step.

He gave her a curious look.

"Your dog."

"Ah. . ." He glanced at the black wingtip.

Melody descended a few more steps. "She's a bundle of energy this afternoon."

Lexi wagged her tail and chomped at the tassel on the top of the shoe. Luke raised his hand, and she jumped for it. "Hey, this isn't yours."

Mel smiled and let go of the leash. Freed once more, Lexi forgot the shoe and pranced into the kitchen. She then slurped noisily from her water dish.

"She hasn't been outside yet," Mel explained. "She was running around your house like a maniac."

A look of amusement wafted across his features as he tossed his shoe up the stairs. Next he removed his dark-rimmed glasses and rubbed the perspiration from around the bridge of his nose.

"Say—um—Melody, have I done something to offend you?"

"No, why?" In the next second, she guessed the reason he asked. "Oh. . . You're referring to the last few days."

"Yes, I am." Luke put his glasses back on, leaned against the corner of the stairwell, and folded his arms. "What's going on? It's like you've been purposely avoiding me."

Melody saw the look of hurt flash in his tawny eyes, and she felt guilty for being the one to inflict it. On the other hand, she didn't want to admit to being such an idiot. After all, she should have known long ago that she was none other than Mystery Girl. The telltale signs had been right in front of her face.

"I—well, I've been struggling with some issues. I needed time to sort everything out in my head." She pushed out a tentative smile. "But the good news is I'm on the right track now."

The explanation sounded lame to Mel's own ears, but it was the best she could come up with—and it wasn't as if she lied.

Luke gave several subtle nods, although the confusion never left his features. "Glad to hear it."

Melody walked down to the next step. She wished she could wipe away Luke's wounded expression. "I'm sorry if I was rude. Please forgive me, all right?"

"Of course. All's forgiven." He searched her face, and Mel felt her cheeks warm under his scrutiny. "I just wondered if I'd done something to upset you."

"No, it's not you at all. It's me."

Now he looked concerned. "Want to talk about it?"

Mel shook her head. She sat down on the third step up, deciding she'd feel like an imbecile if she revealed the truth behind her standoffishness the past couple of days. "It really doesn't matter anymore, Luke. Like I said, it's all good. I'm squared away."

Luke put his foot on the first stair and leaned forward, his forearms resting on his thigh. "I hope I didn't do something to lose your confidence."

"No." She wagged her head once more. "No, you've been terrific. I know I can always count on you."

Chagrin inched its way up her neck and face. She wanted to blurt out her misunderstanding about him and Alicia, but the words felt wedged in her throat.

"I'm glad you feel that way. I want you to be able to depend on me."

He reached out and tucked several strands of her hair behind one ear, and Melody found herself hoping he'd kiss her. He appeared to be considering the idea, and the anticipation caused her heart to skip a beat.

But instead of inching closer, he pulled his chin back and narrowed his gaze. "There is another matter we need to discuss. I'll have you know you broke your promise."

Melody drew her brows together. "What?"

"You promised me you wouldn't take off in your car all alone, but that's exactly what you did on Monday night."

"But, Luke, I didn't have anywhere to go."

Melody told him about the way Scott nearly knocked her over after she'd cleared the dinner table.

Luke shook his head in disbelief, and Mel saw the muscle work in his right jaw. She sensed he experienced the same indignation now as she had felt that night.

"Things are making more sense. That's what you wanted to tell me, isn't it?" Luke asked. "That's why you came over Monday night, and when you saw Alicia and the pastor here, you realized we couldn't hold a private conversation."

Melody nodded as relief filled her being. She wouldn't be forced to admit her utter stupidity.

Luke sat one step below her. "Well, I'm sorry I let you down, even if it was unintentional."

"You didn't let me down." She put her hand on his broad, muscular shoulder. "I think that would actually be impossible."

He stared up at her with vulnerability pooling in his honey-colored eyes, a reminder to Melody of his sensitive nature. She loved that quality about him. But just as those very words—"I love you"—were about to slip off the end of her tongue, a crash in the other room dispelled the moment's magic.

A naughty puppy needed to be reckoned with in the kitchen.

Chapter 18

Melody entered the large bedroom she shared with her sister feeling as if she were part of some incredible fantasy. The birds seemed to sing a little louder. The sunset tonight had looked more vibrant, with silver and violet-red streaked across the horizon. Mel had seen the Master's handiwork as she and Luke left the church tonight—after choir practice—and she could easily imagine those stunning shades as bridesmaids' dresses and in a bridal bouquet.

Her only disappointment came when two of their friends, Marlene and Sarah, asked Luke for a ride home. He obliged them, of course, being the kind and considerate guy he was, and neither woman lived too far out of the way. However, their presence meant Mel couldn't speak with Luke privately, and she'd been eager to tell him how she felt.

But then it occurred to her that God had intervened so she couldn't share her heart with Luke. She had concluded quite some time ago that he was a bit old-fashioned—like the way he always called her Melody or Mellie, but never Mel. Having realized all that again tonight, she decided she would show him how deeply she cared about him, but allow him to speak words of love to her first.

The only problem was that Luke hadn't completely outgrown his bashful nature, especially when it came to expressing his emotions.

Oh Lord, is this going to take forever?

Mel sighed as she set down her purse on the bureau and turned on the lamp. Patience had never been one of her strong points, and where Luke was inhibited, she was ingenuous.

Maybe that means we'll make a good pair.

Melody kicked off her sandals and strode across the plush peach carpeting.

And that's when she spied Bonnie sitting at the head of her bed with her legs pulled up to her chest.

"Bon-Bon, what are you doing?" Mel thought it odd that her sister would sit in the dark all alone. "Are you sick or something?"

In reply, Bonnie lowered her head onto her knees. Her shoulders shook, and Mel knew she was crying.

"Let me guess. You and Scott had your first fight."

Bonnie raised her head and glared at her. "How can you be sarcastic when you can see I'm upset?"

Melody blinked at the comeback. "Sorry. I didn't mean to come off as insensitive."

Bonnie didn't answer but buried her face once more, and Mel thought about all the times she'd cried out her own heart over Scott. That creep wasn't worth even one single tear, and she wished her younger sister would realize it.

"Look, I'm here if you want to talk," Mel said. "But if you don't, that's fine, too."

Again no response, and Melody didn't push it. She went about her business. After changing her clothes, she booted up her computer and checked her e-mail. She chuckled as she read the joke Luke had forwarded to her.

"How can you laugh when my life is falling apart?" Bonnie murmured.

"Sorry, it's this dumb thing Luke sent me."

"You mean you two spend practically every waking hour together, and then he sends you e-mail on top of it?"

Melody shrugged and decided not to add that Luke called her at work at least once a day. "Doesn't Scott send you e-mail?"

"No, he's much too busy."

The note of defensiveness in Bonnie's voice caused Mel to bristle. "What's he so 'busy' doing? I mean, he's not in school and he only works part-time."

As the last word left her mouth, Mel wished she could suck them all back inside. No doubt she'd just started World War III.

But much to her surprise, Bonnie didn't have a retort, and the silence made Mel feel doubly sorry she'd spouted off.

"Bon-Bon, I apologize."

"Forgiven." Bonnie unfolded her limbs and began to change her clothes. "I know you don't like Scott."

Melody clamped her mouth shut, deciding to quit before she really did incite a battle.

"Do you mind if I ask how much Luke knows about your relationship with Scott?"

"Luke knows every ugly detail."

"Does he dislike Scott, too?"

"I don't know." Mel swiveled in her chair to face Bonnie again. "I never asked him point-blank and he never said."

She appeared to think it over, then slipped her nightshirt over her head. "Well, if he doesn't like Scott, he hides it pretty well. He was really polite when he showed Scott and me around the Thornton place." Bonnie's voice trembled. "I had high hopes of buying that house. But Scott dragged his feet and someone else's bid was accepted before ours."

"Think of it like this—you were spared a total nightmare."

"Did you see it?"

"Yep." Melody sent Bonnie a teasing grin. "I happen to know the Realtor personally."

"Yeah, I guess you do." Bonnie stretched her slender body. "All our friends are buzzing about the two of you."

Melody tipped her head, digesting the remark. "Yeah, I figured."

"Some of them think you're using Luke to—oh, you know, get over Scott."

"Those who think that aren't *my* friends. And you know what else? Our career group has some serious issues. Instead of extending mercy to their brothers and sisters in Christ, too many people gossip about them and think the worst."

"I agree."

Mel tried to hide her surprise. She had expected Bonnie to argue the point.

"Jamie's been bad-mouthing Scott."

"Oh?" Mel decided she'd probably agree with Jamie, but she kept her thoughts to herself. Her relationship with Bonnie seemed to be on the mend, and Melody didn't want to do—or say—anything to jeopardize the reconciliation process.

"Yeah, and tonight Scott and I exchanged such terrible words. And it's all because I listened to my friends. I got this crazy idea in my head that Scott doesn't love me anymore."

Bonnie's voice broke, and she began to cry again.

Melody ached for her. She sensed that in this case, their friends might be right. She stood, crossed the room, and pulled Bonnie into a sisterly embrace. What more could she do? Words only sparked resentment. Bonnie would have to learn the hard way.

Just like she had.

∽

The next morning, Melody was busy at work. When her lunch hour arrived, she grabbed her purse and left the office. She had every intention of driving to Luke's and taking care of the puppy, but as she stepped into the parking lot, someone seized her upper arm in a painful grip. Surprise mingled with irritation rose up inside of her until she turned to face her captor. Then fury set in.

"Scott!" She tried to twist out of his grasp. "What do you think you're doing, sneaking up on me like that?"

"Settle down, all right? I have to talk to you. It's important."

Melody stilled, and he released her arm. She rubbed the place where he'd held fast, wondering if he took some diabolical delight in hurting her just now.

"What do you want—and how did you know where I work?"

"Bonnie told me." Dressed in beige cargo shorts and an avocado green T-shirt with a bold black stripe across the chest, Scott gazed down the sidewalk. Dr. Leonard's dental office was one of six businesses comprised in this small strip mall. "Let's go have lunch at that Chinese place. Then I'll explain."

"I can't. I have to let Lexi out."

He looked back at her. "What I have to say is more important than a dog, I can assure you."

"Lexi is not *just* a dog."

"Whatever. Look, I need to talk to you about Bonnie. But not here." He glanced around. People walked in and out of nearby stores and offices. "Please, I need your help."

Melody recalled her conversation with Bonnie last night about her spat with Scott. No doubt that's what he wanted to discuss. Did he want to know how to make it up to Bonnie?

"Try flowers and candy, Scott. They work every time." Mel grinned, then looked at her watch. "I really have to go, or I'll be late getting back. Just tell Bonnie you're sorry. She'll forgive you."

"Mellow, it's not as simple as flowers and candy, and if you don't have lunch with me and hear me out, the consequences will be on your shoulders."

"What?"

"You heard me."

The hard tone of Scott's voice prevented Melody from taking another step. She slowly lifted her gaze to his face. It was met with a stony expression.

Melody mulled over the ultimatum. "I don't want to get in the middle of anything."

"There is no middle."

Mel thought it over some more and finally relented. Something was up, and she knew better than to underestimate Scott's motives.

"Oh, fine, but I have to call Luke and let him know I won't make it home." She reached into her purse and retrieved her mobile phone. "Why don't you get us a table?"

"No, I'll wait." Scott folded his arms.

Mel didn't even try to hide her annoyance as she searched for Luke's office number in her phone bank. When she found it, she pressed the SEND button. To her disappointment, she got his recorded message. Next she called his cell phone but again reached its voice mail feature. This time she left a message.

"Hi, Luke, it's Mel. I can't get home for lunch, but I'll call you later."

She ended the call, tucked the phone back into her purse, and then grudgingly walked to the restaurant with Scott.

Inside, the place was dimly lit, and the walls were papered in red and gold. Imitation Chinese lanterns hung from the ceiling, and the tables were covered with red plastic cloths. After being escorted to a table for two against the far wall, they sat down. The hostess, a young Asian-American woman, gave them a smile before handing them menus.

Mel already knew she'd order the buffet. "So what's going on?"

Scott sent her a look of disbelief. "Can we order first?"

"I really don't have time. I'm on my lunch break." Melody tapped her wristwatch to emphasize the point. "Some of us have to work for a living, you know?"

Scott took her teasing to heart and slapped the menu on the table. "Why do you hate me so much?"

"I don't hate you. I just—well, to be perfectly honest, I think you're a jerk. Now tell me what's so important that I had to change my plans."

He narrowed his gaze, but before he could reply, the waitress showed up.

Melody and Scott both ordered the buffet. Then they stood and helped themselves to the various Chinese-American dishes.

Back at the table, Melody bowed her head and thanked God for her meal. She also asked for wisdom and grace to get through this discussion with Scott, although she couldn't imagine what he wanted to tell her.

Scott returned and began eating his lunch. Melody noticed he didn't pray first, but many times she said a swift and silent *Thank You, Jesus*, before eating, so she reminded herself not to be too hard on Scott—this time.

"Okay, now tell me what's up."

Scott chewed, swallowed, then wiped his mouth with the white paper napkin. "I got accepted to the Mayo Medical School in Minnesota on a full scholarship."

"Congratulations." Melody supposed it was good news. He'd already been accepted to the medical college here in Milwaukee, but now, if he moved to Minnesota, the financial burden of his education would be lifted. "Does Bonnie know?"

"Nope." He popped a piece of deep-fried shrimp into his mouth.

"No?" Mel thought it over, then guessed what this was all about. "Oh, listen, I'm sure Bonnie will move wherever she has to in order to get you through medical school. Even if it means leaving her family and friends. Is that what you're worried about?"

Scott shook his head. "Mellow, I can't marry Bonnie."

The remark stole her breath away.

"If I marry her, my financial status will change, and then I'll lose my full scholarship."

Melody felt the blood begin to drain from her face. She sensed what was about to come but felt compelled to reason with him. "Bonnie loves you. She'll wait—"

"No." Scott wiped his mouth again. "I decided I'm not ready to get married."

Mel told herself she shouldn't be surprised. "And you're telling me all this—why? You should be talking to my sister."

Scott didn't look up from his plate. "No, I want you to break the news to Bonnie."

"Me?" Mel gaped at the man. But soon her shock diminished, and her reasoning returned. Scott was planning to pull his old disappearing act once again.

"How totally typical of you to shake off your responsibility and leave someone else to clean up the mess. Life is all about you, isn't it? You don't care who you step on and who you hurt as long as you get your way."

He glanced up at her, and Mel tried to see some sign of remorse in his eyes but couldn't find a single trace.

"For as long as I can remember," he said, "I've planned to attend med school. My entire life has revolved around that goal, and I can't let anything or anyone interfere with my achieving it."

"Shouldn't you have thought of that *before* you left a trail of broken hearts in your wake?"

He shrugged and grinned. "I'm an all-American red-blooded male. What can I say?"

"Oh, spare me." She shook her head at the lousy excuse.

But then, as the graveness of the situation set in, all the fight left Mel. Remorse and trepidation took its place.

"Scott, aren't you sad? Don't you love Bonnie? Won't it devastate you to leave her behind?" Melody just couldn't fathom such callousness. "What kind of doctor are you going to be if you're so unfeeling, selfish, and unsympathetic? How can you act like this if you're a Christian?"

"Do you hear yourself? You're asking me about feelings when emotion can't have a place in my life. A person can't get through all the training it takes to become an MD by being warm and fuzzy. It takes backbone and hard work."

"Yeah, both of which you know nothing about." Melody gathered her purse and stood. She tossed her napkin on top of her barely touched meal. "I'm not saying a word to my sister, Scott. You'll have to tell her yourself."

He caught her wrist as she tried to pass him on the way to the door. "I leave tomorrow."

She pulled out of his grasp. "Good riddance."

The encounter shook Melody more than she cared to admit, and she couldn't flee the restaurant fast enough. She did, however, manage to tell the waitress that "the man sitting over there in the green shirt" would pay the bill. She figured it was the least Scott could do.

Mel jogged up the walk to the dental office. Reaching her desk, she called Luke. Her hands shook with incredulity as she punched in his number. But just as before, she couldn't reach him.

She opted to leave another message on his cell phone. "Luke, something terrible happened. Scott's breaking up with Bonnie and he wants *me* to tell her. What nerve! Can you believe it?" Mel's voice cracked under all the emotion. "Will you call me at work, Luke? I really need to talk to you."

Chapter 19

The sun had begun its evening descent in the western sky when Luke reached the park's baseball field. Earlier today, he'd driven to Chicago for a short seminar with a few business associates, and they hadn't returned to the office until after six o'clock. He had attempted to call Melody several times, but his cell phone didn't seem to be working. There hadn't been time to use a pay phone, and Luke just figured he'd catch up with her at some point. When he arrived home, Melody and Lexi were nowhere to be found. He presumed Melody had taken the pooch for a walk, but the disappointment he experienced amazed him. His house had never felt emptier. Even so, he did his best to set aside his feelings for the sake of his teammates and changed from his suit and tie into faded blue jeans and a green T-shirt sporting the name "Faith Bible Church." Then he scribbled a note to Melody, grabbed his gear, and set off in his SUV for the baseball diamond.

Luke parked and glanced at the digital clock on his dashboard. He had fifteen minutes to get warmed up and into position. Tonight his team played Creekwood Community Church.

"Luke! Over here!"

His gaze followed the familiar voice until he spotted Keith and his shock of dark curly hair. Luke jogged toward him, and reaching the bench on which his buddy sat, he deposited his duffel bag against the chain-link fence just behind home plate.

"Glad you made it."

Luke nodded. "Yeah, me, too." Unzipping his bag, he removed his bat and began to stretch. "I spent six hours on the road today—and the seminar in Chicago was only four hours long."

"Worth the drive?"

Luke shrugged. "Sort of, although I'm glad my company picked up the tab."

"I can relate." Keith sat forward and folded his hands over his knees. "So, uh, where's Melody?"

"I haven't talked to her today, but I'm hoping she'll show up to watch the game."

Keith bobbed his head and pursed his lips as if thinking over the remark. "You've got it bad for her, don't you?"

Luke replied with a tight smile. He wasn't about to discuss his feelings for

Melody with a third party, even though he'd known Keith since junior high. In fact, he was probably one of Luke's better friends, in spite of the fact that, at times, Keith could be as impetuous as the apostle Peter had been when he cut off the guard's ear.

"Listen, Luke, what if I told you that there's—um—someone else she's seeing that you don't know about?"

"I'd say ignore the rumors and mind your own business." Luke had heard all the talk, and the truth was it hurt Melody more than it bothered him.

"They're not rumors."

Keith stood. He was shorter than Luke by about four inches, but he made up for the lack of height with his broad shoulders and sinewy biceps. He unclamped his cell phone from its holster that he wore on his belt.

"I ate lunch with a friend today at a Chinese place, and guess who I happened to see there." He flashed his picture phone at Luke. "Melody—with her sister's fiancé."

Luke took the phone and stared at the picture. It wasn't the best quality, but he could clearly see Melody and Scott Ramsay, seated at a table. It appeared they were having an intimate conversation.

He handed the phone back to Keith but said nothing.

"I know it hurts, man, but someone had to set you straight. Mel dated that guy in college, and—"

"I know all about it." Luke held up his hand to forestall further comment, although he had to admit he was curious as to why Melody had met Ramsay for lunch. She hadn't said anything about it last night—except she did tell him she'd been struggling with something. Was that "something" Scott Ramsay?

Luke reined in his imagination; he wasn't about to jump to conclusions.

"Look, for all we know, Melody and Scott were discussing a surprise party for Bonnie. Her birthday's next month."

"I don't think so." Keith wore a dire expression. "I couldn't hear exactly what they were saying, but I do know this—Mel was doing her best to talk that guy out of *something*. Then she left in a huff."

"Now *that* I can believe." He grinned. Ramsay did aggravate Melody to no end.

Keith, however, wouldn't be assuaged. "Hey, I know love is blind and all that, but come on. A picture is worth a thousand words."

"Pictures can also be deceiving."

"But—"

Luke cut him off. "I'll talk to Melody."

"And she'll lie to you. What? Do you think she'll admit to secretly seeing her sister's fiancé?"

Luke sighed. "Look, Keith, I know your last girlfriend lied to you, and that was terrible. But you can't judge Melody—or any other woman—by the way Amanda treated you. I know Melody. We both do. She's not a liar."

"Yeah, well, I thought I *knew* Amanda, too." Keith wore a sour expression.

"I know." Luke gave his buddy's shoulder a sympathetic slap. "And I also know the Lord has someone good out there for you. I've been praying for you."

"Thanks." Keith's features lightened, but Luke didn't think his pal was totally convinced of Melody's innocence.

His next words confirmed it.

"I appreciate the prayers, but in the meantime, I've got your back, Luke. We've got the evidence right here." Keith shook his phone at Luke, then returned it to its hard plastic holder.

Luke tamped down his irritation. "I don't need evidence. What's more, I'd appreciate it if you'd delete that picture. It's not going to edify anyone, but it could hurt a lot of people if they buy into all the gossip floating around."

Before Keith could utter another syllable, he and Luke were called onto the playing field. The baseball game was about to begin.

∽

Melody read Luke's note and felt relieved when she saw the words "cell phone not working." It explained why she hadn't heard from him all day. Mel had wondered about it since Luke always returned her calls.

But at the rest of his scribbled message, she groaned. The last thing she felt like doing was sitting on hard bleachers, getting eaten alive by mosquitoes, and watching an amateur baseball game. She was physically tired and emotionally spent. She'd fretted all afternoon about the bomb Scott had dropped in her lap at lunchtime. Melody just wished she could spill out her troubles to Luke and get everything sorted out in her head. She knew talking to him would calm her troubled spirit. But obviously any discussions had to wait until after his game. She sensed by his note that it was important for her to attend the ball game.

She crated Lexi, then ran home to change out of her scrubs and into plaid walking shorts and a red sleeveless shirt. She slipped leather sandals on her feet before scurrying out the door. But when she reached her car, she felt sorry for the dog. The poor thing had been cooped up all day, and to leave her again seemed almost inhumane.

Returning to Luke's place, Melody lifted the leash from its hook in the back hall and opened the crate, setting Lexi free. "Come on, girl. You get to see your very first baseball game."

The puppy replied with a vigorous wag of her long tail.

With Lexi in the backseat of her yellow Cavalier, Mel drove to the county recreational area and found the location where the games were typically held. She'd been here numerous times in the past. Most often she came to gab with her friends and seldom paid attention to the game. As for Luke, she had seldom paid attention to him, either. Until now. Suddenly the church's baseball team held some interest for her.

Mel pulled into the asphalt lot, parked, and climbed out of her car. With Lexi in tow, she strode toward the bleachers. She saw Jamie, Sarah, and Marlene right away and then scanned the dirt diamond and the lawn beyond it. She spotted Luke playing center field. The other team was up to bat.

"What's the score?" she asked, reaching the stands.

"Four to two," Jamie said. She flipped up her sunglasses and set them on top of her head. "We're losing—and we've got an injured player. Keith sprained his ankle."

"Bummer."

Melody looked past her girlfriends to see Keith on the bench with an ice pack covering his foot. But before she could tease him, and express her sympathies afterward, of course, several kids ran over to pet Lexi. Mel was able to get the puppy to sit while the children talked to her and stroked her soft fur.

With Lexi and her admirers occupied for a few moments, Mel glanced out over the field just in time to see Luke catch a fly ball.

"*Woo-hoo!* Way to go, Luke!"

"Will you cut it out?" Jamie teased, giving Mel a rap on the arm. "All these guys have egos the size of the Great Lakes region. Luke was the only one left who didn't. Now you ruined it—and him."

Melody laughed. At the same time, she caught Luke's gaze and waved. He smiled and waved back. Then out of the corner of her eye, she glimpsed Keith's fierce stare. Melody figured his ankle really must be bothering him to make him so grumpy. He was normally a fun-loving guy.

She sat on the edge of the bleacher next to Jamie and watched a little more of the game.

"Cute dog," Jamie remarked, plucking her sunglasses off her short dark hair. "Are you puppy-sitting tonight?"

Mel grinned. "Yeah."

"So where are Bonnie and Scott tonight?" Sarah asked, peering around Jamie's narrow shoulders.

"Don't know." Mel tried to sound nonchalant, but her stomach crimped with the reminder of what transpired during lunch today.

"I can't decide if I like Scott or not," Jamie said. "Sometimes he seems charming and very nice, and other times I get the feeling he's a creep."

You're right on with the creep business, Melody thought. But she kept silent, because when this entire situation blew up, she didn't want to be anywhere near the fallout.

"Hey, Mel, c'mon over here."

At Keith's request, she gazed at him and he motioned her over to the bench.

"I'll hang on to the dog for you," Jamie offered.

Mel handed her the leash.

Sarah leaned forward, and her reddish-brown hair fell against her cheek. "Keith probably wants you to run and buy him soda."

"Or a pizza." Jamie rolled her brown eyes.

"Yeah, probably." Mel strode over to where Keith sat with his muscular arms stretched out along the top of the bench.

"What's up?" Mel stood over him, arms akimbo.

"Siddown."

Mel lowered herself onto the bench and watched as Keith extracted his cell phone from where he wore it on his belt. He flipped it open, and Mel wondered if he was making a call while talking to her at the same time. Dialing the pizza parlor? Maybe Jamie was right.

"How was lunch today?" he asked, still toying with his phone.

Melody shrugged, wondering what the question was supposed to mean. Was Keith implying he didn't get any lunch and justifying his pizza order?

Then he flashed his phone at her. "I caught you."

"What?" Mel groped to understand what he was saying.

"Look at this picture. I caught you, Miss Two-Timer."

Melody gaped at him and ripped the phone out of his hand. She stared at the photo, and suddenly her head began to swim. The photo clearly depicted her and Scott at the Chinese restaurant today.

"How'd you get this picture?" Mel's first thought was that this could be Scott's handiwork. She'd told him she wouldn't cooperate. Was this his way of getting even?

"I was at the restaurant," Keith said.

"I didn't see you there."

"Well, I saw you two with my own eyes, and I took a picture because I knew Luke wouldn't believe it unless I had proof."

Luke. Melody glanced out over the field. He had his back to her, watching another player chase a ball.

She looked back at Keith. "I have every intention of explaining what happened today at lunch to Luke. He'll believe me."

"Mel, you could tell that guy the moon was made of cheese and he'd believe you. That's why God gave Luke a friend like me. To set him straight."

"Set him *straight*?" Mel's heart banged inside her chest so hard that its pulsating beats filled her ears. Luke would believe her—wouldn't he? Or would this be the last straw? Maybe Luke would decide she wasn't worth all the time and trouble.

And she could only imagine what would happen when the gossips, who already believed the worst, saw the picture. They'd have a heyday. What would

Luke do then? Believe all of them—or her?

And Bonnie. . . When she saw the picture, she'd assume Mel had something to do with Scott breaking off their engagement. Melody's plan to keep her mouth shut had just been obliterated. Now she'd have to say something. But how? What would she say? Bonnie would be devastated. Her parents would never trust her again. She'd have to move out. Find a new church. Everyone would hate her!

Miss Two-Timer.

Indescribable anguish filled Melody's being. She closed her eyes against the horror of what she imagined the future would bring. "I can't believe you did this, Keith."

"Me? What about you?" He snatched back his phone.

Mel disregarded his question. "Who have you shown that picture to? Wait. Never mind." She shook her head. "It doesn't matter."

She knew better than anyone that Keith liked to talk. Mel wouldn't put it past him to relay the whole sordid untruth to anyone who'd listen. Even if he didn't have a picture of her and Scott, Keith had seen them together. It was too late.

She pushed to her feet, willing her legs to hold her. Her mind whirred as she grappled for a solution. There was none. Her breath came and went in rapid succession as panic threatened to overtake her.

Keith caught her wrist, but Mel twisted out of his grasp. She heard him say something, but the words were indiscernible. Her brain screamed, *What am I going to do? What am I going to do?* Melody had never felt so helpless in all her life.

Everything seemed surreal as she took the leash from Jamie and then jogged to her car. She felt as though she was in a vacuum and the only voice she heard was her own, crying and pleading for help. *Oh God, what am I going to do?*

❧

Luke trudged off the playing field. The Creekwood guys had scored another two points. It looked like they'd win this game.

He scanned the stands for Melody but didn't see her. Curiosity and disappointment caused his shoulders to sag. She hadn't left, had she?

When Luke reached the bench, both Jamie and Sarah were barraging Keith with questions and accusations. The terseness in their voices caused Luke to experience one of those proverbial sinking feelings.

"What's going on?" He almost didn't want to know, but he could guess: Keith and his picture phone. . .

"Luke, Mel's really upset," Sarah told him. "I don't know what this knucklehead said to her—"

"Hey!" An indignant frown furrowed Keith's dark brows.

"Let me repeat—we don't know what this knucklehead said, but Mel left looking really stressed."

"Totally stressed," Jamie agreed. "I've never seen her like that."

Luke stared at Keith, who squirmed beneath his scrutiny. "Give me that phone."

"What?"

Luke held out his hand, and Keith reluctantly slapped the device into his palm. Flipping it open, Luke set about deleting the infamous photo, which was obviously the cause of Melody's grief.

"I'm trying to reach Mel on her cell," Sarah announced.

"She won't answer until she's calmed down." Luke realized Keith's phone wasn't all that different from his own and soon figured out how to operate it.

"She drives like a lunatic when she's upset."

Luke glanced at Jamie. "She promised me she wouldn't do that anymore." He fiddled with a few keys and searched through several files.

"I'll try her at home," Sarah said.

"Don't bother." Luke didn't think she'd seek refuge at her folks' place. He hoped Melody was at his house.

He found and removed the offensive picture from Keith's phone. Then he tossed it back and gave him what he hoped was a withering glare.

"The game's as good as over. I'll catch up to Melody. You two just pray, all right?" He glanced at Sarah, then Jamie.

Both women nodded.

"And you," he said to Keith, "better keep your mouth shut."

Keith raised his hands in surrender. "Look, buddy, I'm sorry," he said with an earnest expression. "I was just trying to help."

Luke didn't reply but collected his gear and strode to his Durango. He prayed Melody would keep her promise and wouldn't drive like a "lunatic," as Jamie described it.

Lord, let me be her hero again, he prayed as he drove home. *This time I won't leave any questions or doubts in her mind. This time. . .* Luke paused to gather his resolve. *This time I'll tell her that I love her.*

Chapter 20

Melody heard Luke enter the side door and walk into the kitchen, but she stayed riveted to the leather-upholstered sofa in his living room. Lexi, however, bounded through the dining room to greet him. Mel listened as Luke calmly instructed the puppy, "Stay down. Don't jump," and she almost cracked a smile.

Almost.

Had Keith shown Luke the iniquitous cell phone snapshot? Luke's voice sounded composed. What if he didn't know about it yet?

Well, it would only be a matter of time. But would he, like everyone else, believe she was capable of the same treachery that Keith accused her of?

Luke strode into the room, and Mel turned to watch his approach. He didn't look angry, but his expression was hard to gauge. Concerned? Confused?

He walked toward her, then paused long enough to push aside the magazines on the coffee table before he sat on it, facing her. The fabric of his blue jeans rubbed across her knees.

Melody searched his face but didn't know where to begin. She wanted to tell him everything, but how much did he already know? What did he believe?

Fat tears filled her eyes and obstructed her vision. She put her face in her hands. Life seemed so totally hopeless.

"Mellie." Luke whispered her name and pressed his forehead against hers. He rubbed his palms up and down her bare arms. "Why are you crying?"

"Because I never want to hurt or disappoint you."

"You've done neither. So what's the problem?"

She glanced up at him and tried not to wince. "Keith didn't talk to you?"

"Oh, he talked to me, all right. He showed me the picture he took of you and Ramsay."

Mel felt sick. "Well, it's not like it seems."

"I figured."

She tried to defend herself. "I tried to call you twice today—"

"Look at me." Luke put his hands on each side of her face, forcing her gaze to meet his. "I love you, Melody. I think I've loved you since we were ten. I'm not about to believe hearsay—or even a photograph—over you." His thumb brushed the top of her upper lip.

She blinked. "You said you love me?"

Luke momentarily closed his eyes. "Oh, Melody, isn't it obvious?"

"Well, yes, but. . ." Her doom and gloom fled. She couldn't stifle a giggle. She felt almost giddy. "I love you, too, Luke. I don't know exactly when it happened, but it did." She covered his wrists with her hands. "And what I feel for you, I never felt for Scott or any other guy. It's the real thing. I know it."

His eyes grew teary. "Melody."

"It's true, Luke. I love you with all my heart."

He drew her forward and placed a sweet, undemanding kiss on her lips that left her longing for another.

"I promised your father I'd be a gentleman at all times." Luke touched his nose to hers.

"What did you promise that for?"

Luke sat back, his hands capturing hers, and wagged his head in feigned exasperation.

She grinned. "All kidding aside, I'd like nothing better than for you to kiss me for the next three hours. But I know it wouldn't be right. And as much as I never want to sadden or disappoint you, I especially don't want to disappoint the Lord Jesus." Past mistakes scampered across her mind. "Not again."

"I want our relationship to glorify God, too." Luke glanced down at their entwined fingers, then looked back at her. "Will you marry me?"

"In a heartbeat."

He sat up a little straighter. "Really?"

She grinned at his amazed expression. "Really."

"You just made my day—my year—my whole life!"

Melody's smile grew, and she saw the love he felt for her shining in his honey-brown eyes. She'd finally be a bride—and marry the man she loved so deeply.

"Oh, but—um, Luke? You'd better talk to my dad."

"I already stated my intentions. He knows."

"When did you do that?" Melody frowned—and then another piece of the puzzle fell into place. She sucked in a breath. "Wait. It was that Saturday morning in the garage, wasn't it? The day you brought Lexi home. . ."

Luke arched a dark brow and grinned. "Very good, Mystery Girl; you finally figured it out."

She laughed and gazed at their clasped hands. But moments later, she realized it was much too quiet.

"Hey, speaking of Lexi. . ." Mel scanned the area. "Where is she?"

"In her crate." An expression of chagrin wafted across Luke's face. "I didn't want her kissing you because *I* wanted to kiss you."

They shared a chuckle.

Luke stood and dropped down onto the couch next to Melody. "Okay, want to tell me what happened today?"

"Yeah." Mel turned and tucked one leg under her, sitting sideways on the sofa.

The whole lunchtime fiasco tumbled from her lips. She told Luke every detail. When she finished, despair reared its ugly head once more.

"What am I going to do?"

Luke stared straight ahead, his mouth pursed in a thoughtful manner. Then, finally, he looked at her. "You're going to tell the truth." He stood. "Right now."

He held his hand out to her, and Mel took it. Luke helped her to her feet.

"What do you mean 'right now'?"

"As in *right now*. We're going next door so you can tell your family exactly what you just told me."

Mel pulled her hand free. "Are you nuts?"

"Look, I'll help you every step of the way." Luke put his hands on his hips. "But if you don't say anything, you run the risk of being accused for not sounding the alarm in time for Bonnie to do something."

Mel didn't get it. "What do you mean? What can she do?"

"You said Ramsay's leaving tomorrow, right?"

"Yeah."

Luke glanced at his wristwatch. "It's just after ten. The night is young."

He took her hand, and Mel allowed him to lead her through the house, toward the door. She prayed he was right. Luke had always been a commonsense sort of guy.

"Oh, one more thing. . ."

He stopped so fast that Mel almost tripped over his heel.

"Let's not say anything just yet about the two of us getting married. If it's okay with you, I'd like to wait a few days until I can put an engagement ring on your finger."

His words touched Mel to the core. "All right. It's our secret until then."

But as they walked hand in hand around the yards, Mel's heart broke for her sister. Bonnie never did get an engagement ring, and now she'd be deprived of the wedding that she and Mom had been planning for months.

Anxiety snaked its way around her midsection. "Luke, I don't think I can do this. What if my family doesn't believe me?"

He paused. "Then they don't believe you, and we'll deal with whatever happens next. All you can do, Melody, is tell them the truth in love. You're not responsible for their reactions."

He rang the doorbell, then smacked his forehead. "Duh. You can walk right into your own home."

"Yeah, they haven't changed the locks yet."

Hearing Luke's rumble of laughter caused her to smile and relax a bit.

They entered the house, and Mel willed herself to stay calm. She prayed for wisdom to "tell the truth in love," as Luke put it.

Dad sat in his recliner in the den, wearing sweatpants and a navy blue T-shirt. "Well, hi, you two." Lifting the remote, he turned off the TV. He reached for the handle on the side of chair and positioned it upright. Then he stood. "Where have you been?"

"Luke played baseball tonight. He's on the church's team."

"So I see by his T-shirt." Dad grinned at him. "Good for you."

"Thanks, Bill." Luke shook his proffered hand. "Unfortunately, we lost."

"Ya win some, ya lose some."

Mel watched as her father gave Luke a friendly slap between the shoulder blades.

"Where are Mom and Bonnie?"

"Shopping, as usual. I'm going to be broke by the time Bonnie gets hitched."

Mel tried not to grimace as she slid her hands into the pockets of her shorts. She looked up into her dad's suntanned, age-lined face. "Could I talk to you before they get home?" She glanced at Luke. "Maybe it's better we tell my father first."

He inclined his head.

"This sounds serious." Dad sat back down in his recliner.

"It is." She and Luke took a seat on the striped cover of the daybed.

She felt less intimidated talking to her dad, and after a rocky beginning, Mel spilled the whole story.

Dad sat forward. "You gotta be kidding me. He told *you* to tell Bonnie that he can't marry her?"

Mel bobbed her head, feeling as though she might cry. Luke slipped his arm around her shoulders.

"What a rotten thing to do." Dad clenched his jaw. "Scott's aware there's been strife between you two girls. He had to know this sort of thing could ruin your relationship with your sister—maybe forever."

"I don't think Scott really cares."

"Obviously."

The sound of the side door opening signaled Mom's and Bonnie's return. Shopping bags rustled, and Bonnie's laughter accompanied their entrance into the dining room, where they set their purchases down on the table with a thud.

"I'll tell them." Dad rose, then left the den. He closed the door behind him.

Mel leaned against Luke, wondering what would happen next.

"Let's pray."

Luke took her hand, and Mel fought against all the angst in her spirit long enough to follow his petition to their heavenly Father.

Minutes later, Melody's mother entered the room. Her expression was one of shock. "I can't believe it," she murmured, lowering herself onto the wooden desk chair across from the daybed. "And of course Bonnie won't believe it until she sees it—or hears it from Scott's mouth. She and your father are on their way over to his place right now."

"So you think I'm a liar?"

Luke squeezed her hand. "No, Melody, don't you see? It's good that Bonnie is checking things out for herself—and it's doubly good that your dad's going with her."

Melody stared at him, a frown pulling at her brows.

He explained. "If Amber said you decided not to marry me, you'd best believe I would want to discuss the matter with you *up close and personal*."

Melody's defensiveness crumbled, and she laughed. At this rate, Luke would blow their secret before she ever did.

"Luke, you're a marvelous mediator," Mom told him, sending Melody a look of warning. "And this whole thing with Scott. . . Well, it's got to be some horrible misunderstanding."

Mel wanted to shout at her mother and say that she and Bonnie were so caught up in wedding plans they wouldn't know the truth if they crashed into it with their shopping carts! But the pressure Luke applied to her hand once more kept her angry words at bay.

Minutes passed. Mom left the room, and Melody could hear her putting dishes away in the kitchen. Luke flipped on the television and occupied himself with his favorite cable news program. Soon more than an hour had gone by.

At long last Bonnie and Dad returned home, and Melody made her way into the kitchen to meet them. Luke trailed in behind her. But Bonnie ran up the stairs to their bedroom without saying a word, so Mel assumed she'd discovered the truth for herself.

With a grim expression, their father confirmed it.

"We found Scott at home, all right. But he was there with his *other* fiancée, who happens to be a few months pregnant. Well, maybe more than a few. It's quite obvious the woman's expecting."

"What!" Mel gaped at her dad. She'd known all along what a creep Scott was, but she'd never imagined he was that much of a scoundrel!

On second thought, maybe she had.

Mel glanced at her mother, who paled at the news.

"We didn't discuss anything in front of the expectant mother, who can't be any older than Bonnie," Dad went on. "And Scott tried to dance around answering my questions, but finally he confessed to everything. It's true he's leaving for medical school tomorrow. He's breaking it off with Bonnie, but he's not taking the other girl with him, so my guess is he's running out on her, too." Dad exhaled a weary sigh. "I feel bad for her, but my first concern is Bonnie."

"He actually told Bonnie he was—was calling off the wedding?" Mom's voice sounded strained.

"Yep. 'Course I had to threaten him within an inch of his life, but—"

"Oh, Bill, this is no time for hyperbole."

"Honey, I'm not kidding. I'm a little ashamed over how I lost my temper with Scott, but no one messes with my daughters and gets away with it!"

Mel's gaze flitted from one parent to the other before settling on Luke, who stood beside her.

"Luke's already been fairly warned."

He gave Dad a nod before sending Mel an affectionate wink.

"I'm sure Bonnie's devastated," Mom remarked.

Melody turned and saw tears in her mother's eyes. She could well imagine how hurt Bonnie must be.

"I suppose I should go up there and comfort her, but I know I'll just end up sobbing right along with her." Mom swatted at the moisture trickling down her cheeks. "Scott seemed so—so perfect."

"Perfect?" Mel couldn't keep silent a moment more. "Mom, how can you allow yourself to be so ignorant? Scott has been a major instigator, wreaking havoc between Bonnie and me. He's stirred up all kinds of trouble in our career group. I tried to warn all of you, but no one would listen. You thought I was the hateful one, and I've been miserable for the last few months. If it weren't for Luke, I probably would have flung myself off some cliff."

"She's right," Luke said. "Well, not about the cliff part." Stepping behind her, he placed his hands on Mel's shoulders and gave her a shake.

She nearly grinned.

"But Melody did sound the alarm more than once."

"I know she did," Dad said.

Mel saw the remorse in her father's eyes.

"She wanted to do something to prevent this very thing from happening," Luke added, "except each time she stepped in, things backfired."

"I should have listened," Dad admitted, "but you know, as Christians, we want to forgive a person's past and move on." He looked at Melody. "Your mother and I decided Scott made his mistakes, and you made yours, and since God forgave the both of you, so should we."

"Scott never changed," Mel said, lifting a defiant chin and folding her arms.

"Yeah, well. . ." Her dad ran a hand over his balding head. "I guess we all found that out the hard way."

Mom crossed the room and gathered Melody in an embrace. "I'm so sorry you've been hurting all this time and I couldn't see it." She began to sob. "I'm so sorry, Mellie."

Mel's stony facade disintegrated. In seconds, she returned her mother's hug while tears dribbled down her own cheeks.

It was then—only then—that Melody sensed she'd gotten her family back.

∽

"Just look at those stars."

Her hand in Luke's as they strolled toward the alley, Melody lifted exhausted eyes and gazed at the sky. "It looks like black velvet with pinholes."

"No, no, you're supposed to say they look like diamonds—as in engagement rings."

Mel laughed. "Oh, right." She was so tired, she felt punchy. The time was somewhere after three in the morning, and she already knew she'd have to call in to work. But she rarely missed a day, so her supervisor would understand, considering the circumstances. Fortunately, Bonnie seemed to be coping with Scott's rejection amazingly well—now that the initial shock had worn off.

They reached the end of the walk.

"I'll wait here and watch so you get back inside safely."

"Then who's going to watch you get in safely?"

"Melody." Luke's gentle reprimand hung between them.

She tipped her head and regarded him beneath the bright beam of the streetlamp. "You know, you're really hunky with that five o'clock shadow."

Luke rubbed the side of his face. "Would that be a 5:00 a.m. shadow?"

"I guess so." She giggled.

He gave her a sweet grin, then lifted her hand. "Good night, Princess Melody," he said, placing a kiss on her fingers.

An electric current zinged up her arm. "Good night, Sir Luke. You're my knight in shining armor."

"That's because I love you."

"I know." Melody smiled. Her heart swelled with joy. "I love you, too."

Epilogue

S unshine spilled through the autumn treetops as Melody held Luke's hands while he recited his vows. Standing beneath the leafy canopy, she'd never felt more beautiful dressed in her short-sleeved, off-the-shoulder white satin gown with its beaded lace appliqués. Melody had never imagined she'd agree to an outdoor wedding ceremony, but when Luke's sister, Amber, and her husband, Karl, offered the use of a pretty corner of their property—the spot right beside a little creek—Mel couldn't refuse. She knew it'd be perfect.

". . .to have and to hold, from this day forward, as long as we both shall live."

Luke gazed into her eyes and gave her fingers a meaningful squeeze.

She smiled.

Then it was Melody's turn. As the pastor led her, she promised to "love, honor, and cherish."

When the vows were finished, Bonnie, Mel's maid of honor, read from 1 Corinthians 13: "Love is patient, love is kind. It does not envy, it does not boast, it is not proud. It is not rude, it is not self-seeking, it is not easily angered, it keeps no record of wrongs. Love does not delight in evil but rejoices with the truth. It always protects, always trusts, always hopes, always perseveres. Love never fails."

Tears gathered in Melody's eyes. This was the first time Bonnie made it through the reading without breaking down and sobbing. But she had insisted that she wanted to read this passage. Bonnie claimed she wanted this portion of God's Word etched upon her soul forever.

Mel knew her younger sister's wounds were still raw. It had only been four months since Scott left. Bonnie now clearly saw how wrong she had been to trust and believe him over Melody. He'd baited Bonnie with his charm, good looks, and empty promises, and she'd fallen for it hook, line, and sinker. She'd let the idea of getting married and having a home and family outweigh her common sense—as well as warnings from others, particularly her older sister. But Melody could well understand how it happened, and all was forgiven. She and Bon-Bon had renewed their close relationship.

And then there was Cassidy Chambers, Scott's pregnant "fiancée." After Scott's departure, Melody and her family felt God leading them to help the young woman in any way possible. They reached out to her, and Cassidy allowed them to take her in under the protective wings of their friendship. Several weeks ago, they all rejoiced when she accepted the Lord Jesus Christ as her Savior, and in just another month her baby would be born. As for Scott, no one knew where he'd vanished to. Bonnie did some digging, and not surprisingly, the Mayo Medical School had never heard of him.

"I now pronounce you man and wife," the pastor said. "Luke, you may kiss your bride."

Flutters of anticipation filled Melody's insides. She'd dreamed of this moment. After their initial kiss, they hadn't shared another until now.

Luke drew her into his arms and pressed his lips to hers in a way that made Mel's knees threaten to give way.

Their guests applauded.

Afterward, friends and family members tossed birdseed as Melody and Luke made their way toward the white canvas tent. Beneath its billows, the bridal party formed a queue so they could greet everyone who entered the makeshift reception area for food, wedding cake, and punch. True, it wasn't the pricey wedding Melody had always fantasized about, but she felt dizzy with happiness nonetheless.

"I love you, Melody," Luke whispered close to her ear.

She smiled. He told her that at least twenty-five times a day. "I love you, too, but those words can't come close to comparing to how I feel right now." She looped her arm around his. "I guess I'll just have to take the rest of our lives to show you how much I love you."

"I'll look forward to it." He kissed her again.

"All right, that's enough." Jamie Becker appeared wearing a black dress with white and yellow daisies and a matching yellow knit jacket. "No smooching while the guests are trying to congratulate you, okay?"

The sparkle in Jamie's brown eyes let Mel know she was teasing. Next Jamie hugged both her and Luke.

Then Keith came through the receiving line. They had long since patched things up, and now Keith was one of the most loyal friends she and Luke knew. The entire career group, in fact, had experienced something of a spiritual revival. Gone were those days of gossiping and repeating negative things about others. Instead, every member of the group vowed to adhere to the Golden Rule.

Keith grinned at Mel before giving her a crushing bear hug. "I'm so happy for you two."

"Thanks," Luke said as he and Keith clasped hands.

After Keith sauntered off, Luke whispered to Melody, "That guy's bachelor days are numbered. I have a hunch that he and Marlene will be tying the knot soon."

Mel smiled and nodded. She thought the same thing.

"And, Melody. . ."

She stared up into her new husband's gaze. Luke kissed her once more.

"No matter how old we get, I'll always see you the way you look today. You'll always be my beautiful, blushing bride."

Her eyes filled with tears of joy. Life couldn't get any better than this.

Then again, she reminded herself that with God all things are possible!

The Long Ride Home

Dedication

To my friends at Froedtert Memorial Lutheran Hospital, especially Kathy M. and Danielle A. and the other wonderful people working in the Emergency and Trauma Center.

A very special thanks to Dusty Rhodes, PRCA clown, and Debra Ullrick for patiently answering my questions and sharing their rodeo expertise with me.

Chapter 1

As Lara Donahue penned the date in the departmental log, she shook off the inkling of impending doom. She'd never been a superstitious person. She liked black cats, walked under ladders, and had cracked her share of mirrors. Nothing horrible ever happened to her, and she didn't believe in bad luck. As a Christian, she acknowledged God's will.

So why did she feel so. . .*unsettled*?

As if in reply, her black digital pager squawked out several high-pitched beeps. Lifting it off the scuffed walnut desktop, Lara pressed one of the gadget's four front buttons. A message from Paramedic Base appeared on its tiny screen.

FFL. 29 YO MALE THROWN FROM HORSE.
UNCONSCIOUS. PULSE 85. BP 170/90.
GCS 13. ETA 20 MIN.

Lara grimaced. *FFL*—the Flight-for-Life helicopter—was flying him from the accident site, and the last line of the electronic page indicated their estimated time of arrival to be in twenty minutes. The guy must be in bad shape.

Thrown from a horse. . .

Oddly, Lara felt an immediate interest in the new patient. She considered herself a horse lover—had been since junior high school. Now she volunteered at the Regeneration Ranch and taught physically challenged kids how to ride. It was something she looked forward to doing one Saturday out of every month.

Lara replaced the pager on her desk and continued logging the patients she'd cared for today. Like poor old Mr. Drummond. He was an eighty-six-year-old who obviously had difficulties caring for himself. After a nasty fall down his front porch steps, the older gentleman had been taken by ambulance to County General's emergency department, or "ED." The nurses discovered his personal hygiene was deplorable, his clothes filthy, and his matted white hair infested with head lice. After Mr. Drummond was washed, examined, and diagnosed in good health, aside from his bruised hip, Lara found him a clean shirt and a pair of trousers in the boxes of donations in her office. Next she implemented his transfer to the neighboring mental health complex where he'd be evaluated further and enrolled in various social programs that might preserve his independence.

Lara ceased her journaling long enough to wish she could take Mr. Drummond home with her. He seemed like such a sweet man. He said his son and two daughters lived too far away to care for him. He was lonely. . . .

She shook herself for the second time. What an absurd idea. Of course she couldn't take home a complete stranger—and she wouldn't. Nevertheless, some cases broke her already bleeding heart.

Lara logged another patient before glancing at her wristwatch. The accident victim would be arriving any minute. As a hospital social worker, she was assigned to the trauma team, which also included a surgeon, residents, nurses, an X-ray tech, a chaplain, and a registrar, and she was expected to be present when Flight brought in the patient.

Leaving her office, Lara fastened her pager to her skirt's belt, then headed for the trauma room located on the far side of the emergency department. Walking through the bustling "arena," the center part of the emergency department, Lara passed the nurses' station. It was an area squared off by gray faux-marble counters used for writing orders and prescriptions and documenting in patients' charts. Desktops had been installed inside the parameter and ran along all four of the half-walls. At the helm sat two unit secretaries who answered ever-ringing phones, entered lab and X-ray orders, and paged specialists on call. Outside the emergency room was a four-bed observation unit, with the trauma room positioned cater-corner to it. Just down a short hallway to Lara's left, ambulances pulled into the garage, or ambulance bay, and critical patients could be wheeled through the doors and right into the trauma room. Not-so-critical persons went into ED. When Flight brought in patients, its staff used the nearby service elevators. Everything was set up perfectly, as County General was a "level one" trauma facility.

As Lara entered the trauma room, residents and nurses were suiting up in fluid-resistant disposable gowns, masks, and plastic goggles. The ED doctor and chief neurosurgeon sat in the back, ready to make the necessary calls. Many of the nurses wore lead vests to protect themselves from the harmful rays of the portable X-ray machines. But Lara had no need for a vest. She'd learned to stay out of the way.

Her leather-bound portfolio tucked into the crux of her arm, she found a place to stand and wait for Flight. Within moments, the signal came that the helicopter had landed, and minutes later, the unconscious patient was wheeled in.

Doctors and nurses went to work at once, cutting away clothes and checking vital signs. Lara hadn't gotten a glimpse of the patient, which wasn't at all uncommon. One of the Flight staff handed the registrar the patient's driver's license, and the young woman hurried away to create an account number, wristband, and plastic plate that would be used to stamp up other paperwork and labels for lab work.

Lara opened her portfolio and began to write down specifics on her yellow legal pad.

"This is Kevin," the flight nurse said loudly enough for all to hear. A petite woman with short strawberry blond hair, she wore a blue jumpsuit and spoke in a commanding voice. "He's with a rodeo going on in Waukesha County right now, and he was thrown from a horse."

Lara frowned as the name struck a familiar chord in her memory. She'd known a guy named Kevin who competed in the rodeo circuit. They'd grown up in the same neighborhood, and he'd been the one who sparked her love for horses when she was thirteen years old.

That awkward time in her life flashed across her mind, and Lara recalled her pudgy frame traipsing after tall, blond, and extremely cute Kevin Wincouser, who patiently taught Lara everything he knew about riding and grooming horses. He hadn't been required to spend time with her—he was four years older, on the football team, and popular with all the girls in school. But since their parents were well acquainted, attended the same church, and lived in the same neighborhood, Kev was kind enough to show Lara "the ropes," so to speak.

Eighteen months later, a year after his parents were tragically killed overseas, Kev took off for the excitement of the rodeo, and his younger brother moved in with an aunt and uncle in a neighboring state. That was over a decade ago, and nobody had seen the Wincouser boys since.

This couldn't be the same guy. . . .

Danielle, the registrar, returned and handed Lara the driver's license along with a sticker on which the patient's account number, medical record number, and date of birth had been printed.

"There are some folks in the lobby asking about this patient," she told Lara. The attractive African-American woman handed off the rest of her paperwork to the ED technician. Pausing near Lara again, she added, "I told 'em you'd be out in a few minutes."

"Thanks."

Holding up the driver's license, Lara looked at the patient's name. Her heart sank. It *was* him! Kevin Wincouser!

Oh Lord, I can't believe it. . . .

She glanced across the room where medical personnel still assessed Kevin's injuries. She felt numb and in shock. Nevertheless, Lara knew she had to be a professional despite the sudden personal angle in this situation. She forced herself to concentrate on the team's ongoing evaluation and take notes. Minutes later, Kevin was wheeled off for a CT scan, and the trauma room emptied out.

Collecting herself, Lara made her way over to the neurosurgeon. "What's your initial diagnosis, Dr. LaPont? The patient has friends and/or family members in the lobby, and I'll have to tell them *something*."

"Well, we're obviously looking at a head injury," the physician said. He towered over Lara by nearly a foot, and the way he combed his straight dark brown hair forward gave the specialist a somewhat ominous appearance. "I won't know for sure until I get the CT results."

"All right, I'll relay that message."

Closing her portfolio, Lara headed for the lobby. She feared the worst for Kevin. He might have suffered a brain injury. Would he ever be the same? Many times, head injury patients never fully recovered, although Lara couldn't help but be hopeful. Medical advancements had come a long way.

And, of course, the Lord was able to do exceedingly, abundantly, and above in the way of healing. The Kevin Wincouser Lara once knew had been a committed Christian, although his dedication to the Lord seemed to have waned after his parents' deaths. Had Kevin ever renewed his faith?

Making her way back through the arena, Lara's mind whirred with questions. She wondered if Kevin had married. Was his wife among the people waiting for an update on his condition? She steeled herself, planning what to say and what not to say.

Lara reached the emergency department's waiting area and walked down the center aisle until she came to a small cluster of people. To her right, she spotted a clown dressed in dusty denims and a red, white, and blue striped shirt. His face had been painted with colorful makeup, and on his head he wore an oversized Stetson. He was juggling for some kids who cackled at his antics. The lobby suddenly looked as though the circus had come to town.

Make that the rodeo.

"Any of you here for Kevin?" Lara asked, careful not to use his last name and violate patient confidentiality laws.

The clown ceased his act, and two cowboys stood along with a woman. Turning to face Lara, she stepped forward. Petite and slender, wearing blue jeans that were as snug as a second skin, she tossed her head, sending a thick lock of auburn hair over her shoulder.

"Mackenzie Sabino." She extended her right hand. "I'm with Kevin. Are you the doctor?"

"No." Lara took her hand in a quick, polite introductory greeting. "I'm a social worker. I just wanted to give you a brief update. The doctor will be out shortly, and he can give you more details." Lara pointed to a door at the end of the waiting room where they could speak in private. "Please follow me."

Lara drew a set of keys from her skirt pocket and unlocked the door to the "quiet room." It was a place where friends and relatives of trauma victims could sit and talk—sometimes cry—and not be gawked at by the general public.

"Please make yourselves comfortable. Can I get you anything? Coffee? Soda?"

The redheaded female whirled around. "Look, Miss *Whoever-You-Are*, I don't want anything except news about Kevin, got it?"

"Whoa, Mac, take it easy," one of the cowboys said, grabbing hold of her elbow and reining her in. "This little lady's just tryin' to be nice."

The woman raised a doubtful brow.

Lara felt herself tense. "I apologize. I didn't introduce myself. My name is Lara Donahue." She met the other woman's intense gaze but kept her voice low and even. Wife, fiancée, or maybe just a friend, Mackenzie Sabino was probably sick with fear over Kevin's well-being. Everyone handled stress in a different way. Lara had learned that much in the last two years on the job. "Mr. Wincouser is having a CT scan right now. Once the results come back, the neurosurgeon will discuss them with you." Lara tipped her head. "Are you his wife?"

"Possibly."

The clown laughed, a deep, jolly sound. "In your dreams, Mac." He chuckled once more, and the two cowboys joined him.

"Shut up, you guys." Mac whirled on her heel and walked several feet away from them.

"She's Wink's rodeo sponsor," the clown informed Lara.

"Wink?" Lara frowned in confusion.

The cowboy grinned. "Yeah, that's what we call him."

"Oh. . .I see."

Lara chastened herself for feeling relieved to learn the woman wearing the tight jeans and snobbish demeanor wasn't Kevin's wife. Kevin's taste in women wasn't any of Lara's business. Sponsor or wife. . .why should she care? She hadn't even seen him in over a decade.

Except she'd practically grown up with the Wincouser boys. Lara couldn't help feeling worried about Kevin.

Forcing herself back into her professional mode, she lowered herself onto the plaid sofa. She opened her portfolio and took out a pen. "Would you mind telling me what happened today? How did the injury occur?"

Mackenzie gave her an indignant look. "He got bucked off a horse. What more is there to tell?" She raised her arms in exasperation.

"Aw, Mac, take it easy, will ya?" the second cowboy said, taking a seat in a tan leather armchair adjacent to Lara. He appeared to be younger than the other two men. His blondish-brown hair was shaved in the classic crew-cut style. "Wink is a two-time world champion bareback rider, and he was riding as good as ever today. Stayed on the bronc for the entire eight-second ride. But the horse must have calmed down some, and Wink relaxed enough so when the horse started bucking again, Wink flew off like a rag doll."

Lara grimaced, imagining the scenario.

"He didn't stay on for eight seconds," Mackenzie Sabino spat with sarcasm. "He fell off just before the buzzer." She cursed. "And now with this injury, he's going to be out points and money."

Lara's mouth fell open, knowing Kevin stood to lose so much more.

"Don't mind her," the other cowboy said with a little smile. He sat down and held his black wide-brimmed hat between his knees. His face was tanned, and his hair was the color of cherrywood. "Mac's mouth tends to run faster than her mind."

"Oh, quiet," she snapped. "I don't need you making excuses for me."

"Someone's gotta do it," the younger cowboy mumbled under his breath.

"I heard that, Jimmy."

The clown took the chair beside the quipping cowboy and grinned at Lara. "So how is Wink *really* doing? C'mon now. You can tell us."

"I honestly don't know. The doctor is waiting for the CT scan results."

"Do you have a business card, honey?" the older of the two cowboys asked.

Taken aback by the way she'd been addressed, Lara glanced at the man across from her, noting for the first time his very rugged appearance. From the tips of his well-worn boots to his daring brown-eyed gaze, he seemed every inch the classic cowboy. She suspected he called every woman "honey."

Lara pulled a card from her portfolio and wondered if the guy didn't believe she was whom she claimed. After handing it to him, he seemed to study it for several long seconds before dropping it into the breast pocket of his white pinstriped shirt.

"This is a very nice hospital," the clown remarked.

Lara sensed he was attempting polite conversation, so she did the same. "We take very good care of our patients here."

"That's good to know."

The other cowboy with the cropped hair cleared his throat. "You mentioned a neurosurgeon. . . . That doesn't sound too good."

"The neurosurgeon is part of the trauma team that responds to head injuries."

"See, Jimmy, just a formality," the clown said.

Mackenzie Sabino had taken to pacing the carpeted floor behind Jimmy and the clown. "I can't believe it. I'm going to have to cancel the television interview for tomorrow," she muttered, "and after I worked so hard to get Wink on that local morning show, too."

Lara's pager chirped, and she snatched it off her belt and read the phone number on the screen. *8745.* She recognized it as the trauma room's extension.

"Excuse me while I make this call." She stood and smiled at the clown and cowboys before crossing the room and plucking the receiver from the wall phone. She dialed the number, and after two rings, one of the nurses answered her call.

"Dr. LaPont is taking the head injury patient to surgery. He started to go downhill in CT, and it looks like he's got a head bleed."

Lara closed her eyes as regret filled her soul. "All right. I'll let his friends know it might be a long night."

"Good. And let them know that after surgery, he'll go to the NICU."

"Okay. Thanks."

Lara hung up the phone. Pivoting, she at once became aware of the curious faces staring back at her.

"I'm sorry to tell you this, but. . .Kevin. . .he's on his way to surgery right now. He's got what we call a subarachnoid hemorrhage or, in simpler terms, some bleeding in his brain. The neurosurgeon will go in and—"

"Brain surgery?" Mackenzie shrieked. "He'll be nothing but a. . .a vegetable! He'll never ride again!"

"Oh, now, calm down, Mac," the clown said. "It's not like they're doing a lobotomy. Surgeons can perform amazing things nowadays. Wink'll be back to his old self in no time." He turned and gave Lara a wide, white-painted smile. "Isn't that right?"

She smiled back and nodded, praying it was true.

Chapter 2

In a dreamlike state, Kevin floated through space and time. Peace flooded his being like the perfect drug. He felt full and satisfied as though he'd just gobbled down a bountiful Thanksgiving Day meal. He felt weightless, confident, and competitive, and imagined he was about to take the ride of his life.

"He who has an ear, let him hear what the Spirit says...."

What?

Kevin tried to discover where the voice had come from, but his limbs felt restricted somehow. That tranquil feeling vanished, and he suddenly felt trapped.

"Those whom I love I rebuke and discipline. So be earnest, and repent."

A wave of panic engulfed Kevin. He recognized the scriptural passage, but it had been years since he'd cracked open a Bible. He'd decided long ago that religion didn't work. Look where it got his devout parents. Dead. Instead, Kevin chose to be the decider of his own fate. He lived life hard and fast, and he knew he was no saint. Experience had taught him that sinners had a lot more fun.

But was God really talking to him now?

Naw. Couldn't be. This was just some weird dream.

On the other hand, if it wasn't, Kevin figured he was in for a heap of trouble. What could God want with him except to pour out His wrath and judgment?

"For I know the plans I have for you...plans to prosper you and not to harm you, plans to give you hope and a future."

Kevin knew that verse. He'd memorized it as a teenager. But that was a lifetime ago. He wasn't the same person anymore.

"You did not choose me, but I chose you and appointed you to go and bear fruit— fruit that will last."

Not me, God. You've got the wrong guy for that job.

The reply couldn't even take root, for all at once, Kevin felt himself free-falling, like a man who'd jumped from an airplane without a parachute. Fear gripped every muscle and robbed him of his next breath.

Help me! Help me! Don't let me fall like this! God, please help me!

∽

Lara glanced at her watch. Seven o'clock. This wasn't exactly the way she had planned to spend her Friday night. However, she couldn't get herself to leave the hospital without knowing Kevin was all right. Earlier, she had shown his friends to the Family Center, where they could wait out the long and delicate procedure in some comfort. With that accomplished, Lara had returned to the ED, where she finished her work. After a couple of hours of overtime, she made her way up to the Neurological Intensive Care Unit, or NICU, where she planted herself next to Polly Nivens, a unit secretary and one of Lara's good friends.

"I'm off work in a half hour," Polly said, "and I have no intentions of hanging around."

Lara shot her brunette friend a look of irritation. "I'd wait with you if you were in my situation."

"Yeah, I suppose you would." Reluctance laced her tone.

Lara grinned. She and Polly had been hired around the same time and met during their orientation week here at County General. They'd hit it off, and with so much in common, including their Christian faith, they'd remained friends ever since. Together, they had even joined a local Christian singles' group that met once a month. Some of the situations that occurred during those get-togethers kept Lara and Polly laughing until the next month's meeting.

"Well, maybe we won't have to hang around too long after your shift. I called the recovery room," Lara said, "and one of the nurses told me Kevin would be out of the OR soon. That was an hour ago. I imagine he'll be brought up here to the unit anytime now."

Polly shrugged in reply as she separated paperwork.

Lara smiled and watched her friend complete her task. Wearing light blue scrubs with a colorful cotton cover-up, Polly stood an average five feet four and had average proportions. She and Lara shared a similar figure—although they both admitted they'd like to shed a good twenty pounds. They swapped articles of clothing, an inexpensive way to enhance each other's wardrobe, and they tried all types of diets. However, the latter more often than not resulted in a drive to Snoopy's Ice Cream Parlor after a stressful day, where they ordered double scoops of "Death by Chocolate."

In fact, if Snoopy's were open right now, Lara would be tempted to order a triple chocolate sundae or a banana split.

"Are you thinking of your friend?" Polly asked with a sympathetic note in her voice.

Lara laughed. "No, I'm thinking about how much I need an ice cream fix."

"Oh yeah, that'd be good. I wonder what the Friday Flavor was today." Opening her desk drawer, Polly removed a menu from Snoopy's. "Cherry Cheesecake. Good, we didn't miss much."

"We're hopeless," Lara said, shaking her head and smiling.

"I know it."

Untwisting the cap on her diet cola, Lara took a drink. The sugar-free beverage would have to suffice for now. Looking over at Polly again, she decided to change the subject. "What do you think the odds are that Kevin Wincouser would be flown to this hospital and I would be the social worker on call and in the trauma room?"

"Not very likely, but when God's involved, there are no such things as coincidences."

"I agree, but I'm too much in shock to think about what God might have in store for the future. I've been praying so hard that Kevin will be okay."

"What do you think you'll say to him when he wakes up? 'Where have you been all my life?'"

"Oh, quiet." Lara cast an exasperated glance toward the ceiling. She and Polly had been admiring Kevin's picture on his Missouri State driver's license. Judging by his photo, Kevin had gone from a cute boy to a rakishly handsome man. And how many men—women, too—ever looked so good on their driver's licenses? Those government snapshots always seemed to capture people at the worst possible angles.

But not Kevin's.

"You know, seriously, Polly, I hope I get the chance to thank him for sharing his knowledge about horses with me. It's because of him that I've been able to teach my kids how to ride."

"Your kids?" Polly grinned. "That's neat how you refer to them. You're a true saint for volunteering your time over at the ranch. Handicapped kids require a lot of patience."

"You're more than welcome to join me anytime."

Polly chuckled. "Yeah, so you've told me. . .about a hundred times. Maybe even two hundred. The problem is, I'm lacking in the patience department."

"Maybe God will teach you patience when you donate your time."

Polly gave her a skeptical look.

At that moment, a transporter and a nurse from recovery wheeled a gurney through the doors of the NICU.

"Is that room 7?" Polly asked.

"Sure is," the husky transporter replied.

Lara strained to get a look at Kevin, but all she could see was his bandaged head. Minutes later, Bill Kitrell, one of Dr. LaPont's residents, walked in. He slapped down the metal-encased chart. Without a word, he began to write out orders.

"Hey, Bill, is the guy in 7 going to be all right?" Polly asked, stealing the words right off the tip of Lara's tongue.

"Yeah, I think so," the young man said without even glancing up.

"I'm asking because Lara grew up with him."

Bill raised his dark head and peered at Lara. "Oh yeah?"

She nodded.

The soon-to-be neurosurgeon, a nice—and very married—guy, gazed at the chart again. "I was wondering what you were still doing here. Although. . ." He cast a hooded glance in Polly's direction. "I know you two are cohorts, so I didn't think too much about it."

"Cohorts?" Polly put her hands on her hips. "Who uses that word in this day and age?"

"I just did. Didn't you hear me?" He slid the chart in Polly's direction.

"A wee bit crabby tonight, eh, Bill?"

"Just a little," he confessed. "I haven't slept in two days."

"Is it all right if I go in and see Kevin?" Lara asked, interrupting the banter.

"Sure." Bill forced a tight smile. "But your friend is in a coma-induced state, and we're keeping him that way for a while to make sure no more swelling occurs in his brain."

Lara stood and stepped out of the nurses' station, only to glimpse several RNs at work in Kevin's room. She paused, deciding to wait until they had him settled.

"Bill, has anyone been to the Family Center to let Kevin's friends know he's out of surgery?"

"Yeah, I think LaPont went down there." He gave both ladies a curt nod. "Now if you'll both excuse me, I need to catch a few winks."

The word "wink" reminded Lara of Kevin's nickname. She straightened and glanced into his room again. The nurses were just finishing up. She walked to the doorway, and the male RN waved her in.

"Working overtime, aren't you? I don't think this fellow's up for an interview."

Lara smiled at the glib remark. Since her assigned areas as a social worker consisted of the emergency department and the three intensive care units, she was recognized by most of the personnel who worked there. "This is actually a personal call."

The nurse, a lanky blond with a goatee, suddenly looked concerned. "Is this patient a friend of yours?"

"Yes. A friend from the past. I haven't seen him in about ten years."

"Tough way to get reacquainted," the other RN said as she peeled off her protective gloves. Without waiting for a reply, the slender woman with short light brown hair and a pockmarked complexion brushed past Lara.

Stepping over to Kevin's bedside, Lara cringed at all the ticking, pulsing machinery and plastic tubing coming and going from various parts of his body. He'd been placed on a ventilator to help him breathe, and the IV fluid that kept him hydrated and nourished ran into his arm. Surgical staff had bandaged his head so Kevin appeared to be wearing a white cap. His face resembled the Kevin Wincouser Lara used to know, and contrary to the celebrity smile on his driver's license, his expression was now one of unconscious bliss.

The other nurse left, and Lara touched the back of Kevin's hand. Compassion engulfed her. *Oh Lord, please heal this man. I have no idea what sort of person he is now, but he was nice to me at a time when a lot of other kids weren't.*

Lara could still recall how some of the boys in the neighborhood called her "Larda," poking fun at her chubby size. But neither Kevin nor his brother ever taunted or teased her. The Wincouser boys had always been kindhearted and polite.

She stood there a few more moments before giving herself a mental shake. She felt suddenly exhausted and knew it was time to go home. At least she'd learned Kevin had made it through surgery, and according to Bill Kitrell, he would recover.

Leaving his room, Lara made her way over to where Polly stood gathering her belongings. The third-shift unit secretary had arrived and appeared busy at the computer.

"Ready to leave?" Polly asked. "I sure am!"

Lara nodded, and together she and Polly walked out of the NICU. They reached the elevator, and Lara suddenly remembered she had Kevin's driver's license.

"Pol, I need to stop at the Family Center. I should return Kevin's license to his friends."

"Okay. I'll go with you so neither of us has to brave the parking structure alone."

"Great."

Rounding the corner, the two women ambled into the surprisingly busy Family Center. Lara glanced around and spotted Dr. LaPont on the telephone nearby, but she didn't see any of the four people who had been in the emergency department earlier. Once LaPont finished his call, Lara managed to catch his attention as he started to head out the door.

"No one's here with the patient," the surgeon informed her. "I even had them paged overhead. I don't have a phone number. Nothing."

"That's odd. I got the impression Kevin's friends were going to stick around until he came out of surgery."

LaPont shrugged, then proceeded to give Lara the rundown on Kevin, all of which she'd heard from the resident.

"If I see his friends, I'll be sure to tell them," she said, wondering how she'd manage to keep her promise since she was off for the weekend.

Dr. LaPont inclined his head in a parting nod, then left the Family Center.

Feeling helpless, Lara looked at Polly, who shrugged.

"Nice friends."

Lara groaned. "If Kevin is from Missouri, like his driver's license states, then he's a long way from home. I don't have a clue as to whether he has family. . .a wife. He could be married with five kids for all I know."

"That'd be a bummer." Polly's green eyes shimmered with the jest.

Lara couldn't help but laugh as they headed for the employee parking structure on the other side of the hospital. "I must confess, I did have a crush on Kevin my freshman year of high school. He was a senior, and every time he saw me in the hallway, he'd wave or smile or say hello." Lara chuckled at the recollection. "I was the envy of all the freshman girls—maybe even *all* the girls."

"He sounds like he was a nice guy back then. I wonder if he's still a nice guy."

"Don't know." Lara hitched her purse strap up higher onto her shoulder. "Doesn't seem like he has very nice friends."

"Maybe they went to get something to eat. If they come back, they can call Admitting and find out where Kevin is, although they won't be allowed in the NICU at this time of night. Maybe someone told them that, so they left."

"Yeah, maybe. . . ." Lara thought it over. "Do you think they'll know to call the admitting department?"

"Well, if they don't, it's not your problem, Lara. You're off duty now—you have been for the last six and a half hours."

"I know, but—"

"But you knew the guy way back when. . . . I understand, except it's still not your problem. Who's the social worker on call this weekend?"

"Sarah Jackson."

"Good. It's Sarah's problem, and since it's our weekend off, we're going to enjoy it!"

Stepping out into the balmy June night, Lara pushed out a smile. She agreed with everything Polly told her; however, her heart didn't seem to be listening. Kevin Wincouser was her "problem." The niggling deep inside her chest told her so. What's more, she had an odd feeling that he would likely be her problem until some family member claimed him.

Chapter 3

What's the matter, Muffin? You seem a million miles away this morning." Lara snapped out of her musings and realized she'd been staring sightlessly into her coffee cup. Lifting her gaze, she smiled at her grandmother, who was spreading jam across her slice of toast. "Guess I've been a rude breakfast companion."

"Not at all. You obviously have a lot on your mind."

"Yeah, I do." Lara looked back down into her black coffee.

"Anything you'd like to talk about?"

Lara considered the offer. She'd been thinking about Kevin ever since Flight-for-Life flew him into the ED yesterday, and now, this morning, she wondered how to get in touch with his friends. She supposed she could drive out to the rodeo in Waukesha. It wasn't all that far away. What gnawed at her was the fact she hadn't gotten the chance to say she and Kevin knew each other as kids and. . . Were they going to contact Kevin's brother, Clayt? Somebody should!

"Gram, do you remember the Wincousers?" Lara warned herself to be careful. If she said too much, she'd violate patient confidentiality laws. Looking up from her coffee, she peered into her grandmother's face with its delicate features bordered by white hair that she wore in a short, classy style.

"The Wincousers. . .yes, of course I remember them. Ted and Roberta were the ones killed in that tragic train wreck in Japan, isn't that right?"

Lara nodded.

"And they had two sons, both fine young men, if I recall." Gram took a sip of her freshly brewed green tea. "I wonder what ever happened to them."

"Kevin left to compete in the rodeo." That hadn't been a secret. Lara recalled hearing her parents discuss the topic in hushed voices. The pastor had been unsuccessful in talking Kevin out of moving away. Various other well-intentioned church people tried to dissuade him also, but Kevin seemed determined to leave Wisconsin.

"He was the older boy, right?"

"Right."

"Seems to me he took his parents' deaths extraordinarily hard."

"That's what I heard, too."

Gram bit into her toast, chewed, and swallowed. Then one of her light brows dipped in a frown. "Why are you thinking about the Wincousers?"

"Oh, something happened yesterday that caused me to remember them. I can't go into details, though."

"I see."

Lara scooted her chair back and stood. Lifting her cereal bowl and coffee mug off the kitchen table, she carried them to the sink.

"Don't worry about the dishes, Muffin. I'll take care of them."

"Thanks, Gram. I've got some errands to do, and the sooner I leave the better."

"Well then, don't let breakfast dishes keep you."

Smiling, Lara kissed her grandmother's cheek before ambling down the hallway of the spacious flat they shared. The lower half of the duplex was occupied by Lara's parents and her younger brother, Tim. An older sister lived on the other side of town with her husband and their three small children.

Entering the large bathroom with its white ceramic-tiled floor, Lara shed her nightgown, stepped into the tub, and turned on the faucet. She heard the familiar knocking of the pipes before she pulled up the knob activating the overhead shower.

Lara had grown up in this house. It had been built in the 1930s, and even with remodeling and updates, some things never changed, like noisy plumbing and handcrafted charm. When she was a kid, Lara's grandparents and Aunt Eileen lived up here, but since then, Gramps had gone to be with the Lord, and Eileen had moved to Colorado, where she remained happily unmarried and now taught high school science. Over the past few years, Gram's health had declined, so Lara had volunteered to move in with her. The elderly woman enjoyed the company, and Lara liked caring for her, the little bit that she did. Gram was still quite self-sufficient for the most part.

After washing up, Lara padded to her bedroom. Gram had insisted she take the master bedroom when she moved in, and seeing it would do no good to argue, Lara agreed. She painted and wallpapered to make the room feel like her own. In fact, the entire flat was beginning to look like "her own," but Gram adored the changes.

Once she'd dressed in jeans and a blue-and-red-striped T-shirt, Lara gathered her light brown hair, with its blond highlights, and clipped it up at the back of her head. Snatching her purse off the desk in the living room, she called a good-bye to Gram and left. As she passed the downstairs unit, Lara opened the back door and hollered a greeting.

"Anybody need anything while I'm out?"

"Don't think so," her father answered from the direction of the living room.

Lara continued on her way out. Behind the off-white vinyl-sided house with its burgundy shutters and next to the garage, her father had erected a carport under which Lara and Tim parked their vehicles. Unlocking the door of her teal compact car, Lara climbed in and started the engine. Next she backed into the alley, deciding her first stop would be the hospital. Lara hoped she'd find Kevin's friends there so she wouldn't have to search for them at a crowded rodeo.

When she arrived at County General, Lara was unprepared for the sight that met her in the spacious lobby. Television crews and cameras filled the area, and several feet away, Lara recognized the director of public relations talking to media personnel.

She took cautious steps forward, wondering what was going on. Then someone caught her elbow, and Lara whirled around to face a man about fifty years of age with a stocky build, graying brown hair, and a suntanned face.

"You don't recognize me without my makeup, do you?" He laughed. "I'm Quincy Owens, otherwise known as 'Quincy the Clown.'"

Lara blinked until finally the realization struck. "Oh. . .from yesterday. Kevin's friend."

"That's right." Quincy smiled, then nodded toward the reporters. "This here's the press conference Mac arranged right after Wink went into surgery. She's determined to make him famous one way or another."

"Oh. . .so that's what's going on here."

"Yep. We're all gettin' updated on Wink's condition. The doctors say he's going to be okay, even though he's in a coma right now."

Lara noticed the worry lines that formed on Quincy's forehead.

"I sure hope he's okay. . . ."

"I hope so, too." Lara opened her purse and pulled out her wallet. From it, she extracted Kevin's driver's license. "I need to return this." She handed the plastic card to Quincy. "The registrar in the emergency department gave it to me yesterday, and somehow I never gave it back. I apologize."

After giving the ID a quick glance, Quincy handed it right back. "Maybe you oughta keep it till Wink wakes up. See, the rodeo is over after tomorrow. We're all pulling up stakes and heading out. Wink'll have to catch up with us when he's better."

"What about his sponsor. . .Mac?"

The large man shrugged. "She might stick around. Her daddy's company has a lot of dough riding on Wink—pardon the pun."

"I see."

"You can give the license to Mac if you want, although she's not the most responsible person in the world."

Lara slipped the driver's license back into her purse. "I'll find out where Wink—I mean, Kevin's belongings are. Security will know. I'll be sure to add his license to his other things."

"Sounds good."

After a hesitant look, she decided to forge on. "I never got a chance to tell you and the others that Kevin and I grew up in the same neighborhood right here in Milwaukee—Wauwatosa, actually. Our part of town borders Waukesha County."

Quincy brought his chin back. "I never knew Kevin was from around here." He turned. "Did you know that, Brent?"

"What?"

Several feet away, another man pivoted and looked their way. Lara recognized him as the ruggedly handsome cowboy who had asked for her business card.

"Woman here says she grew up with Wink. I didn't know he hailed from Wisconsin, did you?"

The man called Brent sauntered over. He gave Lara an appraising glance from head to toe before meeting her gaze. A blush warmed her face.

"Yeah, I knew Wink was from Wisconsin. Didn't realize it was this particular area, though." He tore his stare from hers and looked at Quincy. "But if she says he is, I imagine it's true."

Lara felt oddly flattered that Brent would give her the benefit of the doubt.

"I can't imagine there's more than one Kevin Wincouser in the world," Lara added, "at least not one who's twenty-nine years old and in the rodeo."

"Heaven help us if there is," Brent quipped with a slight grin.

Quincy chuckled.

Pulling something from the breast pocket of his plaid shirt, he offered it to Lara. An instant later, she realized he'd handed her two tickets.

"Bull-riding competition is tonight. Want to come watch?"

"Um. . ."

"Bring a friend."

Lara glanced at the thick blue tickets before looking back at Brent. She couldn't think of any other commitments she had this evening.

"You do have a friend, don't you?"

"Huh? Oh yeah." She shot him an exasperated frown. "Of course I have a friend."

Brent shifted his weight. "Just one? Or do you need more tickets?"

Lara smirked. She was beginning to understand the man's sarcastic wit. "My brother and his fiancée might like to come."

Brent pulled out two more tickets from his shirt pocket.

"My sister, her husband, and their three kids—"

"I said 'friends,' not your entire relation."

Lara laughed. "I'm just giving you a hard time. Four tickets are plenty. Thanks."

Quincy stood by chuckling. "And notice she didn't even mention a husband, Brent."

"I noticed."

A twinkle entered his brown eyes, and Lara could feel another blush burn into her cheekbones. She had a feeling Brent probably charmed the ladies from coast to coast. But he certainly seemed nice enough.

"Well, thanks for the tickets."

"Don't let 'em go to waste, now," Quincy the Clown said with a grin.

"I won't. I promise."

With a smile, Lara walked past the men and into the throng of media people. The press conference had just finished, and Lara realized, much to her disappointment, she would now have to wait until the evening news to hear what was said publicly about Kevin Wincouser's medical condition.

Chapter 4

"Do I look okay to go to the rodeo?"

Standing in her bedroom, Lara scrutinized Polly's outfit, faded jeans and a red sweater. "You look fine. It's not like the rodeo is a black-tie affair or something."

"I know, but. . ." She pushed out a pretty pout. "I don't even own a pair of boots. I'm wearing athletic shoes. Some cowgirl I am."

Lara laughed. "Don't worry about it. There'll be plenty of folks in athletic shoes tonight. You'll see."

"Well, you look like a cowgirl."

Lara turned to gaze at herself in the full-length mirror attached to the closet door. She'd chosen a lightweight, long-sleeved blue plaid shirt and a newer pair of jeans. But unlike Polly, Lara had boots.

"I'm feeling out of sorts here," her friend confessed.

"Want to change?"

"I thought you'd never ask. Yes!"

Grinning, Lara swung open her closet door and helped Polly select a soft chambray shirt. Lara found an old pair of brown boots that had obviously seen better days, but Polly accepted the offer to wear them despite the leather's many scuffs and scrapes.

"Now I feel like I'm dressed for the rodeo," Polly declared, admiring her outfit in the mirror. "Yee-haw! Let's go."

Laughing, the girls walked down the hallway, heading for the back door. Lara called a farewell to her grandmother, who sat in the living room watching reruns of *The Lawrence Welk Show*.

Outside, the setting sun cast golden hues against the cloudless evening sky. Lara decided to drive, so they walked to her car and climbed in.

"So this Brent is really a hunk, eh?" Polly asked, snapping her seat belt into place.

"I don't believe I ever used the word *hunk*." Lara grinned and backed out of the carport, then drove down the alley. "But he is quite the charmer."

"Aren't all cowboys charming? I mean, when I think cowboys, I think of that cute actor in that recent Western. . . . What's his name?"

"I can't remember his name, but I know which one you're talking about, and Brent strikes me the same way. Hollywood handsome. But he's almost too charming for his own good."

"Well, you know, looks can be deceiving. Maybe the guy is really an upstanding Christian who adheres to good moral values."

"Yeah, maybe."

Lara wanted to be careful. She wasn't a prude, and she knew she ought not to pass judgment; however, God wanted her to be discerning. There was nothing wrong with handsome and charming—unless it went along with boozing and womanizing. Lara had heard too many tales involving the latter, especially when it came to rodeo cowboys, and it caused her to be suspicious of Brent's motives.

"Tim once told me that some guys see an innocent woman as a challenge."

"Oh, what does your brother know? He's a committed Christian with a sweet fiancée. Besides, how would Brent know you're *innocent*?"

"I think men can tell, Polly."

She merely shrugged.

Lara decided there was no point in debating the issue. She wanted to have fun tonight. "Personally, I think the reason Brent turned on his charm and gave me free tickets to the rodeo is because he wants me to spend money there—and bring some friends who'll spend money, too."

"Bingo. I think you're right."

Lara laughed. The good times were already beginning.

A half hour later, they arrived at the fairgrounds, paid to park, then walked through the dusty gravel parking lot to the arena with a crowd of other people. After a quick stop in the restroom to brush their hair and touch up their lipstick, Lara and Polly headed out to find their seats. An usher came forward and offered his assistance, handing them both a program. Lara and Polly were soon shocked to discover that their "tickets" were actually VIP passes and that they would watch the bull-riding competition from the stands right behind the bucking chutes.

"We're going to be able to hear the bulls snort from these seats," Lara teased.

"Are you kidding? We're so close we'll feel their hot, angry breath!"

Lara grimaced, imagining that bulls' breath didn't smell all that pleasant. Then, amid the growing din of the crowd, she sat down and took in the sights.

The arena consisted of an enclosed oblong area that had bucking chutes on one end and a roping chute on the opposite side. The flooring consisted of a clay and sand mixture spread around and loosened with some sort of harrow. Watching the grounds crew finish its final preparations caused Lara to feel bad for Kevin, who had been injured somewhere out there. She wondered if he was any better this evening.

"Is this where we're sitting?" a feminine voice asked, although it sounded more like an exclamation.

Shaking herself from her reverie, Lara turned to see her brother, Tim, and his fiancée, Amanda, standing in the aisle.

"This is it," she replied, waving them in. "We're practically in the front row."

"So I see." Tim allowed Amanda to scoot in first. He then sat down on the end of the metallic bench. "Did you and Polly get programs?"

In reply to her brother's question, Lara nodded and held hers up so Tim could see it.

"Kevin Wincouser's part of this rodeo. Remember that guy, Lara? Open your program, and you'll see his picture. Mom said she heard on the news that he got hurt."

Lara laughed at her brother's rapid-fire remarks. "I was at the hospital when Flight brought Kevin in yesterday."

"And you didn't say anything?" Tim appeared insulted.

"I couldn't. There are laws I have to abide by, or I'll lose my job, you know?" Her brother shrugged.

"But now that the media is reporting Kevin's injury, I don't have to keep it a secret anymore." Lara glanced at her program, knowing she was prohibited from discussing his condition. What the media reported was all she could confirm.

"Wow, Kevin Wincouser. . ." Tim shook his head. "He was like my hero or something."

"Yeah, mine, too," Lara admitted, leaning over Polly and Amanda in order to converse with her brother."

"Is this the guy you're talking about?" Amanda asked, pointing at a photo in her program. Her long, straight, platinum-blond hair hung past her shoulders, adorned by a simple red plastic headband.

Lara tried not to envy her future sister-in-law's flawless beauty. Bright blue eyes, a trim figure, and gorgeous locks, Amanda Erikson was model material. But what caused her to be so special was that the younger woman was just as attractive on the inside. She had a sweet, caring heart and would do just about anything for anybody.

Tim, a sweetheart himself, was a tall, lanky brunette. He was the veritable computer geek of the Donahue family, and he had found a gem in Amanda. They made an adorable couple, and Lara was looking forward to their wedding in the fall.

Polly gave Lara a nudge. "Look. There's some activity in the bull pens."

"Bull pens? That's baseball, you nut. What you're staring at are called bucking chutes."

"No, what I'm staring at is a cowboy in a black Stetson heading this way."

Lara whipped her gaze to the left and saw Brent striding toward them. In one smooth move, he jumped up on the side of the stands and clasped the overhead green metal railing. "Glad you could make it," he said with a dashing smile.

Lara returned the gesture, then began introductions. "This is my friend Polly Nivens."

With his left arm wrapped around the rail, Brent pulled off his tan leather glove and stuck out his right hand. "Pleasure to meet you, Polly."

"Same here." Reaching over Lara, she clasped his hand in a friendly shake.

"And this is my brother, Tim, and his fiancée, Amanda."

Lara watched Brent's expression as he glanced down the row and bobbed out a polite nod. He didn't seem starstruck by Amanda's good looks, which upped Lara's estimation of him.

"Mac heard from the docs at your hospital," Brent said, focusing on Lara. "Apparently they're going to try to wake up Wink on Monday."

"Really? They're bringing him out of his coma so soon? That's awesome!"

Brent narrowed his brown-eyed gaze. "We'll see."

Lara wondered what he meant but didn't get the opportunity to ask.

"I'd better go. Just wanted to, um, swing by," Brent stated, indicating the railing he still gripped, "and say hello."

Lara and Polly smiled, and Brent tugged on the brim of his hat before jumping off the edge of the bleachers.

"Why didn't you tell me he's drop-dead gorgeous?" Polly shrieked, putting her hands around Lara's neck and giving her a playful shake.

"I did tell you."

Amanda leaned over. "I think I'll buy Tim a Stetson for Christmas. What do you think?"

"Can't turn a frog into a handsome prince," Polly quipped. "Correction— handsome *cowboy*."

Lara frowned. "Hey, that's my brother you're insulting."

"And my fiancée." Amanda raised her perfectly shaped chin in mock indignation.

"Right. You two love him. That's why you need *me* to point out the obvious."

"Amanda, let's both spill our sodas on Polly's lap later, accidentally, of course."

"Not good enough. I think we should volunteer her as a clown during the bull-riding competition tonight."

Lara laughed, Polly smirked, and Amanda wore an expression that said she'd get even—in one amusing way or another.

The rodeo began with a booming overhead announcement that came on so fast it startled Lara. Then a preshow commenced with a parade of pretty white horses wearing decorative headpieces. Dancers stood on the animals' backs, performing a variety of acrobatic moves and all to a popular Western tune that soon had the audience clapping their hands and singing along.

Once the preliminary entertainment ended, the contestants were introduced. A familiar song played in the background, warning mothers not to let their children grow up to be cowboys.

"Next, and currently in third place, is Brent Yiska."

Lara applauded with the rest of the audience but soon felt Polly lean toward her.

"What kind of name is Yiska?"

"Beats me."

"Polly Yiska. . . Has a nice ring to it."

Lara stopped in midclap and gaped at her friend. "Polly Yiska?"

She turned and smiled. "I think I'm in love. I'll never wash my right hand again."

The two started laughing so hard that before long, their sides ached.

Then the bull riding began. Contained in the chutes just several feet away, the fierce animals stomped and snorted. Cowboys stood on something that looked like a catwalk on top of one end of the chute. When the rider lowered himself on the bull's back, other cowboys held on to his vest until he nodded, signaling he was ready for the chute to be opened. The bull lunged out, kicking its hind legs and twisting its massive body in one direction, then the other, determined to unseat the man astride it.

Lara found herself tensing and cringing each time a cowboy was bucked off. Even Brent couldn't hang on long enough, and Lara feared he'd be trampled after he hit the ground. But several clowns immediately appeared to distract the bull, and riders on horseback, or "pickup men," according to Tim, showed up to haze the bull out of the ring.

As the rodeo neared its end, Brent stopped by once more, but this time he encouraged all four of them to come back out for tomorrow's events. He offered them another set of passes.

"Thanks. That's really nice of you. But I'm involved with my local church," Lara informed him, "and ministry fills up most of my Sunday."

"Same goes for Amanda and me," Tim said.

Polly sighed. "Me, too. . .but I wish I could come back. I had a fun time tonight."

Brent grinned. "That's good." He paused while the ladies collected their purses and Tim gathered their trash. "It's been nice to meet you all, and next time the rodeo's in town, you'll have to come visit again." He turned his head, catching Lara's eye. "I imagine I'll see you at the hospital on Monday."

"It's very possible."

He gave her a parting nod, then bid farewell to the others and returned to wherever it was the cowboys hung out when they weren't competing.

On the way home, Lara and Polly stopped to pick up a pizza, which they planned to eat at Lara's place.

"You're awfully quiet, Polly. Is anything wrong?"

"No. . .not *wrong*. I'm just wrestling with an issue."

"Can you tell me about it?"

"I'd rather not, at least not now. Maybe later."

"All right." Lara didn't push her friend to say more, although she had a feeling the "issue" had something to do with Brent Yiska.

Chapter 5

"Kevin, can you hear me?"

A commanding male voice penetrated the darkness. Kevin opened his mouth to reply, but it felt as dry as Oklahoma dirt, and all he could do was croak out a vowel sound. He swallowed, only to discover his throat was raw and tender. Before he could wonder why, another question came at him.

"Kevin, can you count backwards from ten?"

From beneath some dark, heavy shroud, he began, "Ten, nine, eight, seven, six, five, four, three, two, one. . ."

⟡

On Monday morning, Lara could hardly concentrate on her work. The emergency department bustled with sick patients, and tensions ran high. It didn't seem she'd ever be able to sneak away to the NICU to find out about Kevin.

By midafternoon, she found a few minutes to pull up his name on the computer. Lara discovered he had been transferred to a regular floor, meaning his condition had improved. Rejoicing and thanking the Lord, she went about her work with renewed enthusiasm.

At four thirty, Lara punched out, feeling the exhaustion weighing on her limbs. The day passed in such a flurry, she hadn't even found time for a lunch break. The second-shift social worker had come in at three, and the overlap helped Lara catch up so she could leave work on time.

Now to see how Kevin fared.

Walking around the hospital, using the lower level tunnel that took her past the cafeteria, Lara arrived at the patient elevators and took the car to the fifth floor. She found her way to Kevin's room and met Brent and Mac standing just outside the doorway.

"Well, look who's here. The little social worker."

Lara forced a smile in Mac's direction, despite the woman's sarcastic greeting. She looked at Brent, hoping for an ally. "I came up to see how Kevin's doing."

"Not so good," he replied in a tight voice. "He doesn't remember any of us."

"After all I've done for him," Mac muttered.

"You got paid for all you did." Brent slid an annoyed look in Mac's direction.

"Maybe Kevin's memory lapse is only temporary." Lara glanced between the two, then back to Brent. "What do the doctors say?"

"Don't know. Haven't seen 'em."

153

"If you'd like, I can ask the unit secretary to page the doctor on call."

"Yeah, maybe. . ."

"I'll ask her." Mac pushed past Lara in a huff.

"Don't mind her," Brent said. "She feels a little insulted. I s'pose we all do. We've been Wink's friends for years—we've been more than friends. We're like family."

"What about Kevin's brother? I meant to ask all weekend if he'd been contacted."

"Wink has a brother?" Brent's brown eyes widened in surprise. "I never knew that. Maybe you've got the wrong Kevin Wincouser after all."

"Hmm. . ." Lara didn't think so. But at the same time, she wondered why his good friends, his family, didn't know about Clayt.

Leaning forward, she peeked into Kevin's room.

"Go on in," Brent drawled. "He's kinda groggy, but he's awake. Quincy's in there along with Jimmy."

Lara glanced at Brent, acknowledging his reply with a nod. Then she slowly stepped up to Kevin's bedside. It heartened her to see him without all the tubes and the ventilator from Friday night. She smiled a quick greeting to Quincy the Clown and the young cowboy. The two men sat in chairs near the window.

Looking back at Kevin, Lara touched his arm. She spoke his name, and he blinked.

"Don't expect too much," Lara heard Brent say as he came to stand beside her.

"I don't." She tried again. "Kevin?"

His lids fluttered open, revealing startling blue eyes that Lara thought she'd know anywhere. She'd dreamed of those eyes hundreds of times.

She smiled. "Hi, Kevin."

His gaze lingered on her face for a long moment, and then a grin pulled at the corner of his parched-looking lips. He closed his eyes. "Lara Donahue. You're a. . .a sight for sore eyes."

Her smile widened. "You remember me?"

"Sure." He looked at her again before his lids dropped closed, as if they were too heavy for him to keep open. "You've changed a little."

"A little? Since my sophomore year of high school? I would hope that I've changed a lot." She laughed and noticed a hint of an amused expression on Kevin's face.

"How's. . .family. . .parents? Ruth and Timmy?"

"Everyone's fine. Dad just retired, but Mom still teaches part-time at the grade school. Ruth is married with three kids, and Tim is getting married this fall."

"You married? Kids?" He asked the question with his eyes closed, and his words sounded slurred, probably from any number of medications Kevin was being given.

"No husband," Lara teased, "but I have kids. About twelve last time I counted."

Brent shifted his stance and now regarded her with a look of shock. "You're kidding. You? Twelve kids?"

"Yep."

"No way!"

Lara looked back at Kevin and saw that his chapped lips had split into a grin. "Lara, you're a. . .a terrible liar."

"You're right. But I really do have twelve kids. I volunteer at the Regeneration Ranch. It's a place where physically challenged children can learn to ride horses. And I can do that, Kevin, because you taught me how to ride."

"I remember."

So did Lara, and she suddenly felt as though she had a crush on him all over again.

Brent sat down on the end of Kevin's bed. "I should have known you didn't really have twelve kids—of your own, I mean."

"No, not of my own." Smiling, Lara focused on the patient. "So, um, Kev," she said, using his childhood nickname, "you're kind of banged up."

"Yeah, that's what they say."

"Do you remember how it happened?"

"No."

Mac walked into the room, and Brent relayed the news. "Wink knows her. That's a good sign."

"Sure is," said Quincy, wearing an ear-to-ear grin.

Mac only scowled at Lara.

Tamping down the intimidation she felt around the snarly woman, Lara looked at Kevin, only to find him staring back at her.

"Who are these people?"

"They're your friends."

Brent stood and leaned on the bed's guardrail. "I'm your best friend, Wink. You don't remember me?"

"You *were* his best friend," Mac added with a snide grin, "until he stole your girl right from under your nose."

Lara widened her eyes at the remark. "Kevin would never do that!"

Brent straightened and pursed his lips, regarding Kevin all the while. "Sure he would. . .and he did."

Kevin stared back, his blue-eyed gaze obviously drawing a blank. Lara realized in that moment that she didn't know this man anymore.

"Well, listen," Brent drawled, "it doesn't matter. Emily wasn't worth my time anyhow."

"You can say that again," Jimmy interjected.

The stress level in the room suddenly skyrocketed, and Lara felt as if she was about to break out in a cold sweat.

Kevin reached out and took hold of her forearm, and Lara decided that, for an invalid, he had a strong grip as he pulled her nearer to him.

"Lara, you've got to help me," he whispered. "I feel like I'm in a nightmare."

Her heart ached for him. "It's okay. Don't worry. Just rest, all right?" She placed her free hand over his. "Things will get better as you recuperate."

She saw doubt flicker in his eyes, so she gave him a reassuring smile.

"It'll be all right," she repeated. "Go back to sleep and get some rest."

He let his eyes drift shut.

Lara slid her arm out from beneath his grasp and noticed the eerie silence that had crept into the room.

Finally, Brent dispelled it when he blew out an audible sigh. "I hope I'm never in such sad shape that a woman has to fawn all over me that way."

Lara grew embarrassed for a second time. "I didn't mean to 'fawn,' as you put it. Kevin is a longtime friend, that's all."

She saw Mac roll her eyes, but not before she glimpsed the mischievous expression on Brent's face.

"What kind of *longtime friend*?" he asked.

"Not like you're thinking," she retorted.

Brent chuckled. "So now you can read my mind, huh?"

Lara changed the subject. She disliked sparring with this man, mostly because she was afraid she'd lose. "Say, can I treat you all to dinner in the cafeteria? I didn't get lunch, so I'm starved, and today's special is one of my favorites. Homemade gyros."

"I'm game," Jimmy said.

"You're always game when there's food involved," Mac muttered.

Quincy rose from his chair. "Well, I sure could use some supper."

"Not me," Mac said. "I have work to do. I'll see you boys back at the fairgrounds."

Lara tried not to look relieved when the petite redhead in snug blue jeans marched out of the room.

"Gyros sound okay," Brent said. "You're on, Miss Lara, the social worker."

She smiled, a gesture that belied her sudden awkward feelings.

Suddenly she thought of Polly and decided to call and invite her. "My friend works a split shift, and it's about time for her dinner break. I'm going to give her a quick call."

Using the phone on the side table, Lara lifted its receiver and dialed the NICU's extension.

"Hey, Pol, I'm taking Kevin's friends, Quincy, Jimmy, and Brent, to the cafeteria for dinner. Want to come along?"

"Brent's there?"

"Uh-huh." Lara forced herself not to glance over her shoulder at him.

"Oh, wow, is it my lucky day or what? Sure, I'll come. I'll meet you in the cafeteria."

"Great. See you in a few minutes."

Grinning, Lara hung up the phone, and her odd uneasiness waned. Then she recalled her friend's comment on Saturday night—"Polly Yiska... Has a nice ring to it"—and Lara had to stifle her amusement.

Polly Yiska indeed!

Lara paused by Kevin's bedside, touched the back of his hand, and sent up another prayer for God's healing. Moments later, she left the room and caught up to his friends already in the hallway and nearing the elevators. She told herself Kevin's memory loss wasn't anything to fret about. God could do anything!

Chapter 6

Traumatic brain injury. Those three words struck terror into Kevin's soul. He wanted to believe this was some sort of bad dream. However, the weakness he felt on his right side as the doctor maneuvered his limbs was all too real. Still, he listened to the neurologist explain the injuries and talk of extensive rehabilitation.

"What about his memory loss?"

Startled by the soft, feminine voice, Kevin glanced to his left and saw Lara Donahue standing at his bedside. When had she appeared, and how was she involved in all this? Maybe this was some crazy nightmare after all. He hadn't thought about Lara Donahue in. . .well, in half of forever.

He stared at her, noticing the look of concern in her hazel eyes. Her honey-colored hair with its blond streaks had been combed back and clipped, while feathery bangs covered her forehead. She looked professional. Of course, the dark green suit she wore only added to that upper-management image, and Kevin decided the plump ugly duckling he'd known in high school had definitely turned into a lovely swan with curves in just the right places.

He sighed with relief. At least *that* part of his brain hadn't been damaged.

Closing his eyes, Kevin fought the grogginess that dogged him. He realized he was drifting in and out of consciousness and missing portions of the conversation.

"Short-term memory loss is actually quite common in this sort of situation," he heard the doctor say. The man had a dark complexion and a thick accent. Kevin wondered where the guy was from—India, perhaps. "I think he will get his memory back in a day or so."

"What if he doesn't?"

Kevin opened his eyes to see the same three men who had been in his room earlier standing next to Lara. The one who asked the question claimed to be Kevin's "best friend."

"We cannot deal with the what-ifs at this time," the wiry doctor said, setting Kevin's right arm back onto the sheet-covered mattress and pulling the light blue coverlet over the top of his body. "For now, we're glad that he's conscious and that he can speak because it means he's processing information. All very good signs so far. We will have to take things one day at a time. Okay?"

Kevin grinned at the way the man's voice went up an octave when he said,

"Okay?" Then he followed the doctor out of the room with his gaze before looking at Lara.

She smiled at him. "Pretty good news, Kev."

He had so many questions. "Why are you here?"

"Me?" She appeared taken aback. "Don't you want me here? I'm sorry. I can leave—"

"No, that's. . .not what I meant." It was an effort to form even the simplest of words. When he finally managed it, they sounded as if he'd consumed two six-packs of beer.

His head sort of felt like he'd been drinking, too.

"Lara, I haven't seen you in. . .ages. What. . .what are you doing here?"

"Oh." She smiled. "I work here. I'm a social worker." Her voice had that same happy lilt as when they were kids, and somehow it made Kevin feel that everything might really be all right. "I was part of the trauma team on duty when Flight-for-Life brought you in. I recognized your name and. . .well, I hope you don't mind that I involved myself in your case."

"I don't mind."

"My parents and Tim heard about your accident on the news. They want to come and see you. Is that okay?"

"Sure."

"I told them tomorrow night might be better, since you just got out of the NICU today."

"I imagine I'll be here."

"Well, we won't." The cowboy with the reddish-brown hair sat down on the end of his bed. "We're all hitting the road tomorrow morning."

"Where to?"

"South Dakota and the Cyprus Ranch Rodeo."

The name lit a spark in Kevin, and he knew he had to be there. "I'll catch up."

"Now, Wink, the doctor said you've got months of rehab ahead of you." Kevin watched as an older man stepped around his bedside. He looked familiar. And an image of a clown flashed across his mind. "Didn't you hear what that doctor said?"

"I know you," Kevin managed. "Quincy. Quincy Owens."

The older man let out a whoop that ping-ponged off all four walls of his hospital room. "Your memory's comin' back, Wink. That's great." Quincy placed a wide hand on Kevin's shoulder. "That's just great."

Kevin did his best to grin at the man who had been a father figure to him the past nine years.

"Do you remember me now?" asked a fresh-faced kid with a buzzed hairstyle.

Kevin studied his facial features but drew a blank. He looked at the other man, his "best friend," but again he couldn't recall a name or how he knew him.

"No. . .not yet."

"It'll come," Lara said.

"Just don't strain yourself, Wink," the other cowboy said, narrowing his brown eyes. "Weren't too many brain cells in your head to begin with."

The younger man laughed, and Quincy told them both to have a little decency.

"Can't you see Wink's hurtin' right now?"

Kevin couldn't suppress the grin that reached his lips, and as he regarded his supposed best friend, intuition told him he'd met his match—in more ways than one.

∽

"So tell me everything you know about rodeos."

Sitting outside on the second-story porch of her parents' home with Polly, Lara laughed. "I know about as much as you do."

"No, you know more. You knew what a bucking chute was. Please. . .I want to be able to talk to Brent about something."

"You might start by talking to him about Jesus."

"I will. Whenever I get a chance."

"Sorry to say, but I don't think you'll get that chance."

"How do you know?"

"He's leaving tomorrow morning. I think you should just forget about Brent Yiska."

Lara lifted her long legs, planting the heels of her bare feet on the porch railing. Tonight as they had dined in County General's cafeteria, it seemed to Lara as though Brent purposely tried to catch her eye. In a word, flirt. Once she realized it, she tried not to glance in his direction as he sat catercorner from her across the long table. The whole scene had made Lara feel uncomfortable, especially since Polly appeared to be hopelessly infatuated with the handsome cowboy.

"He's too charming for his own good," Lara told her friend. "He's a lady's man."

"Are you interested in him?"

"Me? No!" Realizing her reply sounded overly enthusiastic, she calmed her voice, adding, "I want a man who's walking with the Lord, someone who will care about my spiritual well-being."

"You don't know that Brent's *not* a Christian."

"True. He's a nice enough person, and I've never heard him curse. He's never given me a reason to think he isn't a believer. But, Polly, you know me. I would rather err on the side of caution than get emotionally involved with a man who doesn't share my beliefs."

"I know, I know—and I feel the same way." She paused for a long moment. "Lara, this is going to sound insane, but when I first set eyes on Brent, it's like

God said, 'That's him.'"

"Are you sure it was God?"

"Positive. Who else speaks to my heart like that?"

Lara shrugged. Leaning her head back, she gazed up at the dusky sky. A soft breeze rustled the treetops that canopied the Donahues' front yard.

"Whenever I imagined myself married to someone, I imagined. . .Brent and everything about him. His dark brown hair and somewhat cynical brown eyes, broad shoulders—"

"Okay, okay. Spare me the details."

"You don't like him?"

"It's not that, Polly. Brent seems nice. But he's a. . .a *player*."

"You really think so?"

"Yep."

Polly grew quiet, obviously thinking everything over. Silence filled the space between them, except for some chirping birds in one of the nearby treetops.

"Do you think Brent is worse than Bob Robinson?"

Lara deliberated, recalling the last time she'd seen Bob at one of the Christian singles' functions. "No one is worse than that dude."

"Good, he's got one up on Bob, anyway."

Lara laughed.

Just then, Tim burst through the screen door and stepped onto the porch. "Hey, look what I printed off the Internet. It's the PRCA's unofficial standings as of yesterday. Brent's in third place in bull riding with 9,236 points. Kevin slipped to seventh place in bareback riding, but there's an article about his accident and a couple of pictures."

Tim handed the pages to Lara. She glanced over the information before handing them to Polly.

"What's PRCA stand for?" Polly wanted to know.

"Professional Rodeo Cowboys Association," Tim informed her.

"Boy, do I have a lot to learn."

Lara grinned and looked at her brother. "Kevin said you could visit him tomorrow evening."

"Oh, great, I'll plan on stopping at the hospital after work. Mom said Kevin is doing better today."

Lara nodded. "Yes, but one of the residents told me that he'll be surprised if Kevin ever returns to the rodeo circuit." Her heart broke for him, and she wondered how he'd take the news.

"Well, you never know," Tim said. "Doctors have been wrong before."

"That's true." Lara stood. "I'm going to make some popcorn. Be right back."

As she walked through the living room and into the kitchen where her grandmother stood at the sink, peeling an apple, Lara prayed that Kevin would make a full recovery. The rodeo had obviously been his whole life for the past ten years—and even before that. Kevin was always involved in the statewide junior rodeos in high school. As Lara recalled, he always did well. It didn't surprise her that Kevin was a two-time world bareback champion.

Suddenly she remembered Brent's claim that Kevin had stolen "his girl." Was it true? If so, what sort of life had Kevin been living?

He's a Christian. Things happen like that. . .even to believers. Besides, it's none of my business.

"You're deep in thought, Muffin," Gram said.

Lara extracted herself from her musings. "Yeah, just thinking about Kevin."

"Doing a lot of that lately."

"More than I should."

"Well, you were awfully fond of that boy," Gram said with a knowing twinkle in her rheumy eyes. "Maybe you still are."

"No, Gram." Lara chuckled. The insinuation sounded as foolish as Polly hearing God tell her that Brent Yiska was "the one."

Nevertheless, deep in her heart of hearts, a question sparked. Lara quickly extinguished it. She wasn't about to get emotionally involved with one of her patients. True, Kevin was a childhood friend, but it was also true that she had a job to do, and Lara took it seriously.

Shaking off Gram's implication, Lara flung a package of unpopped corn into the microwave, punched in the time, and waited for it to cook.

Chapter 7

"I came to say good-bye."

Kevin stared at the woman hanging over his bedside. For the life of him, he couldn't remember who she was. She did look familiar. . .but probably because she'd been in his room yesterday with Quincy and the other two cowboys. Kevin had concluded that she was a redheaded spitfire with a tongue so sharp it could shred a man in seconds flat. He'd seen her rip apart that younger guy named Jimmy after he'd made some inane remark.

"I'll miss you, but I have to get back to Houston," she said in a sultry tone. "Daddy's expecting me."

"Okay." Kevin didn't know what else to say. With no one else in the room, he felt vulnerable, defenseless. Only one word described this woman—scary. He wished a nurse would walk in right about now and take his vitals. Give him a shot. Anything.

Taking a deep breath, she leaned closer. Kevin smelled her heavy perfume, and it made the bridge of his nose ache. "Of course, Daddy's upset about your accident. It'll cost the company millions. But I've got a plan. We'll play up your injuries, get some magazines to write your story, and once you return to the rodeo, you'll be a hero—and so will we for standing by your side through thick and thin."

"What company?" Kevin felt more confused than ever.

The woman straightened and gave him a glare. "Sabino's Authentic Mexican Foods, of course. You must remember. We're the leading brand of salsa, con queso, hot sauce, and bean dips." She heaved an impatient sigh. "Come on, Wink."

"Sabino's. . .yeah. . ." He'd heard the name before.

"We're your sponsor."

Kevin might not remember much, but he knew that cowboys needed their sponsors.

"But don't worry," she said, turning on her velveteen voice again, "I'll soothe Daddy's ruffled feathers."

"Well, thanks."

Seeing the smile curve her red-painted lips, Kevin gave her a polite grin.

Then, in a flash, she put her hands on each side of his face and brought her mouth to his in a devouring kiss. She might have even crawled into his hospital bed, had Kevin not pushed her back with his left hand.

"Whoa," he said, catching his breath. "What do you think you're doing?"

"I love you, Wink. Tell me you love me, too. Say we'll get married just as soon as you're out of this horrible place."

Kevin opened his mouth to inform her that he didn't even know her name, let alone love her.

"Better yet, let's transfer you to Houston's medical center so I can keep my eye on you."

Kevin knew he didn't want that.

"Say you love me."

"I–I. . ."

"Yes? Say it, Wink."

"What are you wantin' him to say, Mac?"

Kevin swung his gaze to the doorway and sighed with relief when he saw Quincy standing there.

"I told you I needed some time alone with Wink," the woman spat. "What are you doing here?"

Quincy stepped forward, met Kevin's gaze, and shook his head. "You've got lipstick all over your face, son."

Taking the small Kleenex box off the rollaway tray, he tossed it at Kevin, who caught it with his strong hand. Pulling out several tissues, he proceeded to wipe his mouth.

"You're nothing but a meddling old man," Mac spat, making her way around Kevin's bed. "You're a has-been bull rider reduced to being a clown people laugh at—even when you're not made up and dressed in your ridiculous outfits."

"Hey!" Kevin felt defensive for his friend. He tried to sit up, but Quincy placed his hands on his shoulders and held him back.

"You need to stay still, boy."

Mac had long since stomped out of the room.

"Whoo-whee, that woman has a wicked tongue." Kevin felt suddenly exhausted after the encounter. "Who is she?"

Quincy grinned. He seemed unaffected by the insults flung at him only moments before. "That's Mackenzie Sabino. Her father is owner and CEO of Sabino's, your sponsor. Mac has followed your career for years. She's a regular rodeo groupie and tells everyone that she's in love with you."

"Do I love her back?"

"I sure hope not; otherwise I'll have to give you another head injury."

Kevin laughed, causing his temples to throb. "Oh man, I think my pain medicine is wearing off."

"Want me to get the nurse?"

"Yeah, would you?"

"Sure, and I think Miss Lara was on her way in to see you. I met her by the elevators. Maybe she saw Mac kissing you and decided you were indisposed."

"Oh no. . ." Kevin rolled his head toward the windows. The blinds were partially open, allowing in a sprinkling of morning sunshine.

"What's wrong?"

He looked back at Quincy. "When we were kids, Lara thought the world of me, and well, I know this sounds odd considering my track record with women, but I don't want Lara's opinion of me to slip because of that. . .that redheaded vixen."

Quincy hooted. "You're right. It does sound odd coming from you. You're a regular Casanova. Won't be long, and you'll have every female nurse on this floor fawning all over you. But if it'll make you feel any better, I'll stop by on my way out and tell Miss Lara what really happened up here."

"Yeah." Kevin disliked Quincy's character description, even though he knew it was true. "Yeah, will you straighten Lara out for me?"

"Will do."

∽

Lara felt troubled and distracted when she returned to her office. With the ED relatively quiet, she'd made the trek to the fifth floor to say good morning to Kevin. Unfortunately for her, she'd walked in on a love scene that wasn't exactly PG-13.

In her mind's eye, she could still see Mac plastered against Kevin's chest, her delicate hands with their long, red, manicured fingernails caressing his face. Kevin had placed his left hand on Mac's shoulder, and Lara imagined he drew Mac nearer to him. Obviously, the two of them were involved in a serious relationship. Kevin must have suddenly remembered Mac, and perhaps the intimate exchange was their way of celebrating.

Lara tamped down her jealous feelings. Where had they come from anyway? *Probably Gram and all her teasing about my schoolgirl crush on Kevin. . .*

Doing her best to dismiss the less-than-professional thoughts from her mind, Lara tucked her portfolio under her arm and headed into the ED. At the physician's request, she entered a patient's room and began an amicable conversation that soon became a lengthy interview. Lara discovered the young woman named Amber was three months pregnant and wanted help with her drug addiction. Lara scheduled an appointment for her, then supplied Amber with a bus ticket, courtesy of County General, so she'd have transportation to the treatment center.

"Thanks," Amber said with a shaky smile. Her complexion looked so pale, it seemed almost transparent.

"You're welcome. Call me and let me know how you're doing." Lara held out one of her business cards. After accepting it, Amber gave her a hug.

Feeling satisfied to have helped someone, Lara returned to her office. She sent up a prayer for Amber, asking the Lord to somehow reach the young lady during this crisis. Sitting down at her desk, Lara began to make some notes, and then her pager sounded. She dialed the extension illuminated on the device's tiny screen and was informed by a registrar in the front lobby that someone was waiting to speak with her.

Gathering her portfolio once more, Lara left her office. When she entered the lobby and saw Quincy chatting with the security guard near the front doors, she hid her surprise.

"I thought you'd be long gone by now," she said, walking toward him.

"Couldn't leave town without saying adios to Wink."

Lara replied with a tight smile.

"I also wanted to thank you for being so kind to Jimmy, Brent, and me. Mac, too."

"Just doing my job."

Quincy narrowed his gaze, and Lara looked away, glancing down at the end of the lobby where a tall African-American man dropped coins into one of the vending machines.

"You're upset, aren't you? Wink thought you might think badly of him, so he asked me to explain. See, what you saw up there—"

Lara touched her forefinger to her lips, silencing Quincy. The last thing she wanted was to become the subject of gossip, and judging from the security guard's interested expression, he was all ears. "Why don't we discuss this in my office?"

"Good idea."

Lara led the way back to her cramped work area at the far end of the emergency department.

"It's cozy," Quincy said.

Lara laughed. "That's a nice way of describing my cubbyhole. It's not even mine, either. I have to share it with two other social workers."

Quincy chuckled and lowered himself into one of the two armchairs near her desk. "Now about Mac. . ."

Lara held up a hand. "You really don't have to explain. Kevin's personal life isn't any of my business. I involved myself in his case because we knew each other as kids."

"Well, since you're involved now, you need to know that Mac throws herself at Wink anytime she sees an opportunity. She's like gum on his shoe, and Wink's gotta be nice to her because her father owns the company that sponsors him. Making the gum even stickier is the fact that Mac convinced her daddy to invest more money in Wink and promote his career with the idea that the more famous he gets, the more money Sabino's will make. Personally, I believe Mac thinks if she has a hand in furthering Wink's career, he'll marry her. Little does she know that Wink's not the marrying kind."

Lara sent him a polite smile. She wondered if Quincy was trying to warn her in some roundabout way. But, of course, there was no need for cautionary words. "Look, it's true that I do care about Kevin more than if he was a regular patient here at County General. Our parents attended the same dinner parties, and the Wincousers went to our church. But that's the extent of it."

"You told me all that, and it's understandable why you'd take a special interest in Wink. That was clear from day one—or maybe day two."

Lara's smile broadened. "I love people in general. That's why I went into this profession."

"And that's about as obvious as a bull in a tea shop. I'm not concerned," Quincy said with a hint of a smirk. "Wink sent me here because he didn't want your opinion of him to lessen. . .you know, since you happened to walk into his room during that latest Mac Attack."

Lara laughed. "Mac Attack?"

"Yeah, that's what me and the boys have taken to calling those. . .um. . . incidents."

"I see." Another giggle escaped before Lara could stop it.

"But the good news is Mac's flying home to Houston today, although I doubt that's the end of her."

"I appreciate that bit of warning."

"Yep, I thought you might." Quincy stood to his feet. He wore a black cotton shirt with silver buttons and black jeans. A rather dark outfit, Lara decided, for a guy employed as a rodeo clown. Regardless, he was a likable fellow.

"Quincy, it's been a pleasure to meet you." Lara stuck out her right hand, and he gave it a firm shake.

"Likewise. We'll check in with Wink every couple of days. We drive from here to South Dakota for this next weekend's rodeo. The summer schedule is intense."

"I understand." Lara escorted Quincy to the lobby.

"It's a blessing you're here, Miss Lara," he drawled. "At least we're not leaving Wink in the hands of complete strangers—bad enough we've got to leave him at all."

Lara caught the word "blessing," and it piqued her curiosity. "Quincy, are you a Christian?"

He paused. "I have my own faith."

She sensed no open door, so she didn't pursue the matter. "Oh, I see." She smiled. "Again, it was really nice to meet you."

Quincy's guarded expression crumbled, and he smiled. "Nice to meet you, too." He took a few steps forward, then paused. "Oh, and. . .I got the impression your friend Polly's set her cap for Brent."

"It's that obvious, eh?"

"Sure is. But she should know that he's not the marrying kind, either."

"I suspected as much, and I tried to warn her. Polly wouldn't listen."

"Tell her again." Quincy grinned. "Both he and Wink learned from my mistakes. I made 'em swear they wouldn't follow in my footsteps."

"Oh?" Lara tipped her head, curious.

"Yep. I was married three times, and I can honestly say there's no such thing as wedded bliss."

"Talk to my parents about that subject," Lara countered. "They've been married for thirty-five years."

A frown crinkled Quincy's brow. "I'm referring to happiness."

"So am I." He seemed to weigh her reply before giving her a friendly smile. "Well, there's always an exception, isn't there?" He chuckled, then continued the trek into the lobby.

Lara watched him go, thinking how sad it was that Quincy thought "for better or for worse" was an exception. To her, marriage vows meant forever, and for herself, Lara wouldn't consider anything less.

Chapter 8

Lara debated whether to stop in and see Kevin before leaving work. Her parents and Tim and Amanda were planning to visit, so he wouldn't be without company, and Lara felt exhausted. She wanted nothing more than to go home, change clothes, eat supper, and watch a few mindless television programs. But she surmised that by not stopping in after Quincy made a point to explain about the "Mac Attack" this morning, Kevin might think she was disappointed in him or worse. The truth was, Lara couldn't have cared less. At least she kept telling herself that.

Riding the elevator to the fifth floor, Lara exited and made her way to Kevin's room. She walked in and immediately spotted all the flowers lining the wide window ledge. Glancing at Kevin, she saw that he slept despite the noise from the TV hanging up in the corner.

Lara strode to his bedside, located the controls, and muted the local newscast so it wouldn't disturb Kevin. She noted the steady rise and fall of his broad chest, then her gaze moved upward to his shadowy jaw. The small cleft in his chin was still visible through the stubble. Without intending to, Lara found herself studying the perfect shape of his mouth, and after remembering this morning's passionate scene, Lara wondered what it would feel like to be the recipient of Kevin's kisses.

What am I thinking? I must be deranged!

Glancing at the flowers again, she steadied her thoughts. But when she looked back at Kevin, she discovered his blue eyes staring at her.

"Lara," he said, sounding groggy. "I'm sorry. Did I fall asleep while you were talking?"

Her cheeks burned with embarrassment. She hadn't meant to ogle him while he lay sleeping—and now he'd caught her at it!

"I–I wasn't saying anything. I just came up to see how you're doing."

"You're a sweetheart, Lara. You've always been a sweetheart."

"Oh, I don't know about that." She glanced down at her hands, resting on the metal guardrail.

"Well, I do. You always rushed to the aid of someone in need." Kevin's words came out in slow succession, as if it took a great effort to form each one. "You were like the little mother of the neighborhood, taking care of everybody, running to the grocery store for the old ladies, comforting little kids who fell off their bikes. That's the Lara Donahue I remember."

Lara grinned. "I tried. I guess I wanted people to like me since most of my peers made fun of me because I was fat."

"Kids can be mean."

"You and Clayt were never mean. Your parents raised you right, that's for sure."

Kevin's blue eyes widened, and an anguished expression washed across his face.

"Did I say something wrong? I'm sorry."

Kevin blinked back whatever emotion had momentarily gripped him. "That's okay. I'll be fine."

"Are you in pain? Should I get your nurse?"

Kevin didn't reply, and Lara began to worry. Was this some reaction to medication? Was something occurring because of his head injury?

She put her hand on his forearm. "Kevin?"

He stared straight ahead, looking across the room at nothing.

"Kevin, please tell me what's wrong."

His gaze inched its way to the left until it reached hers. "I haven't seen or talked to my brother in nine long years."

Lara raised her brows at the unexpected reply. "Oh—"

Kevin bent his arm at the elbow and clasped her hand. "We had a big fight the second Christmas after Mom and Dad were killed. I didn't feel much like celebrating. I hadn't planned on staying through the holiday. That made my aunt and uncle mad. Then, when I told Clayt I just wanted my half of our parents' estate so I could be on my way and live my own life, things got really nasty. In the end, I had to hire an attorney to get what was rightfully mine. You see, my aunt and uncle were control freaks. Still are, as far as I know."

"I'm so sorry, Kev."

"Why are you apologizing?" He gave her hand a squeeze. "Not your fault."

"I'm sorry for you—that you've been estranged from your brother. That's sad. You're flesh and blood. Family."

"The only family I need is my rodeo family. But I could use all the friends I can get." He paused and searched her face. "Will you be my friend, Lara?"

"Of course." She smiled into his deep blue eyes. "You won me over in junior high by being nice to me and teaching me how to ride. I'll always be your friend, Kev."

∽

As the week progressed, Lara made a point to visit Kevin every day on her lunch breaks and after work. Her parents, Gram, and Tim stopped at the hospital twice to say hello, and Kevin remembered them. Lara noticed he enjoyed reminiscing—to a point. However, when the subject touched on his brother Clayt, their deceased parents, or the Lord, Kevin grew quiet, his discomfort evidenced by his silence. The Donahues, out of politeness, changed the topic of discussion.

Then, on Thursday, Mackenzie Sabino called, insisting that Kevin be transferred to a facility in Houston. But when Lara presented him with the option, Kevin refused it.

"My rodeo family is traveling," he said, still sounding groggy, "so I might as well stay put. This hospital is as good as any, I imagine."

Lara relayed Kevin's decision to Mac, and the woman put up such a fuss that Lara was forced to involve the patient relations department. They managed to deter the unrelenting Texas belle, but Lara figured it wouldn't be for long.

And it's none of my business, she reminded herself on Friday night as she changed clothes. Tonight marked the monthly Christian singles' group dinner, and neither she nor Polly felt like attending. Lara grinned as she recalled Polly's suggestion for their weekend plans. She wanted to drive to South Dakota to watch Brent in the bull-riding competition.

"By the time we get there, you nut," Lara had replied, "we'll have to turn around and come home."

"It can't take that long to drive to South Dakota. . . ."

The telephone rang, startling Lara out of her thoughts. Walking to the other side of her bedroom, she lifted the portable phone and pressed the TALK button.

"Hey, it's me."

Lara smiled, hearing Polly's voice. "Hi. What's up?"

"I'm getting bold in my old age."

Lara laughed. Polly was only twenty-six. "What did you do?"

"I called the Cyprus Ranch and left a message for Brent. He called me back."

"How did you manage that? You're still at work." Lara recalled all the many times Polly showed up late at their singles' dinner because her shift ran from eleven in the morning to seven thirty. Polly worked what was called a "split shift."

"I took a break and used my cell phone, and Brent called me back in the unit. We're really slow tonight. Only three patients up here. Anyway, I told him you and I were looking for something to do this weekend and that we thought about making the drive to South Dakota. Brent said it wasn't much more than ten hours from Milwaukee, and he sounded pleased that we wanted to come. He also mentioned that he's got some of Wink's things he'd like to send back with us. So what do you say? If you can't do it for me, do it for Kevin."

Lara rolled her eyes. "Nice try."

"No, listen. Seriously. I figure I can get home, throw some stuff into a suitcase, and pick you up by nine tonight. We'll get to South Dakota by seven tomorrow morning. We'll check into a hotel, sleep until about one o'clock, then head over to the rodeo. It doesn't start until eight at night, but—"

"But you'd like to get some time to talk to Brent."

Polly gasped. "Why, Lara, you read my mind."

"You're crazy!" She laughed as the words tumbled out of her mouth.

"Lara, we never do anything exciting. It's the same thing all the time. Let's live a little. Let's do something impulsive for once."

"Impulsive can be dangerous. Besides, I already told you what Quincy said about Brent. He's not the marrying kind, not to mention he might not even be a believer."

"The same is true about Kevin. You told me that, too."

Lara frowned. "What's Kevin got to do with anything?"

"You are as hung up on Kevin as I am on Brent. Admit it."

"No, I won't *admit it*, because it's not true."

"Yes, it is. You never got over your eighth-grade crush on him."

Lara clenched her jaw, feeling defensive. She opened her mouth to lash out at her friend for stating such untruths but caught herself just in time.

Collecting herself, she said, "If I'm acting like I still have a crush on Kevin, then I need to adjust my behavior."

"Why?"

"Because. . .I'm a professional."

"You're a woman—and he used to be a friend."

He is my friend, Lara thought. At least, she'd promised to always be his friend.

Polly sighed. "Look, we'll have ten hours to hash this out. Be ready at nine." With that, she disconnected the call.

Lara's jaw dropped, and she stared at the telephone as if it had suddenly grown horns—bull's horns, to be exact.

I can't believe I'm going to do this. But I am!

Walking to her bedroom door, Lara opened it and sauntered into the living room, where her grandmother was watching television and crocheting a gorgeous afghan for Tim and Amanda.

"What's the matter, Muffin? You look like you just lost your best friend."

"No, Gram, I'm okay. I just came to tell you that, well, that I'm driving with Polly to South Dakota for the weekend. We're going to another rodeo."

Chapter 9

Kevin stared at the white porous ceiling tiles as he lay in his hospital bed. He had a phone number whirling around his mind, but no clue as to whom it belonged. Feeling more cognizant than he had in days, Kevin lifted the phone off the rolling table and placed it on his abdomen. Then, with his left hand, since his right still felt a little more than useless, he pressed in the number and brought the receiver to his ear. It rang at the other end twice, then a familiar male voice answered.

"Hey, it's Wink. Who's this?"

"Well, hey yourself. It's Brent."

A memory flashed across Kevin's mind. A bull rider. His dark brown chaps flinging outward with each kick of the animal's hind legs.

"Brent."

"You remember me yet?"

"Sure do." Kevin realized he'd been here at the hospital with Quincy.

Then another image. A woman with golden blond hair and lying blue eyes. Emily.

"She wasn't good enough for you."

"What? Wink, what are you talking about?"

"Em. Every time you turned your back, she was giving me calf eyes. One night I gave in to her just to prove to you that she wasn't what you thought."

"I don't want to talk about it."

"She ain't worth bustin' up our friendship," Kevin drawled, "that's for sure."

"You feeling better?"

"Sort of." Kevin realized Brent had changed the subject on purpose. "The doctors still have me pretty doped up. They don't want me moving around and injuring my brain worse than it is."

"How would they tell if that happened?" Brent chuckled. "You've been falling on your head for the last decade."

Kevin smirked, figuring half of Brent's remark was probably true. How much could a head take, anyhow?

"So guess who's coming to see me this weekend?"

"Who?"

"Lara, the sweet social worker, and her friend."

The news surprised Kevin. "Where are you?"

"South Dakota."

Kevin still remembered his geography. "What does Lara want to travel all that way for?"

"Guess I'm worth it."

Kevin could hear the animosity in Brent's voice. Obviously, he wasn't over Em yet. But did he think he could use Lara as payback? Kevin failed to see how that plan would unfold since he had no romantic designs on Lara, but he hoped he was wrong. Lara didn't deserve to get caught in the middle of this skirmish.

"A couple of things you'd best know about her," Kevin began, suddenly feeling exhausted. "One, she's a born-again Christian, and two, she's a package deal, comes with an entire family, including an overprotective father. So consider yourself fairly warned."

"Don't worry about me. But do you think you can live without that woman fawning all over you? It was a pitiful sight if I ever saw one."

Kevin grinned. "Yeah, you're just jealous."

"Oh, right. I sure wish I was lying in a hospital bed, losing points and money, not to mention my standing."

The dig struck the core of Kevin's being. While part of him figured that Brent was still sore about his two-timing girlfriend, another part of Kevin sensed his friend was taking his cutting comment and going for the jugular. Maybe their friendship had already been irreparably damaged.

"Time to hang up," Kevin said, trying to keep his emotions in check. "You have fun this weekend."

He hung up the phone, and for the first time in a very long while, he felt as though he might cry. He replaced the phone on the rolling table and located the remote. Pressing the ON button, he sought some distraction from the TV. He flipped through the channels, then the loud jangling of the telephone almost startled him.

He lifted the receiver, hoping it wasn't Mackenzie Sabino. That's about all he needed right now.

"Yeah, hello?"

"Wink, it's me. Hey, look, I'm, well, I'm sorry about what I said. I hit an all-time low rubbing your injuries in your face like that."

Hearing Brent's apology, Kevin swallowed hard. What was wrong with him anyway? When had he become such a softie? "Forget it."

"Okay, it's forgotten. Get better, you hear?"

"Will do."

Hanging up the phone for the second time, Kevin couldn't restrain the tears that blurred his vision. He squeezed his eyes shut. Then the oddest feeling overtook him. He suddenly yearned for Lara, wishing she were at his bedside, "fawning all over him." She made him think everything was going to be okay. Her presence comforted him.

My head must be a mess. I've turned into a regular sissy.

Clearing his thoughts, Kevin willed himself to fall asleep.

∽

"Okay, I admit it. I never got over my childhood crush on Kevin Wincouser—and I probably never will. He was the first and only guy who treated me with dignity and respect when I was a chubby, self-conscious junior higher." Hiking the strap of Tim's video camera case back onto her shoulder, she glanced at Polly, who walked beside her. "There. Are you happy?"

"After ten hours of listening to your denial. . .yeah, I'm happy now."

Smiling, Lara rolled her eyes as they neared the trailer in which Brent lived. Another cowboy on the grounds had pointed it out to them.

They reached the door, and Polly knocked just as Lara's cell phone rang. Fishing it from her purse, she pushed the tiny green button, answering the call.

"Hi, it's Tim. I'm at the hospital—"

Sheer dread poured over Lara. "Is Kevin all right?"

"He's fine. But he wants to talk to you. I'll put him on."

At the pause, Lara waved to Brent, who had answered the door and was now beckoning them inside.

"I'll be right there," she said, and a moment later, she heard Kevin's voice.

"So you're in South Dakota."

Lara grinned. "That's right."

"What made you go?"

Since her friend had stepped into the large trailer, Lara decided to divulge the truth. "Do you remember meeting my friend Polly?"

"Umm. . ."

"She stopped in while I was visiting you last week, and I introduced her."

"I'm sorry, Lara, I don't recall."

She heard the drowsiness in his voice. "That's all right. You were pretty out of it the evening she showed up. But anyway, this trip was Polly's idea. She's rather, um, attracted to Brent, and that's putting it mildly."

"How does she know Brent?"

"She doesn't. I mean, she's seen him get thrown from a bull, and she's talked to him twice." Lara started giggling, realizing how silly it must seem to Kevin. "Sounds like true love, eh?"

"You're kidding me. Your friend? I thought maybe it was you."

"Me? No!"

Before Lara could even wonder about the remark, Brent appeared at the trailer's door. "You comin' in?"

Lara met his gaze and nodded. "I'm talking to Kevin. I'll be right there."

"Lara, listen to me. I want you to be careful, okay? I have a feeling Brent wants to settle an old score, and I'd hate to see you get hurt. He and I had a conversation this morning, and well, I've been thinking about things all day."

"That's really nice of you to be concerned, Kev, but. . ." Lara watched Brent descend the three metal stairs that led down from the trailer before he strode in her direction. ". . .I'll be fine."

"Keep your guard up."

"I always do."

An instant later, Brent reached out and snatched Lara's cell phone.

"What do you think you're doing?" Surprise and indignation caused her to gape at the man.

"Wink? It's me. I don't mean to be rude, but this little social worker is off duty right now. Call back later, after the rodeo tonight, and I'll catch you up on the current standings." Without waiting for a reply, he dropped her phone into her purse. Then, taking hold of Lara's elbow, he guided her toward the trailer. "Wink'll survive for a couple of days. You need a break, a chance to have some fun and enjoy yourself."

Lara bristled. She didn't appreciate being bossed as though she were a little girl. Pulling out of his grasp, she stepped up into the trailer. She'd never been inside what was commonly known as a "fifth wheel," and the sight impressed her, even though it smelled sort of weird—like strong coffee, leather boots, and horseflesh intermingled with dirty socks.

Out of politeness, Lara tried not to grimace as she glanced around. The trailer was much bigger inside than she imagined. To the right was a cozy living room where Polly stood chatting with Quincy. On her immediate left was a small kitchenette; a narrow hallway led away from it to the back of the trailer where Lara assumed the bedrooms were located.

"Welcome to our humble abode," Quincy said with a grin. He extended his right hand, and Lara took it. "Didn't think I'd see you again so soon, but I'm glad for it. Have a seat."

"Thanks."

"Here, let me take your bags," Brent said.

"No, thank you." Lara lowered herself into one of the two swivel rockers and placed the leather-encased video camera and her purse right beside the chair.

"Oh, now, don't be sore at me because I ended your phone call," Brent said, sporting a charming grin. "Wink can be a demanding guy, and Polly just got done telling Quincy and me that you two wanted a little excitement this weekend."

"Can't get more exciting than the bull-riding competition," Quincy added with a laugh. "Would you two ladies like something to drink? A can of pop?"

"No, thanks," Polly replied.

Lara declined the offer, as well. She could feel Brent's penetrating stare, but she refused to validate his boorish behavior with even a brief glance. It troubled her that Kevin had taken the time to warn her about the "score" Brent wished to settle, and a heartbeat later, Lara wanted nothing more than to turn tail and go home. This was a stupid idea. Why had she let Polly talk her into it?

"Looks like a camera in that black leather case. Is it?"

Lara drew herself from her thoughts and nodded in reply to Quincy's question. "I volunteer at a ranch for physically challenged kids. When the weather isn't good for riding, we'll play games or watch a movie. The original version of *National Velvet* is one of my kids' favorites. They love any story involving horses, so I thought I'd film the rodeo tonight. The kids will enjoy seeing it."

"That's mighty thoughtful of you," Quincy said. "If you'd like, Quincy the Clown can do a little juggling for the kids."

"Anything to get on camera," Brent quipped.

Lara ignored him. "A juggling act would be great. Thanks." She looked over at Polly, whose gaze seemed glued on a certain handsome bull rider. A feeling of disquiet plumed inside of her, and Lara stood. "Well, I guess we should be on our way."

"What?" Polly gave her an incredulous glare.

"I'm hungry," Lara told her with a meaningful glance. "And these gentleman need to get ready for their performances tonight."

"Honey, that's five hours away," Brent said. "We've got plenty of time. But if you'd like something to eat, there's a place nearby that serves up some of the best barbeque beef you've ever tasted."

"Mmm, that sounds good," Polly replied, standing to her feet.

Lara felt the invisible noose around her neck tightening.

"Quincy, want to come along?" Brent asked.

"No, I think I'll let you tend to our guests while I take a quick nap."

"All right, then." Brent gave Lara and Polly an engaging grin. "Let's go."

Chapter 10

I don't like him. He acts like an egomaniac."

Sitting at the picnic table across from Lara, Polly gave her a disappointed pout. "Brent took our orders and went up to buy the food. He's paying. I think he's a gentleman."

Lara glanced over her friend's left shoulder and saw Brent waiting his turn in line at the service window. Located on the far side of the vast ranch on which the rodeo took place, Dakota Dave's BBQ was only a little bigger than a hut in a row of food stops and lemonade and beer stands.

"I still don't like him."

"What happened to 'love your neighbor as yourself' and 'forgiving one another as God, for Christ's sake, forgave us'?"

"All right, all right. You don't have to scripture-whip me."

"Well?"

Lara shrugged. "I just don't appreciate Brent's macho demeanor. He acts like he's used to women falling at his feet because he's a big rodeo star, and he's wondering why we're not swooning."

"Hey, speak for yourself."

Lara rolled her eyes at the tart reply.

"Okay, fine. You don't like one particular quality about Brent. But you can still be nice and a good Christian witness to him."

"I just feel like going back home."

"Why?"

Picking at the splintery top of the table, Lara shrugged.

"You're going to let a macho cowboy steal your joy? That's silly, Lara. Let's just enjoy ourselves."

Lara glanced across the table and noticed Polly's short walnut-colored hair shimmering in the afternoon sunshine. She was right. No one could steal Lara's joy unless she allowed him to—and she wouldn't.

"We're in South Dakota at a rodeo. How cool is that!" Polly declared. "Wait until I tell everyone on Monday what I did over the weekend."

Lara grinned. "Yeah, we're finally doing something out of the ordinary." She glanced over her friend's shoulder and saw their host heading toward their table. "Here comes Brent."

Polly sat back, straightened her shirt, and combed her fingers through her hair, and Lara laughed.

"You're a hoot."

Polly replied with an impish wink.

"Here we are, ladies," Brent said, setting down a cardboard tray. "If this isn't the best barbeque you've ever tasted, I'll eat your sandwich for you."

Another laugh escaped Lara, and she felt herself begin to relax. Brent set a plastic glass of lemonade in front of her and handed her a straw before offering her a foil-wrapped sandwich.

"Thanks."

"You bet." Brent served Polly in the same manner.

"Thank you."

"You're very welcome."

"Should I ask the blessing, or would you like to do the honors, Brent?" Polly asked.

He paused. "Um, you go ahead."

Polly bowed her head, and Lara followed suit. "Thank you, Lord God, for this meal. Thank you for Brent, who purchased it for us. We ask that You protect him tonight as he competes in the bull-riding championship. Bless him. . .and Lara and me. In Jesus' name, amen."

"Amen," Lara echoed.

She looked up just in time to see Brent lift his gaze. As they began eating, Lara sensed his discomfort.

"Are you a Christian?" Before she could stop it, the question bubbled out of her mouth. "I, um, hope I'm not being too personal."

"I went to church as a kid," Brent said, taking a large bite of sandwich.

"This barbeque is delicious," Polly said.

Lara's mouth was full, so she nodded.

"You ladies like it?"

"Very much."

"Mmm-hmm. . ."

Brent chuckled. "You even sound like you're enjoying it, Lara."

She swallowed, smiled, and stuck the straw into her plastic glass of lemonade. "Now, getting back to my question. . ."

"About religion?" Brent asked with a glance in her direction. "Wink told me you're a born-again Christian, so I imagine you're looking for recruits."

"All the time."

Polly laughed. "We try not to be obnoxious about it. I'm a born-again Christian, too."

"I figured," Brent replied. "It's like that old 'birds of a feather' cliché."

"So are you or aren't you?" Lara felt rather sassy. It must have been the ten hours she'd spent in the car with Polly.

Pushing up on the rim of his black Stetson, Brent peered at Lara. The expression on his face said he was contemplating her inquiry. "I guess I'm a Christian like some people are Irish. It's in my background, but I don't think about it too much."

"You seem to be confusing religious beliefs with heritage," Lara pointed out. "Being Irish isn't something you can control. Becoming a Christian involves exercising your will."

His brown eyes locked on Lara, Brent narrowed his gaze.

Polly touched his forearm. "If you'd prefer not to discuss this issue, we can talk about something else."

"No, that's okay. I don't shy away from controversial topics." He smiled at Polly, then looked back at Lara. "Okay, Little Miss Social Worker, why don't you tell me all about being a Christian, and I'll tell you whether I am one or not."

The challenge caused Lara to smile with delight. God had just flung open a door of opportunity that she couldn't—or wouldn't—pass up. After a glance at Polly, and seeing the prayerful expression on her friend's face, Lara opened her purse and extracted a gospel tract.

"This is pretty simplistic," she stated apologetically. "I use this pamphlet to talk to my kids about Jesus."

"The kids on the ranch?"

Lara nodded. "God's plan of salvation is so easy that even children can comprehend it. Look—" She directed his attention to the tract. "There are four things you've got to understand in order to become a Christian. One, you're a sinner. We're all sinners. No one's perfect, right?"

Brent nodded. "Right."

"Two, sin has to be punished. When you were a kid, did you get spankings when you were naughty?"

"Sure did."

"Same thing, except sin is punishable by eternal death in an awful place called hell." When Brent didn't reply, Lara continued. "Three, Jesus took the punishment for our sin when He died on the cross. I tell my kids that Jesus took the spanking we were supposed to get from our heavenly Father so we didn't have to get punished."

Brent pursed his lips, thinking it over.

"Four, anyone can be saved if he or she will just ask."

"That's it?" Brent gave her a suspicious look.

"Yep." Lara pushed the small, colorful pamphlet toward him. "You can keep this tract. There are some Bible verses on the back that you can look up and read whenever you get a chance."

"Brent," Polly began, "was there ever a time in your life that you asked Jesus Christ to save you?"

"No, not that I can recall."

"Well, will you give it some thought?"

He nodded, then balled up the foil from his sandwich. "But if what you're saying is true, and those four things are what it takes to be a Christian, then how come no one's told me till now?"

"Maybe your heart wasn't ready to receive the good news until now," Polly replied.

"Hmm." A grin tugged at the corners of Brent's mouth. "You know what? Instead of hospital work, maybe you two should have gone into sales."

∽

Kevin lay awake, holding the telephone to his ear. After five rings, Brent finally answered.

"About time you picked up."

"Wink?"

"Yeah, it's me. Where've you been? It's one o'clock in the morning."

"I've been out having a good ol' time. Just walked in, as a matter of fact."

In his mind's eye, Kevin could see the trailer he shared with Brent, Quincy, and Jimmy.

Jimmy! He remembered him.

"My memory's comin' back."

"That's a good thing."

"So what kind of 'good ol' time' were you out having?"

"Well, I'm now in second place, Wink. That was cause for celebration, don't you think?"

"Yeah. Congratulations." Kevin tried to raise his right hand, but the limb felt as if it had been filled with cement. He was beginning to fear he'd never ride again.

I'll ride again. Of course I'll ride again! Sheer determination gripped his heart. He'd rather die than give up rodeoing.

"Lara and Polly are real nice girls," Brent was saying.

Hearing Lara's name, Kevin forced himself to pay attention.

"They're the kind of women a guy wouldn't mind taking home to meet his mother."

"If he *had* a mother." Kevin's mom was dead, and Brent's left home when he was a boy, never to be heard from again. Neither of them were "mama's boys."

"You know what I'm getting at."

"I think I do. You'd better have Quincy tell you a bedtime story about one of his three disastrous marriages again."

"Oh, right." Brent chuckled. "I've heard enough of them stories to last me a good part of forever. And speaking of. . ."

"Forever?" Kevin frowned, wondering where all this was going.

"Yeah, Lara and Polly tried to sell me on their faith. Did a pretty good job, too. I promised to take 'em to the sunrise church service tomorrow morning. I can't believe I actually said I'd crawl out of bed at the crack of dawn on a Sunday morning."

"It'll be tough, especially if you've been drinking."

"Wink, are you kidding? I haven't had a drop of alcohol. I've been in the company of two Christian women all night. Well, and one mean, angry bull."

Kevin chuckled, and the left side of his head felt sort of weird. It didn't hurt, exactly.

"You know, I was thinking. I'll be thirty years old in less than six months. Maybe it's time to settle down."

Kevin could hardly believe what he'd just heard. Was his mind playing tricks on him? Was he hallucinating?

Was Brent hallucinating?

"I'm of the persuasion you *have* been drinking, my friend—or indulging in something else."

"Nothing, Wink. I've never been more sober in my life. What about you? You ever give marriage a thought?"

"Maybe just a thought, then my sanity returned."

"What about Christianity? Ever think about it?"

"Sure. My parents were Christians; so was my brother—"

"How come you never told me you had a brother?"

" 'Cause we kind of disowned each other."

"Well, better not tell Little Miss Social Worker that, or she's liable to initiate some sort of kiss-and-make-up session." Brent laughed.

Kevin, on the other hand, didn't find the remark a bit amusing. His eyelids suddenly grew heavy. The shot the nurse had given him a half hour ago was beginning to affect him. "Lara already knows about my brother and me. She grew up with me and Clayt. Remember?" He paused, thinking over Brent's "Little Miss Social Worker" comments. "Sounds like you and Lara aren't getting along so well." In some odd way, the notion comforted Kevin.

"What makes you say that? We're getting along just fine."

Disappointment engulfed him. Lara wasn't Brent's type. His friend had to realize that much.

"It's just too bad she's had a crush on you since her junior high years."

Kevin frowned. "What? Why is it too bad?"

" 'Cause she's still got a crush on you, that's why. But isn't that the way it always goes? If I'm even remotely interested in a woman, it turns out she's got eyes for you."

"You're interested in Lara?"

"I'm not telling you anything about anyone I might be interested in," Brent growled, and Kevin imagined him clenching his jaw while his brown eyes sparked with contained fury. "After what you did with Emily, you're lucky I'm even speaking to you."

"I didn't do anything with Emily—except kiss her after she flung herself at me."

"You're a liar."

"No, friend, *she's* the liar."

A long pause filled the airspace. "Well, look, it doesn't matter anymore. Neither does Emily. But I will say this—the man who lassoes Lara Donahue's heart won't have to worry about her being unfaithful."

"No, I don't suppose he will." Kevin felt as if he'd been socked in the gut.

"And I can contend with a schoolgirl crush. It's nothing compared to true love, right?"

"Leave her alone, Brent. Don't try to get back at me by using Lara."

Brent chuckled. "Is that what you think? Listen, pal, I have a lot more integrity than you give me credit for." Another pause. "I'm not like you."

Moments later, the phone line went dead, and Kevin felt a deep regret fill his soul. Memory after memory rushed forth like waves against a shoreline. He'd been and done all the things he learned as a kid that God condemned, and yet Brent had been a true friend through it all.

Until the situation with Emily occurred—but that hadn't been Kevin's fault.

Still, in spite of his self-defense, sadness washed over him. The word "integrity" described nothing about Kevin Wincouser. He was about as honorable as a rattlesnake.

Oh God, why did You let me live? The world would be a lot better off without me in it.

On that dark thought, he tumbled off into a restless sleep.

Chapter 11

After the uplifting sunrise service, Polly convinced Brent to eat breakfast with them instead of returning to his bed as he'd threatened to do ever since they took their seats in the grandstands. However, after consuming several cups of coffee at a quaint diner in town, he came to life. Still, as they drove back to the Cyprus Ranch where the rodeo was being held, Lara had to wonder if anything from this morning's message had penetrated his heart. The gospel couldn't have been presented any more clearly, and Lara rejoiced that Brent had heard God's plan of salvation not only from her and Polly, but from another cowboy, too—a cowboy-preacher. But had Brent been too tired to comprehend the truth?

"Why are you frowning so hard, Lara?"

He's watching me. . .again. Embarrassed, she looked up from where she sat in the backseat of Brent's black pickup truck and smiled. "Oh, it was nothing. I didn't mean to frown."

Stopping at an intersection, he twisted around and tossed a glance at her, and Lara felt that familiar angst settle around her. Ever since yesterday afternoon, she'd done her best to hang back and try to be invisible, but Brent sought her out time after time. It seemed he paid more attention to her than to Polly—and that wasn't supposed to happen. Worse, Lara had gone from disliking Brent to finding his charm and good looks rather appealing. But each time the thought formed in her head, Kevin's warning rang in her ears. *"Brent wants to settle an old score, and I'd hate to see you get hurt."*

Lara recalled that first day up in Kevin's hospital room when Mackenzie Sabino mentioned that "Wink" had stolen Brent's girl. But Lara couldn't figure out how Brent would use *her* to settle any score. It wasn't as if Lara was Kevin's present girlfriend, although she imagined she wouldn't mind the title.

Then again, in all reality, maybe she would. Ten years changed people—the years had changed her—and now Lara knew Kevin about as little as Polly knew Brent.

Brent pulled onto the vast ranch, and the truck bumped along dirt roads until it slowed as he steered toward the small colony of trailers and tents. Finally, he parked beside the one in which he lived, pulling in alongside Polly's car.

"You ladies want to come inside for more coffee? Quincy and Jimmy are probably awake by now."

"Actually, I'd like to get some pictures of the horses to take back to my kids," Lara said. Turning to Polly, she added, "Let's go for a quick walk before we go back to the hotel."

Polly bobbed her head. "Okay."

"While you two do that, I'll pack up some of Wink's things," Brent said. "I imagine he'll need 'em once he gets better."

Lara met his deep brown gaze.

"You don't mind taking them to the hospital, do you?"

She blinked, feeling oddly flustered. "No, of course I don't mind."

Lara watched as a slow grin spread across his face before he pivoted and strode toward the trailer. "Don't get lost, now."

With a flickering skyward glance, Lara turned to Polly. "How could we possibly get lost?"

"I don't know, but if there's a way, we'll be the ones to do it."

Lara laughed as they took off toward the arena. She hoped Polly hadn't noticed her sudden peculiar behavior with Brent.

Lord, please intervene here. I'm acting like an insipid junior higher with an unattainable schoolgirl crush, and I don't want to hurt Polly for the world. She mulled over her petition, examining her heart. *Lord, is that all I'm capable of—schoolgirl crushes? Will I ever know what it's really like to fall in love?*

"Hey, look. Horses."

Lara gave herself a mental shake and gazed up ahead, where she saw a cowboy walking toward them leading two frisky mares. When he got within earshot, Polly asked for his picture with the horses, and the husky man of average height obliged them.

They strolled on, pausing here and there to snap a photograph. Reaching the arena, Lara and Polly stepped inside, and to Lara's delight, some cowboys were perfecting their roping techniques. With her video recorder in hand, she filmed their practice.

"My kids'll love watching this video," Lara said as she and Polly traipsed back to Brent's trailer. More than an hour had lapsed, and the noonday sun rose high in an overcast sky.

"I suppose we should start driving back home soon," Polly murmured, pushing strands of hair off her forehead.

Lara agreed with a nod.

"I had fun this weekend."

"I did, too."

Polly glanced Lara's way and grinned. "Then it was a worthwhile trip, wouldn't you say?"

"Uh-huh."

"And just wait until the singles' group hears about our adventure."

Lara laughed. "They'll all wonder why we didn't ask them to come along."

"Oh yeah, right. Could you imagine *that* field trip?"

Again Lara had to chuckle. With so many stoic souls in their Christian singles' group, it was amazing anybody had fun. But they did try. Lara had to give them a little credit.

They reached the trailer just as Quincy and Jimmy were exiting.

"Brent's getting worried about you ladies," the younger man said with a boyish grin. "But he should be used to having women run out on him by now."

Quincy gave the youthful cowboy a shove, and Jimmy hooted.

"Don't mind him," Quincy said on a note of apology. He drew in a deep breath. "So you two are going to be heading home soon, eh? Drive safely, now."

"We will," Polly said.

"It was real nice seeing you both again. And, Lara. . ." He turned to face her. "You take care of Wink for us."

"Sure." She smiled. "I'll tell him you all say hello."

"You do that." Quincy gave the rim of his wide-brimmed hat a polite tug, then turned on his heel and followed Jimmy.

Lara moved toward Polly's car, preparing to deposit her video camera into the backseat just as Brent emerged from the trailer carrying a large blue suitcase.

"Thought I heard you girls out here," he said with a smile. "Finally found your way back, huh?"

"We were never lost, contrary to popular belief." Polly opened the trunk for him, and Brent set the luggage inside.

Brent chuckled. "That's a good thing." He glanced at Lara. "These are most of Wink's clothes. I packed his socks, underwear, shoes, razor—everything he'll need once he's out of the hospital and on his way to meet us wherever we might happen to be at that time. There are also some get-well cards in here from friends and admirers."

"Do you travel a lot, Brent?" Polly wanted to know.

"Honey, traveling is my life."

Oh good, he called her "honey." Lara grinned as she gave the back door of Polly's sedan a push. For the better part of the last twenty-four hours, Lara had been "honey," and the title felt a little demeaning somehow.

"That's the biggest part of the rodeo. Getting there."

"Do you think you'll be back to see Kevin?" Lara asked.

Folding his arms, Brent leaned up against the car. "Guess it all depends."

"On what?" Polly ventured.

"On whether I'm still speaking to him. You see, me and Wink had a bit of a falling out before his accident." Brent held up a hand, forestalling further questions. "I don't care to discuss the particulars, all right? But I wish Wink a speedy recovery."

"I didn't mean to pry," Polly told him. "I just feel like you're a friend now, so I thought I'd ask."

"I am a friend, and don't you forget it," Brent replied, and Lara didn't miss the warmth of sincerity that entered his brown eyes. She felt glad that he'd bestowed the expression on Polly. "And I hope you girls'll come to another rodeo soon. You've got my itinerary. Illinois isn't so far from Wisconsin."

"A lot closer than South Dakota," Lara quipped.

Brent grinned. "Yep. So maybe you can make that competition. It's over the Fourth of July weekend."

"We'll certainly try," Polly promised, and Lara knew she meant every word.

Brent stepped forward and wrapped Polly in a better than "friendly" embrace. Watching on, Lara wanted to giggle, imagining she'd hear all about the weak knees and pounding heart on the way back to Milwaukee. Moments later, Lara got a hug, too.

"Drive careful, now," Brent told them after both women climbed into the car.

"We will," Polly promised.

Lara couldn't stop smiling as they drove off the Cyprus Ranch. *Thank You, God, for turning things around.*

❧

The next day, Monday, proved a veritable challenge for Lara. She felt tired from the long hours of traveling over the weekend, and the number of patients who required her services caused her to forgo a lunch break and work a couple of hours overtime.

When she finally punched out, she decided to go straight home and skip a visit with Kevin. She figured if she missed one night it wouldn't matter. Maybe he'd even feel relieved if she didn't go up to his floor and see him tonight. But as she walked toward the parking structure, she felt a twinge in her spirit, as if she was disregarding a certain, important responsibility. Of course, that was silly. Kevin wasn't her responsibility.

But he was her friend.

Expelling an audible sigh, Lara pivoted and strode in the opposite direction. After walking through several meandering hallways, she reached the hospital elevators. However, when she arrived on Kevin's floor, she discovered he'd been transferred to the rehab unit, so she made her way over there. Finding Kevin's new room, she entered to find him sitting in a wheelchair. Except for his glassy stare, he made an encouraging sight. The huge white bandage that had covered his head like a winter cap had been replaced with gauze that now resembled a bandanna.

"You graduated to rehab. That's great." Lara sat down in the hard-backed chair next to him. "Did you have a good day?"

"Oh yeah, real good. The highlight was getting my hair washed and brushing my teeth. That's about all the excitement I could handle, though."

Lara laughed and set down her purse and the canvas bag she habitually took to work. She noticed Kevin didn't appear amused. He seemed almost depressed.

"What's wrong, Kev?"

"What's wrong?" His blue-eyed gaze pinned her in place. "How can you ask me that, Lara? Look at me. I just turned twenty-nine years old, and I can barely hold my toothbrush."

"You're recovering from a head injury. What do you expect? It's going to take time for you to get your strength and coordination back. Give yourself a break."

Lara regretted her harsh tone when she saw Kevin's eyes grow misty.

"I'm sorry," she said, resting her hand on his forearm. "I didn't mean to bark at you just now."

Kevin blinked, and a slight grin tugged at the corners of his mouth. "And I don't mean to be such a little sissy."

The phone began to ring before Lara could reply. Kevin looked at it, then at her.

"Want me to answer it, Kev?"

He nodded.

Leaning forward as she stood, Lara kissed his cheek. "You're not a sissy, either." With that, she walked to the metallic beside table and lifted the receiver. "Hello?"

"Hello," the soft feminine voice replied, "I'm looking for Kevin Wincouser."

"Sure, he's right here. Who's calling?"

A pause. "None of your business who's calling. Put him on."

Lara was taken aback. If she'd "barked" before, this woman was snarling.

"Who is it?" Kevin wanted to know.

Lara covered the mouthpiece of the receiver. She had a good idea as to the caller's identity. "I think it's that red-haired woman."

"Mac?" Kevin made an effort to wag his head. "She's the last person on earth I want to talk to right now. She's been calling here all day."

Lara said nothing.

"Hang up on her."

"Kevin, I can't do that. Our heavenly Father wouldn't be very pleased with me if I did."

He stared at her with those big baby blues, and Lara suddenly felt thirteen years old again.

"Why do you have to be so sweet and nice?" Kevin muttered.

Lara gave him a helpless shrug. She didn't think of herself as "so sweet and nice."

Kevin blew out a long sigh. "Okay, would you mind wheeling me to the phone so *I* can hang up on her?"

Setting down the receiver, Lara tried not to laugh. She walked over to Kevin, and coming to stand behind his wheelchair, she pushed him to the bedside table.

Kevin reached forward with this left arm and grabbed the phone. He lifted it to his ear. "Mac? Don't call here anymore. I don't know when I'll get back in the saddle again, all right? So quit asking!" Without waiting for a reply, he unceremoniously hung up the phone.

"Well, I guess you told her."

"Yeah, for the third time. I doubt she'll listen." He looked up at Lara. "Think you could help me into bed? I'm whipped."

"Sure."

Moving to his left side, Lara helped him stand. Kevin leaned on her to take a heavy step forward. Reaching the bed, he sat down, and Lara straightened the blue printed gown he wore over baggy blue pajama bottoms. She then lifted his right leg up onto the bed while Kevin swiveled on his backside. With the goal painstakingly accomplished, he lay back against his pillows, looking exhausted.

"All that just to get into bed."

"It'll get better day by day."

"And what if it doesn't?" Kevin snapped.

"It will."

Lara lowered herself onto the edge of his sheet-covered mattress. She didn't let his abrasive tone affect her. She'd learned that people handled their illnesses and injuries in different ways. Some turned weepy, some moaned and complained, and some patients became grumpy ol' bears.

Lara gave Kevin a smile. "Just look at the progress you've made over the last ten days."

He gazed at her through sleepy eyes, and finally, a smile escaped. "As I recall, you were always cheerful. I think that's why I liked having you around when we were kids."

"You did?" Lara felt her face warm with the compliment. "I thought I was just the neighborhood pest, and you were just a nice guy."

"Just a nice guy? Brent said you still have a crush on me. Is that right?"

By now, her cheeks were aflame with embarrassment. "All you cowboys have egos the size of Montana." Lara stood, and Kevin caught her wrist.

"Come on now, Miss Happy-Go-Lucky. Let's hear the truth."

"Kevin, I haven't seen you in ten years." Lara hoped she was covering her emotions. "How could I possibly still have a crush on you?"

He released his hold and allowed his hand to fall onto the bed's mattress. His expression lost all signs of humor. "Yeah, you got a point there. And I'm not much to look at these days. I might never be. I could end up an invalid for life."

Lara's heart ached for him. "Where's your faith?" She all but whispered the question. "It's times like this that we need the Lord. We draw our strength and determination from Him."

He rolled his head toward the windows, his face turned away from her. "My faith died with my parents, Lara."

She sat back down, realizing the social worker in her wouldn't let her leave him in this frame of mind. "Will you tell me about it—about how you felt after your mom and dad's tragic accident?"

"What's to tell?" He looked at her once more. "Their deaths shook me up, and I couldn't understand why a good God would let two of the most important people in my life die in a catastrophic train wreck. They'd been on their second honeymoon!"

"I know." Lara glanced down at Kevin's calloused hand. She took a few moments to ponder her reply. "Dying is what really stinks about this sin-cursed earth. We're all going to die sometime, and some of us will face painful deaths while others will leave this world peacefully. God said it would happen. So I've concluded it's what we do while we're alive that counts. Remember what Jesus said about things that are 'bound' on earth will be bound in heaven and things that are 'loosed' on earth will be loosed in heaven?" Lara tipped her head, wondering if Kevin was paying attention. He had his eyes closed. Perhaps he'd decided to ignore her.

But just when she thought the latter was the case, he looked at her as if waiting for her to continue.

"I heard a pastor say the keys that Jesus talks about giving His believers to bind or loose things on earth and in heaven represent opportunities to bring people to Him. So that's our purpose in this life—to lead lost souls to the One who can save them." Lara smiled. "That's *my* purpose, anyway. And if God has to take my life in order for someone else to receive salvation, then I'm willing. It's a cause worth dying for."

Kevin moaned and brought his left hand up, covering his eyes. Then he turned away again.

"Did I upset you? I'm sorry. I didn't mean to."

No reply.

Lara suddenly felt terrible. Even though her tone had been soft, she realized her words may have come across as supercilious and uncaring.

"Kevin?"

He sniffed, sounding suddenly congested.

"Are you all right? Should I call for your nurse?"

His actions were unhurried as he inhaled noisily through his nose, then wiped his eyes. Lara realized to her horror that Kevin was. . .*crying*.

She leaned forward, taking his hand in both of hers. "Kev, I'm so sorry. I didn't mean to hurt your feelings."

"Well, you did," he said. "But the truth sometimes hurts, doesn't it?"

Lara frowned. "The truth? What do you mean?"

He met her gaze, his eyes red-rimmed and sorrowful. "My parents' thinking matched yours, Lara. They would have given up their lives if it meant even one person got saved."

"Maybe one person *did* get saved. Only God knows."

Kevin lay silent in obvious contemplation. Finally, his eyes moved to Lara's face. He seemed to search her features. Then, at last, he grinned. "You're a special woman, Lara Donahue."

"You're special, too." She watched a mischievous twinkle enter his gaze.

"You sure you don't still have a crush on me?"

"Oh, you!" Lara laughed and stood. "That does it. I'm going to visit my friend Polly and get some junk food from the vending machines. If you're *lucky*, I'll stop and say good night on my way out."

Kevin's chuckles followed her out the door. "Hurry back."

Chapter 12

Kevin couldn't say for sure what happened to him the night Lara visited, but for the remainder of the week, he felt less depressed and more determined than ever to get well. Rob, his physical therapist, taught him some strengthening exercises, and Kevin practiced them several times a day. His right arm and leg were showing signs of improvement; however, his speech was still slurred, and frequently Kevin felt as if his mouth couldn't keep up with his mind.

"When do you think I'll get out of this place, Dr. Kitrell?"

The neurosurgery resident looked up from Kevin's chart. "Oh, I'd say a couple of weeks. But I have to be honest with you, it'll be a long time, if ever, before you can compete in a rodeo again."

"What?" Kevin slid himself into a sitting position in his hospital bed. "What are you saying?"

"You suffered a traumatic brain injury, although a fairly mild one, but a bruise to your brain nonetheless. A bruise forms when blood vessels rupture. As you know, there was blood accumulating around the side of your brain, so we had to insert a drainage tube."

"Yeah, yeah, you don't have to remind me."

It made Kevin a little queasy to think of someone drilling a hole in his skull and sticking a tiny strawlike tube inside. He was just glad the awful thing had been removed a couple of days ago.

"Your last CT scan shows things are healing nicely," Dr. Kitrell continued, "but any jolt or bump to your head could cause an injury that might have worse effects than those you've already suffered."

"Like?"

"Like seizures, a stroke, permanent paralysis."

"Look, I've had bruises before," Kevin countered. "Plenty of bruises. They heal up and disappear, and you never know they were there. Why's this bruise so different?"

"Think of it like this," Dr. Kitrell said in a curt, no-nonsense tone. "Some athletes tear ligaments in their ankles and knees, and they're unable to return to sports. The same is true with you, except your 'tear' was inside your head."

"No!" Kevin couldn't accept it. He *wouldn't*. He loved rodeoing. It was in his blood. Riding bareback was his life. "I'll ride again. I'm a two-time world champion, going for three. I'm not about to give up everything I've worked toward for the last ten years. This head injury wants to turn me into a sideline spectator, but I refuse to let it."

"Even if it means sacrificing your health, maybe even your life?"

"Yeah," Kevin replied, undaunted. Then he heard Lara's voice whisper through his memory. *"It's a cause worth dying for."* She'd been referring to her part in converting unbelievers to Christ. Kevin, however, had his own cause, one that he was willing to die for—becoming the best bareback champion such as the world had never seen.

"Well, I'd urge you to reconsider," Dr. Kitrell said. He slapped the chart shut, and holding it in one hand, he let his arm drop to his side. "Have a good weekend."

Kevin almost laughed. How was it possible that he'd have a good weekend holed up in a hospital room?

Glancing toward the windows, he viewed a dark gray sky. He wondered about Brent, Quincy, and Jimmy and found himself resenting the fact he hadn't heard from any of them in a week—ever since Lara and her friend drove to South Dakota.

Kevin's mood plummeted. While he'd received flowers and get-well wishes from friends and fans, he still felt very alone. He thought about the Donahues and how nice it was that Lara and her family took time out from their schedules to visit him. He especially enjoyed conversing with Tim, who loved the rodeo almost as much as Kevin did—and of course Lara, his angel of mercy, who showed up just when he needed her the most. He and Lara had shared some meaningful conversations over the past days. Kevin couldn't ever remember baring his soul with any woman like he had with Lara.

Lara. As Kevin's thoughts strayed to her, he decided Brent had been correct when he said the guy who lassoed her heart wouldn't have to worry about her faithfulness. Lara was about as loyal and dependable as a hound—of course, that's where the similarities ended. Lara Donahue had grown into a lovely woman. She possessed an inner beauty that Kevin hadn't noticed in the women he'd been acquainted with over the years. Even so, Lara had the words "husband" and "children" written on her future, and Kevin didn't want any part of either one of them. Families meant responsibilities, commitment. . .sacrifice. And what did a guy get in return? A busted-up heart—if and when God snatched them away. Just like He did with Kevin's parents. . .

Just like He's doing with the rodeo.

No matter how he summed it up, Kevin felt like an all-around loser.

⌘

As the Fourth of July holiday approached, Lara felt as though she were being stretched in two directions. Brent phoned, inviting her and Polly to Cheyenne Days in Galena, Illinois, and of course Polly wanted to go in the worst way. Polly had even convinced five members of their singles' group that the rodeo was a worthwhile event, so those women planned to make the relatively short drive for a long, fun weekend.

However, Lara wasn't so sure she wanted to join them. For the past several days, Kevin had seemed down in the dumps, and Lara hated the thought of him spending July Fourth alone. Tim and Amanda offered to smuggle a pizza into the hospital, and since Kevin had gotten the okay from his doctor to occasionally leave the rehab floor for the outdoor patio, they'd all be able to watch the fireworks later on in the evening.

"Naw, Lara, that's all right. You don't have to do that," Kevin said when she suggested the pizza plan on the afternoon of July third. "You and your family have already spent an inordinate amount of time with me. I'm sure you've got a life."

Lara regarded him as he sat in a wheelchair wearing faded blue jeans and a light blue crewneck T-shirt with a single navy stripe across the chest. For the last three days, he'd gotten dressed, although Kevin wasn't pleased that it took an hour and some help from a nurse to accomplish what had once taken him mere minutes all by himself.

"Kevin, my life is all about helping other people. Here at the hospital, at church, at home, and at the ranch. I don't mind keeping you company on the Fourth of July."

He shook his blond head, and his blue eyes darkened. "Let's get one thing straight from here on in, okay? I don't need your help, and I sure don't want your pity."

Shocked, Lara gaped at him.

"I'm not a little boy, and I don't need a mommy."

"Fine." She bit back a cynical reply and turned on her professional voice since she didn't trust her emotions. She had thought they were becoming friends— good friends. But it appeared she'd been mistaken. "You know how to contact me if you change your mind. I'm more than happy to be of assistance to you."

After a parting smile, albeit a forced one, Lara pivoted and exited the room.

"Lara, wait. . . ."

She paused just outside his doorway, before slowly turning back around to face him. She fought to keep her expression from revealing the heartache she felt.

"Hey, look, I'm sorry. I shouldn't have said what I did."

"Well, that's obviously how you're feeling, so you needed to tell me. But just for the record, I never intended to thrust my good deeds on you. I never pitied you, and I certainly didn't mean to act like a mother figure. I only thought that if I were the one stuck in the hospital, I'd welcome some company, and I wouldn't want to spend the Fourth of July by myself." She shrugged. "That's all. But it's no big deal."

Spinning on her heel, she headed for her office. She suddenly felt like that awkward thirteen-year-old who'd just been ridiculed by the popular kid in school. Kevin's rejection opened the old wound. However, by the time she reached the main floor of the hospital, she'd collected herself, at least for the time being.

Making her way back through the emergency department and into her stuffy little office, Lara decided Cheyenne Days didn't seem like such a bad option for this coming weekend after all.

∽

Watching Lara leave his hospital room, Kevin swallowed a curse. He hadn't meant to hurt her feelings, and he could tell that's exactly what he'd done. It was just that his head ached, and he felt so weary of not being able to accomplish all the things he used to do. Simple things. Like walking, talking without slurring his words, writing, and feeding himself without getting most of it dribbled down the front of his shirt.

But I'm going to lick this. I'm going to ride again.

Despite a niggling doubt that continually threatened to pull him into the dark depths of despair, Kevin imagined the grand welcome he'd receive when he returned to the rodeo circuit. He envisioned the crowd, cheering from the grandstands as the announcer exclaimed how Kevin "Wink" Wincouser had overcome a traumatic brain injury and was now a world champion for the third time in his career!

A knock on the door brought Kevin out of his daydream.

"Hi," said the brunette woman with a sunny smile, "I'm Kathy, the financial counselor. I came to speak with you about your bill. May I come in?"

"Sure, but I've got insurance. I talked to somebody else about it."

"Right. I know that. . ." The woman entered, and Kevin detected her air of self-confidence, ". . .but your insurance company has only agreed to pay a percentage of your bill."

She began to rattle off the specifics of his policy, all of which went zinging right over Kevin's head.

"Okay, okay," he said at last, holding up his left hand to forestall further explanation. "Just tell me the bottom line. What are my out-of-pocket costs?"

"Twelve thousand five hundred fifty-three dollars and eighty-four cents. Now, that's just the hospital bill. You can expect to get a bill from the doctors, radiologists, the lab, ED physicians, and—"

"I'm getting out of here. This *hotel* is much too expensive—and the food isn't even that good."

In spite of the sarcasm, Kevin's thoughts whirred. Getting bucked off that bronc had jeopardized not only his career but his life savings and then some!

He struggled to stand, realizing there was no way he'd walk out of the hospital on his own. He was going to need help. A lot of help. And he'd need a place to stay.

Kevin considered phoning Quincy and asking him to come fetch him. But even if Quincy agreed, Kevin would need assistance with the basics, and none of his three roommates was likely to volunteer for *that* position.

"I could ask the social worker to come up and talk with you," the financial counselor said. "There might be some federal programs or grants that you qualify for."

He winced. "Um, I don't think the social worker is speaking to me right now."

"Oh?"

Kevin noticed the curious expression on the woman's face and waved off his previous remark. "Never mind. But, um. . ." He cringed before asking his next question. "Will you guys take a credit card?"

Chapter 13

Kevin pondered his dilemma long after the financial counselor left his room. He figured Mac would bail him out if he called her. She'd probably hop the next plane, pay all his medical bills, and nurse him back to health in her Houston penthouse. Of course, Kevin would most likely have to marry her in return.

He considered the idea for all of two seconds before deciding he wasn't that desperate. He'd much rather eat some humble pie and ask Lara to help him out. She was a sweetheart. She'd forgive him.

Once again, Kevin regretted his harsh words. He knew she didn't pity him—but he felt pitiful—and things were only getting worse.

Maneuvering his wheelchair, which was no easy task with his right arm in its weakened state, he made it to the telephone on the side table. He placed the receiver between his ear and shoulder and punched in *0*. The hospital operator then transferred him to Lara's extension. No answer. He hung up, waited awhile, and called back. This time he heard Lara's recorded message saying she had left for the day and wouldn't be back in the office until Monday, July seventh.

Great. Kevin hung up the telephone. *Now what do I do?*

❧

"Lara, cheer up, will you?"

From the front passenger seat of the minivan that Polly had borrowed from her brother, Lara glanced at her friend who sat behind the wheel. "I'm trying. It's just that Kevin's—"

"He's had a head injury," Polly cut in. "He's recuperating. Of course he's going to say things he doesn't mean." Taking her eyes off the freeway, she met Lara's gaze for a brief moment. "Besides, these rodeo cowboys are the kind of guys who abhor being coddled. I mean, they get bucked off bulls and broncos, then climb right back up into the saddle and get bucked off again."

"They sound like masochists to me," Annmarie Watson said from where she sat in the middle backseat. "But then again, what can be more charming and romantic than a cowboy?"

"Particularly if he resembles Clint Eastwood."

Lara laughed and leaned over to look into the backseat. "You're dating yourself, Ramona."

The fifty-three-year-old widow feigned an incredulous glare. "And you think that just because I don't open my mouth, nobody will suspect I'm middle-aged? Ha! Just look at all this gray!" For emphasis, Ramona pointed to her short hair, the color of which reminded Lara of chocolate cookies and cream.

"Clint's a has-been," Betsy Krause declared. "Think Brad Pitt."

"He's no cowboy." Ramona smiled, looking dreamy. "Think Paul Newman and Robert Redford—now there's a pair of good-looking *cowboys*."

"Have you seen them lately?" Polly asked as she put on the blinker and changed lanes. "They're old-timers."

"Ah, but in my heart, they'll always be Butch Cassidy and the Sundance Kid."

"I couldn't agree more," said Barb Thomas. She was about the same age as Ramona.

"My favorite cowboy was Glen Campbell in *True Grit*," Karla Stevens declared from her place next to Betsy in the third backseat.

"Another old-timer," Polly muttered, but only Lara heard her.

She laughed. "Who's your favorite cowboy?"

Polly gave her a wondering glance. "Brent Yiska, of course. Who's yours?"

"Kevin 'Wink' Wincouser."

Polly shot a curious glance at her. "Are you really stuck on him, Lara?"

She turned and stared out the windshield. "I think I've been stuck on Kevin since I was thirteen years old."

⌒

Kevin spent the Fourth of July alone. He told himself that it was just another day and that he didn't care, but he kept thinking about all the past July Fourth holidays he'd celebrated and began feeling depressed and lonely. He remembered Lara's offer and wished once more that he hadn't refused it.

As his thoughts progressed, he recalled some of the heavy conversations he'd had with Lara over the past couple of weeks. They talked about God—rather, Lara talked about God and what He might be trying to accomplish through Kevin's accident. She said Brent had heard the gospel, not only from her and her friend, but from a preacher at a sunrise service. It was to Kevin's shame that Brent hadn't heard it from his best friend. The truth was, Kevin hadn't ever discussed Jesus Christ with anybody—not since he'd left Wisconsin after his parents' death. He'd focused instead on his career and throwing himself into everything that he suspected would further make him a success. Kevin hadn't allowed time to examine his heart, his motives. But now with so much time on his hands and Lara, the social worker, counseling him for free, Kevin couldn't do anything *but* ponder his past and fret over his future.

"It sounds as if you're disappointed with God, perhaps even angry with Him, for allowing your parents' death." Lara's remarks rang in his ears. "But the sad truth is, we're all going to face death one day, and that's not God's fault." She became pensive for several moments. "Do you remember that verse in Second

Peter? 'The Lord is not slow in keeping his promise, as some understand slowness. He is patient with you, not wanting anyone to perish, but everyone to come to repentance.'"

Kevin remembered, although he'd forgotten the chapter and verse of that passage.

"Well, not everyone will come to repentance. That's a fact. There are people who have rejected God's gift of salvation, and they'll suffer for an eternity because of it. They've made a decision that's outside of God's will."

"What are you getting at, Lara?" Kevin had asked, feeling impatient.

"I'm trying to say that bad things happen in this life, and they're not God's fault. There is nothing wicked or bad in God's character. Nothing. Everything about God is good. So stop blaming Him for your parents' death."

Kevin had disputed her claim that he blamed God for *anything*, and Lara had backed off.

Seated in the vinyl recliner positioned near the window, Kevin had to grin. Lara had given in way too easily. She should have stood her ground, but instead she had changed the subject.

And here I am thinking about it.

Kevin suddenly realized Lara's silence had been more effective than a standoff.

I suppose she's right, Lord. Maybe I have been blaming You for taking away my parents and busting up my family. I never even knew I was holding such a grudge. . . .

Kevin's eyes grew misty. Twenty-nine years old and he still grieved his parents' death. He also missed his brother, Clayt's, camaraderie. But in the next moment, the magnitude of his selfishness filled his being. Realization set in.

All these years, he only saw what he lost and not what he took from others. Kevin had looked inward, at himself, at his desires and ambitions, not upward—not at the Lord. He had tossed aside the values and teachings his parents, teachers, and youth pastors had given him. They'd invested a part of themselves in him, and he'd never given anything back.

For the last decade, he never looked outward the way Lara and her family did. Kevin couldn't remember the last time he did someone a favor without having to be asked first. When did he last consider someone else's well-being before his own?

His heart broke. *Oh God, forgive me. . . .*

∞

The sun had set behind the large tent on the fairgrounds. Inside, a band consisting of fiddle, banjo, and guitar players, along with a percussionist, performed a lively Americana folk tune, part of a grand Fourth of July celebration that lasted all weekend. A parade and fireworks had marked the celebration yesterday, and an arts and crafts exhibition, a tractor pull, and an afternoon rodeo had been on today's agenda. But now, as evening fell, battery-operated lanterns illuminated the evening, and from where Lara sat at a rectangular table surrounded by her friends and cajoling cowboys, she felt as though she were on the set for the musical *Seven Brides for Seven Brothers*.

Glancing to her right, Lara caught snippets of Polly's conversation with a guy named Austin. He was a stocky fellow with jet-black hair who was very open about his faith in Christ. Austin's presence put Lara somewhat at ease since Brent was at his flirty best tonight. And being the dashing cowboy he was, Brent took each lady to the dance floor and, one by one, charmed his way into their hearts. Barb and Ramona each declared that Paul Newman couldn't hold a candle to Brent Yiska; however, the two were now engrossed in a jovial conversation with Quincy.

Brent and Annmarie returned from their dance. Since it had been an upbeat tempo, they were both breathing hard when they sat down at the table. Brent claimed the chair to Lara's immediate left—the one Annmarie had occupied minutes before. After a moment's frown of confusion, Annmarie grabbed her purse and sat down on the other side of the table next to Betsy.

Lara knew her turn to dance with Brent was coming, and she stifled a cringe. Up until now, she'd been able to keep her distance. She'd even avoided looking Brent's way because each time she did, he would catch her eye and wink or give her a winsome grin. Lara had to admit it wouldn't be hard to fall under Brent's spell. But each time that thought surfaced, reality tapped Lara on the shoulder. One of her best friends had her heart set on winning his affections, and Lara wouldn't hurt Polly for the world. Besides, Kevin's warning kept echoing in her ears: *"I have a feeling Brent wants to settle an old score. . . ."*

"You having fun?" Brent nudged her with his elbow, jerking Lara from her musings.

"Yeah, I'm having a great time. How about you?"

"Yep." He blew out an audible sigh. "And I'm getting my exercise for the day."

"I'll say." Lara smiled, then glanced at Polly, who still chatted with Austin.

"Hey, Jimmy, hand me that pitcher."

The fresh-faced cowboy grinned and pushed the plastic pitcher half filled with golden liquid toward Brent.

"No, give me the other one, the cola. I drank too much last night, and I don't want to be hung over in the morning when I escort these pretty ladies to church."

Lara thought he'd seemed happier and perhaps friendlier last night, although she hadn't noticed that he was drunk. She almost felt as if she'd been duped. Here she'd thought the laughter they all shared at the fireworks was genuine, when in actuality it had been manufactured by alcohol.

"You coming to church again, Brent?" Austin leaned around Polly as he posed the question.

"Yeah, I figured I would."

"That's two Sundays in a row."

Brent didn't reply but filled the plastic cup in his hand with cola.

"Hey, Brent," Jimmy said, sitting forward so his chest nearly rested on the tabletop, "you're not becoming one of those FCC guys, are you?"

"What's FCC?" Polly wanted to know.

"Fellowship of Christian Cowboys," Austin replied. His barrel-like chest swelled in a silent challenge. "And so what if he is? When you're on the back of a one-ton bull, it's not a bad thing to have the Lord with you. Can't argue with that, now can you, Jimmy?"

"Um, no, guess not."

Lara heard Brent chuckle before he chugged down his cola. Then he changed the subject.

"Tell us how Wink's doing, Lara."

"I guess he's okay." She knew with all the federal regulations concerning patient confidentiality that she couldn't give specifics. "You should give him a call."

"Yeah, I've been meaning to." Brent paused, and other conversations around the table resumed. "But what do you mean you 'guess' he's okay? I was under the impression you went to see him every day."

"I tried, but—" Lara waved a hand in the air. "Oh, don't ask, Brent." She didn't feel like discussing her last conversation with Kevin. It still kind of stung.

"Wink hurt your feelings, huh?"

Lara didn't reply. It smarted even to admit the truth.

The band began playing a slower tune, and when the melodious strains reached her ears, Lara guessed Brent's next thought. Scooting her chair back, she decided to head for the restroom, where she could wait out the set. But when she stood, Brent caught her wrist.

"I owe you a dance, Miss Social Worker."

"You don't owe me a thing, and I'm really not a good dancer. In fact, I can't even think of the last time I danced with someone. . . ."

Brent ignored her ramblings and led her onto the wooden platform over which the huge tent had been erected. Feeling inept, Lara dreaded what was about to come. She'd danced all of three times in her entire life. She'd never been asked to her high school prom, and she didn't frequent establishments that sported dancing. She wasn't a square dancer, didn't practice ballet, and wasn't into the aerobic dances at health clubs, although she knew the latter would probably do her some good.

Brent found an opening and stopped. When he turned around and faced her, Lara tried again to explain.

"I really don't know how to dance."

He took her protest in stride. "It's easy. You put your left hand on my shoulder, like so, and I put my arm around your waist. . . ."

Lara thought she was about to break out in a sweat as Brent pulled her closer to him.

"Now you put your right hand in mine."

Doing as he bid her, Lara shook her head. "I did know *that* much, okay?"

"Okay." Brent wore a hint of a smirk. "Now just move side to side. Follow my lead. I promise I won't try anything fancy."

Lara swallowed her objections, not wanting to be rude, but self-consciousness enveloped her like Brent's embrace. However, all her friends were dancing, so why did she feel so uncomfortable? Perhaps it was her lack of experience.

Brent held her nearer to him, and Lara felt his hand come to rest in the center of her back. Her chin was level with his shoulder, and suddenly the sight that caught her gaze made her pause. There, just ten feet away, stood Polly, dancing with Austin.

"What's wrong?" Brent stepped back and frowned.

"Um, oh, nothing. Sorry."

Brent swung her around so he could see what she'd been gaping at, and Lara laughed when she tripped over the toe of his boot.

"Hey, I thought you weren't going to try anything fancy."

Brent chuckled. "My apologies. Were you surprised to see Polly dancing with Austin?"

"Yes." Lara didn't see any point in fibbing. In fact, now seemed a perfect time to divulge the entire truth. "Polly's got a major crush on you."

"She does not!"

"Yes, she does. Haven't you noticed?"

A slight frown creased his dark brow. "Guess not."

"Even Quincy noticed."

"I suppose I'm a little short on smarts where women are concerned."

"Oh, right," Lara teased. "You're just so used to ladies ogling you that you don't even notice anymore."

Jerking her forward, he tickled her, and Lara let out a yelp. Several heads turned, and Lara wanted to die of embarrassment.

"Quit steppin' on her feet, Brent," a nearby cowboy admonished in jest. "You're gonna hurt the poor thang!"

After a quelling look at the other man, Brent peered into Lara's now flaming face. She met his gaze, and they shared a laugh. But all too soon, she read something in his brown eyes that made her feel uneasy.

Looking away, Lara searched for Polly, who was still in Austin's arms. Polly happened to catch her eye and smiled and waved. She didn't seem a bit unhappy about the dance partner situation.

"Honestly, Lara, I had no idea Polly was interested in me," Brent said so close to her ear that his warm breath sent shivers down her spine. "I hope I didn't do anything to offend her."

"I don't think you did." Lara hoped she hadn't offended her friend, either.

A few moments passed, then Brent lowered his head so his cheek rested against hers. Lara tried not to grimace, but she felt so torn. On one hand, the moment felt so romantic, dancing with Brent to a lovely melody, that she wanted to enjoy it. But on the other hand, it just didn't seem right.

"Relax, Lara."

"I'm trying."

Brent took half a step backward and gave her a curious stare. "What's the matter?"

Again Lara decided on the truth. "Well, in addition to Polly having a crush on you, Kevin told me that you've got a score to settle, and I just don't want to get caught in the crossfire."

"He said that?" Brent's expression darkened. He stopped in midstride. "Let's get one thing straight, honey. I would never use another person to. . .*settle a score.* That might be Wink's way, but it's not mine."

The spark of indignation in his eyes caused Lara to believe him. "Okay, things are straight."

"Good." He drew Lara close to him once more. "Guess it's good we cleared the air."

"Yeah," she said, watching Polly and Austin. Her thoughts were in a jumble. "Guess it's good. . ."

The dance ended, and Lara stepped backward just as another woman approached them. She was red, white, and blue, from her snug denim jeans, red cotton T-shirt, and white cowboy hat. Her long blond hair flowed down past her shoulders in silky waves.

"Brent," she drawled with a pout, "I've been waitin' all night for you to ask me to dance. So after two old-fashioneds, I decided to ask you."

He chuckled, then his gaze slid to Lara in a moment of uncertainty.

"Go ahead and dance if you want to, Brent," Lara said. "I'm sitting this one out anyway."

"You sure?"

"More than sure."

She gave him what she hoped was a gracious smile, but inside, Lara felt troubled—and it would take her the next few hours to figure out why.

Chapter 14

Back in their hotel room later that night, Lara managed to corner Polly in the ivory-tiled lavatory while their two roommates watched TV.

"I've got to talk to you." Lara entered and closed the door behind her.

"I've got to talk to you, too!" Dressed in an oversized nightshirt, Polly had removed her makeup and was now smearing cream onto her face.

"What's going on? I mean, you and Austin tonight behaved as though only the two of you existed."

Polly lowered her gaze.

"I told Brent that you were interested in him, and by the time we left the fairgrounds, I'm sure he thought I was either delusional or terribly misinformed."

"You told him?"

"Well, yeah. He had no idea."

Polly swept her gaze upward. "That figures. Well, it doesn't matter anyhow."

"What?" Lara smacked her forehead with her palm.

"I don't know if Austin is the one, but—"

"Polly, I think I'm seeing a pattern here. Remember back about eight months ago when you thought Peter Fitzgerald was *the one*?"

"I know, I know." Polly held up a hand to forestall further reprimand. "It's just that I've been praying so hard. You know how much I want to get married and have kids. I expect God to answer my prayers and send Mr. Right directly into my path."

Lara lowered herself onto the edge of the bathtub. She could relate to her friend. Lara wanted to get married and raise a family, too. She had been praying for a husband since she began college. She knew God would answer her prayer in His perfect time, but she, like Polly, was still waiting.

"I don't mean to be capricious," Polly told her as an expression of chagrin shadowed her features.

"You're not. I understand more than you know. My dream is to marry a man who loves the Lord first and me second."

"Maybe it's Brent." An ambiguous smile curved Polly's lips. "I'm not blind, you know. I can tell he's fond of you."

"He doesn't even know me," Lara countered. She couldn't help wondering if Polly's new interest in Austin had something to do with Brent's solicitations. "I have a feeling it's a game to him, a challenge to see if he can sweep the naïve

Christian social worker off her feet. But deep down I think Brent's really in love with the thrill of an eight-second bull ride." She paused, mulling over her statement, then added, "Unfortunately, I think Kevin is in love with an eight-second ride, too."

Polly laughed. "Must you analyze *everything*?"

"Of course." Lara stood and faced her friend, then grinned. "*One* of us has to be practical."

"Oh, I guess that's true," Polly said, feigning a reluctant tone.

Lara grinned and left the bathroom, but she sensed some tension between her and Polly. Entering the bedroom of the suite all seven ladies shared, Lara saw that Barb and Ramona had already fallen asleep in one of the two double beds. Out in the living room area, Annmarie, Betsy, and Karla were chatting before bunking down on the hideaway couch and the rollaway bed they'd requested from the hotel.

Picking up the remote, Lara turned off the TV and crawled into the bed she would share with Polly tonight. A few minutes ticked by, and she listened to the other ladies' soft snoring. Lara yawned, turned over, then prayed about this awkward situation.

Men. What a pack of trouble they caused. But in her heart, Lara believed that what she'd told Polly was true; Brent's attentions had to be part of some sort of charade. Lara wasn't his type—and he definitely wasn't hers. Moreover, the rodeo circuit with its competitive pressure to win, to be the best, and its rowdy lifestyle held no appeal for Lara.

Then there was the traveling. . . .

Tonight she'd heard a cowboy fondly refer to himself as a "rodeo gypsy." Lara imagined driving from city to city, town to town, and concluded it wasn't how she desired to spend her life. Lara wanted stability and a husband who came home to her every night—a husband who didn't drink beer and shots of whiskey, whose eye didn't wander, and who didn't slow dance with cute little blonds.

No, rodeoing could never be even a fragment of her world.

✧

The next morning, Lara had to admit she felt impressed with Brent in spite of her decision about him and his profession. He'd roused himself in time for the tent meeting, otherwise known as the Sunday morning church service. He'd even showed up carrying a Bible! Since Lara had strategically situated herself between Betsy and Ramona, Brent took a seat on the end bench beside Polly.

Today's message was about making a difference for Christ and how believers need to behave in a manner that counters worldly trends and standards.

"It might not be popular, and you might lose a few friends," the rugged-looking cowboy-preacher told the small crowd. "But God will honor your obedience. Try it and see."

Thinking back on last night and even the Fourth of July, Lara had to admit she had wanted to fit in. She wanted Kevin's friends to like her—she wanted Kevin to like her. She felt as though she'd been an outcast all her life, but the preacher's next words humbled her.

"Our life's purpose as Christians is to glorify the Savior in everything we do. Praise God we live in the United States of America where we are free to assemble together and worship Jesus Christ. Many a life has been lost over the centuries in order for us to enjoy this freedom."

Cheers broke out along with applause, and some affixed a hearty "amen" to the statement.

When the service ended, Lara and the others ambled out of the tent. The plan was to find a restaurant serving brunch before they checked out of the hotel and headed home.

"Lara!"

Nearing Polly's brother's minivan, she paused while Brent caught up to her.

"Hey, listen, I phoned the hospital right before coming here, and I was told Wink checked out yesterday morning."

"What?" Lara felt sure she hadn't heard him right.

"That's what they told me."

"But he wasn't in any condition to leave the hospital!"

Brent narrowed his brown-eyed gaze. "Where do you suppose Wink would go? I checked with Quincy and Jimmy. None of us got phone calls."

"I don't know." Lara's stomach suddenly crimped with fear. Kevin hadn't been able to sufficiently maneuver his wheelchair, let alone walk. How would he get to an airport? How would he get anywhere?

"Hey, now, don't frown so hard." The corners of Brent's mouth turned upward in a small grin. "We'll find him. Could be that Mac flew into town and took Wink back to Houston with her."

Lara recalled Kevin's last phone call with the woman. "Somehow I don't think that's the case."

Brent smirked. "Well, you know, poor Wink's got a head injury."

"But he's not brain-damaged."

Brent chuckled again, but Lara felt sick. She thought over every possible scenario, but none made sense.

She touched Brent's forearm, and he stopped discussing restaurants with Barb and Polly long enough for her to get a question in.

"Are you sure they didn't say Kevin was *transferred* to another floor or unit?"

"I was told *discharged*."

"That's impossible." Lara opened her purse and searched for her cell phone.

"Get in the van, Lara," Barb said. "We'll talk about it on the way to the restaurant. Brent, Austin, and a few of the guys are riding in Brent's truck, so come on—we're all hungry."

"I want to call the hospital first. It'll only take a few minutes." Lara walked away from the van, across the gravel parking area, until her phone registered a strong enough signal to place the call. She punched in County General's number, and soon the unit secretary answered her call.

"Hi, Kim, this is Lara Donahue, one of the social workers."

"Oh yeah, hi, Lara."

"Hi. Say, listen, I'm calling about Kevin Wincouser."

"He was discharged yesterday."

"Discharged where?"

"To home, I guess. I don't know the ins and outs. You'd have to talk to his nurse."

"Okay, ask the RN if she's got a few minutes to talk to me."

The secretary acted a bit put out, but Lara was determined to find out Kevin's whereabouts. The nurse, however, didn't prove any more helpful.

"A friend came to get him," she said. "He almost checked out AMA, because apparently his insurance isn't picking up enough of his medical bills. But since Kevin promised to keep up his PT, the doctor ended up okaying the discharge."

"AMA?"

"Against medical advice."

"Oh, right." Lara was familiar with the terminology, but in her haste to find out Kevin's whereabouts, her mind momentarily went blank. "Was it a male or female friend who picked Kevin up?"

"Male."

Lara didn't have a clue as to who that friend could be. "All right. Well, thanks for the info."

Ending the call, she walked back to the van. She glanced around at her friends' curious expressions before she met Brent's keen stare.

"You're right. Kevin's been discharged from the hospital." She dropped her cell phone into her purse. "But it's anybody's guess where he went from there."

Chapter 15

Kevin stretched out on the soft double bed and stared across the room at a shelving unit, which held a row of picture frames: Ruthie, Tim, and Lara as kids, then as high school seniors, Ruthie's wedding picture, Tim's engagement photograph. Kevin wondered why Lara wasn't married. By now, she should at least have a steady boyfriend. She would make a great catch for a guy who wanted a wife and kids. Kevin had to chuckle to himself, however, when Tim said that his sister had a way of psychologically assessing her dates and finding them lacking in one area or another.

"Then it's a good thing I'm not dating her," Kevin had quipped. "She'd discover I'm a raving lunatic."

"I think Lara knows that already," Tim had shot right back.

Kevin's smile remained as he allowed his gaze to wander from the snapshots to a watercolor hanging on the wall on the right side of the bed. It depicted a church he found familiar. A second later, he realized it was the church he'd attended with his family before his parents were killed. The sight plucked a sad chord in his heart. On the lower right-hand corner of the painting, it was signed "Ruth Ann Donahue, 1991."

She's a pretty good artist, Kevin decided. He had assumed the painting had been created by a professional. But in 1991, Ruthie had still been in high school.

And so had Kevin. He had graduated in 1993, one year after Ruthie.

At least my memory's intact. Unfortunately, all this time on his hands caused Kevin to remember more than he ever wanted.

He sighed and took in more of his surroundings. If he had to sum up the Donahues' guest bedroom in one word, it would be "homey." From the light blue walls to the fluffy blue carpet to the photos and paintings and the quilt on the bed, the entire room reminded Kevin of his family and brought back a sense of belonging. Indeed, it was a far cry from the trailer he shared with his buddies. Nothing homey about that place.

Kevin wondered if his head injury was causing him to become a sentimental fool, but his heart refuted the notion. There wasn't anything foolish about growing up and acting like a responsible human being, and maybe it was time Kevin grew up. If nothing else, these past weeks had taught him that a man needed a home, a place to which he could retreat when life assaulted him. Kevin's father had been fond of some such saying. What's more, had Dad been alive to witness

Kevin's lifestyle over the last nine years, he likely would have disowned him. Dad wouldn't have put up with it, and Kevin realized he'd acted out his grief and anger by drinking and carousing.

Sadly enough, after all this time, the grief and anger still remained.

Lord, I'm not angry with You. I think I'm more angry with myself these days. . . .

A knock sounded, and the bedroom door opened, revealing Tim's grinning face. "We're home from church, Kev. You okay?"

"Yeah, I just woke up a few minutes ago. What a lazy bum I am, eh?"

Tim opened the door wider and inched his lanky frame into the room. "I think springing you from the hospital yesterday took all your strength, then some."

"Yeah." Kevin had been stunned by his weakened condition.

"Well, Mom's in the kitchen making lunch. How 'bout I help you get dressed and into the living room. We can eat in there and watch the Brewers play baseball on TV."

"I'd like that."

Kevin sat up and ran his fingers through his thick hair. It felt too long and shaggy, except for the bristly part on the left side, above his ear, where the doctors had shaved his head before surgery.

"I should probably get a haircut and even things out a bit." Kevin rubbed the left side of his head, and Tim chuckled.

"My dad could give you a military cut. I think I wore one every summer until my freshman year in high school."

Kevin grinned as he pulled on his jeans, remembering Tim's buzzed head. He tried not to feel impatient with his right hand. It felt stronger, but not up to par yet. "Wasn't your dad in the Navy or something?"

"Marines. He fought in Vietnam."

"That's right."

The chitchat ceased, and embarrassment engulfed Kevin when Tim had to assist him with zippers and buttons. Kevin felt like a two-year-old.

"Man, talk about a humbling experience."

Tim laughed. "Hey, don't worry about it. What are friends for?"

"Well, thanks."

Kevin realized he had never learned how to be a good friend. His focus had been on himself and on competing and winning ever since he understood the concept of "number one." Now, however, he couldn't imagine what he would have done without friends like the Donahues.

Kevin's spirit had hit an all-time low on the Fourth of July. Then Tim walked in, a veritable godsend. He had been on his way to his fiancée's house and decided to stop and say hello. A quick visit had turned into two hours of conversation that ended in heartfelt prayer. The next day, after learning about Kevin's financial dilemma, the Donahues offered him a place to recuperate. Less expensive—free, actually—and the food was a whole lot better.

Tim looped Kevin's right arm around his shoulders. "Ready?"

"As I'll ever be, I guess."

With Tim's help, Kevin managed to limp out of the bedroom and into the hallway. His right leg was weaker than his arm, although Kevin could stand now. But the signals from his brain to his leg muscles were still short-circuiting somewhere along the line.

Once more, Kevin feared he'd never rodeo again—a fate far worse than death for a two-time world bareback champion.

Lara tried to hide her concern over the news that Kevin had left the hospital. She tried to pay attention to the light conversation during breakfast, but both Polly and Brent commented on how distracted she seemed. And it was true. But what bothered her most was the fact that Kevin never even said good-bye. He only said he didn't want her help or her pity.

Perhaps he hadn't planned to check himself out the last time they talked. Still, Lara couldn't help recalling how disheartened she felt the summer going into her sophomore year of high school when she learned Kevin had moved away.

She felt the same way now. Bummed out.

"Hey, will you cheer up over there?" Polly took the plastic straw out of her water glass and shook it at Lara.

The antic worked. Lara laughed, and moments later she realized how silly she was to fret about a man and a situation over which she had no control. Taking a deep breath, she made the choice to turn her feelings over to the Lord.

Then she listened in on Polly's conversation with Brent. The two sat next to each other across from Lara at the long rectangular table, and they were discussing childhood pets, of all things. Minutes later, Lara's melancholy vanished, and she set aside all thoughts of Kevin and his disappearing act—until she arrived home that evening, and Tim met her at the curb.

"Hey, sis, we've got company."

"You came to warn me?" Lara grinned.

"Well, yeah, sorta."

Lara allowed her brother to retrieve her luggage from the back of the minivan. After a wave to Polly and the others, she followed him to the side door of their duplex.

"Kevin moved in with us."

"He did *what?*" Incredulousness pervaded Lara's being, and as Tim spilled the story, everything made sense. "I think Kevin had better telephone his buddies and let them know where he is. They're worried. Brent tried to call him this morning."

"I'll pass that message along." Tim opened the door. "But I wanted to give you a heads-up so you don't come down in your nightgown and robe with a head full of curlers. Kevin never had sisters, you know."

"Oh, so you're worried that I'll scare him, huh?"

"Likely so."

Lara gave Tim a sisterly shove. "Oh, hush."

He chuckled in reply before taking the stairs to the second floor two at a time. Lara passed him on the steps as he ran back down.

"Your suitcase is in the hallway," he said. "Come visit later."

"Yeah, with my hair in rollers."

She laughed and entered the flat she shared with her grandmother. The easy banter with Tim helped the shock to wear off. But now disbelief took its place.

Kevin is here? In my parents' house? He and I are under the same roof?

Well, one thing was certain; Lara wouldn't be stupid twice. She would keep her distance. She'd keep her thoughts to herself and wouldn't offer any assistance, unless Kevin asked, of course.

"Lara, I'm down here." Gram's voice wafted up the back stairwell. "We're having supper. Come and join us."

"I ate already. Thanks anyway. Tell Mom and Dad I'll stop in later."

A nervous flutter filled her abdomen. Why did she suddenly feel doomed?

Chapter 16

"Wink, you dirty dog, you broke her heart."

Sitting on the Donahues' wide front porch, Kevin sighed as Brent railed on him by phone for hurting Lara's feelings three days ago.

"Look, I didn't mean any harm. I'm going through a tough time right now. Doctors say I'll never ride again, and I'm trying to prove them wrong. Lara understands."

"Sure she does."

"I'll apologize, and she'll forgive me." Kevin shifted in the plastic lawn chair. He wasn't very comfortable out here with the mosquitoes and humidity, but his cell phone had better reception outdoors than in the house.

"Well, you're right about that. Lara will forgive you." Brent's voice sounded strained as though he were in the process of reclining. Then he exhaled. "We had a nice time this weekend. All of us. There were seven women to about four of us guys. Great odds, wouldn't you say?"

Kevin grinned in spite of himself. "Yeah."

"On Saturday Lara and I danced the night away."

"Is that right?" Kevin wondered why he felt tense all of a sudden. On second thought, he knew the reason. He didn't want Lara to get hurt as a result of Brent's vengeance. But he wouldn't let on that the remark troubled him. If he did, Brent was liable to continue his spiteful game. "Glad you had fun. You deserve it."

"Yeah, I guess I do. It's been awhile since I had good clean fun." Brent chuckled as if he suddenly recalled something amusing. "Have you met Lara's friend Polly?"

"Once, I think."

"She's a hoot. Pretty, too."

"Yeah?"

"Yeah. Lara says she's interested in me, but. . .I just don't see it."

"Lara's interested in you? She said that?"

"No, no. Lara said *Polly* is interested in me."

"Oh, gotcha." Kevin hoped he didn't sound as relieved as he felt. Then he remembered Lara mentioning her friend's "crush."

"I guess I knew that."

"Anyway, Polly doesn't act interested, so it kind of confuses a guy. Know what I mean?"

"It's a gender thing. Women have confounded us since the Garden of Eden."

"How do you know?"

"Um, I've read a lot of books."

Brent let go of a hearty belly laugh. "Wink, I'll eat buffalo chips for a week if you've read a book in the last five years."

"Yeah, well, good thing for you I can't recall the last book I picked up." Kevin chuckled. He was beginning to enjoy conversing with his pal.

They chatted for a while longer, exchanging occasional barbs, then discussed current rodeo standings. Finally, Kevin felt himself growing stiff and told Brent he'd call back in a couple of days. Turning off his phone, Kevin had just slipped it into his shirt pocket when a soft female voice drifted down from somewhere up above, although her words belied her tone.

"Your friend is a fibber."

Fibber? Kevin twisted around and saw Lara perched on the upstairs porch railing. With the moon directly behind her and her hair hanging down past her shoulders, she made a fetching sight.

"What are you doing up there? Eavesdropping?"

"Yes, except I didn't mean to."

Kevin grinned. That girl was honest to a fault. With some effort, he managed to turn his chair around far enough so he didn't have to crane his neck to look at her. The upper porch wasn't even half the size of the deck, and it only covered the two front doors, as if its original purpose was to protect arriving guests from the elements.

But obviously it had other uses, too.

"I was here when Tim helped you out of the house and into the lawn chair," Lara explained. "I didn't think there was any reason for me to go in. But then you started talking and I realized you were on your cell phone. By that time, there was no way for me to make a graceful exit."

"Okay. No harm done." Kevin wasn't offended in the least. "So what did Brent *fib* about?"

"I'm not interested in him."

"Well, see? You've got it wrong already. I was the one who misunderstood. Brent explained that it's Polly who's got stars in her eyes." *And you've got the moon in your hair*, he thought, feeling oddly captivated.

Lara bent her legs so that she could wrap her arms around her knees. Her back was up against the front of the house.

"Why don't you come on down here so we can talk?" Kevin cajoled. "You can tell me what else Brent's lying about."

Lara didn't move, and Kevin wondered if she was thinking over his offer.

Then he remembered. . .

"Hey, look, I'm really sorry about what I said to you on Thursday afternoon."

"Oh yes, that's right. You said you'd apologize, and you were very confident that I'd forgive you."

"Of course you'll forgive me. You're a good Christian girl." Kevin couldn't see her features in the darkness, but he imagined she had pursed her lips in an effort to stave off a grin and had raised one pretty eyebrow. That look was her habitual expression to weak retorts, and Kevin felt a little amazed that he even knew something like that about her. "Come on down here, Lara. Keep me company for a while."

Once again she didn't move, nor did she reply. Kevin figured she was still miffed, so he tried a new approach.

"You know, just like you didn't intend to listen in on my *private conversation*, I didn't intend to hurt your feelings. I took out my frustration on you, and that was wrong. I regretted it the instant you left my hospital room. Now, are you going to forgive me or not?"

"Yes, I forgive you."

"Good." Kevin smiled with satisfaction. "Now, come down here."

"I can talk to you from where I am."

Kevin thought it over. "Did Brent tell you to be careful around me? If he did, I'm here to say that I'm harmless. More so than dancing with *him* all night, that's for sure!"

"What?"

"Yeah, you heard me. Brent said the two of you 'danced the night away' on Saturday."

Lara started to laugh so hard that Kevin feared she'd fall from her perch. If that happened, he'd be unable to come to her rescue, and the realization made him feel all the more useless.

"You're making me nervous," he barked. "Get off that banister."

Lara did as he said, then entered the house and closed the porch door behind her. As the minutes ticked by, Kevin started to think she wasn't coming out, and the disappointment he felt surprised him. Well, what did he expect? He shouldn't have used such a harsh tone with her. But he hated feeling so inadequate. On the other hand, everyone kept telling him to be patient.

Suddenly he heard a rustling of the bushes, then footfalls on the wooden front porch steps. Moments later, Lara appeared carrying a large candle. She'd come from around the side of the house.

"Where were you?"

"In the backyard. I stopped to pick up this candle from off the picnic table. It's supposed to keep the bugs away." She struck a match, and a golden hue spread across the porch.

Kevin found the soft light rather romantic, although his practical side hoped the candle proved effective on the bugs. The mosquitoes were eating him alive.

He slapped at one on his right arm, then looked over at Lara. She stared back with a curious expression.

"What's wrong?"

"Did you get your hair cut?"

Kevin chuckled. "Yep. The top of my head feels like a tennis ball."

"Must be my dad's handiwork."

"You got it."

A tiny laugh escaped Lara.

Kevin smiled. "Now, about this dancing business. . ."

"One dance. And I didn't even enjoy it."

"No?" Kevin was glad to hear that. "How come?"

"Because, well, I felt uncomfortable." Lara tucked one leg beneath her. "I mean, if Brent were the guy I vowed to spend the rest of my life with, it might be different. But he's not, so such close, personal contact didn't seem right to me. But I suppose I had to learn that lesson firsthand."

"Hmm."

"I sound like a prude, right? Well, maybe I am."

"I take it we're not talking about line dancing here, are we?"

The sound of Lara's laughter made Kevin chuckle.

"Lara, Lara, Lara." He said her name on a long sigh, a feigned reprimand. "Dancing with the cowboys. What are we going to do with you?"

"Shhh." She put her forefinger to her lips. "I don't want my parents to hear. They'll lock me in my room until I'm thirty!"

Kevin grinned, but he felt sure the Donahues weren't at all "lock her up" type of people. They were bighearted folks with a wealth of compassion.

And they'd raised a proper, upstanding daughter who wasn't at all a "prude." In fact, Kevin found her. . .*refreshing*.

❧

The month of July passed in a busy blur at work for Lara, mostly because her heart was at home. She had become accustomed to seeing Kevin around, and even though she reminded herself to keep her distance—to keep her emotions detached from him and his situation—it didn't help. She always ended up sitting on the porch with him, talking and watching the sunset, or just watching TV with him and her parents.

Mike Donahue, Lara's father, had taken Kevin under his wing, so to speak. He drove him to and from physical therapy sessions and assisted Kevin with his exercises at home.

"Mike's Boot Camp for Lame Cowboys," Kevin called it in jest, but he showed obvious signs of improvement. Kevin could walk using an aluminum "elbow crutch," one that fit securely around his upper arm for maximum stability. His speech sounded better, although he still had problems with detailed tasks, such as buttoning a shirt and writing.

Lara's mother had the summer off from her part-time teaching position, so she took pride in cooking, baking, and tending to her small "urban garden." Everyone benefited from Peg Donahue's domesticity; however, Kevin seemed to thrive on it, much to Peg's delight.

For weeks, everything appeared to be progressing at a nice, even pace, until Kevin learned from Quincy that Mackenzie Sabino had plans to sue him for breach of contract. The news troubled Kevin. In addition to rising medical bills, it depressed him to think he'd have to hire an attorney to defend him in court. However, Mike Donahue stepped in and contacted a lawyer he knew from church. After hearing the scenario, the advocate surmised that Mac and her daddy's salsa company didn't have much of a case, given the fact that Kevin had been injured through no fault of his own.

The news brought Kevin a small measure of relief, but he told Lara that, knowing Mac, she'd try to get back at him some other way.

August arrived, bringing with it hot, sticky temperatures. Lara found herself seeking out Kevin's company, yet in spite of the handsome distraction at home, Lara continued her volunteer work at the Regeneration Ranch. She had missed the first Saturday in July because of the holiday. But two weeks later, she spent an entire day with her kids and enjoyed every minute of it. By Lara's first scheduled weekend in August, Kevin was hobbling around well enough that she asked him to go along to the ranch with her. He accepted the offer, and Lara worked out all the details with the ranch personnel. Her kids would finally meet a real rodeo star!

"I can't believe you won't come to Iowa with me," Polly whined on Friday afternoon. It was the day before Kevin's grand appearance at the ranch. A mini-rodeo followed by a picnic had been planned.

At her friend's complaint, Lara didn't even pause in cleaning off her desk for the weekend. Polly knew where she stood. Lara refused the offer to attend this weekend's rodeo and wasn't about to change her mind.

"Since last week when Brent called me, I've really wanted to go."

"I know." Lara recalled how excited her friend had been after Brent's phone call. The two of them shared what Polly termed "a meaningful conversation."

"I want to see him again. I think he might really be the one."

Lara cast an exasperated glance toward the ceiling.

"Please come with me."

"Take Annmarie."

"Yeah, looks like I'll have to."

Grinning at Polly's cynical tone, Lara stuffed her leather folder and other paperwork into a drawer and locked it. "You guys will have a great time."

"You really won't come?"

"No, and I told you before, I enjoy watching the rodeo, but I don't care for what goes on behind the scenes."

"Well, I don't, either, but I care about Brent."

"So Austin's out of the picture for good, eh?"

Polly shrugged. "He only e-mailed me once, and I haven't heard from him since." She tipped her head. "But you and Kevin are certainly hitting it off nicely."

"We're friends."

"Oh, Lara, you are *so* in denial."

She laughed and stepped out of her office. The second-shift social worker had taken over, and it was time for Lara to punch out—and time for Polly to get back to work.

"Listen, it's true. Kevin and I are just friends. I'll admit I wish it were more, but he still talks about rodeoing again. He's determined to return to the circuit a changed man, in more ways than one."

Lara grabbed her purse before she and Polly ambled through the emergency department, past the trauma room, and down the hallway to the time clock.

"It's great that Kevin's been attending church with your family." Polly pulled a stick of gum from the pocket of her multicolored smock top. "Brent hasn't been quite as faithful, but he's been going from time to time."

Lara's heart thrilled at the news. "Kevin's talked to him about the Lord, too."

"We've made a difference in these guys' lives," Polly said. "Nothing more might develop between us in the way of romantic relationships, but God used us to bring them closer to Him. And that's what this life is all about for Christians, isn't it?"

"Yep." Smiling, Lara swiped her badge through the automated time-tracking device on the wall. Then she swung around and gave Polly a hug. "Have fun this weekend, okay?"

"I'll try, but it won't be the same without you."

Lara caught Polly's simulated pout before her friend turned on her heel and walked toward the elevators. With a smile still on her lips, Lara headed for the parking lot, feeling excited about everything God had done. And everything He was about to do.

Chapter 17

On Saturday morning, Lara bounded down the back steps with anticipation flowing through her veins. Today was the big day at the Regeneration Ranch. She just knew her kids were going to be excited!

Turning the corner on the landing, she proceeded down the next set of stairs, only to come face-to-face with a very unhappy-looking Kevin Wincouser. He stood just outside her parents' back doorway wearing faded blue jeans, a short-sleeved blue and white shirt whose bold stripes ran vertically, and a heavy frown.

"What's wrong?"

"Me. That's what's wrong." He lifted his right hand, indicating the crutch he held. "How am I supposed to impress a bunch of kids today?"

"These kids will be impressed. Believe me."

"Lara, I had to wake up Tim and ask him to button my shirt this morning."

She wondered if he worried about finding assistance at the ranch should he require it. "There will be men around who can help you today if you need it."

"I hadn't even thought about that." He groaned.

Lara took a step toward him. "I wouldn't have asked you to come today if I didn't think you could manage. Once we get to the ranch, you'll see what I mean."

Kevin didn't look convinced.

Dropping her shoulder bag onto the steps, Lara reached for his left hand and held it between both of hers. "Please don't change your mind. My kids will be so disappointed. So will I."

"Why? I'm like damaged goods. There are other cowboys in Wisconsin, some that could entertain *your kids* with roping tricks or even a bull ride. I'm sure they'd do it for free, too. Brent, Quincy, and I made charity appearances once in a while."

"But we want *you*. I've talked about you, and my kids want to meet the guy who was my hero when I was thirteen."

"*Was*. That's a good word to describe me." His blue eyes looked misty, and the sight broke Lara's heart.

"Kevin, you have so much to offer. I wish you'd see that." She smiled. "And just for the record, you're still my hero."

He raised his brows, and a hint of a grin tugged at his mouth. "Lara Donahue, are you flirting with me?"

She managed to contain a smile. "Well, maybe just a little."

He twisted out of her grasp, and within moments his arm encircled her waist, and he pulled her up next to him. "A girl could get in big trouble flirting like that."

"You're right. She could." Lara stood so close to him that she smelled the mint on his breath and the spicy scent of his cologne.

Kevin narrowed his gaze. "She could even get kissed."

"Well, it's about time!"

His eyes widened with surprise, and Lara laughed.

"I've only been waiting twelve years for you to kiss me." She said it in jest, but her heart had told the truth.

"Why didn't you say something sooner? I'm more than happy to oblige."

She laughed again, but very suddenly it wasn't funny anymore. Kevin's eyes darkened to cobalt, and an ardent expression crossed his features. The seconds that followed were a million times more romantic than anything Lara had ever experienced, not that she possessed a wealth of knowledge in this particular area. But the instant his lips touched hers, she knew she loved Kevin. In fact, she had probably loved him for half her life.

The kiss ended, and Lara felt oddly disappointed.

"We'd better, um, get going," Kevin stammered. "I mean, folks at the ranch are most likely waiting for us."

"Right."

Kevin released her, and Lara forced her legs backward. She grabbed her shoulder bag and followed Kevin, who had already managed to descend the three steps leading to the outer doorway.

In the car, as Lara drove to the ranch, neither she nor Kevin spoke. The silence told Lara a single kiss had altered their friendship. But why? It couldn't have meant anything to him. Surely he'd kissed a dozen women in his lifetime. Maybe more. But perhaps that was the problem. Lara's kiss hadn't measured up to his expectations. Should she apologize?

∽

Kevin didn't know what to say. Kissing Lara had activated every neuron in his brain, and now his thoughts were in a jumble. Talk about electric currents! That kiss could have lit up Chicago at Christmastime! He stole a glance in her direction. Had she felt it, too?

Lara braked for a stoplight, and Kevin brought his gaze forward. *So now what do I do, Lord? I'm going to fall for this woman, and then what? I leave her? Break her heart?*

Kevin couldn't stand the thought of hurting Lara. *I could take her with me. Marry her. . .* Kevin shook his head, trying to clear his thoughts. *What am I thinking?* He couldn't believe he'd actually considered tying the knot. He had successfully dodged wedding bells for twenty-nine years. Besides, marrying Lara wouldn't work. She had already expressed her aversion to his lifestyle.

Former lifestyle. *That's right, Lord. I've recommitted my ways to You.*

The light changed, and Lara stepped on the accelerator.

"Kevin, I can't stand it anymore. I'm sorry if I offended you."

He looked over at her. "What?"

"You know. What happened before. . . I'm sorry."

"Why are you sorry?"

"Because. . ." She swallowed hard, and her voice sounded strained. It dawned on Kevin that she might be upset. "Because you're not talking to me."

"Sure, I'm talking to you. I just don't have anything to say at the moment." Clutching the steering wheel with her right hand, she lifted her left and proceeded to swat at something on her cheek. Kevin felt like the dumbest mule in the stable. He'd somehow hurt her feelings. "Lara, you're not crying, are you?"

She skirted his question. "I just don't want you to be angry with me."

Kevin chuckled. "I'm not angry. Never was."

"When you didn't say anything, I thought I did something wrong."

"No." Kevin reached out his hand, and she took it so fast it made him grin. "Lara, I'll be honest. I'm developing strong feelings for you, and I'm not sure what to do about them. Seems like we're from two different worlds, and I'm not talking about Venus and Mars, either."

She laughed, and the sound made Kevin smile.

"That's better. No more tears, now, you hear? It sort of rips me apart inside to see you sad."

She took her gaze off the road for the briefest of moments, and although Kevin couldn't read the message in her eyes through the dark sunglasses she wore, he did see her smile.

And that was good enough. For now.

❦

Sitting in the bleachers, Lara watched the mini-rodeo with her kids and several parents. The "rodeo" consisted of an opening act with two funny clowns who looked suspiciously like Caroline and Ron Bramble, the owners of the ranch. But the kids didn't seem to notice, and they laughed at the silly antics.

Next a mechanical bull was placed in the center of the corral, and several of the older kids who had been practicing for weeks got to show off their skills. Not one fell off, either. Of course, the bull's speed had been set so low its riders appeared to be in slow motion. Nevertheless, it was a miracle to watch, given the children's physical disabilities.

Finally, Kevin "Wink" Wincouser rode into the corral on poor old Abby, an ebony-maned, chestnut-brown mare that probably couldn't even trot anymore, let alone buck off a cowboy. But since Kevin was in no condition for bronc riding,

Abby would do just fine. Horse and rider circled the pen once while Kevin waved to the kids. They cheered and clapped. Then, reining in the animal, Kevin stopped and faced his audience. Next he pulled his crutch from behind the saddle as though it were a shiny, silver saber and held it up for all to see.

That's my hero, Lara thought with a smile. Kevin's words from this morning still played in her heart. She tried not to think of forever but forced herself instead to place the matter in God's hands.

And leave it there.

Kevin began to explain why he had to walk with a crutch. He talked about his head injury and admitted it was by God's grace and mercy that he was able to climb back up in the saddle today.

"See, I'm not so different from any of you kids."

Lara grinned, thinking Kevin had unwittingly just endeared himself to the children around her. It was obvious that he had a dynamic way of speaking to youngsters, and Lara felt proud of him.

"And here's something else you should know about me. When I was a little boy, I dreamed of becoming a real live cowboy. Some people told me I'd never make it. Some people even laughed at me."

"That's mean to laugh at other people," eight-year-old Jason Emory whispered to Lara with his adorable lisp.

She nodded. Jason knew firsthand how it felt to be mocked. He had severe learning disabilities, and sometimes the kids at his school picked on him.

"But I worked really hard, and each time I fell down," Kevin said, "I picked myself right back up. I refused to give up. And none of you should give up, either. Now, who wants to learn how to ride a horse?"

Lara laughed as practically every hand around her shot up.

"Well then, you'd better get down here in a hurry and form a single line by the gate over there. I'm going to give you each a special riding lesson."

The kids whooped with excitement, and even though many of them had already ridden astride Abby, none had ever received a lesson from a real rodeo cowboy.

Lined up against the split-rail fence, the children wiggled and waited none too patiently for their turns. Parents who'd brought cameras snapped pictures of their son or daughter getting a tip from Kevin.

Then, suddenly, Lara spotted Maria Kallen at the head of the line. Jogging over to reach her, Lara caught the small girl by the hand.

"I don't think you want a turn, sweetie." Lara knew the seven-year-old was frightened of the animals even though she admired them from afar and often talked about the day when she'd ride a horse.

"Yes, I do. I want to ride."

Lara caught sight of the determined expression on Maria's face and decided to let her try. In the past, the towheaded girl came as close as a foot away from a horse before she panicked. Part of the problem, Lara knew, was the child's poor eyesight.

"Come on, honey. You're next."

Maria's cheeks turned a pretty pink.

Cowboy charm affects females of all ages, Lara thought with a smirk as the child shyly stepped forward.

But just as Lara predicted, the girl got about two feet away and changed her mind.

"Whoa, now, don't run away." Kevin leaned over and halted Maria by taking hold of her arm. Kneeling, using his good leg, he rested his forearm on his right thigh. "You're not scared, are you?"

Lara watched Maria nod a silent reply.

"Well, I'll tell you what. How 'bout I set you in the saddle first, then I'll climb up behind you? Nothing bad will happen if I'm hanging on to you."

To Lara's astonishment, the girl agreed.

Kevin stood and gently hoisted Maria into the worn brown leather saddle before mounting the horse. The two then took a leisurely amble around the corral. Kevin even let Maria hold the reins. When they rounded the last bend, Lara took one glance at the expression of sheer delight on the little girl's face and had to fight back tears of joy. The child was living her very own dream come true.

"I'm riding! I'm riding!" Maria squealed. Her large blue eyes seemed magnified behind the plastic-framed glasses she wore.

"Great job, Maria," Kevin told her after their ride ended. "You're a bona fide cowgirl now." He lifted her off the saddle and placed the child into Lara's outstretched arms.

"I did it, Miss Lara! I did it!"

"Yes, you did." She set the child on the ground.

Maria skipped away. "I did it! I did it!"

"And I didn't have my video camera," Lara muttered, feeling disappointed.

"Guess we'll have to bring it next time."

We? Lara raised an inquiring brow. "Does that mean you're coming back to the ranch with me in the near future?"

"Oh, I dunno." Kevin leaned forward in the saddle. "I could be persuaded."

Smiling, Lara glimpsed the mischievous spark in his blue eyes and decided she might like to take him up on the challenge.

"Hey! Is it my turn now?" A child's voice interrupted.

Lara blinked, and Kevin straightened in the saddle. Dismounting, he was careful to pull his left foot out of the stirrup before he landed.

"Guess you and I will have to finish this discussion later." A note of promise rang in his tone.

"Guess so." Lara couldn't wait. But for now her kids took priority. She glanced at Billy Stievers, the next child in line, and waved him over.

Chapter 18

After the riding lessons and picnic, Lara helped Caroline Bramble and several other volunteers pick up garbage. Tying one of the trash bags, Lara happened to glance at the gray and white barn off in the distance and spotted Kevin leaning against the door frame, talking with Ron. They appeared to be deep in conversation, and Lara wondered what they were talking about.

Ron is probably "persuading" Kevin to volunteer here at the ranch. Lara grinned at the thought. Ron Bramble was a lot more influential than she, although she might have enjoyed giving it a try in Kevin's case.

Once the yard was free of litter, Lara followed Caroline into their large house. The outside of the dwelling matched the barn, and inside, the home looked cozy. The yellow and white kitchen was large, and a vase of daisies sat in the center of the round wooden table. Crocheted afghan blankets covered the backs of the sofa and love seat in the "parlor." Walls everywhere were decorated with snapshots and drawings, given to Ron and Caroline by children who had benefited from the ranch's ministry over the last twenty-four years. In all, it was a very special place.

Lara accepted the can of cola Caroline offered her. Popping its flip top, she took a long drink. She hadn't stopped all day, and suddenly she realized how exhausted she felt. Minutes later, Kevin and Ron entered the house, and Lara sensed Kevin was equally as tired.

"I s'pose we should be on our way," Lara said with a glance in Kevin's direction.

He nodded, obviously ready to go.

They bid farewell to the Brambles, then made their way to Lara's car. Once seated and buckled in, they sighed in unison and leaned against the backs of the front seats.

"This is more excitement than I'm used to."

Lara looked over at Kevin and smiled. "I'm sure you're right. I just hope you didn't overdo it today." She bit her lower lip, realizing her blunder. "Sorry, Kevin, I didn't mean to sound motherly."

"That's okay." He gave her a wink. "I think I'm getting used to it."

She expelled a breath of indignation before laughing and socking Kevin in the arm for the quip.

On the drive home, they chatted about the day's events. Lara commended Kevin for a job well done.

"You know, Lara, it's an odd thing, but when I got on that horse today, I just knew I'd never rodeo again."

"What?" She took her eyes off the road long enough to send Kevin a stunned look. "I can't believe I just heard those words come out of your mouth."

"Well, you did. Part of me feels like I just learned my best friend died, while another part of me is relieved. I mean, I'm retiring a two-time world champion bareback rider. It's not like I'm going out a loser."

"Certainly not a loser."

As she further digested his news, Lara didn't know what more to say. Like Kevin, she had mixed emotions. On one hand, she felt elated that he had decided not to rodeo. It meant he wouldn't get reinjured, and maybe there really was hope for a budding romance between them. But she also knew it was a hard decision for Kevin to make.

"You were great with the kids today," she murmured. It had nothing to do with the present topic, but she couldn't seem to tell him that enough.

"Thanks. Ron thought so, too. He offered me a job."

"You're kidding."

"Nope. And it's actually not a bad-paying position, either. But the salary is probably only half what I'd earn in this year competing."

"What would you be doing at the ranch?"

"Probably anything and everything I'm physically able to do. We didn't get into a lot of specifics. I told Ron I'd give the matter some thought—and, of course, I need to ask God what He thinks."

Lara smiled to herself. Two months ago, praying about a situation wouldn't have occurred to Kevin. He'd come a long way, spiritually and physically.

Their conversation lagged, and Lara felt tempted to ask Kevin what he thought about *them*. Was he interested in pursuing a relationship? However, Lara sensed now wasn't a good time to talk romance. Kevin looked tired, and his thoughts were obviously stayed on one of the biggest decisions he'd ever faced.

She exhaled and, once again, set the matter in her Savior's hands.

*

As the month progressed, plans for Tim and Amanda's wedding took precedence. October fourth, their special day, was creeping ever nearer. Lara had a final fitting for her bridesmaid's dress, and being the groom's sister, she helped coordinate Amanda's bridal shower. To make life all the busier, one of the three social workers quit at the hospital, and Lara and her coworker were forced to divide the job between them until another person could be hired and trained. There didn't seem to be much time for budding romances, especially since Ron had moved Kevin into the apartment above the barn on the Regeneration Ranch. One evening, Lara came downstairs to say hello, and her father gave her the "good news."

Little did he know the information caused his daughter's heart to crimp in misery. But Lara reminded herself that Kevin hadn't made her any promises. When two weeks passed and she didn't see him at church, nor did he call, Lara began to think she had imagined the kiss they'd shared as well as the conversation following it. Perhaps she'd somehow misunderstood when Kevin said he was "developing strong feelings" for her. Of course, he had added that he didn't know what do to about them. Maybe he'd decided they weren't worth pursuing.

"Are you going to our singles' group meeting tonight?" Polly asked on that first Friday evening of September.

Lara held the phone between her ear and shoulder while she arranged an assortment of vegetables on a relish tray for Amanda's shower the next day. "No, I've got too much to do."

"I'm not going, either. I just don't feel like it."

Deciding to take a break, Lara went to the freezer and lopped out two hearty scoops of chocolate ice cream. Then she took the plastic dish and portable phone outside on the little porch off of the living room. Summer was still in the air, even though back-to-school sales raged on at all the local discount stores. Lara's mother had already returned to her part-time teaching position.

"So any news from Kevin?"

"No." Lara spooned a bite of ice cream into her mouth. "How 'bout you? Heard from Brent?"

"No."

She swallowed. "What is with these guys? Don't they know two awesome women when they meet them?"

"I take it you're referring to us? You and me? The two awesome women?"

Lara laughed. "Who else would I be talking about?"

"Well, I wanted to clarify things. . . ."

Again Lara laughed. She thanked God for a friend like Polly who could always find humor in every situation.

"Amanda looks like a fairy princess in her wedding dress," Lara said. "Wait until you see her."

"I'm sure I'll wish it were me walking down the aisle."

"I already wish it were me."

"Hey, I've got an idea. What if we go ahead and start planning our own weddings and just trust God to provide the grooms?"

"Yeah, right." Despite the sarcastic reply, Lara smiled and took another bite of ice cream.

"I'm serious. We trust God for everything else, right? Food, clothing, finances. Why not this area?"

"We are trusting God in this area. But we're supposed to know our grooms before we marry them. The other way around is like putting the cart before the horse."

"No, it isn't. It's stepping out in faith."

Lara laughed. Her friend was such a goof.

"When do you want to get married? Winter? Spring? Summer? Fall?"

"I don't care," Lara quipped. "ASAP."

"What's the rush? It can take *years* to plan a wedding."

"I suppose it could. But if Kevin proposed to me tonight, I'd marry him tomorrow."

"Oh, Lara, really!" Polly lowered her voice and drawled, sounding like a rich, eccentric great aunt. "The perfect wedding takes time to plan. Don't you read the bridal magazines?"

∽

Kevin was hard-pressed not to hoot as he and Tim stood directly beneath the porch on which Lara sat. He'd just ambled up the front walk with Tim, and Lara never heard their arrival.

"At least I know she'd say yes if I ever asked." He whispered the remark so Lara wouldn't hear.

"Don't do it, Kev," Tim whispered back. "You haven't seen my sister with her hair in curlers and green goop smeared all over her face. She looks like she's from outer space."

Kevin chuckled under his breath.

"Once a little brother, always a little brother. That's me."

"Shhh. . ."

"Sorry," Tim whispered back.

"This here's payback time." Kevin grinned, recalling how Lara had inadvertently eavesdropped on him. "I think I'll sneak up there and surprise her." He glanced at his watch, barely able to make out the Roman numerals in the darkness. "I think we've got some time, don't we?"

"About a half hour. Clayt's plane doesn't get in until 8:55, and when I called, it was running on time."

"Okay, I'll see you in thirty minutes."

"Right."

Kevin did his best not to make a sound as he entered the Donahues' lower flat. He made his way back through the empty living room, wondering where Mike was tonight. As he walked into the dining room, he could hear Lara's mother and grandmother discussing something in the master bedroom, and he got the impression the two ladies were discussing wedding particulars and the dresses they had purchased for Tim's big day.

Making his way upstairs without the aid of his crutch, Kevin tried not to let the old wooden steps creak beneath his weight. But he needn't have worried that Lara would hear his approach, because as he sneaked into the upper flat, she was laughing so hard she wouldn't have heard a door slam, let alone footfalls in the stairwell.

Even so, Kevin moved noiselessly through the living room until he came to the screened porch door. Because of the lighting in the house, Kevin knew Lara would be able to see him much better than he could her, so he leaned on the door frame and folded his arms as though he'd been standing there for hours.

"No, Polly, don't choose that color. I don't look good in pinks." Lara paused as if listening to the reply. "Oh yeah, that's right. By the time *you* get married, I'll be expecting my eighth child."

Kevin winced. Lara didn't really want eight kids, did she?

"I'm not a betting woman." Lara rose from her chair. "Besides, you're probably right. The way my life is going, you just might get married before me."

At that instant, Lara glanced at Kevin in the doorway and shrieked.

He laughed.

"Polly, I have to go. I'll call you later."

"I'd love to be listening in on that next conversation." He chuckled again.

Kevin stepped back as Lara yanked the door open and marched into the house.

She glared at him. "What are you doing here?"

"It's nice to see you, too. Say, did you know that when you're angry, your eyes take on a real pretty shade of green?"

Lara narrowed her gaze. "Don't try to charm me, Kevin Wincouser. How long were you standing there?"

"Oh. . ." He pretended he had to think about it. "Long enough to be in on the wedding plans."

At Lara's little yelp of indignation, Kevin laughed again—until she stormed toward him.

"Now, Lara."

She grabbed both sides of his shirt and clutched it in her fists. "You've got a lot of nerve showing up out of nowhere and listening to my private conversation with Polly."

"Are you really mad at me?" Kevin couldn't believe it. "It was all in fun, and since you were discussing *our wedding*—"

"What I was or wasn't discussing is no—"

Kevin kissed her, figuring that would take the wind out of her sails.

He was right.

Slipping his arms around her waist, he realized how much he'd missed her.

"Want to come to the airport with me? I asked Tim if he'd drive."

"Are you leaving?"

"No." Kevin watched as a look of relief spread across her features, and he realized she truly loved him. Lots of women had said they loved him, but he'd never seen the emotion staring back at him like he did now as he gazed into Lara's face. The sight endeared her to him all the more. Holding her closer, he rested his cheek against her forehead.

"What do you have to go to the airport for?"

"Hmm? Oh."

For a moment, Kevin had lost all track of his thoughts. But that's what this woman did to him. Skewed his senses. Made him think about marriage, a home, and even raising a family of his own—everything he'd avoided and even condemned for the last decade.

Collecting his wits, he answered Lara's question. "Clayt and I have been talking. We've sort of patched things up between us, and now he and his wife and my four-month-old nephew are flying into Milwaukee so we can have a long overdue family reunion."

"That's terrific!" Lara pulled back and smiled.

"I figured you'd approve."

"I do."

Kevin smirked. "Was that a practice?"

It took a moment, then she caught his meaning. "Oh, you!" Pushing away from him, Lara whirled around and stomped her way down the hallway.

He chuckled, thinking she was awfully cute when she was mad. "Hey, are you coming with me or not?"

"Yes. Let me get my purse."

Chapter 19

A muggy autumn breeze tousled Lara's hair and clothing as, one week later, she climbed out of her car and traipsed across the wide-open yard at the Regeneration Ranch. She hadn't seen or heard from Kevin since last Friday night. But it appeared that he and Clayt were well on their way to repairing their brotherly relationship, except Lara didn't know for sure. She'd been occupied with Amanda's shower the next day, and for the past month, Kevin had been attending a Bible study and church service with the Brambles so she hadn't seen him on Sunday. Then they both worked all week long, and as a result, Lara never did learn the final results of the Wincouser reunion.

And what about us? Kevin could have called me.

In all her confusion over where she stood with him, Lara bristled. According to Polly, Brent phoned her at least once a week, and they talked for hours.

Kevin and I live in the same city. A date would be nice. He's not exactly broke.

Regarding the latter, Lara had to admit she didn't really know his financial situation, although she suspected it wasn't as desperate as Kevin first imagined. He'd told her the financial counselor at County General had worked out a payment plan and even reduced his out-of-pocket costs because he agreed to pay a bulk of the debt up front.

He could at least afford a pizza for two.

She stomped into the barn, and suspecting Kevin was lurking about, she purposely strode past the office without a glance and headed for the corral where her kids were congregating.

"Hey!"

Kevin's voice hailed her, but she kept on walking.

"I thought that was you. Lara! Aren't you even going to stop and say good morning?"

She paused, remembering the Golden Rule. Pivoting, she manufactured a smile. "Good morning, Kevin." Whirling back around, she continued on her way.

"Um, 'scuse me."

"Yes?" Lara turned to face him again.

"Is something wrong?"

She tipped her head. "What could be wrong?"

Placing his right hand on the wooden edging below the office window, Kevin moved toward her. His limp seemed more pronounced today, and watching him hobble toward her lessened her annoyance.

"Well, I dunno, but I've been looking forward to seeing you today, and I guess I expected a little warmer greeting."

Lara took a few steps toward him. "If you want to have a relationship with me, you're going to have to put forth a little effort. When I don't hear from you for an entire week, I start to think you don't care."

"Look, I've been busy. My motor's running from sunup to sunset, and after I eat supper, I usually pass out from exhaustion. Sometimes I never even bother to change clothes. One day last week, I slept with my boots on. That's how tired I was."

While Lara empathized, she wasn't about to shrug off his inattentiveness. In her heart, she wanted a man who loved her more than his job.

"Life is never going to get less busy, and relationships are like attending church, praying, and reading our Bibles. We have to make time for them. So think about what you want to do and let me know." With that, she spun on her heel and continued her trek to the corral.

∽

Kevin watched Lara sashay out of the barn and decided women were a heap of trouble. She'd accused him of not caring, but he thought about Lara all the time. He'd even gone so far as to mention the idea of marrying her to Clayt. How'd she get it in her head that he didn't want a relationship with her?

He expelled a dismissive sigh. Fine. Let her be mad. Kevin wasn't going to let her wrap him around her little finger. He wasn't going to bend to her every whim. She'd walked in with an attitude today and decided to take it out on him. Great. Just great.

Irritation pumped through his veins and caused his temples to throb. He walked back to the office, where he'd been working on a project. He'd told Ron at breakfast this morning that his gait was unsteady and each word coming out of his mouth felt as thick as maple syrup. Kevin had definitely been overdoing it, and he had to slow down. His neurologist gave him a list of warning signs to watch for, and if he noticed two or more, he had to readjust his schedule or suffer a setback. Fortunately, the Brambles understood. Ron offered him a desk job the next few days, and Kevin accepted.

Planting himself in the worn leather chair, he stared at the spreadsheet before him. He had to admit that he felt rather wounded by Lara's terseness. He'd imagined an entirely different scenario. He thought she'd be happy to see him, and Kevin envisioned wrapping her in an embrace and kissing her pretty pink lips.

Well, maybe she just got up on the wrong side of the bed this morning.

He glanced at the bold-faced clock hanging on the wall. He'd give it until noon and see if she stopped in to apologize.

But noon came and went with no sign of Lara.

Making his way to the house for lunch, Kevin spotted her and a few other volunteers sitting with the kids on the lawn. Colorful plastic thermal-lined lunch containers were strewn all around them. Kevin was tempted to grab his lunch and join them, but he sensed Lara wouldn't appreciate it. Even now, as he paused to stare in her direction, it seemed she deliberately ignored him. Kevin felt surprised at how much that hurt.

Deciding he wasn't hungry after all, he retreated to the office and sat there a little amazed at himself. If this was a taste of how his life would be without Lara, the outlook seemed bleak at best. He needed her. But when had that happened? He had never needed another human being before. When had Lara Donahue wheedled her way into his heart?

A tap sounded on the large glass window, interrupting Kevin's deliberations. He looked at the doorway to see the object of his thoughts standing not even ten feet away, holding a tray.

"Can I come in?"

"Sure."

She entered and set her burden on the corner of the desk. "Caroline wanted you to have some lunch, and since she's juggling several minor crises right now, I offered to bring it out here."

"Thanks."

"She made you a ham sandwich, sliced tomatoes, cucumbers, and a fat slice of peach pie."

With his insides so stirred up, it was hard to think about food.

Kevin rose to his feet. "Lara, please don't be angry with me. I'll try to do better, okay? A lot of this is new for me, the relationship thing. It shouldn't be at my age, I realize that. But it is."

She slipped her fingers into the front pockets of her blue jeans. "Okay."

Stepping around the desk, he pulled her hands back out and held them, one in each of his. Then he leaned forward and kissed her cheek. "I missed you, and believe it or not, you were never far from my thoughts."

"Well, Kevin, you have to tell me that. How else am I supposed to know? I can't read your mind." There was a sweetness in her voice that soothed his soul.

"I'll try to remember that."

"And you might want to look into a cell phone package that offers free nights and weekends." Lara cleared her throat.

"Point taken."

She gave him a grin.

"Now, can I have a hug? Man cannot live by Caroline Bramble's cooking alone."

∽

Sunlight trickled through the flaming treetops as Kevin entered the church for

Tim and Amanda's wedding. *They couldn't have asked for better weather,* Kevin decided as he claimed a seat in the second pew from the front. He had arrived early, and as they'd discussed last night at the rehearsal, Kevin's job was to save seats for some Donahue cousins who were driving in from Ohio today. Tim's parents and grandmother would sit in the pew in front of him, and Lara, a bridesmaid, would be standing in the front.

A small ensemble near the platform began to play their stringed instruments, and more guests filed into the sanctuary. Kevin willed his tense muscles to relax. He felt edgy, especially since last night's practice. While he knew it wasn't a big deal and it didn't mean anything, Kevin hadn't been able to stop a knot of envy from forming in his gut when he watched Lara walk up the aisle with her hand hooked around another man's elbow.

"Excuse me. This seat taken?"

Kevin turned to his left and grinned when he saw Brent. "What are you doing here?" He stood, and the two men shook hands.

"I told Polly I'd be her date for today." Brent scooted into the pew and sat beside Kevin. "Would you believe there's not another guy in all of Wisconsin who would escort her?"

"No, I wouldn't believe that."

"Me, neither. But here I am anyway."

Kevin chuckled. "Where's Polly?"

"Talking to some friends in the lobby." Brent unbuttoned the jacket of his black suit.

"Look at you, all dressed up. Spiffy lavender shirt. Where'd you find that?"

"Bought it."

"Did you buy the suit, too, or is that rental?"

"I'll have you know I own my clothes, okay?"

Kevin laughed, and a few heads turned, so he quickly lowered his voice. "Well, if you never wear it again, they can always bury you in it."

"Yeah, that's what I figured, too."

Kevin grinned. He'd forgotten how much fun it was to razz Brent. Phone calls just weren't the same.

"You're lookin' mighty spiffy yourself, Wink."

"Thanks." He tugged on the lapels of his jacket. "I'm meeting all of Lara's family today, so I rented a tux."

"Cheapskate."

Kevin snickered at the quip.

"Polly tells me you and Lara are real serious."

"Yep. I'm going to marry her and live happily ever after."

"Asked her yet?"

"Not yet, but she knows it's coming. And she'll say yes. I heard her talking to

Polly about it awhile back."

"Well, I need to tell you something." Brent's voice sounded just above a whisper.

"About marrying Lara?" Kevin narrowed his gaze, studying his buddy's profile. Brent's jaw was clean shaven, and his dark brown hair appeared to have some special goop in it so it spiked up right above his forehead. Kevin wondered if the style of Brent's cut was that "bed-head" look that Lara said she disliked.

"I haven't been the friend you think."

"Shut up." Kevin stared straight ahead, knowing Lara would have told him if something had gone on between her and Brent.

"Wink, listen. . ."

Kevin whipped his gaze at him. "Do I have to remind you that you're in church?"

"I know where I am. In fact, I believe it's God who wants me to do this." He paused. "I need to apologize."

Kevin clenched his jaw.

"I purposely tried to make you jealous right from the start. I could see Lara cared for you that first day in your hospital room. I wished a girl would fawn all over me the way she fawned all over you. But back then, I was too proud and stubborn to admit it. So now I want to tell you I'm sorry."

"You serious?"

"Dead serious."

Kevin felt rather impressed. He could count the number of times on one hand that he'd heard Brent apologize. The recipients were all women, and Brent hadn't been genuinely repentant. In short, the act of contrition had served his purposes in one way or another.

But Kevin sensed this was very different.

"Apology accepted." He stuck out his right hand.

Brent clasped it, their gazes locked in silent challenge, then each man began to squeeze.

"Grip's still a little weak."

"Yeah, I'm workin' on it."

"Good. Wouldn't want you to turn into some kind of cream puff."

Kevin retracted his hand and grinned. "Not a chance."

People continued to fill the large, octagon-shaped sanctuary in anticipation of the ceremony. Polly showed up and claimed the seat beside Brent. Kevin found it amusing that the lilac print on her black dress matched Brent's attire.

Kevin leaned over to Brent. "Did you two do that on purpose?"

"Actually, no."

"Everyone's going to think you did."

"So what?"

Straightening in the pew, Kevin decided Brent must truly care for Polly if, one, he agreed to miss a Saturday rodeoing to escort her to a wedding, and two, he didn't care that they looked like a set of bookends.

The Donahue cousins arrived, and after the usher brought them to the pew, Kevin introduced himself. Then, out of courtesy, he, Brent, and Polly slid down to the other end. Minutes later, a heavyset woman in a stylish skirt and blouse took a seat at the organ's keyboard, and the processional began. When Kevin caught sight of Lara in the flowing emerald green dress, he had to force himself not to gape. Her light brown hair had been pinned up, but several tendrils spiraled down and brushed the tops of her shoulders. But along with admiration, Kevin felt a surge of jealousy rip through his being at the sight of the man guiding her down the aisle.

"Whoa, boy. Easy now. That poor groomsman can't help it that he was picked to walk down the aisle with Lara. Your turn's coming."

Kevin's gaze slid to Brent. "When did you start mind-reading?"

"I didn't." Brent smirked. "But it wasn't hard to tell what you were thinking when you turned the color of Lara's gown."

Swallowing his laughter, Kevin realized how foolishly he was behaving. He looked forward and found Lara's gaze on him. He sent her a wink. She smiled in return, and two pretty spots of pink appeared on her cheeks.

Brent leaned over again. "You've got nothing to worry about."

"You're right," he replied, feeling captivated as he regarded the woman with whom he planned to spend the rest of his life. "I don't."

Chapter 20

Lara thought her younger brother's wedding day had been beautiful. The ceremony went off without a hitch, and the fall weather was perfect for outdoor pictures afterwards. Making the day all the more wonderful for Lara was the fact that her relatives and friends seemed to like Kevin. Then again, what wasn't to like? Handsome with an endearing limp that was becoming less noticeable with each passing week, Kevin charmed his way into the Donahue women's hearts and laughed and joked with the men as if he'd been part of the family forever. With Brent to egg him on, the cowboys were the life of the party—second only to the bride and groom.

By six o'clock, a scrumptious fare was served by candlelight in an elegant banquet room, and by eight, a shiny white limousine arrived to whisk the newlyweds to an undisclosed location. Tomorrow they planned to board a plane to Nova Scotia, where they would honeymoon for the week.

"Tim and Amanda make such a sweet couple," Polly murmured.

Lara couldn't have agreed more as she stood outside the restaurant watching the limousine's taillights vanish into the night.

"But you know what I've learned?"

"What?" Lara looked at Polly.

"I've learned a bride to be can save a ton of money if she forgoes the DJ or live band."

"Are you still planning your wedding?"

"Sort of. I'm gathering data and deciding what I do and don't like as far as ceremonies and receptions go. I even found my dress and put a down payment on it."

Lara chuckled. "You are so silly."

"I beg to differ." Polly raised her chin. "I'm trusting God to provide the groom. I don't know who he is, and I've given up trying to figure it out. I'm hanging on to Psalm 37:4."

Lara listened as Polly recited the passage.

"In other words, as I delight myself in the Lord, His desires become my desires." She smiled. "The Lord gave me that verse when I was feeling sorry for myself one night. Afterwards, I started thinking and soon concluded that Jesus has to be my first love before I can have a husband."

"Sounds as if you're right on target." Lara gave her friend a smile.

"It's about time, eh?" Polly laughed. "Listen, it's freezing out here. Let's go in."
Lara agreed.

Reentering the building, Polly excused herself and headed for the ladies'
rest-room. Lara decided not to wait in the dim hallway and continued on to the
banquet room, where they'd left Kevin and Brent. But as she scanned the guests,
she didn't see any sign of them. Spinning on her heel, she strolled back into the
hallway. A heartbeat later, she thought she heard Kevin's voice and headed in that
direction. She passed the restrooms until she came to another darkened corridor,
where she found Kevin and Brent deep in conversation. When they spotted her,
however, neither man spoke another word.

"My apologies for interrupting."

She turned to walk away, but Kevin halted her.

"It's okay, Lara." He smiled and held out his right hand. Taking it, she stepped
forward. "You should probably hear this, too. Mac's up to her old tricks."

"Oh?" Lara glanced from Kevin to Brent.

"Mac says she's through talking. She's filing a lawsuit against Wink come
Monday morning."

Lara frowned and looked back at Kevin. "But I thought Mr. Blivens said she
didn't have a case."

In reply, Kevin expelled a weary-sounding sigh.

"She probably doesn't, but that woman's thinking is all backwards," Brent
said. "She somehow believes that if she sues Wink, she'll get his attention. If she
gets his attention, Mac thinks he'll marry her."

"Ain't gonna happen," Kevin drawled, giving Lara's hand a little squeeze.
Gazing into her eyes, he added, "Guess I'll have to get a lawyer after all."

"Well, maybe not."

Lara and Kevin simultaneously glanced at Brent.

"Why don't you plan to attend the championship in Kentucky, Wink? They're
looking for an announcer. We all think you'd fit that part, and if you accepted the
position, you could still rodeo."

Lara ignored the cry of opposition from her heart. She sensed Kevin cared
for her in a special way, but she felt certain she couldn't compete with the rodeo.

"What's attending the finals got to do with Mac?" Kevin asked, letting go
of Lara's hand and causing her to wonder if the gesture was indicative of his true
feelings.

Brent grinned. "I've got a plan." He caught sight of Polly, who appeared in
the corridor's entryway, then looked back at Kevin. "I'll tell you 'bout it later."

Disappointment filled Lara's being. She would have liked to hear Brent's
"plan."

The four of them ambled back to the reception area and socialized for a bit
longer. Lara tried to enjoy herself, but all the while, as she stood at Kevin's side,

she feared losing him to what he loved most—the life of a pro rodeo cowboy.

⁓

Fall continued on its course with sunshine, dry air, and cool temperatures. The days and weeks went by in a whir as Lara continued her job at the hospital, but she spent most of her free time at the ranch. She helped Kevin with chores, although it was obvious he didn't need her anymore. A social worker who loved people, Lara realized her deepest desire was to be needed. However, with Kevin on the mend, surpassing even the doctors' prognoses, he could pull his own weight at the Regeneration Ranch.

She attempted to convey those very thoughts to Kevin one evening.

"Lara, you know what your problem is? You think too much." He tossed her a smirk before disappearing behind one of the two horses the Brambles had recently purchased.

"I'm just trying to tell you how I feel." Exasperated, Lara scooped up a handful of straw and threw it at him.

Moments later, Kevin emerged around the backside of the mare, his blond hair and the shoulders of his red plaid shirt littered with prickly shafts. Lara had to swallow a laugh.

"I already know how you feel."

She raised her chin.

"But now you're gonna get it."

Seeing the glint of determination in his blue eyes, she bolted out of the barn. It dawned on her then that the one thing Kevin couldn't manage yet was to outrun her.

⁓

Since October was "Brain Injury Awareness" month at County General, special ongoing seminars were held for the general public, and Kevin's doctors asked him to speak at one of them. Lara felt so proud of Kevin's progress, and she thanked God every day for answering her prayers and healing him.

Yet despite those many uplifting and fun times they shared, discouragement began to nibble away at Lara's sense of peace. Kevin skirted discussions about the future, which only inflated her insecurities about the two of them. He now said he loved her, and Lara could see in his eyes that he meant each word. But she wondered if Kevin struggled with the idea of commitment. Determined to find the answer, she applied both their personality traits and their situation to every psychological evaluation she'd learned in school, although she only felt more confused at their inconclusiveness. At last, she decided Kevin was right. She *did* think too much. From that point on, she once again endeavored to give her fears to God and leave them in His all-powerful grip.

Polly, on the other hand, proved to be very little support, since she was distracted beyond reason by a certain handsome bull rider. She soon spouted off

PRCA standings with the proficiency of a doctor rattling off lab orders. However, because of her influence, Brent had "settled down," to the amazement of his friends. Best of all, he'd asked Jesus into his heart, and no one could have been happier to hear the news than Kevin—with Polly running a close second.

At long last, November arrived, and Kevin couldn't stop talking about the finals in Kentucky. In fact, Lara likened his excitement to that of a little boy at Christmastime. But as ironic as it seemed, his happiness only saddened her all the more. To her, it appeared that his former lifestyle still possessed his heart, and Lara wondered if it would ever belong to her.

"Lara, I'm not fool enough to entertain thoughts of bareback riding again." Kevin leaned against the side of her car and folded his arms. Rays from a faraway autumn sun shone through the now-barren treetops near the Brambles' gravel driveway. "What are you worried about?"

"I'm not worried." It was the biggest fib she'd ever told, and Kevin's expression said he saw right through it. Lowering her gaze, Lara kicked at the stones beneath her brown high-heeled shoes. She was still dressed in her Sunday attire, having come right to the ranch after church this morning so she and Kevin could have some time together.

"I don't need or want a·mother hen clucking at me the rest of my life."

Is that how he sees me? A mother hen? Clucking?

Lara felt the blood drain from her head and stop somewhere in her chest. Her heart threatened to explode with anguish.

"I apologize, Kev. I never meant to *cluck*."

He had the audacity to laugh.

"You know, if it bothered you so much, you could have said something sooner." Lara felt like she was choking on each word. "When people talk to each other, it's called *communication*."

A little frown knitted his brows. "Are you angry?"

"Why would I be angry?" The reply dripped with sarcasm. "You only called me a clucking mother hen and said you didn't want to spend the rest of your life with me."

Kevin pushed himself off the car. "I said no such thing."

Lara stomped around to the driver's side, but before she could fish her keys from her purse, Kevin caught her arm and spun her around to face him. By that time, however, she felt so wounded, tears leaked from her eyes.

"What's wrong?" He cupped her face and brought her gaze to his. "Are you crying?"

"You're a genius." She sniffed back an ounce of emotion.

Kevin swiveled around so her back was to the Brambles' farmhouse. "Cut it out, Lara. If Ron sees that I made you cry, he'll come out here with his shotgun."

She laughed in spite of herself. Ron was such a peaceable man that she wasn't sure he even owned a shotgun.

"There. That's better. You're pretty when you smile. I mean, you're pretty when you cry, too. It's just that I like it better when you're happy."

His stammering caused her to grin.

"Now, look, I didn't mean to hurt your feelings. But I've told you before I'm not going to ride again."

"I know. That's not what I'm worried about." Lara wiped the moisture off her cheeks with her fingertips. "I've been trying to tell you for weeks that I feel like the rodeo is the love of your life."

"Not so. Jesus has the number one slot."

"I'm talking about second to our Savior. It's the rodeo, not me. At the finals, I'm afraid you'll get around the rest of the cowboys, remember the thrill of that eight-second ride, and won't want to come back home."

"Home." A rueful smile curved his mouth. "This city, you. . . I'm really home, aren't I? Maybe I shouldn't have ever left."

His soft words tenderized her heart.

"Look, Lara, you've got nothing to fear. I'm not going to ride again. Ever."

"What if your friends find something else for you to do?"

Kevin shook his head. "I never thought I'd say it, but you're acting like an irrational female. All this time I thought you were levelheaded."

"That just proves you don't know me very well." Hurt mingled with irritation coursed through her veins. Glancing at the leather purse slung over her shoulder, she shoved her hand inside it and rummaged for her car keys.

Kevin grasped her upper arms and brought her around to stand in front of him. "I know you as well as I know anybody. Look at me."

Lara slowly raised her gaze to meet his unwavering stare.

"I love you. And this weekend at the finals, you'll see that I love you more than any rodeo. Even more than a championship."

"I don't want to go anymore." The truth was, she hadn't wanted to go in the first place.

"Hey!" He gave her a gentle shake. "Do you love me?"

"Yes."

"Okay, then." He grinned. "You just keep practicing. That's the right answer."

Lara wrenched herself free of his hold and gave him a playful sock in the arm.

∽

"There you are!" Polly came running at Lara at a full gallop. "Where have you been?"

Lara turned and pointed toward the refreshment stand. "I was in—"

"Come on!" Polly grabbed her wrist and led her into Freedom Hall, the midsection of the vast Exposition Center. "Oh, sister, if you missed this, Kevin would never speak to me again."

"You?" Lara was hard-pressed to keep up with her friend.

"Yeah, it's my job to make sure you're standing in this particular aisle at this particular time." Polly glanced at her watch. "Whew! I think we might even be three minutes early."

Lara didn't even ask. By now, she knew something was up—and she knew that "something" involved Mackenzie Sabino. For the past two days, the woman had all but planted herself in Kevin's path so he practically tripped over her. But that neither surprised nor upset Lara. She actually felt sorry for Mac. The petite redhead fell into that "poor little rich girl" typecast, and she thought she could buy anything she wanted, including Kevin's love. Moreover, Mac was obviously used to getting her own way and would rather wield manipulative threats than take no for an answer.

"Ladies and gentlemen, may I please have your undivided attention?"

Lara grinned at the announcer's Kentucky drawl.

"Back in June, our own Kevin Wincouser, known as 'Wink' to most all of us, got bucked off a horse and took a bad spill during a competition. He suffered what's called a traumatic brain injury."

"Yeah, and good thing he landed on his head, or he really might have hurt himself."

Glancing over her shoulder, she saw Brent walk up the aisle and stand next to Polly. Lara rolled her eyes at his smart remark, but several folks in the stands heard it and laughed.

"As a result of his accident," the announcer continued, "I'm sad to say Wink's rodeo days are gone forever."

The crowd moaned and booed.

"But he's here tonight to say good-bye to his fans and friends alike. . .and here he comes right now."

To her left, Lara watched as a lone figure of a man walked into the ring, leading a dapple gray horse behind him.

"Where's Mac?" Brent wanted to know.

"Sitting in the most expensive seat in the house, of course." Polly laughed.

Lara arched a brow. "This is all for Mac's benefit, I take it?"

"No. No, it isn't," Brent said. His somber expression told Lara he spoke the truth. "But this public farewell will put an end to Mac's plans right quick. Trust me."

"Okay." Lara was all for any solution that halted Mac Sabino's scheming ways.

Kevin came to stand in the center of the ring. The big-screen JumboTron magnified his entrance for all to see. He stopped and waved to the now-cheering crowd; then, once the noise level dropped, he began to speak into the microphone he evidently wore on the collar of his chambray shirt.

"I want to thank you all for your support over the years and for your prayers over the last five months. I mean it when I say it's by God's grace that I'm standing here, talking to you. But I had top-notch physicians, the best of friends, and I even found a brand-new family who helped me get through some tough times. Now I'm ready to start a new life. But there's just one thing I have to do first, so you'll have to pardon this rather personal moment."

Kevin cleared his throat and turned Lara's way, pinning her with his blue-eyed gaze.

"Lara Beth Donahue, I love you, and I'm asking you to be my wife. Will you marry me?"

Freedom Hall suddenly grew so quiet, everyone in attendance could hear a coin that clattered on the cement floor. But Lara couldn't get herself to move, let alone utter a syllable. She felt paralyzed by a strange mixture of awe and embarrassment.

Kevin took a step forward, his expression one of earnestness. "Lara, I need you."

Those were the very words she longed to hear.

Just then, Brent leaned over. "Honey, the world is watching. If you say no, Wink's in big trouble."

Lara shook off her shock. "I'm not going to turn him down. Are you crazy? I've been waiting half my life for this!"

Stepping past the grinning security personnel, Lara ran out to Kevin and flung herself into his outstretched arms. The cheers and whistles from the crowd were deafening, but Lara managed to hear Kevin's chuckles.

"So are you going to marry me or not?" His lips brushed her ear.

"Yes, I'll marry you," Lara replied with tears of joy in her eyes. "A thousand times yes!"

Wearing a triumphant smile, Kevin mounted the horse and pulled Lara up into the saddle behind him. Together they circled the arena, and Kevin waved to the bystanders. Lara thought it was as perfect an ending to his rodeo career as riding off into the sunset was to a good Western. But in reality, they had found love. They had found each other.

Even though Kevin had taken the long ride home.

Epilogue

The makeshift dressing room in the back of the church had been crowded while Lara and her bridesmaids carefully donned their gowns and applied their cosmetics. But now as "Cannon in D" melodiously resonated through the building's sound system, only Polly and Lara remained. They were minutes away from the bridal procession.

"I told you we'd save a ton of money by purchasing that wedding CD on the Internet."

"I had my doubts at first," Lara admitted, "but it sounds just as good as a live orchestra."

Polly agreed. "But honestly, I didn't think we'd pull this wedding off."

"Oh you of little faith."

Polly's emerald-green eyes widened. "Less than three months to plan an entire wedding and the reception…and here I've been planning mine for—" She paused. "For forever, it seems. When you and Kevin chose January of *this year* for your special day, I almost had apoplexy."

"Yes, I know." Lara smiled. "So did my folks."

"And with just cause." A smile curved Polly's red lips. "But we did it. . .and just look at you. You're gorgeous in that wedding gown!" She stepped back to take in the full view. "Just wait until Kev sees you. He won't be able to think straight. Let's just pray he's able to recite his vows."

Lara laughed. "Well, you're gorgeous, too." Polly's pale skin contrasted with her crimson bridesmaid dress in a flattering and very feminine way. The garnet pendant with its delicate gold chain around her neck added just the right touch. "Brent will take one look at you and forget which pocket of his tux he stashed our wedding rings in."

Polly appeared pleased by the remark.

Lara turned toward the mahogany-framed full-length mirror and gave her own appearance one last inspection. She felt beautiful in her white, pearl-studded, lacy gown, and she hoped Kevin decided she looked as good as she felt.

She faced Polly again. "I can't believe this day has finally arrived. I'm finally marrying the guy I've loved since junior high." She hugged her special friend and maid of honor. "Thanks for all your help with the planning."

Polly arched a brow. "I do expect reciprocation, you know."

"You got it," Lara promised. "As soon as you snag a groom, I'm here for you, girlfriend." She laughed. "But seriously, I have a feeling it won't be long before Brent proposes."

"I'm praying to that end."

The door opened, and Lara watched as her sister-in-law, Amanda, entered the dressing room. She was another of Lara's bridesmaids, so her attire matched Polly's.

"It's time, ladies." Amanda paused, then pointed to the speaker overhead. "The 'Bridal Chorus' is just beginning."

Lara and Polly gasped in unison. Then the three rushed out to join the rest of the bridal party in the church's foyer.

Lara found her father and took his elbow. She thought he looked quite dapper in his charcoal gray suit.

He bent his head and whispered, "You're a lovely bride—almost as pretty as your mother on our wedding day."

Lara smiled at the compliment and hugged his arm.

Polly handed her the bridal bouquet, a striking combination of white and burgundy roses. Then she clutched Brent's arm and they strode to the altar.

Finally it was Lara's turn to walk up the carpeted aisle, escorted by her dad. Step. Pause. Step. Pause. Cameras flashed from all around. Aunts, uncles, cousins, and friends smiled with pleasure. But Lara barely noticed the attendees' reactions. Instead her gaze was stayed on Kevin in his classic black tuxedo, awaiting her arrival at the front of the church. His sky-blue eyes had fastened onto only her, and Lara felt foolish for wondering over his reaction. Happiness filled her being. While it was a blustery winter day outside, it was forever summer in Lara's heart.

Dad slipped out of her hold and handed her over to Kevin.

"Who gives this woman in marriage?" The pastor asked.

"I do."

Lara thought her father's voice sounded thick with emotion, and a sentimental lump formed in her own throat.

Kevin took her gloved hand and placed it around his elbow. "You're beautiful," he murmured with a glimmer of love in his gaze. Next he led her up the few steps to the platform on which the pastor stood.

Lara felt dazed as the ceremony proceeded. She couldn't help but marvel at everything the Lord had done since June of last year when Kevin was airlifted into the emergency room with a head injury. He'd gone from a backslidden bareback bronc rider to a God-fearing cowboy in the ministry at the Regeneration Ranch, and, once upon a time, Lara never would have dreamed this day was possible.

Then again, all things were possible with God.

And when the pastor gave the cue and Kevin kissed her, sealing their vows to love, honor, and cherish from this day forward, Lara knew once more that God's Word was truth.

The Summer Girl

Dedication

To my former neighbors and precious friends
who resided on the 3900 block of Prospect Avenue
in Shorewood, Wisconsin, from 1965 to 1975.
Ours was a closely knit neighborhood
made famous by its Fourth of July block parties
and Mr. Sheldon's motorcycle rides up and down the street.
The memories I have of you all will remain near and dear to my heart.
A special hello to Patty Andrews. I hope you don't mind that I moved
my characters into your childhood home. . .and then remodeled it!

Chapter 1

Needs a *"Summer Girl."* Jena Calhoun glanced at the piece of paper Mrs. Barlow handed to her at church yesterday, then looked back up at the Spanish-looking house looming in front of her. According to Mrs. Barlow, the owner and occupant of this place, a lawyer by the name of Travis Larson, would be expecting Jena.

"You'll be perfect for the position," insisted old Mrs. Barlow, who lived next door to the Larsons. "Travis's daughters will adore you, and the job will solve all your problems."

Yes, it sure would, Jena thought as she neared her destination. Located on the corner of Prospect Avenue and Shorewood Boulevard, the two-story hacienda had a white stucco exterior with a red tile roof. It looked like it belonged in Mexico, not in this small suburb of Milwaukee, Wisconsin. A tall redwood fence surrounded a tiny courtyard, and a narrow roof above the back door joined the house to a little apartment that sat above the two-car garage.

Jena made her way up the front steps, her palms sweating and her stomach filled with perpetual flutters. She hadn't ever been good at impressing others. She only knew how to be herself: Jennifer Ann Calhoun—Jena for short.

But would that be enough to get her the job?

Lord, I need Your help. . . .

Taking a deep breath, she pressed on the doorbell. Within a minute, the door swung open, and she found herself looking up into the face of a very handsome man with a very stern countenance.

"Yes?"

"Hello," she began, smiling politely, "I'm Jena Calhoun, and I'm here to interview for the summer girl position."

The dark-headed man's expression changed from severe to surprised. "You? You're Jena?"

"Why, yes. Is there a problem?"

"Well, no. . . ." The man opened the door a bit wider and beckoned her inside. "I was just expecting someone a little younger—like, fifteen years old."

"Oh?"

The man indulged her with a patronizing smile. "Usually summer girls are teenagers," he explained. "I was expecting a fifteen-year-old."

"I see." Jena chewed her lower lip in contemplation. Her friend Mary Star had given her a lift to Mayfair Mall, a popular shopping center on Milwaukee's west side. From there, Jena had taken two city buses to get here to the small village of Shorewood, a suburb on the shores of Lake Michigan. It seemed such a shame that now she wouldn't even get an interview. "Well," she said at last, "thanks anyway."

She had turned to leave when the man grabbed her elbow. "Whoa! Where you going?"

Jena swung around and looked at him, taking note of his frown and the concern in his chocolate brown eyes. "I'm twenty-six. I guess I'm too old to be a summer girl."

The man chuckled. "Perhaps, but let's talk anyway." He guided her into the well-lit living room. Six tall white wood-framed windows graced the entire front wall. A sofa and matching love seat, upholstered in greens and mauves against an ivory background, had been expertly placed on plush cream-colored carpeting. Jena wondered if the man was going to ask her to slip out of her shoes before she walked on the immaculate wall-to-wall rug.

He didn't.

"Come in, please, and sit down. Maybe I'll redefine the summer girl position and interview you as a possible nanny." He grinned.

Jena, however, wondered if she'd just been insulted. She thought the title of "nanny" sounded so. . .subservient. She sat down on the sofa anyway as the man took a place on the love seat across from her.

"So you're the girl—I mean, the woman Mrs. Barlow recommended."

"Yes, I guess I am."

"Hmm. . ." The man appeared thoughtful. "Mrs. Barlow kept referring to you as 'such a sweet girl,' so, obviously, I pictured a girl."

"Sorry." Jena didn't know what else to say, and she was beginning to regret even coming here.

"Oh, no need for apologies." Travis cleared his throat. "I understand you and Mrs. Barlow attend the same church."

"Yes, that's right."

"In Menomonee Falls."

Jena nodded.

"You know," he began with a puzzled frown, "I never did figure out why Mrs. Barlow went all the way out there just for church when there's one not even a mile away from here."

"Her son's family lives in the Falls," Jena told him, "so she spends Sundays with them, and of course, she's a proud grandmother."

"Oh, right. I forgot about her son and his family." The man rubbed his palms together. "Well, enough chitchat. Let's get down to business. I'll tell you about the job. I have two daughters, Mandi and Carly. Mandi is six, and Carly is three.

My sister has cared for them since my wife died, shortly after Carly's birth. But then Glenda, my sister, decided to elope." Traces of sarcasm suddenly tainted his voice. "Not only did Glenda leave me without child care, but she ran off with my assistant, which leaves me overworked at the office. Nice sister, huh?"

"Nice assistant," Jena quipped.

"Yeah, that too," he muttered.

The man relaxed against the back of the love seat, and Jena noticed the sleeves of his crisp white dress shirt were rolled to the elbow. He wore a loosened necktie and black dress pants. Jena thought he looked like he belonged on the cover of *GQ Magazine*.

Her gaze moved back up to the man's face. His gently angled jawline was clean shaven, and his lips appeared soft and tender, though bent into a natural smirk. His eyes were a deep brown, and Jena noticed they mirrored her assessment. From his expression, Jena couldn't tell what he thought of her, but in just two words, she figured she could sum him up: handsome and arrogant.

"By the way, my name is Travis Larson."

"Yes, I figured as much."

The smirk broadened. "Well, it's a pleasure to meet you, Miss Calhoun."

She smiled a reply, unsure if she could return the sentiment.

"Do you drive?"

"Yes."

"Good. My girls are involved in a lot of activities. Swimming, gymnastics, a weekly playgroup."

"I don't own a car."

Travis waved off her remark. "I do. I own two, in fact. You can use the station wagon."

Jena lifted an inquiring brow. "I can?"

"Maybe this won't be so bad after all," he mused aloud, gazing off into the direction of the sleek black grand piano, which jutted out from the corner of the living room. His gaze shifted back to Jena. "Do you like children?"

"Yes."

"Are you in school?"

"Yes. I attend Lakeview Bible College."

"Bible college, huh?"

"That's right."

"Are you taking summer classes?"

"No."

"Good."

"Good?" Jena raised surprised brows.

"I wouldn't want your schooling to interfere with your caring for my children."

"Oh."

"What's your major?"

Jena cleared her throat. "I majored in home economics with a minor in child development."

Travis looked taken aback. "Do women still major in those things? Sounds kind of obsolete to me, considering this day and age."

Jena merely shrugged. He was entitled to his opinion, faulty as it was.

"What do you hope to do once you graduate?"

"Manage a daycare center or teach kindergarten in a private school."

"Hmm. . ." He didn't look very impressed. But after a moment's deliberation, a slow grin spread across his face. "You know what? This is perfect! You can practice your home economic skills here in my household and use your child development techniques on my girls. You're hired." Travis stood.

"I am?" Jena stood, too. "But—"

"I'll pay you three hundred fifty dollars a week plus room and board. You'll have access to a car, but I'll take care of all expenses, like gas, tires, tune-ups. In return, I'll expect you to care for my girls from six o'clock a.m. until they go to bed at eight o'clock at night. . .six days a week. You may have Sundays off."

Jena's eyes widened. To her, a poor college student, it sounded like a great deal! She had run out of money last week, after getting laid off nearly a month ago from her part-time job as a waitress. Fortunately, her wee bit of savings and an unexpected grant had carried her through a few weeks. Then her roommate and best friend, Lisa, moved out of their apartment. Lisa had decided to go back home so she could save money for her upcoming wedding, and now Jena had to be out by the end of the month.

But this job seemed a perfect solution to her financial situation. She'd make a lot more money as Travis Larson's summer girl than she had earned waitressing, and she'd have a car and a place to live until the fall. By then, perhaps she'd have enough money saved to finish her final semester of college and get another apartment.

"Miss Calhoun?" Travis drawled, sounding as though he was preparing to cross-examine a witness. "What do you say? Do Mandi and Carly have a new summer girl?"

Jena looked across the room and straight into Travis Larson's mahogany eyes. Something about his self-assured demeanor troubled her. She wondered if she'd really be able to work for him effectively, a handsome widower with dark, chestnut-colored hair and an ego the size of Montana. . . .

"I want to accept, but—"

"But what?"

"Well, I do need the job; however—"

"However?" He shook his head before arching a perplexed dark brow. "I don't understand your hesitation."

Jena sighed. Maybe she could work around his ego. She really needed the money. "Could I think about it?"

"Of course." Travis glanced at his wristwatch. "I'll leave the room for, say, ten minutes. How's that?"

Jena gave him a subtle nod. She had really wanted more than ten minutes, but the time allotment would have to do.

True to his word, Travis exited, and Jena sat back down on the sofa. Leaning forward, she folded her hands over her knees and prayed for wisdom. *Lord, what do I do? You know my financial needs. Should I take this job? And what about Mr. Larson? Can I work with him?* She paused in thought. *Can I somehow minister to this family? Is this Your will?*

She mulled over the details. The money sounded great, and she wouldn't mind caring for children all summer. She could be outdoors with them, take them to the beach. "Miss Calhoun?"

Jena lifted her head. "Yes?"

"May I call you Jena?"

"Certainly," she said with a little smile.

"Please call me Travis."

"I'll try," she stated honestly. However, with such a commanding presence, he seemed more like a Mr. Larson.

He left the room again, and Jena continued her inner debate. Maybe he'd turn out to be a really nice guy once she got to know him. She frowned. Were lawyers really "nice guys"?

"Jena?"

She looked up at Travis, standing at the entrance of the living room once more. "Yes?"

"May I show you photographs of my girls?" He stepped forward, holding a picture frame in each hand. "These are this year's school pictures." He handed one to Jena. "That's Amanda Lyn—Mandi for short."

"Oh, she's cute," Jena said, looking at the little blond girl with the toothless smile and cocoa-colored eyes.

"And this is Carlotta Leann—Carly. She's named after my wife's grandmother."

Jena smiled. "I'll bet she's just as precious as she as looks." Huge brown eyes in a little round face surrounded by blondish-brown curls peered out from the picture frame. "They're both darling," Jena said, handing back the photographs.

For the first time, Jena saw Travis's face split into a full-fledged smile. "Thank you." He glanced from one picture to the next. "I'm very proud of my girls, and. . . I think the three of you will get along."

Jena still hesitated. After all, her ten minutes weren't up.

Suddenly his expression fell, and his attitude crumbled along with it. "Look," he said, sitting down beside her, "I'll be honest with you. I'm in a terrible bind.

I've got no one to take care of my children and a law firm to run. I've interviewed dozens of summer girl applicants, and I wouldn't leave my goldfish with any of them, let alone my daughters. You are the first decent one to ring my doorbell. And if Mrs. Barlow says you're a sweet girl, I trust it's true. Mrs. Barlow has been my next-door neighbor for the last eight years, and she's one tough old lady—no offense intended," he added quickly. "I mean, quite the opposite, really."

Jena was stunned by his candidness.

So stunned she accepted the job.

"Oh, that's great," Travis said, smiling, and Jena thought he actually looked. . . grateful! Then he glanced at the framed photographs, still in his hands, before looking back at her. "Just one more thing, Jena."

"What's that?"

He paused, and his gaze returned to hers. His dark eyes held an almost pleading look. "Can you start today?"

Chapter 2

Okay, you can come down now," Travis called up the stairs.

A couple of doors squeaked open, and two pairs of feet came running down the carpeted steps.

"Was she another dud, Daddy?"

Jena looked expectantly at Travis, but he didn't even glance her way. He just smiled fondly at the little girl hugging him around the knees.

"Hardly a dud, sweetie. We've got ourselves a summer girl. Look." The little girls peered curiously at Jena, and Travis made the introductions.

"She doesn't look like a summer girl, Daddy," Mandi said precociously.

"Well, maybe we'll call her your new nanny, then."

"You know, I really would rather be a summer girl," Jena interjected. She smiled at Travis's surprised expression and added, "Summer is my favorite time of year."

"Mine, too!" exclaimed Mandi.

"Mine, too!" little Carly mimicked.

"Terrific!" Travis said with a clap of his hands. "I can tell you two girls are going to like Jena."

"Miss Jena," she corrected. At Travis's wondering glance, she explained, "During my internship last year, I learned that it's best for children to address adults respectfully by using a preface such as Miss, Mr., or Mrs. But your girls don't have to use my last name, since I think that would be too formal for this situation. They may simply refer to me as Miss Jena."

"I see." The smirk returned, and Travis looked much like that handsome, arrogant man Jena saw just minutes ago. "Any other rules that I should be aware of. . .Miss Jena?"

"Hmm. . . Well, no, I think that's it," she replied, feeling her face warm with embarrassment.

"Good." Travis turned to his daughters. "Mandi, Carly, Miss Jena is going to be your new summer girl." He suddenly frowned and looked back at Jena. "Somehow that doesn't sound quite right, the words 'Miss Jena' and 'summer girl' in the same sentence."

"I know, Daddy," Mandi said, "Miss Jena can be our summer lady."

Travis laughed. "All right. Summer lady it is."

Jena shrugged, feeling more than a little chagrined now.

"Can the girls and I show you the apartment you'll be staying in?"

"Sure." She followed Travis and his daughters, who bounced and skipped beside their daddy. They walked through the kitchen, out the back door, and into the courtyard, which was more like an enclosed patio complete with a round white wrought-iron table and matching chairs. They passed under the walkway until they arrived at another door. It was painted white, and a little half-moon seemed to be smiling lopsidedly at her.

Travis pulled a ring of keys from out of his pocket and unlocked the door. "The apartment is pretty much furnished," he told Jena. "My sister used to live up here."

"But then she married Tony," Mandi stated informatively. "And now Daddy has no one to watch me and Carly."

"Yes, I do," Travis replied as they all walked up the polished wooden stairs. "I have Miss Jena to watch you."

"Oh yeah."

Chuckling at his daughter, Travis unlocked another door at the top of the stairs. They all entered the living room, where the two girls made for the overstuffed sofa and flounced on it as though they'd done it a thousand times before. They sank into it, all giggles and flailing limbs.

Smiling, Jena looked around the room. The walls were a dusty rose, the woodwork painted white. Ivory draperies hung on four large windows that looked out over the quiet tree-lined avenue. A deep maroon fabric covered the sofa, the same color as the carpet. In the corner stood a small tea table and chair, and on the adjacent wall were two built-in bookshelves.

"After my wife, Meg, died," Travis explained, "I supplied this apartment with our old furniture so my sister would be comfortable up here. Then I bought new items for my place, thinking they would somehow ease the pain of losing my wife."

"Did they?" Jena inquired softly.

Travis gave her a pointed stare. "Nope. Not a bit." He quickly changed the subject. "Mandi, Carly. . .let's show Miss Jena the rest of her new home, shall we?"

"Okay, but I'll do it, Daddy," Mandi said. She jumped off the sofa and took Jena's hand. "This is where you eat," the little girl said as they entered the dining room.

Jena surveyed the soft-pink walls, the same color of the living room. A white dining set and four matching chairs occupied the center of the dining area. Against one wall was a built-in china hutch, and Jena decided that this was nicer than any dining room in any apartment she had lived in since she'd left home.

Then suddenly, she thought of her family. Jena wished she could phone them and share the news of this blessing—and, yes, she already sensed this job was a godsend. Unfortunately, her family probably couldn't care less. They'd never been close, and only Jena claimed Christ as her Savior; the rest of her family members resided in determined unbelief.

Still, she prayed for them daily and trusted the Lord to change their hearts as only He could. Jena also prayed that she'd have a close-knit family someday—a family that loved each other and enjoyed doing things together, unlike her own parents and brother who had always operated independently of each other. In fact, her family background was why Jena had selected home economics and child development as her fields of study—she longed for a real family someday, and she was determined to do the best job possible caring for it.

"And this is where you cook," Mandi told her, pulling her into the kitchen.

The room was tiny, but the whitewashed walls and matching mini-blinds made it seem like less of a cracker box. An apartment-sized refrigerator and stove, a standard-sized sink, and a very narrow counter were the kitchen's only fixtures. Nevertheless, it appeared practical enough.

"This is your bedroom," Mandi said, running forward, then sailing headlong onto the bed. Carly followed right behind her, and soon both little girls were jumping on the bare mattress.

"All right, that's enough," Travis told them, lifting each child off the bed. "I have no time to take you to the hospital for stitches today." He looked at Jena. "My sister had her own bedding and towels which she took with her, so I'll have to purchase some for you."

"That's not necessary. I own those essentials."

Travis shrugged his broad shoulders. "Well, okay. But if you need anything else, let me know."

"I will. Thanks."

"Here's the bathroom, Miss Jena!" Mandi cried excitedly. Her dark eyes sparkled, and when she smiled, the entire hallway seemed to light up.

"I see your front teeth have come in since you had your school picture taken," Jena remarked, and Mandi smiled even more broadly to show off her two new pearly whites.

Jena peered around the pixie and looked into the bathroom. It was more than adequate, and she whispered a prayer of thanks for such a comfortable place in which she could live.

"You can do your laundry in my washer and dryer," Travis offered. "Just do it during the day, because I usually wash our clothes at night. My sister would usually throw in a load while the girls were watching TV and while dinner was cooking."

"So I'm to make supper?"

Travis nodded, but then his expression turned to one of concern. "You can cook, can't you?"

"Oh yes," Jena replied, smiling. "In fact, I love to cook!"

"Well, that'll be a nice change," Travis said on a facetious note. "Glenda's specialty was macaroni and cheese out of the box."

"And peanut butter and jelly," Carly piped up happily.

Travis smiled at his youngest, then back at Jena. "I don't often make it home for dinner, though," he informed her, "so you don't have to worry about me. Just feed the girls—and yourself, of course."

"Sometimes Aunty Glenda let us eat up here with her," Mandi said.

Carly nodded. "We had a picklenic."

"A picnic," Mandi corrected.

Little Carly just nodded.

"How fun," Jena said warmly, although she felt a little sorry for Travis. *He doesn't often make it home for dinner with his daughters,* she mused. And, sadly, it reminded her of her own upbringing, her parents working constantly with little or no time to spend with their children. Jena and her brother often fended for themselves in between the wide gamut of sitters who came and went.

"Well?" Travis asked, bringing Jena out of her thoughts. "What do you think?"

"I think I'll be very comfortable here," she replied gratefully. "Thank you."

"You're welcome. When can you move in?"

Jena chewed her lower lip in contemplation. She had to be out of her apartment by the end of the month, which was just days away, and she didn't have much to pack. "I don't know," she said at last. "Anytime, I guess."

"Great." Travis pulled three keys off his ring. "This is for the car," he said, putting it into Jena's palm, "this is your apartment key, and this is for my house."

Jena looked them over and nodded.

"Move in whenever you like. Today would be fine with me, and I'm sure the girls would love to help you move."

Mandi and Carly both nodded exuberantly.

"But my apartment—it's in Jefferson County," Jena said. "Or don't you mind me taking the girls that distance?"

"Are you a good driver?"

"Well, yes, I suppose I am."

"Speeding tickets?"

"Never!" she exclaimed.

An amused expression crossed Travis's face. "Okay, just make sure the girls wear their seat belts. You can use the station wagon to haul all your stuff over here."

"Well, the good news is I'll only have to make one trip," Jena informed her new employer. "I don't have a whole lot." She snapped her fingers. "Oh, but I forgot—I'll have to return my apartment key at my landlord's house if I move out today."

"Where does your landlord live?"

"Just a few miles from the college I attend, but it'll take extra time. Then I'll have to put in a change of address at the post office. . ."

"Jena, do whatever you have to do; just take Mandi and Carly with you. Have them help you. It'll be good for them, and it'll be great for me," he added emphatically.

"Okay, sure."

They all walked back through the apartment and out the front door. Travis waited for Jena to lock it before continuing down the stairs.

"Anything else I should know?" she asked.

Travis thought it over, then shook his head. "I don't think so. But here," he said, pulling out his wallet, "let me give you my business card so you can phone me if something urgent arises. I have an extra cell phone you can use." He handed her the card, followed by a fifty-dollar bill.

Jena gave him a quizzical frown. "What's this for?"

"Dinner—and whatever else you might need to pick up. There's not a lot of food in the house." He turned pensive before pressing another twenty-dollar bill into her palm. "Come to think of it, we really don't have any food in the house."

Jena tried not to laugh. "Don't worry. The girls and I will go grocery shopping right after we get my things and finish my errands." She turned to the little faces gazing up at her. "Mandi and Carly," she said with a smile, "we have our work cut out for us today!"

Chapter 3

Jena dialed the cell phone number of her friend Mary Star Palmer to say she didn't need a ride back to school. When Star heard Jena had gotten the job, she was almost as relieved as Jena.

"Now we just have to find me a summer job," Star said. "I'm not getting any bites here at the mall."

"Well, let's keep praying about it. . .and I'll call you later."

After hanging up the Larsons' phone, which hung on the kitchen wall, Jena scooted the girls into the car. Taking a few minutes to familiarize herself with the dashboard, she stuck the key into the ignition and backed out of the garage. As she neared her apartment, Jena stopped at a local fast-food restaurant and ordered lunch. A deep-fried aroma of cheeseburgers and French fries filled Travis Larson's Volvo wagon, and Jena promised herself they would eat healthier at dinnertime. After they arrived at the dingy shoe box of a place that Jena called home, she seated Mandi and Carly at the scuffed-up table, then served lunch.

"Wait, don't eat yet," Jena said just as Mandi bit into her burger. "We have to pray."

The girls glanced at each other, then looked, wide-eyed, at Jena, who folded her hands and bowed her head. Peeking over her lashes, she watched as Mandi and Carly followed her lead.

"Thank You, Jesus, for this food. Please use it to make our bodies strong so we can get all our work done this afternoon. In Your name, we pray. Amen." Lifting her gaze, she smiled at the girls. "Okay, now we can eat."

They regarded her with curiosity shining in their brown eyes.

"Do you pray at your house?" Jena asked.

With mouths full, they both shook their heads.

"Do you know who Jesus is?"

Mandi and Carly bobbed their heads and smiled.

"He's God," Mandi said after swallowing her food. "Mrs. Barlow told us about Him."

"Wonderful!"

"And God made this whole world," Carly declared, spreading her arms with a dramatic flare that caused Jena to grin. "He even made this hamburger!"

"No, people at the restaurant made the hamburgers," Mandi retorted.

"You're both right," Jena cut in before a heated debate ensued. "God made the cows, and cows are the beef, and the beef is what the cooks at the restaurant use to make the hamburgers."

"See," Mandi told her little sister.

The reply was all but lost on Carly, who started a new subject about cows that lasted for the remainder of lunchtime. Once they'd finished eating, Jena instructed the girls as to how to clean up.

"My mom died," Mandi blurted as she tossed her hamburger wrapper in the trash.

"Yes, I know," Jena said on a rueful note. "Your dad mentioned it. How did she die?"

"She had cancer."

"I'm sorry to hear that." Jena's heart went out to the little girl.

Carly, on the other hand, seemed oblivious to the conversation as she balanced on her tiptoes and deposited her garbage into the tall blue plastic bin.

Mandi didn't say any more about her mother, so Jena didn't push the subject. Instead, she assigned tasks. She pulled out the small canister vacuum cleaner and showed Mandi how to use it. Next she gave Carly a spray bottle of the organic orange nonpoisonous "cleans everything" solution her friend Lisa used to sell and showed the little girl how to wipe down the furniture.

"Do a good job for me so I'll get my security deposit back, all right?"

"What's a s'curity posit?" Carly asked as she sprayed the liquid onto a table.

"That's the money I had to put down on this apartment when I first moved in. If I leave this place nice and clean, my landlord will give me my money back."

"Down worry," Mandi said, "we're good cleaners. You'll get your money back."

Jena smiled, and with Mandi and Carly now occupied, she began opening drawers and closets, stuffing things into boxes. Since the apartment came furnished, there wasn't much to pack. Before long, the air smelled like a ripe orange grove. Mandi had finished vacuuming and decided to dust with Carly. The two left no surface untouched.

Awhile later, Jena had the Volvo packed with everything she owned. *My life in the back of a station wagon,* she thought, feeling a bit blue. But then she heard the girls giggling as they jumped off the apartment building's front steps, and she realized that things weren't all that important in life. What mattered most were people.

"Mandi. Carly," she called, opening the door to the backseat. "Let's go. We've got to drop off my keys and stop at the grocery store."

Carly pouted. "But that's going to take twenty weeks!" she said, waving her hands in a theatrical manner.

Jena laughed. "It better not."

"How come?" Mandi wanted to know as she climbed into the deep-green car.

"Because in twenty weeks, I'll be back in school. My last semester, then I graduate—Yes!"

"How come you can't stay with us forever?" Carly asked as Jena fastened the seat belt around her.

"Well, because—" Jena felt her heart constrict. *These poor kids! First their mother dies, then their aunt takes off and gets married, and now I'm counting the days until I'm back in school.* "I can't stay with you forever," she tried again, "because I'm not part of your family. But we can always be friends, okay?"

"Okay," Carly agreed with an easy smile.

"My Aunty Glenda is part of our family," Mandi countered with a perception far beyond her six years, "but she can't stay with us forever because she married Tony."

Jena didn't know what to say. Relationships in her own family unit had been cast off, discarded. Did anything last forever in this throwaway society?

"Know what? The truth is, only Jesus lasts forever. He'll stay by you and never leave you for anything. Now that's a happy thought, isn't it?"

The girls nodded, and Mandi turned to gaze out the window. Carly kicked her sandaled feet up and down.

"Can we go now, Miss Jena?" Carly asked. "Twenty weeks is gonna come really fast."

"Yes, it is," Jena agreed with a little laugh. "And you're right. We can't sit around chatting all day. There's lots of work to be done before twenty weeks are up!"

∽

"I'm glad you got your babysitting problems taken care of, Trav."

He nodded in reply to Craig Duncan's comment. As the senior partner of Duncan, Duncan, and Larson, Craig had shouldered the burdens caused by Travis's many absences since Glenda left.

"Do you think you'll be prepared to take the Hamland case tomorrow?"

"Oh sure. Not a problem. I'm very familiar with the case."

"Good."

Craig sat back in his burgundy leather office chair and put his feet up on his paper-laden desk. "So what's this girl like?"

"What girl?" Travis asked, preoccupied with the file he held.

"The one you hired to babysit!"

"Oh. . .sorry, Craig." Travis looked up and gave the grizzled older man his undivided attention. "She's great. Her name is Jena. She's in her midtwenties, just finishing up college, and she needs a job for the summer."

"Interesting. . ."

"And she's a home ec major." Travis gazed back at the contents in the file.

"Oh, is she?" Craig rubbed his grizzled jaw. "Well, this does sound like a perfect match, doesn't it? Too bad she can't earn a couple of college credits while she works for you."

Travis shrugged. "That's her department."

Craig chuckled. "You're all heart, Trav."

The quip caused him to grin, and he glanced back at his business partner. Since the day they met, Craig reminded him of a mad scientist. Fluffy gray hair, keen blue eyes. An intelligent man, but somewhat scatterbrained. Capable, but highly disorganized. Craig's son, Josh, on the other hand, was the extreme opposite. Stout and blond, Josh threw a conniption if paper clips in his desk drawer weren't in their proper place. Most of the time, Travis felt his duty in the office was to serve as some sort of balance between the two men and to encourage Marci, their secretary who threatened to quit every other Friday.

Then there was Yolanda. The dark-haired beauty was the firm's intern, and if there ever existed a woman whom Travis would hate to come up against in court, it would be her. She could dig up dirt on Mother Teresa.

"So is she pretty?" Craig asked.

"Who?"

"Your summer girl!"

Travis gave himself a mental shake. "Oh yeah, she's okay." He thought about Jena's full figure—a little too full for his liking. But she had pretty hair, shoulder length and strawberry blond. She had an oval, freckled face with a healthy complexion. But her blue eyes said more than her naturally pink lips, and as she sized him up this morning, Travis could tell he didn't measure up to her standards. He saw it in her expression, as cut and dry as the Hamland's lawsuit. Of course, he really didn't care what Jena Calhoun thought of him personally. He'd hired her to take care of his daughters, not him.

"Okay? Just okay?" Craig chuckled and lifted his feet off the desk. "Well, she must have impressed you if you left your most precious commodities with her, having only made her acquaintance this morning."

"Sure, she impressed me. She's got that wholesome motherly look about her, and she goes to a Bible college, which means she's probably honest and trustworthy, and my neighbor Mrs. Barlow gave her a glowing recommendation. That pretty much cinched it for me."

Craig pursed his thick lips and sniffed. "Look, Trav, I hope it works out for you. You're a partner in this law firm, and we need you here."

"I understand, and things are going to work out great," he replied, perceiving the comment as something of a threat. If he didn't pull his weight, Craig and Josh could easily let someone buy him out. Yolanda might be a candidate. She had the ability to sway Craig with amazing ease, and he frequently took her side on the various issues that had emerged in recent weeks. Moreover, Craig owned the deciding shares.

That's why he needed Jena, and Travis felt a twinge of desperation at the thought of her quitting her position. He had muddled through the last month while Mandi was in school and Carly in daycare. But now that summer was here, he would much prefer the girls be at home, enjoying the sunshine and a less hectic schedule. If they caught a cold, Jena could nurse them back to health, and he wouldn't have to ask a colleague to cover him in court as he'd done in the past. On the nights he worked until midnight—or beyond—Jena could have the girls fed and tucked into bed by the time he came home so he could pick up where he'd left off at the office.

Yes, Jena had to work out. And if there truly was a God in heaven like Meg used to insist, then He would see to it that these arrangements were a success. Mandi and Carly's well-being depended on it.

And so did his career.

Chapter 4

When Travis walked into the back hall at 7:55, the enticing smell of oregano and garlic met him. He made his way into the kitchen and placed his briefcase on the table, along with the bag of greasy tacos he'd purchased on the way home. The glass pan on the stove caught his eye. He crossed the brightly decorated room and peeled back the tin foil.

"Lasagna." Travis's mouth began to water, and his stomach rumbled.

Suddenly he heard a loud boom above him, and he suspected his oldest daughter had just jumped off her bed—something he was forever telling her not to do. She'd crack the plaster ceiling one of these days—either that or crack her skull.

He listened as thundering footfalls raced across the second floor and down the steps.

"Daddy's home!" the girls cried in succession. "Hi, Daddy!"

He knelt down to receive their welcome. His exuberant daughters nearly knocked him onto his back. "Hey, little princesses. . . ." They smelled good, like baby shampoo and lotion. He kissed them and gave them each a squeeze. "What are you still doing awake?"

"Miss Jena said we could come down for a good night kiss," Mandi informed him.

"Ah. . ."

"But now we hafta go back up to hear the rest of our story," Carly chimed in.

"Winnie the Pooh," Mandi announced, "but it's not the baby picture book. It's the real book."

Travis lifted his brows, hoping he looked impressed.

"But Miss Jena is letting Carly look at the picture book while she reads to us."

"I see." Travis stood. "Well, don't let me keep you."

He grinned as his girls took off running, then Mandi did a one-eighty.

"I forgot to tell you. . .we made lasagna."

"I see that. Looks great!"

"And there's salad in the fridge that we made, but it has chunks of stuff in it." The six-year-old wrinkled her nose. "I didn't like it. But Miss Jena says we should try new things."

"Chunks of stuff?" Travis almost laughed aloud at the description. "What kind of stuff?"

"I don't remember what it's called," she said, padding to the refrigerator, swinging the door open, and pulling out the wooden salad bowl. She picked a 'chunk' out of the leafy green contents and handed it to him. "That's it. Yuck."

"That's an artichoke heart," Travis said, popping it into his mouth. "Yum."

"Glad you like it, 'cause I sure don't," Mandi said, handing him the bowl and trotting out of the kitchen. "'Night, 'night."

"Good night." Travis smiled as he picked out another artichoke heart and ate it.

This is great, he thought, *lasagna, salad. . .* He set the bowl on the table and, on a hunch, peeked into the oven. There it was, wrapped in foil—garlic bread. *All right!*

Plate in hand, Travis carved a wide slab out of the pan. He put the lasagna in the microwave for a minute, then added the salad, lightly seasoned with oil and vinegar, and the garlic bread. Carrying his dinner into his study, he decided he could get used to this, coming home to find supper all ready for him. But he wouldn't. He figured Jena had just set out to impress him on her first day, and—after one bite—he was impressed. After all, Glenda never cooked.

His sister's elopement still angered him. Glenda knew he needed her. She had promised to stick by him, help him out—but, of course, it had cost him plenty. Jena's salary paled next to his sister's.

Travis tried to focus on the newspaper as he ate, but he kept thinking of Glenda, which rekindled his aggravation. He loved his sister, but her leaving had put him in an awful bind, and life in general had been incredibly difficult since Meg died. Many a night Travis had cried himself to sleep, knowing he'd never again hold his beloved wife in his arms. But it wasn't as if he didn't have time to prepare for her passing. Just after discovering she was expecting Carly, Meg learned she had ovarian cancer. The doctor urged her to give up her baby, but Meg refused, and the cancer spread quickly. By the time Carly was just about full term, Meg had barely the strength to deliver her. But she sure had the determination, and a healthy baby girl arrived in the world. Travis had never resented Carly, and he was always surprised when friends mustered the courage to ask that question. No, Carly was a special gift from the woman he loved with all his being. In fact, he was hard-pressed at times not to show partiality toward Carly. Mandi was a special little girl, too.

Setting down his fork, Travis stared at his half-eaten meal. He'd been so hungry when he delved in, but he'd suddenly lost his appetite.

"Excuse me."

Travis jumped at the feminine voice—one he was very unaccustomed to hearing. He looked toward the doorway and found Jena standing there, dressed in the same outfit she'd worn this morning, a loose-fitting navy blue shirt and a gypsy-looking skirt. On her feet were strappy brown sandals.

"Sorry," she said, "I didn't mean to sneak up on you."

"No problem," he fibbed. "What's up?"

"Well, the girls are just about asleep, and since it's after eight, I thought I'd go next door and start unpacking."

"Sure. Go ahead. . .and you did a great job today. Thanks." He nodded at his plate. "Food's delicious."

"Good."

She smiled, and Travis noticed the two bright pink spots that suddenly appeared on her cheeks. It amazed him a little. He didn't know many women who blushed these days.

"Um. . .if you don't mind me saying so, you look really tired. Can I get you anything before I leave?"

"Naw." He sat back in his desk chair and crossed his foot to his knee. "I'm fine."

She looked disappointed, and her expression piqued his curiosity. He furrowed his brows.

"Okay, I'll confess," she said, obviously noting his frown. "I had an ulterior motive for asking that last question. You see, I have a ton of things to get done, and I'm a coffee freak, so I was hoping you'd say you wanted some coffee, then I'd have a great excuse to make a pot and help myself to a very large mug of it before I left."

Travis chuckled. "Why didn't you just say so?"

She shrugged. "I was trying to be polite."

"I see. . . . Well, sure. . .I'll have a cup. I'm planning to burn the midnight oil myself. But do we have coffee?"

"Ohhhh yeah," she drawled. "We have coffee. That went into the shopping cart before the milk and eggs."

He laughed again. "Go for it. Brew to your heart's content."

"Great. Thanks."

She spun around, her skirt flaring, and headed for the kitchen. Travis pushed his plate aside and tossed the newspaper onto the floor. Then he opened his attaché case and withdrew the Hamland file. After some time of reading through the case, the rich aromatic smell of some sort of flavored coffee teased his nostrils and distracted him enough that he decided to take his plate into the kitchen and pour a cup. When he entered the kitchen, he found it empty, save for the gurgling coffeemaker. Through the space between the lacy valance and yellow and white café curtains, he saw that Glenda's light was on.

But it's not Glenda's place anymore. It's Jena's. . .at least for the summer. Travis tried not to think about what he would do come fall. *One day at a time.*

Exhaling a long, weary sigh, he figured he might as well throw in a load of wash before he buckled down to work. He made his way to the basement, noticing the girls' toys were picked up in the playroom. For the first time in a very long time, he could actually see the red, yellow, and green geometrically designed carpet, and—he took a sniff—it smelled oddly of oranges.

Sure hope the kids didn't spill something down here.

He walked into the laundry area and stopped dead in his tracks. There on top of the shining white washer was a basket of folded clothes.

She did the laundry, too?

Travis couldn't believe it. Dinner, clean playroom, clean children. . .and clean clothes.

But, of course, it was too good to be true.

Okay, she earned her money today. Travis walked up the stairwell. *But let's just see how long this lasts.*

He thought of his sister, Miss Lazybones herself. She barely dragged herself out of bed before he left for work. Most times, Travis had to send the girls over to wake their aunty up. Her idea of "making supper" was ordering Chinese food or pizza or buying frozen dinners that she could just heat up. Just as he'd informed Jena, macaroni and cheese out of the box was Glenda's specialty. Rarely were the girls ready for bed when he got home, and often they were dirty from playing outside or at a neighbor's house. Glenda watched every daytime drama on TV, and those shows were often the topic of heated debates, since Travis didn't want his young daughters exposed to the adult themes and steamy love scenes. Her nighttime television habits weren't much better.

But at least she'd been a responsible person, for the most part. She practically raised Carly. She sang to the girls and played games with them. For all her faults, the girls loved her.

So did Travis. Glenda was his baby sister, after all—except he still felt a strong urge to take her over his knee for abandoning him without notice. However, he quickly reminded himself that his worries were over. He had hired a summer girl now. He had hired Jena.

༄

The sun crept up the eastern sky amid splashes of pink, maroon, and gray, and the wind felt warm against her skin as Jena traipsed across the teeny courtyard to the main house. She stuck the key into the lock and let herself in. Day two on the job was about to begin, and the weather promised to be beautiful.

As she made a pot of strong coffee in the charming kitchen, papered in blue and white checks with tiny pink flowers at each corner, Jena began thinking over the things she wanted to accomplish. Of course, she would have to confer with Mr. Larson before she set her plans in motion. He'd mentioned the girls had scheduled activities. . . . Did he say swimming lessons?

Extracting a slip of paper from the back pocket of her denim skirt, Jena scanned the recipe for her favorite scrambled egg casserole. She had hurried to copy it by hand out of a fat recipe book before leaving her apartment. Within minutes, she had all the necessary ingredients on the counter. Eggs, milk, green pepper, a package of precooked sausage, which she'd put in the fridge overnight to thaw, and cheddar cheese. She sliced and mixed, then turned it all over into a casserole dish and slid it into the oven.

Jena stood back, feeling elated. A family to cook for and dote upon—what a dream come true. Best of all, she'd get paid for it.

As a girl growing up in a bustling suburb of Los Angeles, she usually did all the cooking and cleaning at home. Her mother worked a full-time job, and her father was a fireman who wasn't home much. Consequently, Jena mothered her mother, took care of her father, and practically raised her brother—and those were the good days. The bad days began while Jena was in high school. Her mother had her career, her father had his, and Geoffrey, her baby brother, was enrolled in every sports program and co-curricular activity the school offered. They had their own lives, apart from each other, and worse, apart from God. There were no in-depth conversations taking place in the home. No one cared how the others fared, as long as somebody didn't interfere with schedules and appointments.

Watching her family grow further and further apart broke Jena's heart. She tried to round them up for dinner, but it didn't work. She tried to corner them individually so she could tell them about her faith in Christ, but they were too busy to listen. When she chose to attend Lakeview Bible College in Wisconsin, her father said he wouldn't pay for it—he wouldn't even help her out. He thought she should join the military and get her education paid for through the government. But Jena prayed about it and felt the Army wasn't God's will for her life. Her mother thought she should go into interior design and attend the junior college in LA. But again Jena knew God wanted her in Wisconsin. So she saved her money and stepped out in faith. She hadn't seen her family in nearly four years. She phoned them every once in a while, but there wasn't much to say. She wrote letters and sent e-mails, but replies were few and far between. Her mother, father, and brother were her blood relatives; she had lived with them for most of her life, but Jena didn't know them at all.

The drumming of little feet running upstairs brought her out of her reverie. Next a scripture verse flittered across her mind. *"No one who puts his hand to the plow and looks back is fit for service in the kingdom of God."*

Jena shook herself. *Dear Lord, forgive me for dwelling in the past. You brought me halfway across the country to grow me up in Your Word, and You've got a job for me to do.*

At that precise moment, Mandi and Carly skipped into the kitchen.

Chapter 5

W hat's all this?" Travis asked, entering the kitchen. Dressed in a starched and pressed light blue dress shirt and dark pants, he held his attaché case in one hand while juggling his matching suit jacket and a coordinating tie in the other.

Jena gave him a polite smile and set Carly's plate of eggs in front of her. "This is breakfast." She caught a whiff of the sweet woodsy scent of Travis's cologne and thought it smelled quite appealing.

"So I see. . .but we usually don't do breakfast. I mean, the girls might have cereal or something. . . ."

"Breakfast is the most important meal of the day," Jena said, scooping out some of her scrambled egg casserole for him. Next she placed it on the round table and held her hand out, indicating he should sit down in between the girls.

Travis gnawed the corner of his lip, appearing contemplative.

"It's really good, Daddy," Mandi said.

"I'm sure it is."

"And look how we set the table!" Carly exclaimed.

"I noticed." He glanced at his wristwatch. "Well, okay, I've got a few minutes."

Travis deposited his briefcase, jacket, and tie on the long counter. Taking his seat at the table, he lifted his fork and began to eat.

"Daddy, you forgot to pray," Mandi chided him.

Jena couldn't help a grimace as she stood with her back to the table pouring Travis a cup of coffee. She hoped he wouldn't mind that she'd taught the girls to ask God's blessing on their food at every meal.

"Your prayer counted for me, too," Travis replied with a mouthful.

Jena rolled her eyes. *Okay, Lord, I guess I have a way to go here. . . .*

She set the steaming mug in front of him. "Cream or sugar or both, Mr. Larson?"

He peered up at her with a puzzled expression. "Just sugar. . .and I thought we were on a first-name basis. . .Jena."

"It's Miss Jena, Daddy," Mandi corrected him.

Carly nodded, her little cheeks bulging with food.

When he glanced back at her, Jena had to laugh at the bested look on his face. "I'll get the sugar bowl for you. . .Travis."

"Hey, that's Mr. Travis," Mandi scolded.

"Stop being so bossy and eat your breakfast," he told her.

"That's Miss Bossy," Carly said.

Travis chuckled, and even Jena had to laugh as she placed the sugar on the table. But then she noticed Mandi's indignant expression and quickly walked over to the little girl. Standing behind her, Jena gently massaged her upper arms.

"It was just a little joke. Don't be upset. We know you're not really Miss Bossy." She kissed the top of Mandi's blond head. "You just like things done right—and that's good."

She nodded, and peering around her, Jena saw that her scrunched-up features had softened.

Travis gave his oldest a charming wink, and Mandi returned a shy smile.

Jena straightened and rubbed her palms together. "So what's on the agenda for today, Mr. Travis? Do the girls have any lessons or playgroups that I need to get them to at a certain hour?"

He wiped his mouth with a paper napkin. "Today's Tuesday, so that means Mandi has swimming lessons this morning at ten o'clock. After that, the day's yours."

"Okay. We'll think of something fun to do this afternoon."

"Great, and I'll get a schedule together for you. I'll give it to you tonight."

"That would be most helpful," Jena replied, thinking Travis Larson didn't appear to be half as egotistical as she'd first thought yesterday.

After a few more bites and a swig of coffee, he wiped his mouth and stood. "I've got to get going." He gave each of his daughters a loving smooch before adding the old fatherly warning "Be good."

Then he strode over to Jena, who moved aside so he could reclaim his tie and briefcase.

"I wasn't sure if you needed it or not, but I packed you a lunch." The fat brown bag sat on the counter near his tie, and she slid it toward him.

He stared at it, wearing a curious look. "I don't usually take a lunch, but. . . what is it?"

"Oh, nothing really, just a piece of leftover lasagna and a small salad. I didn't put dressing on it so the lettuce wouldn't get soggy."

Travis scooped up the bag. "Thanks."

Jena followed him through the kitchen to the back hall in case there were any last-minute instructions.

"Um. . .thanks for doing the laundry. You didn't have to."

"Yes, I did. I needed to wash some clothes, and your stuff was in both the washer and dryer."

Travis pivoted, and she saw him wince. "Sorry 'bout that. I wasn't expecting you, so—"

"It's okay. Not a problem."

He replied with a hint of a smile and opened the door.

"Have a good day," she said.

"Yeah, you, too."

With that, he exited the house, and Jena walked back into the kitchen. Mandi and Carly both watched her with expectant grins, causing her to feel like doing something silly. Lifting her arms, she let out a whoop before shouting, "We're going to have a fun day today!"

The girls caught the excitement. They laughed and jumped off their chairs.

"C'mon, Carly, let's go get dressed."

Jena chuckled as the girls ran out of the room, imitating the hoot she'd just produced. Glancing around at the glasses, plates, and crusty casserole dish, she figured she had about ten minutes—if that—in which to clean up the kitchen.

∽

Life seemed good again as Travis drove back to his office. After six hours in court, the judge had ruled in his favor in the Hamland case. Travis felt like he was back on top of the world.

Parking his sleek black Lexus, he sauntered into the busy downtown office building and rode the elevator to the tenth floor. Stepping out of the car, he walked down the muted yellow marble thoroughfare to the glass doors on which the names DUNCAN, DUNCAN, & LARSON were etched in gold lettering.

"We–ell, congratulations." Craig greeted him in the lobby of their office suites. "Nice day in court."

"Oh, honestly," Yolanda Timmerman muttered from behind the receptionist's desk, "an idiot could have won that case. It was obvious the company was negligent in Mr. Hamland's injury."

Travis bit back a retort. He'd worked hard and done his research, and he'd won fair and square—and he wasn't an idiot, either!

"Trav, I need to talk to you," Craig said. "Follow me into my office."

"Sure."

He didn't bother to look in Yolanda's direction. He didn't need to see her exotic dark features to know that her lips were curved in a mocking smile.

Entering Craig's office, Travis shut the door behind him. "Isn't her internship up yet?"

Craig chuckled. "Sit down, Travis."

Setting his briefcase on the adjacent armchair, he did as Craig bid him. "What's up?"

"Oh, nothing really—just a minor inconvenience."

Travis began to worry. "What kind of inconvenience?"

"Isabella Minniati."

Travis winced at the name of the top executive of a local sports team—one that DD&L was courting and hoped to represent. "What hoops does Bella want us to jump through this time?"

"Oh. . ." Craig waved a nonchalant hand in the air. "She's suddenly big on families, kids, and pets." He lifted a bushy brow. "She's expecting, you know?"

Travis lifted a brow of his own. "Is she? Well, congratulate her for me."

Craig grinned. "You can congratulate her yourself. I've invited her to dinner on Thursday night to celebrate her newest, um, discovery."

"Obviously you want me to be there."

"Well, of course. . .seeing as dinner will be at your house."

"What? My house?" He shook his head. "No. Won't work."

"Travis, it's a perfect backdrop. You have a comfortable home. Your daughters are as cute as koalas, and your home ec summer girl can whip something up for dinner."

"I can't ask Jena to do that."

"The firm will pay her. Tell her we'll give her. . .oh, a hundred bucks."

"A caterer would cost two grand."

"Yes, well, all the more reason to have your summer girl put her skills to good use."

"What if she bombs? What if dinner is a complete disaster?" Travis didn't really believe it would happen, but there was always that possibility.

"The answer's simple. We'll explain to Bella that your summer girl is but a mere college student, and we'll laugh it off. Then we'll order a pizza."

"Let's just order pizza to begin with."

"Now, Travis, we owe it to your summer girl to prepare her for life. What if she winds up marrying some businessman whose job requires him to entertain? You don't want that poor girl to be completely in the dark, do you? We're offering her a chance to gain valuable experience."

Travis laughed. "That's quite a stretch, Craig. How long did it take you to think up that logic?"

"About as long as it took you to convince Judge Thompson that Dwight Hamland is now permanently disabled because he bent over to pick up a quarter that accidentally flew out of the vending machine he was working on at the shop."

"There was a little more to it than that." Travis stood and lifted his briefcase. "But I'll talk to Jena and let you know what she says. I'll warn you, though, I'm not going to coerce her into doing anything that she's not comfortable with. The last thing I need is for her to quit on me."

"True, true. . ." Craig leaned back in his chair. "But give it your best shot. You're a persuasive guy, and there's millions of dollars riding on this deal."

Then why be so cheap? Travis wondered, leaving Craig's office for his own. Then again, that was Craig Duncan's middle name—Cheap. He sighed and entered his office. Maybe he'd just go ahead and hire a caterer and leave Jena out of this.

"Are you sure your new boss won't care that I'm here visiting you while you're on the job?" Mary Star Palmer asked.

Kneeling on the pavement in the tiny courtyard as she and the girls planted flowers, Jena glanced over her shoulder. "No, I don't think he'll care. It's not like I'm neglecting my duties."

"Do you want some help?"

Jena smiled at her blond, blue-eyed friend. "No. We're just about finished. You just relax and drink your lemonade. You've had a rough day."

"Amen! I'm telling you, there's not a job to be had in this entire city." Star sighed.

"Maybe somebody else needs a summer girl," Mandi said, her hands covered in rich dark topsoil and a black smudge across her nose.

"Naw, I don't think I could be a summer girl," Star announced, her hoop earrings wobbling as she spoke. "Too much work."

"Yeah, too much work," Carly parroted. "Just like planting flowers."

"This isn't work," Mandi argued. "This is fun."

Carly didn't reply right away but watched as Jena dug a hole and carefully placed a geranium into the earth before filling the space around it with dirt.

"I'm hungry," Carly whined. "I don't wanna plant flowers anymore."

"We're almost done, and then I'll make dinner," Jena said.

"Noooo, right now."

Jena stared up at the pouting little girl. "How about a few crackers while you wait? Would you like some crackers?"

Carly nodded.

Standing, Jena brushed herself off and entered the house. She plucked the graham crackers from the cupboard and returned to the yard. Sitting Carly on one of the two picnic benches, she opened the box.

"Hey, what are you making for supper?" Star asked.

"Grilled chicken and a tossed salad."

"Yum."

"Want to stay for dinner?" Jena asked, going back to her knees to finish the flower-planting project.

"Will your boss care if I stay?"

"I don't think so. He's not that kind of guy. Besides, he doesn't get home until eight."

"Well then, sure. I've got no plans tonight other than to soak my tired feet. I must have walked ten miles today and filled out just as many applications."

Jena inserted the last of the geraniums into what would become a colorful border. She stood and stretched out a kink in her back. Carly began to cry for no other reason than the fact she was overtired. At three years old, she still eeded an afternoon nap.

Taking the little girl by one of her dirt-covered hands, she led her to the ose and washed her off. Carly protested the entire time. Next came Mandi's urn for her grubby bare hands and feet to be hosed off. After that, Jena cleaned ff the gardening tools and sent Mandi over to Mrs. Barlow's next door to return hem. Jena had looked but couldn't find a hand spade and rake in the garage and asement—although she hadn't felt comfortable performing an in-depth search. t seemed easier to borrow them from kindly Mrs. Barlow.

Carly's whines and complaints suddenly became a raving tantrum. Carrying he kicking and screaming child into the house and upstairs, Jena managed to vash her red, tear-streaked face and change the little darling into her nightgown. Minutes later, Jena left her in her bedroom to finish her temper fit.

Star crossed her eyes. "I don't know how you stand it. I couldn't put up with kid acting like that!"

"She's overtired. She'll probably sack out up there." Jena glanced at her wrist-vatch. Five thirty. That wasn't too terribly early. There was a good chance Carly vould sleep through the night.

Just then, Mandi skipped into the house. Jena instructed her to go upstairs nd change clothes, which she did without a single objection.

"Hey, Star, will you keep an eye on things while I run over to my apartment nd take a quick shower?"

"Um. . ." Her tall, willowy friend gave her a skeptical look. "I don't know, en. . . ."

"It's quiet upstairs now. Carly probably passed out from exhaustion. Mandi's n angel, and it'll only take me twenty minutes. When I come back, I'll start the rill, and—"

"Okay, okay. Just make it quick."

"I will. I promise."

With that, Jena dashed out the back door and up to her apartment. The girls vere safe and clean. She would be back in time to make a nice supper. What ould go wrong?

Chapter 6

Travis braked in front of his house when the gold, orange, and russet bloom of marigolds in front of the hedges caught his eye. When had he phone the lawn and garden company? Had someone there called him? Life ha been so hectic, he couldn't even remember.

Puzzled, he maneuvered his Lexus the rest of the way into his driveway ar parked. Grabbing his briefcase off the passenger seat, he walked into the sma courtyard that divided the house and garage. The girls' bikes were out, and Carly favorite doll had been forgotten on the picnic table. Travis picked it up and no ticed the pink buds of geraniums that now graced the edge of the house. Alor the fence were several tall leafy green plants.

Since when does the lawn and garden company plant stuff without even askir what kind of flowers I want?

Miffed, he stalked into the house only to find a tall blond young woma standing in his kitchen wearing blue jeans and a light blue top that barely covere her tanned midsection.

"Who are you?" he asked, sounding brusque to his own ears. However, h didn't care for the ring in her navel. "Where's Jena?" He hoped she hadn't qu and left this person in charge. With her hair going every which way, she had ditzy look about her.

"Uh-oh," the young lady said, her blue eyes widening. "I just knew this wa going to happen. . . ."

"You knew what was going to happen?" Travis stepped into the kitchen.

"Well, lemme start by introducing myself. I'm Star."

Travis felt his frown deepen. *Star? What kind of name is that for a huma being?*

"I'm Jena's friend," she continued, and as she spoke, Travis saw the braces o her teeth. "Jena said you wouldn't care if I was here. I'm just holding down th fort until she's done with her shower. She and the kids were planting flowers th afternoon, and—"

"Daddy!" Mandi zoomed into the kitchen, and Travis braced himself befor she flung her arms around his waist.

"Hi, baby," he said, bending over and kissing her. "Where's Carly?"

"She had a meltdown, and now she's asleep. I'm watching TV."

"Great. Here, take Carly's doll with you."

"Okay, Daddy."

Mandi spun around on one bare foot and hightailed it out of the room. Straightening, he glanced back at. . .Star.

"So you're one of Jena's friends, huh?"

"Yeah, she led me to Christ, and now she's discipling me. . .as well as trying to help me find a job."

"I see." Travis sort of understood the religious implications of the young woman's remark. His wife had been a born-again Christian, and she'd often spoken about "leading" someone to Christ, although "discipling" was a new one to him. He presumed it meant Jena was some sort of mentor. "You're in college?"

"Yeah, I'm going to begin my junior year. But I don't go to the same school as Jena. I attend the University of Whitewater."

Travis blinked as Star tipped her head from side to side while she talked, the hoops in her ears jangling. Nevertheless, he felt himself unwind. Things weren't so bad—they weren't so out of control as he'd first imagined.

"You said Jena and the girls planted flowers?"

"Yeah, that's why she needed the shower. It's hot, and she got kind of sweaty, you know?"

Exiting the room, Travis rolled his eyes. "Sweaty" was really more than he wanted to know. He traipsed into his office, a room with mahogany paneling and leaded glass-paned doors.

Setting his briefcase on a nearby armchair, he spied some envelopes stacked on the corner of his desk and figured Jena had put today's mail there. He lifted the small pile and rummaged through it. Hearing the back door open and close, he deduced that either Star had left or Jena had returned. He realized the latter had occurred when strains of female voices reached his ears.

Moments later, he heard footsteps and glanced up from the mail. Jena gave him a smile. Her strawberry blond hair appeared a deeper color since it was still wet, and she had secured it on the back of her head with one of those plastic pinchy-comb things his sister used to leave all over the house.

"You're home early."

"Yeah, I've been known to do that every so often." Travis briefly noted the white T-shirt and tan straight skirt she wore. He also noticed her bare feet.

"I'm getting ready to light the grill."

"How come?"

"So I can cook the chicken that has been marinating all afternoon."

Travis pursed his lips and nodded. He thought about asking her if she'd cater Thursday night's dinner party but hesitated.

"Carly's sleeping," Jena said.

"I heard. Mandi told me."

"She was exhausted beyond reason."

Travis nodded. "That happens sometimes when she doesn't get a nap."

"So I've discovered."

He grinned at the quip.

"I hope you don't mind that my friend Mary Star came to visit me."

"Mary Star?" With the prefix, the name sounded a little more normal. "No, I don't mind. But what made you decide to plant flowers?"

"I saw an ad in the paper this morning promoting a big sale at a nearby garden center." Jena casually leaned against the door frame. "I thought it would be fun for the girls to plant flowers, water them, and watch them grow and bloom all summer. You know—give them a sense of accomplishment. So after Mandi's swimming lesson, we went over and bought some flowers."

"Okay." Travis decided "a sense of accomplishment" was probably worth some flowers. "How much do I owe you?"

"I've got the receipt in my purse. I'll give it to you later." With that, she pushed off the door and headed for the kitchen.

"Jena," Travis called, wearing a smirk, "get back here."

She complied, but the innocent expression she mustered didn't work.

Travis crossed his arms. "Jena, you forget that I know this old female trick of diversion. Now, I'm not going to get angry. Just tell me how much I owe you."

"Eighty-nine dollars and ninety-four cents," she blurted. "In addition to the flowers, I bought some tomato plants and bags of topsoil."

Travis wanted to laugh. That was a whole lot less than the cost of his usual lawn and garden company. "I'll write you a check tonight."

"Okay," she replied, but her face was a bright shade of pink.

She made off for the kitchen again, and this time Travis couldn't contain his chuckles.

∽

"Was he mad?" Star wanted to know.

"No, of course he wasn't mad." Jena tried not to audibly expel her sigh of relief.

"What can I do to help with dinner?"

"Want to put the salad together for me?"

"Sure, I can do that."

Jena laughed at the understatement. Her friend had a flair for the culinary arts and hoped to operate her own restaurant someday. Walking to the fridge, Jena pulled out the lettuce, a tomato, and scallions and handed them off to Star.

"Jena, I'll light the grill," Travis said, giving her a start as he strode through the kitchen. "You shouldn't barbecue without shoes on. So unless you want me to burn the chicken, you'd better find something to put on your feet."

He marched out of the house, and Jena saluted in his wake. She looked over at Star, who laughed at her antics.

"He's a hunk," she said.

"Yeah, and he knows it, too," Jena whispered in case Mandi was within earshot. "But I have to say he's been very nice so far. A little bossy, but nice."

"A good-looking guy like him—a lawyer, too—I'll bet he's got a line of women waiting to go out with him."

Jena nodded. The same thought had crossed her mind. But from what Mrs. Barlow said, Travis Larson was a family man through and through. Of course, that didn't mean he wouldn't have an occasional date. In fact, Jena had a hunch he would ask her to babysit later than eight o'clock once Friday and Saturday night rolled around.

"Jena, come out here, will you?" Travis's deep voice boomed through the kitchen.

"Orders from headquarters," Star murmured with a laugh.

Jena had to chuckle as she walked outside. "What's up?" she asked Travis, who was busy pouring lighter fluid onto the charcoal.

"I've got a big favor to ask you."

"You've got a date and want me to stay late one night."

"*Urrrnt*, you're wrong," Travis replied, sounding like a game show host. He flashed her a captivating smile.

Must be a serious favor, she thought. *He's turning on the charm.*

"Unbeknownst to me, until late this afternoon, Craig Duncan, one of my partners, invited a prospective client to dinner on Thursday night. . .here. To my house."

"Oh." Jena thought it awfully presumptuous of his business partner to do such a thing but refrained from saying so.

"Anyway, this client is Isabella Minniati. Ever heard of her?"

Jena shook her head.

"Well, she's a top executive for the Milwaukee Mavericks."

"Who?"

"It's an indoor football team."

Jena hoped she appeared impressed for propriety's sake. In truth, she wasn't crazy about football—outdoor or indoor.

"My firm is vying for the position of the Mavericks' corporate attorneys. Bella, that's her nickname, just found out she's expecting a baby, so Craig decided my house would be a cozy little backdrop for cinching this deal, seeing as I have two adorable daughters—and a summer girl who knows how to cook."

Jena's eyes widened with horror. "Me? Cook for somebody important?"

"Well, you cooked for me the last two days. What am I? A nobody?"

Jena noted his wounded expression and wondered if it were part of the presentation. "Of course you're not a nobody. I didn't mean that. I just. . .well, I like to cook, but I don't have a lot of confidence in my ability. . . ."

Then suddenly it dawned on her. "Star. Star's a great cook! And she needs a job." She tipped her head. "Are you willing to pay extra for this?"

"Absolutely. Name your price."

"Um. . ." Jena was stumped. She hadn't a clue as to how much the job should pay. Fifty dollars? How much did cooks make an hour?

"Tell you what; I'll pay you each a hundred bucks—plus expenses."

"A hundred bucks each?" she repeated. "Hey, that sounds great." Jena thought the money would tide Star over until she found a real job, and she herself could always use an extra one hundred dollars.

"So you'll do it? You and your friend Star?"

"I have to ask her, but if she agrees. . .sure, we'll do it!"

"Nothing fancy. Think homey."

"Like homemade vegetable soup and a loaf of home-baked bread?"

"Yeah," Travis said with a pleased grin. "Like that."

"Well. . ." Jena put her hands on her hips and glanced at the cloudless blue sky. "In that case, we'd better pray a cold front blows through. I have no intentions of slaving over a hot stove in ninety-degree weather."

Striking a match and igniting the charcoal in the grill, Travis smiled and stepped back from the flames. "Jena, I don't care what kind of food you prepare. Just make it homey and impress Bella."

"Star and I will certainly do our best," she replied.

"That's all I ask."

Pivoting on the ball of her bare foot, Jena reentered the house, hoping Star was as receptive to Travis's idea as she had been.

Chapter 7

Jena and Star spent much of the next day planning and preparing for Thursday night's homey dinner. But when the day arrived, it was too hot to make the soup and bread they had selected, so they quickly changed the menu to steaks on the grill and seven-layer salad. Jena phoned Travis at work, and he gave his approval.

"I think everything's ready," Jena announced, entering the kitchen where Star put the finishing touches on the salad. "Now that's how I like to eat my vegetables." She gazed at the bacon bits Star sprinkled on top of the shredded cheddar cheese. "It looks fabulous."

"Thanks." Star beamed. "This is one of my summer specialties."

"I can tell."

At that moment, Jena glanced out the kitchen's picture window and spied the top of Mrs. Barlow's snowy-white head. Half a minute later, a knock sounded on the back door.

"Come on in," Jena called.

The older woman stepped into the back hall carrying a small cardboard box. "After you told me how the two of you have been fussing, I wanted to help, so I baked a rhubarb pie this afternoon."

"In this heat?" Star placed her cold soda bottle against her temple.

"Oh, it's not that hot." Mrs. Barlow's green eyes snapped with amusement. "Besides, a cold front is coming through tonight. Anyway," she said, looking at Jena, "the pie just came out of the oven, and I figure by the time Travis and his guests are done eating dinner, it should be cooled enough to slice and serve with a scoop of vanilla ice cream."

With her hands in oven mitts, she extracted the pie from the box. Then she pulled out a round container of ice cream.

"Thanks, Mrs. Barlow." Jena took the frozen treat and set it inside the freezer. While she had planned to serve cheesecake for dessert, the rhubarb pie and ice cream sounded ever so much more "homey"—especially since Jena had used a no-bake boxed recipe.

Suddenly Mandi came dashing into the kitchen. "Miss Jena, can you tell Carly to be quiet? She's crying, and I can't hear the TV."

"Why is she crying?"

Mandi shrugged. "I don't know. Come see. Make her stop it."

"All right."

The six-year-old ran out of the kitchen. Jena followed, and reaching the de
she paused at one of its two doorways. Carly lay on the red and blue plaid sof
whimpering.

Jena frowned as concern surged through her. "What's wrong, Carly? Wha
the matter?"

Sitting on the couch, she pulled the three-year-old onto her lap. Carly qu
eted and snuggled into her arms. Jena rocked her, and not to be left out, Man
bounded onto the sofa and slipped her arm around Jena's, leaning her blond hea
on Jena's arm.

Mrs. Barlow's tall, broad-shouldered frame appeared at the doorway. Sh
folded her arms and shook her head, smiling. "You're mother material if I ev
saw it."

Jena smiled. "Well, I want to be a mother. . .someday."

She peered down at Mandi, who regarded her with curiosity.

"How come you're not a mom now?" she asked.

"Because I'm not married. I have to find a husband first."

"Hey, I got it!" she cried, popping upright. "You could marry my daddy, an
then you'd be our mom."

Jena felt her face begin to flame. She'd walked right into that one. "God ha
to find me a husband."

"That's right. It can't be little Miss Mandi Larson," the older woman sai
with a broad grin.

The girl pouted, and her brown eyes shifted from Mrs. Barlow to Jen
"Could Carly and me just pretend you're our mom?"

"Yeah," Carly murmured, "just p'tend."

"I don't think that's a good idea," Jena told them. She didn't want to sta
something she couldn't finish. Besides, she wasn't Travis Larson's type. She ha
seen pictures of his deceased wife, and the woman had been model gorgeous wit
a slim figure and clear complexion—not a freckle face like Jena. Moreover, sh
sensed from the various photos she'd viewed that Meg Larson had been trendy an
modern—not old-fashioned, which was more Jena's style. On the flip side, Trav
Larson wasn't the sort of man who would capture Jena's interest. Ever since she'
moved to Wisconsin, she had been praying for a husband in the ministry—a mis
sionary, a pastor. A lawyer wasn't even a consideration. "I'm just your summer lad
remember?"

"Good," Mandi said, curling up beside her once more. "Then summer's neve
gonna end."

"Of course it is, silly." After a roll of her eyes, Jena gazed at Mrs. Barlov
"These two act like they're starving for affection."

"I don't think it's an act, dear."

Jena felt a tiny piece of her heart tear. . .until she remembered seeing their father kiss and hug the girls. "Travis gives them affection."

"But it's not quite the same as a mother's tender nurturing. And while you're not a mother per se, you have a motherly way about you. That's why I knew you'd be perfect for this job."

Jena smiled and glanced down at Carly, whose eyelids were drooping. Next she peered at Mandi, who had once again become absorbed by *Anne of Green Gables* on the television.

"Hey, Jen," Star said, entering the den, "your boss just got home, and a couple of other cars pulled up in front of the house. I can only assume his guests have arrived, too."

"I'm going to leave," Mrs. Barlow said, giving Star a hug and blowing a kiss to Jena. "You're both going to do fine tonight. Travis is lucky to have you helping him out."

"Thanks for the pie," Jena called after her.

She turned and waved.

Gathering Carly, Jena stood. "You know, this little girl feels awfully warm. What if I have to mind a sick child tonight? Will you be okay?"

"Sure. Everything's basically done."

Star's confidence caused Jena to relax a bit.

"Daddy!" Mandi cried, jumping off the couch and running toward him with arms outstretched.

Travis met his oldest in the living room and swooped her up into his arms as his guests traipsed in through the front door. Smiling like a proud papa, he and Mandi greeted the two couples. Then he glanced toward the den as if looking for Carly, and Jena seized the moment to wave him over.

"I'm going back into the kitchen." Star spun on her heel and exited through the den's second doorway.

Jena watched as her friend made her way through the dining room. Glancing into the living room once more, she stepped toward the other door and watched Travis's approach.

"Are we ready?" he asked, rubbing his palms together. Behind him, Jena could hear a woman exclaiming over Mandi.

"Well, yes—food-wise we're set. But I'm afraid we might have a sick little girl on our hands." She nodded at Carly, whose head rested against Jena's shoulder.

Travis gave his daughter a dramatic frown, intended to make her grin. Then he put a hand over her forehead. "She's got a fever." A worry line formed above his dark brow. "Did you give her anything yet?"

She shook her head. "I just noticed how warm she felt a few minutes ago."

"Hmm. . . Well, if she's not better by tomorrow morning, I'll call Dr. Becker, the girls' pediatrician. In the meantime, there's medicine upstairs in the linen closet."

"Great. I'll go get it."

"And I'll introduce my youngest daughter to our guests." Travis held his arms out to Carly, but she whimpered and buried her head deeper into Jena's chest.

"Carly!" Jena couldn't believe the child refused her father. Usually she was as excited to see him as Mandi was.

"Oooh, you little heartbreaker." Travis tickled his daughter; however, Carly yelped and clung more tightly to Jena.

"I think she's sicker than we first believed."

Travis narrowed his gaze. "I think she just knows which one of us is going to spoil her." Grinning, he winked at Jena.

She smiled back, but her heart suddenly beat in the strangest way. Maybe she was coming down with something, too.

"Travis, is this your wife?"

Wide-eyed, Jena glanced at the doorway in time to see a slim woman with white-blond hair enter the room. Clad in a fitted black sleeveless dress, she carried herself with an air of confidence.

"Hi," she said, "I'm Isabella Minniati. It's a pleasure to meet you. And who's this?" She sidestepped Travis to peer at Carly. "What an adorable little girl!"

Carly turned her face away.

"She's not feeling well," Jena tried to explain, "and I'm not—"

"Oh, what a shame," Isabella declared, touching the top of Carly's blond head. "Yes, she is a bit warm."

"Bella, this is Jena," Travis began. "She's my sum—"

"She's lovely, Trav," the woman cut in, whirling around to face him. "When I saw the two of you together in here and that darling child in your wife's arms, well, I. . . Well, it was picture-perfect. You make a charming couple!"

Jena's jaw dropped, and she stared at Travis, who rolled his eyes and shook his head just as two men strode into the room.

"Honey, this is Travis's wife, Jena," Isabella said to the husky man in a white polo shirt and dark slacks.

"A pleasure to meet you," he said with a genuine smile and a nod of his ebony head. "I'm Joe Minniati."

Jena forced a small smile and repositioned Carly in her arms. She looked back at Travis, who was conversing with another man who appeared to be in his early sixties.

"Their little girl is sick," Bella went on.

"What a shame."

"So when did you and Travis get married? Poor Travis has been a single dad for so long." Bella pointed a well-manicured finger at him and laughed. "You needed a wife. You were getting awfully grumpy!"

"He certainly was!" the older man said.

He strode toward her, and Jena inadvertently took a step backward, but he halted her process by placing his hands on her shoulders. "Great to see you again, Jena," he told her, batting one eye. Oddly, this wink didn't have the same effect on her that Travis's had earlier. "Well, folks," he said, turning to face the Minniatis, "let's leave Jena to do her motherly thing and put her sick child to bed. Then we'll eat. Right, Trav? Jena's prepared a homey meal for us to enjoy. She's the picture of domesticity."

With that, he ushered the others into the living room, and Jena glanced at Travis.

"What in the world. . . ?"

"I'm so sorry. We've traumatized you, haven't we?"

"Well, no. . .not traumatized exactly."

"Not to worry. I'll take care of everything." He swallowed hard. "After I throttle my partner. I bet I could get off with the insanity plea."

Jena ignored the quip. "That man with the bushy white hair—he's your partner?"

Travis's features softened. "Right. His name is Craig Duncan. He's senior partner at my firm." He shook his head and took several steps in her direction. "Look, Jena, I'll straighten things out. I promise. Craig's not thinking like a normal person right now. He's so desperate to sign this deal with Bella, he'd beg, borrow, and steal if he had to. But instead, he's letting her believe a lie because. . .well, she obviously likes the idea that you and I are married."

Jena felt her face heating up at the implication.

"Again, I apologize." Travis ran a hand through his hair, a nervous gesture if Jena ever saw one. "Don't get mad and quit on me. . .please."

"Don't worry. I have no intention of quitting."

He expelled a weary-sounding sigh. "Good. That's the last thing I need."

Jena gazed down at Carly, deciding this was her chance to change a most uncomfortable subject. "I guess I should go tend to the little one here. What kind of medicine am I looking for upstairs in the linen closet?"

"It's a bottle of children's fever reducer. Give her two tablets. I'll send Mandi up, and she can get in her pajamas. Meanwhile, I'll clear up the misunderstanding down here."

"Okay." That sounded like as good a plan as any. "Star's in the kitchen, and she'll put the steaks on the grill whenever you tell her to. The meat will only take a few minutes."

Travis nodded.

With Carly asleep in her arms, Jena felt as though her limbs might give out. Nevertheless, she marched purposely out of the den, making her escape to the second floor.

Chapter 8

With Carly sleeping restfully and Mandi settled in for the night, Jen strode down the carpeted hallway, heading for the stairs. She hoped Star fared all right in the kitchen without her. Reaching the top of the stairwell, Jena paused, hearing footfalls ascending at a rapid pace. A heartbeat later, Travis rounded the landing and took the next flight two steps at a time, nearly colliding with Jena as he reached the second floor.

He caught himself in time and backed up. "Sorry 'bout that."

She gave him a forgiving grin. "That's okay."

"Are the girls sleeping?"

"Carly is, and Mandi's almost there."

"Good." He raked a hand through his dark brown hair. "We've got a problem."

"What is it?" Jena asked with a frown. "Did Star burn the steaks?"

"No, no, nothing like that." Travis drew in a deep breath. "You see. . .there hasn't been a good time for me to straighten out the matter of you being my summer girl and not my wife. I'd have to practically call Craig a liar in front of the Minniatis, and I can't do that."

Jena started to protest, but Travis held up a forestalling hand.

"He told Bella and Joe that you and I went to Paris for our honeymoon."

"No, he didn't!" she exclaimed incredulously.

"Shhh. . ." He glanced over his shoulder. "Yeah, he did. Bella asked to see our wedding pictures, and Craig said we haven't gotten them back from the photographer yet."

Jena stood there gaping at him. "So now what?"

"Well, I wondered if you'd. . .well, if you'd play along."

"No!"

"Just for tonight."

"Absolutely not!" She folded her arms and prayed she looked adamant, because her insides were quivering with sudden anxiety.

"You'll probably never see these people again, Jena."

"I can't lie. . . ."

"You won't have to. You don't have to say a word. Just be polite and follow my lead."

"Travis, if I agree to this pretense, it's a lie."

Putting his forefinger to his lips, he glanced over the stairwell wall. "Jena, I'll give you and Star five hundred bucks each if you help me out."

"I can't be bought."

Travis smirked. "Your friend can. Star thinks this whole thing is hilarious, and she agreed to my offer."

"Then tell your guest that Star's your wife."

"Too late now." Travis stepped up to the landing, causing Jena to retreat. Taking hold of her elbow, he led her a few feet away so they wouldn't be overheard below. "Listen, it's for a few hours, Jena. That's all. Pretend you're an actress at your college performing in a play. . . ."

She raised a dubious brow. "Comedy or Shakespearean tragedy?"

Travis chuckled. "I think it's a little of both. But hopefully none of us will die at the end." He gave her a charming smile that made Jena's face flush. "Say yes. Please? This deal's important to my law firm."

Jena didn't feel right about being part of such deception. But on the other hand, she didn't want to be the one responsible for his firm losing a big contract. Perhaps if she went along with this, she could somehow bring the truth to light without publicly embarrassing Travis's partner.

"What's the verdict, Jen?"

Jen? She swallowed her surprise and continued her struggle with indecision.

Unfortunately, he interpreted her silence as acquiescence and propelled her toward the stairs.

"Bella's tired," he said in hushed tones. "This dinner won't last long. It'll be the easiest five hundred dollars you ever made."

"You don't have to pay me."

"Of course I do."

"No, I wouldn't feel right about it."

They reached the bottom stairs and strode to the living room.

"We'll discuss the matter later. . .dear."

Jena's jaw dropped in indignation; however, she managed a recovery before they made their entrance.

"Well, here they are," Craig Duncan said, standing from the delicately patterned green and mauve sofa on which he'd been sitting. "Hope everything's okay, Trav."

Jena perceived the subtle warning in the older man's tone, and she felt suddenly sorry for Travis. True, she hadn't liked her boss much the day she first met him. But over the course of the last few days, it hadn't been difficult to see that he adored his daughters, and much could be said for a guy who loved his kids as much as Travis Larson did his. It made Jena wish her father had been as doting.

"Everything's fine," Jena shocked herself by replying. Then, seeing as she was on a roll, she decided to go for broke. "I hope I didn't appear rude, but with Carly sick and all. . ."

"Rude? Absolutely not!" Bella said from several feet away in the love seat beside her husband. "Your stepdaughter is more important than guests."

"I didn't even realize she had a fever until just before Travis got home."

"No need to explain," Bella insisted with a warm smile.

Jena felt a pinch of guilt for duping the woman. For some reason, she rather liked Bella Minniati.

"Now, who's in your kitchen cooking?" Bella asked before taking a sip of her iced tea.

"No one," Craig blurted. "Jena is just a fabulous homemaker all the way around. Isn't that right, Jena?"

"Well, usually. . .yes," she answered with an inward chuckle, thinking this acting stuff was kind of fun. But she had to laugh outright at the curious stare Travis gave her. Nevertheless, she saw an opportunity here for Star to get a summer job and chose to nab it. She turned to Bella. "I asked a friend to help me tonight. She's a great cook, and. . .well, she'd make a terrific caterer. So I said she could practice on us."

Craig Duncan nearly choked on his beverage.

"But you won't be sorry, I promise."

"I'm sure you're right," Bella said, glancing at Craig, then back to Jena. "And it so happens that I'm holding a garden tea party next month, and I'm in need of a caterer. Perhaps your friend would be interested in the position."

"Yeah, maybe she would be. Would you like to meet her? I'm going into the kitchen right now to make sure everything's ready. Want to come along?"

"I'd love to."

"I'll come along, too," said the petite older woman who had been sitting next to Craig. She wore a red cotton short-sleeved sweater, white linen pants, and co-ordinating accent jewelry, and her regal bearing made it known that she identified with society's upper crust.

"What do you want in the kitchen, Miriam?" Craig's frosty, bushy brows almost touched the bridge of his nose as he frowned.

"I'm going to need a caterer for Samantha's bridal shower."

"Oh, right. I forgot about that." Craig rolled his eyes and waved his wife on.

Flanked by two obviously wealthy women, Jena refused to feel intimidated as they ambled to the kitchen. God wasn't impressed by a person's wealth; He saw the heart—and so did Jena, or at least she tried to.

"I just adore blue and white kitchens," Bella exclaimed as they entered the room. "Don't you, Miriam?" Before the woman could reply, Bella added, "Did you decorate this yourself, Jena?"

"No, I didn't." Standing next to Star, she quickly changed the subject and then made the introductions.

"I mentioned that you were thinking of starting your own catering business, like we discussed this afternoon." That wasn't a lie, either. Jena had listened patiently to Star ramble on about wanting to run her own restaurant business someday, and catering was sort of like a restaurant business. "Mrs. Duncan and Mrs. Minniati might be interested in hiring you this summer."

"Oh?" A light flickered in Star's blue eyes as understanding set in. "Oh! Oh yeah. . .my own catering business."

"Are you experienced?" Mrs. Duncan asked. "You look awfully young."

"I'm entering my junior year of college. I'm twenty-two. So, yeah, I'm young. But I do have experience."

Jena smiled as her friend rattled off all the school functions she'd helped cater at Whitewater, including two alumni balls.

Bella Minniati looked impressed. "Do you work alone?"

"Usually, but I can find help if the guest list is too large to manage myself."

"You seem quite capable. I'll bet you could handle my garden tea party single-handedly." Bella tipped her head, and her brown eyes darkened. "Let's talk business. How much do you charge?"

Jena glanced toward the entryway and saw that Travis had entered the room. With one hand on his hip, the other dangled next to his head as he leaned against the door frame. He watched the transaction with interest.

"Okay, I have to claim ignorance here," Star said, raising her hands as if in surrender. "I have no idea what caterers charge." She extended her hand, indicating Travis. "He's paying me five hundred dollars for tonight."

"Five hundred dollars?" Bella looked aghast. "I can do better than that." Turning to Travis, she said, "You cheapskate."

"Hey, now, didn't you hear Jena?" He countered with a good-natured smirk. "Star's practicing on us tonight."

Bella gave him a doubtful glare and turned back to Star. "Another catering service quoted me a price of close to twenty-five hundred. Will you do it for a thousand dollars plus expenses?"

"Sure!"

Jena grinned at Star's enthusiasm before chancing a look at Travis. His expression said he found this entire incident quite amusing. His gaze eventually found hers, and he pushed himself off the side of the doorway and headed in Jena's direction.

"If we don't get those steaks going," he said, "Star will have to cook in the dark."

Jena gave him a nod. "Right."

Pivoting, she strode to the refrigerator, opened the door, and found the meat marinating on a baking sheet.

"Oh, now, Jena, don't go doing my job for me," Star said, crossing the kitchen. "Mrs. Duncan, may I call you tomorrow so we can finish working out the details of your daughter's shower?"

"Of course, dear. And if this pans out, I have a friend who needs a caterer on the third of July at the yacht club." The woman smiled. "You may need help with that one."

"No problem." Star glanced at Jena. "Right?"

"Right."

"Ah, wait a second here," Travis cut in, giving Jena a pointed look. "We're going to have to discuss this matter of you moonlighting as Star's hired help. I don't know if I—"

"Oh, Travis, honestly!" Bella exclaimed with a laugh. "If it's appearances you're worried about, no one is going to care that your wife is helping her friend's business get off the ground. I think it's quite admirable. Star is working her way through school, and Jena wants to assist her."

Little does she know I'm working my way through college, too.

Travis's gaze shifted between the two women, but it came to rest on Jena. She knew that he didn't want anything to interfere with her job as his summer girl, but of course, Bella had been purposely misguided, and so she'd drawn another conclusion.

As they stood there, regarding each other, Jena thought he appeared chagrined, and while she wanted to laugh, she instead put on her sweetest, most wifely expression—whatever that was.

"We'll discuss it later. Not a problem. There are other people besides me who want to help Star out."

A slow smile spread across Bella's face. "You're a doll, Jena." She turned to leave the kitchen but paused to give Travis a rap in his midsection. "She's too good for you, Larson."

Travis narrowed his gaze, and once Bella was out of earshot, he said, "I can't stand that woman."

"Really?" Jena lifted the seven-layer salad from the fridge. "That's a shame. I like her."

"That's because you're a nice person so you think everyone is nice." Travis came up behind her and took the rectangular glass pan out of her hands.

"I didn't think you were nice. . .at first."

Depositing the dish into its fitted serving basket, Travis shot her a curious glance. "We'll have to discuss that later, too," he said, carrying the salad to the dining room.

Chapter 9

Jena hurried to set two more places at the table, one for herself and the other for Star. She suspected it wasn't proper etiquette to have hired help eat with society's upper echelons, but Jena figured that since she'd been coerced into this farce of playing Travis's wife for the next couple of hours, she could invite whomever she pleased to dinner.

Back in the kitchen, Star sliced the individual tenderloins into succulent strips so that there would be enough for everyone. She arranged the meat on a shiny silver meat platter, then carried it into the dining room. Jena followed.

"We're ready."

"Great." Nervous flutters filled Jena's stomach.

Star frowned. "Are you sure you want me to eat in here? I feel kind of weird about it."

"How do you think I feel?"

"What's the next step up from weird?"

"Mortified."

"Yeah, that, too."

Jena found the quip amusing. "Please, Star? I'd feel more comfortable with you at the table."

"Sure." A slow smile spread across the younger woman's face. "Whatever you say. . .Mrs. Larson. Hey, maybe since you're his wife for the night, you ought to ask for the credit card."

"Oh, stop!"

Star laughed.

"Are we ready, ladies?" Travis asked, striding toward them with a purposeful expression. He lowered his voice. "I'd like to get this over with as soon as possible."

"Food's on the table," Jena said. "Call the guests in."

"No, I'd rather if you, being tonight's, um, hostess, would direct the guests to the table."

"Oh. . .well, if you say so." Jena gave her curly strawberry-blond hair a self-conscious pat, although she felt glad she'd clipped it up off her perspiring neck.

"You look great," Travis muttered. "Just get them in here so they can eat and leave."

Something inside Jena wondered at the compliment. She looked great? Since

289

when? Well, Travis was desperate. He'd most likely say anything so she would continue the acting.

She walked into the living room, where she politely interrupted the amicable chitchat. "Dinner's ready."

The guests ambled into the dining room, and once they were seated at the handsome cherry table, Travis reached for the plate of meat.

"We should ask the Lord's blessing. Travis, will you do the honors?" The words were out before Jena could stop them.

Travis shot her a wondering look. "Um. . .sure."

To her left, the Minniatis initiated handholding while they prayed, and Jena fought her smiles over the sight of Travis clasping Joe and Craig's hands. Funnier still was the perturbed expression on Craig's aged face.

They bowed their heads.

"God is great. God is good," Travis began. "Thank You, God, for this food. . . . Amen."

Bella collapsed against her husband's arm, laughing. "Oh, that was precious, Trav. Now pray for real."

His expression said he had prayed "for real." But to appease his guest of honor, he lowered his chin once more. Everyone followed suit.

"Thank You, God, for this food. And, um, thank You for the hands that prepared this meal."

Star squeezed Jena's hand. Jena squeezed back.

"Thank You for the good company here tonight. Bless us all. Amen."

Jena looked up as Travis reached for the meat platter again and passed it to his right.

"Are you one of those people who gets nervous when he has to pray in front of others?" Bella asked.

"Yeah," Travis replied in a crisp tone. He watched as Mrs. Duncan helped herself to the seven-layer salad and passed it to her husband.

"What about you, Jena?"

"Oh, she loves to pray," Star blurted.

Abashed, Jena simply confirmed her friend's statement with a tiny nod.

"She taught my girls to pray," Travis said, scooping salad onto his plate. Catching his blunder, he gazed across the table at Jena. "I mean, our girls."

Jena felt her face begin to flame.

"Why didn't you teach them to pray?"

Watching the exchange, Jena noted that Bella didn't mean the question in a derogatory manner but asked it quite offhandedly as she sliced into her grilled beef.

"I, um, found it very hard to pray ever since. . .well, since Meg died." He passed the salad to Joe.

"Meg? Who's Meg?" Bella asked.

"That'd be Travis's sister," Craig stated.

"Meg was my wife," Travis countered, sounding as though his shadowy jaw was clenched as he spoke.

Craig laughed off his lie. "Oh, of course. Meg. Your wife. I'm terrible with names."

Bella looked aghast. "I'm. . .I'm so sorry, Travis. I was under the impression you were divorced."

He shook his head. "Widowed."

"You're so young. Our age." Bella looked at her husband, then at Craig. "You said Travis was divorced."

"Me?" Craig appeared taken aback by the accusation. "I said no such thing."

"I beg your pardon," Joe cut in, "but you did indeed say Travis was divorced. It was right after we arrived here tonight."

"Oh, well." Craig waved his hand in the air, dismissing the issue. "I must have been thinking of my son. He's divorced."

Jena saw Mrs. Duncan's shocked expression, which she hid by staring down at her plate. Next Jena observed the Minniatis exchange curious glances, but all the while, her heart ached for Travis. Was he bitter with God for taking his beloved wife? Was he a Christian? Mrs. Barlow didn't think so. She had mentioned the many times she'd attempted to tell Travis about the love of Christ, although the older woman had informed Jena that Meg had been a believer.

"My humble apologies," Craig said, looking in Travis's direction before focusing on the Minniatis. "I've got a busy mind, and I meet so many people. Sometimes the names and faces just blur together."

"Perhaps you need your eyes checked—or your head examined." Bella gave him a tight smile.

Jena picked at her salad as the tension in the dining room mounted. Things weren't going well, but it was Craig Duncan's own fault for spouting off such lies tonight. Now Travis seemed completely disgusted, and Bella gave the impression of feeling just as aggravated.

She turned to Jena. "Your friend said you like to pray. Is that true?"

"Yes. I'm a born-again Christian." She set down her fork. "I'm not always as faithful as I want to be, but I do enjoy conversing with the Lord."

"I know what you mean." The taut lines around Bella's perfectly shaped lips relaxed. "I'm a Christian, too. So is Joe."

He grinned.

Jena smiled back.

"Jena's the one who led me to Christ," Star said. "I went to her church's Christmas program last year. At the end of the play, her pastor preached a short message about why we celebrate Christmas. It's 'cause of Christ. If He hadn't left heaven and been born a man, there'd be no way for salvation and eternal life."

"Amen!" the Minniatis exclaimed in unison.

"I was one of the trained counselors milling about during the invitation," Jena further explained, recalling that snowy night a week before Christmas. "I was matched with Star, and well, the rest is history."

"Now I'm like gum on Jena's shoe. She can't get rid of me."

"I'll vouch for that," Travis quipped.

Jena tossed him a quelling glare. However, she couldn't help a small grin. Then Star snorted with indignation, making things all the more humorous.

To Jena's left, Bella laughed. "What church do you attend?"

"Countryside Community Church in Menomonee Falls."

Bella brought her chin back. "Way out there?"

Jena nodded.

"Well, Joe and I go to Parkside Baptist. It's not far from here. Would you and Travis like to join us this Sunday? Bring the girls," she said, looking at Travis. "We'll all go out to lunch afterwards."

"Umm. . ."

Jena caught his eye and tried to shake her head without being obvious. "I have nursery duty on Sunday."

Travis feigned disappointment. "Aw, too bad."

"Can't you get out of it?" Bella persisted. "Trade Sundays with someone?"

"I think it's a great idea," Craig interjected. "You young couples can get better acquainted, and—"

"Us 'young couples' nothing!" Jena retorted. She'd had just about enough of this man and his endless fibs. It would do him good to go to church on Sunday. "I insist you and. . .and Miriam join us."

Mrs. Duncan appeared startled at Jena's familiar use of her given name.

Her husband, however, looked suddenly very irritated. His face reddened, making his white hair seem a shade lighter. "You insist?"

"Craig—"

"No, no, Travis. Don't try to defend her."

Bella gaped at the older man, and Jena felt as though she were a witness about to be cross-examined.

Craig's steely gray gaze bore into her. "You insist?"

Jena forced herself not to squirm; however, in the next moment it was as if the Lord revealed to her that she held the upper hand in this little game.

"Yes, I insist," she replied, lifting her chin. "You're coming and that's that."

"What?"

She held his gaze, silently daring Craig Duncan to say one more word. If he did, Jena planned to confess the grand sham Craig had so thoughtlessly instigated tonight. She'd probably lose her job, but. . .

The words of Queen Esther suddenly flittered through Jena's head. *"If I perish, I perish."*

"I think you've overstepped your bounds, young lady." Craig said. "No one's going to insist I do anything. Particularly you."

Jena turned to Bella, who watched the exchange with an expression somewhere between confusion and curiosity.

"There's something you need to know about tonight. I'm not—"

"Sunday morning it is!" Craig exclaimed, bringing his palm down on the table with a bang. "You know, Trav, I haven't been in church in years. This'll be refreshing."

Bella placed a hand on Jena's arm. "Ignore him. What did you want to tell me?"

"I'm not the person you think I am."

"Jena. . ."

Hearing what sounded like surprise mingled with hurt in Travis's voice, she looked across the table at him. "Travis, I can't lie anymore."

An almost wounded expression crossed his face, as if he'd been slapped, and for whatever the reason, Jena couldn't get herself to betray him. She searched her mind for a way to back out of what she'd begun to say.

"You see, I'm not as domestic as Craig has made me out to be." She stood and began to clear her place. Next she took Star's plate. "I let you all believe I baked that rhubarb pie in the kitchen. But the truth is, our sweet neighbor, Mrs. Barlow, did."

Exiting the dining room, Jena caught Travis's look of relief.

Chapter 10

The sun was just beginning to set when the guests finally departed. The last three hours had seemed like a week to Travis. Even so, he glanced up Shorewood Boulevard and felt a moment's appreciation for the maroon and gray streaks painted across the sky. After a *beep-beep* from the Minniatis' white SUV, he waved and forced a parting smile as the couple drove away.

"If Bella doesn't sign with us because of tonight," Craig muttered, "I'm taking that little upstart summer girl of yours to court for breech of contract."

"Don't be ridiculous. She never signed a thing. Where's your evidence?"

Craig grumbled. "I'll have Yolanda dig up something on her, and I'll go from there."

Travis laughed. "Good luck. Your chances of finding dirt on Jena are about as good as the chance of it snowing tonight." Unknotting his tie, he wished he had turned on the central air when he got home.

"Listen, that girl's got a lot of nerve insisting I go to church on Sunday morning."

"Yeah, well, I want to go to church about as much as you do." He waved away Craig's next remark. "I'll talk to Bella. I'll make up some excuse for tonight's. . . misunderstanding."

"No, you can't do that. Not unless she signs first."

Travis inhaled and willed himself to stay calm. He blew out a deep breath. "If we lose this contract, Craig, it's your fault. You might as well accept responsibility for it now. You started everything, and if I were Jena, I'd have socked you right in the nose."

"Then I would have had a good lawsuit, wouldn't I?" Craig chuckled, and his good-natured disposition returned. "Well, all in all, I think it was a productive evening."

Travis wanted to argue the point, but he felt too tired.

Craig walked around to the other side of the car. "See you tomorrow at the office, Trav."

"Right-o." He waved to Miriam through the window of the passenger side. She'd been waiting in cool comfort while he and Craig said their good-byes.

With his hands on his hips, Travis watched the Duncans' green Lincoln Town Car pull away from the curb and make its way up Prospect Avenue. Turning on his heel, he walked back to the house. One step inside the front door and he could hear Star's laughter over the din of the garbage disposal and running water. Next came Jena's reprimand.

"Mary Star Palmer! I cannot believe those words came out of your mouth! ust for that, I'm going to tell Tom. . ." Her voice trailed off.

Travis figured there was some big-time teasing going on. Over the last couple of days, he'd gotten to know Star a little better. She seemed intelligent, but a little on the ditzy side, and she had a hankering for poking fun at Jena in a way that made Travis wonder why Jena put up with the girl. He sighed. *Oh well, what are friends for?*

He strode to the kitchen and entered just as Jena backed up to the doorway, dodging a flying wet dishrag. She stepped on his foot, and as a reactionary gesture, he set his hands on her waist to steady her. In doing so, he caught the soaking cloth in the shoulder.

Star's eyes grew as round as dessert plates. "Oops."

Jena swung around, and her face turned two shades of pink. Travis held her blue-eyed gaze with his as he balled the rag in his palm. Then without warning, he whipped it at Star. She yelped and jumped out of the way, but it splattered against her right elbow.

Jena whirled around and laughed. "That's what you get."

Star chuckled along before tossing the rag into the sink. "Yeah, I suppose so."

Smiling, Travis shook his head at both of them. "You girls need to lighten up."

The sarcasm wasn't lost on either of them, and they replied with chagrined smiles.

"Listen, I'm sorry about tonight. Jena, I'm really sorry about tonight."

She lifted her shoulders in a quick up-and-down motion and resumed loading the dishwasher. Dressed in a white T-shirt and a crazy-patterned skirt and matching vest, she had ditched her sandals already, and Travis had to grin at the sight of her bare feet. She was as bad as his daughters.

"Guess I'll go up and check on Carly," he said, deciding he'd wait until Star left before talking to Jena about tonight.

"I did already." She glanced his way. "I don't think she has a fever anymore, and she's sound asleep."

"Oh, good." Travis looked from Jena to Star. "Then I guess I'll go up and change my shirt."

Chuckling at her guilty expression, he left the kitchen and took to the stairs with his usual two-at-a-time pace.

⁂

"He always does that."

"Does what?"

Jena turned to Star. "He always runs up the steps like that. Practically shakes the whole house."

"Yeah, so?"

Jena shrugged. "Just something I noticed, that's all."

"Hmm. Well, I hope you're noticing the guy running up the steps, too."

"Oh, Star, honestly! Will you stop it already? I've told you—"

"I know. I know. You're waiting for God to bring the right man to you. You don't have to go looking. Our heavenly Father will take care of it." Star shook her blond head. "But I'm telling you, Jena, I think He has."

"A lawyer? Yeah, right." Jena pointed toward the dining room and lowered her voice. "Look at his friends. I could never be one of those kind of people. Besides, I don't think Travis is a Christian."

"If God saved me, He can save anybody!"

Jena didn't reply, even though she agreed with Star. Nevertheless, Jena wished her friend would stop trying to pair her with Travis. It was most frustrating.

They finished cleaning the kitchen, and Jena started the dishwasher.

"You should see how he looks at you. I'm not kidding."

Jena moaned in aggravation. "Star! Drop it already!"

"All right, all right." The younger woman stepped back, her palms raised in surrender. "I will not say another word. Not one more thing."

"I'd get that in writing, Jen," Travis said, entering the room, checkbook in hand. He laughed at his own quip.

Jena prayed he hadn't heard what preceded it.

She watched as now, wearing a green polo shirt and khaki trousers, he clicked his pen and began writing out a check.

"Just pay Star," Jena told him. "You don't owe me anything."

"Yes, I do, and I'm going to pay you." His voice sounded kind but adamant.

"No." Jena's tone was just as firm.

"She's in an argumentative mood tonight," Star said, throwing Jena a dubious glare.

"I need to repent for lying tonight, not get paid for it." She looked at Travis. "I don't want your money, and if you pay me, I'll rip up the check."

With that, she spun around and left the house. She walked across the small courtyard wondering why she felt so ornery. Normally Star didn't get on her nerves, but tonight for some reason, Jena felt perturbed with her friend.

She reached her apartment's lower door and turned the knob.

"Jena. . ."

Travis's deep voice halted her, and she thought that maybe he was getting on her nerves, too.

Slowly she turned around and watched as he came toward her. Star was right behind him.

"I'm leaving," she announced. "I'll call you tomorrow, Jena."

"Okay." She let her gaze follow Star out of the yard, then looked back at

Travis, who now stood only a couple of feet away.

"If you're angry with me, I can understand why. But I promise I'll straighten everything out with Bella."

Nodding in reply, Jena opened the door and stepped up into the hallway. She turned on the light, then brushed the hair that had fallen out of its clip back off her face.

"If you won't take the five hundred dollars I promised you, fine. But you might as well take it. I'll see to it my law firm reimburses me." Travis put his foot up on the threshold and leaned forward on his knee. "It's money for school."

Jena wanted to tell him how accepting the money would make her feel. But she felt too embarrassed.

"Take it, Jena. I'll make out the check right now."

"I said I don't want it." She inched the door forward, only to have it connect with the toe of Travis's brown shoe. He didn't take the hint and move his foot, either.

"You earned it. Take the money."

"No, I didn't earn it. Don't say that."

"Why not?"

"Because it makes me feel. . .cheap."

There! She said it!

Jena drew in a calming breath and lifted her chin. She almost cracked a smile at Travis's stunned expression.

"I. . .I had no idea you felt that way. I'm very sorry. Nothing like that ever entered my head."

"It didn't really enter my head, either. . .until you tried to pay me."

"My sincere apologies, Jena."

"All's forgiven. Let's just forget it, okay?"

"Okay."

He removed his foot, and she began to close the door when Travis caught it before it met the latch.

"Yes?" She peeked around the door.

His brown eyes filled with apprehension. "You're not going to quit on me, are you?"

She rolled her eyes as a smile edged its way across her face. "No, I'm not going to quit on you." She must have told him that four times this week. "I do need the summer girl job, you know."

"Good." He took several steps backward, but he still wore a wary expression.

"I'm not going to quit on you," she reiterated. "I promise."

Halfway into the courtyard, he managed a cordial smile. "Good night."

"Good night."

On that, Jena closed the door, locked it, and ran up the steps—two at a time.

Chapter 11

The next morning, Travis awoke to the sweet smell of cinnamon, fresh bread, and coffee. By the time he'd showered, shaved, and dressed, the girls were at his bedroom door exclaiming over the fact that they'd made sweet rolls.

"Daddy, you have to come downstairs and eat breakfast now."

"Yeah, all right." He gazed at Mandi through the mirror while knotting his tie. "You're awfully bossy for a six-year-old, know that?"

She gave him a sassy smile before climbing up on his bed. He could tell she had every intention of using it as a trampoline.

"Hey, off the bed. No, don't jump. Get off."

She took a flying leap and landed on his back, causing him to lose his balance. He fell into his bureau, knocking over a couple of cologne bottles and a picture of Meg.

"Amanda Lyn Larson, what do you think you're doing?" Travis peeled off her arms from around his neck and swung her over his shoulder so that she hung upside down.

She giggled so hard her lanky body shook, and Travis tossed her onto the bed.

Some example I am. He shook his head at Carly, who was in the process of mimicking her older sister.

"Don't do it," he warned her.

But, wearing an impish grin, Carly started jumping on his bed despite the words of caution. With each bounce, she jostled Mandi, who laughed so hard she couldn't sit upright.

Travis snatched his youngest in midair. She giggled and he tickled her, tossing her on the bed, too. Then he tickled both of them until they squealed and screamed, pleading for mercy.

"There." Holding them around their forearms, he brought them both to a standing position. "Now I'm the dad, and I say. . .no more jumping on the bed. Got it?"

"Tickle us again, Daddy," Carly said, a huge smile on her cherubic round face.

He gazed upward, shaking his head. So much for authority and influence. "Sorry, fun's over. I've got to be in court this morning. Here," he added, hoping to distract them, "Mandi, you carry my briefcase, and Carly, you carry my suit coat."

He folded it in her arms so she wouldn't trip on it.

"Daddy, this is too heavy for me," Mandi declared, setting the attaché case on the top of the steps.

Carly flung his jacket down and followed her sister down the stairs.

"Some help you two are."

Gathering his things, he made his way to the first floor. After a quick stop in his office, he entered the kitchen. Jena glanced at him, then did a double take, and he watched her gaze take in his appearance. Suddenly he realized the tails of his shirt had come untucked, and his tie was askew.

"I'll have you know I was all spit 'n' polished before my daughters attacked me." He combed his fingers through his hair in case it, too, had been mussed.

"I didn't say a word."

He caught her smirk. "You didn't have to."

Travis watched as Jena flitted around his kitchen in a yellow and white patterned jumper and white T-shirt. Her hair hung to her shoulders, and it looked like it was still wet from a shampoo. His gaze traveled down to her feet—which were bare, just as he expected. But today he noticed the berry-colored polish on her toenails. And then he noticed that Jena had very pretty feet—as far as feet go—and she had nicely turned ankles, too.

"I hope you don't mind that I walk around your house barefoot."

"What?" Travis looked up, realized what she'd asked, and shook his head. "No, of course I don't mind. Why would I?"

"I don't know. Just thought I'd ask."

He ignored her curious expression and reached for a frosted cinnamon roll.

"Want a cup of coffee?"

"Yeah, thanks."

From the dishwasher, she pulled out his travel mug and held it up in question, and he nodded. Funny how quickly she learned his routine. Travis didn't particularly like sitting down to a formal breakfast. He wanted something to grab and go, and he enjoyed taking his coffee with him.

"Where'd the girls take off to?" he asked, watching Jena add cream and sugar to his brew.

She smiled. "I bought them each a little plastic watering can, and they're just outside giving our flowers a morning drink."

"Oh, good. That'll keep those two urchins busy for a few minutes."

Finishing off his sweet roll, he reached for another. He munched on it while observing Jena as she twisted on the lid of his stainless thermal mug. Her fingers were long and graceful, and a smattering of tiny brown freckles covered her capable hands and traveled up her arms. Before he could contain the thought, he wondered if her skin felt as soft as it appeared. . . .

"Did I do something wrong?"

Travis swallowed the food in his mouth and met Jena's questioning stare. "No, why?"

"Well, I don't know, but. . ." Her freckled cheeks turned petal pink. ". . .you're looking at me kind of weird."

"Oh, sorry."

He stuffed the rest of the cinnamon pastry into his mouth before he could contend that his appreciative glances had never been called "weird" before.

Jena handed him his mug. "Are you going to talk to Bella today?"

He sipped his coffee before answering. "I'll talk to her. . . soon."

"Today?"

Her eyes beseeched him, and Travis suddenly noted their unique color. A dark blue-gray—like the color of a summer sky before a storm.

"Travis?"

"Hmm?"

"Today? Are you going to speak with Bella today?"

"If I get a chance. . ." Travis tried to make his reply as vague as possible, knowing Craig would shoot him if he told Bella the truth before she signed the contract.

Jena, however, didn't look satisfied with the implied promise.

"Listen, don't worry." He touched her arm, a gesture of reassurance, but a tiny thrill passed through him when he learned her skin felt, indeed, quite soft. "I'll. . . I'll take care of it. I'll explain about last night, okay?"

A small worry line marred her brow. "Are you feeling all right, Travis?"

"No! I think I've gone crazy!"

"Oh, is that all?" Jena laughed, breaking whatever spell he'd fallen under.

"You sound like your friend Star," he muttered, leaving the kitchen. If there was one thing in this world he abhorred, it was a sarcastic woman.

In his office, he straightened his clothes, combed his hair, grabbed his briefcase and suit coat, then made his way toward the back door.

"See you tonight," he said, walking through the kitchen.

"Bye, Travis. Have a good day."

Jena's soft voice plucked a chord in his heart, one he'd never heard or felt before—even when Meg was alive. Every day this week, with the exception of last night, he had felt like he'd entered some kind of storybook fantasy where everything was perfect and wonderful. It was a world where delicious smells wafted from the kitchen, laundry never piled up, and children were always clean and happy.

He shook himself. *I have gone crazy.*

∽

Gazing out the window, Jena lifted her coffee cup to her lips and sipped. She saw Travis kiss Mandi and Carly good-bye before walking into the garage. He sure acted strange this morning. Maybe he just had a lot on his mind. She only wished Star hadn't put those silly thoughts in her head about Travis "looking at her" in some romantic way, because she could almost swear that's what he'd done this morning.

The phone rang, and Jena moved to answer it where it was stationed on the wall near the back hall. "Larson residence."

"Is Travis gone?"

"Um, just leaving now. Who's calling, please?"

A feminine laugh. "It's Bella Minniati. How're you this morning?"

"Fine. Thanks." Jena tried to tamp down the feeling of impending doom. "Do you need to speak with Travis? I'll try to catch him."

"No, no, I want to talk to you, Jena. I just don't want him in the vicinity while we converse."

That's what she was afraid of. *Oh dear God. . .*

"Jena, I might be blond, but I'm not stupid. I could sense some odd undercurrent last night, and I want you to tell me what was going on. I think you were about to tell me while we were at the dinner table. Am I wrong?"

"No. . .but Travis said he'd rather be the one to discuss the matter with you."

"I see. Are you two having marital problems?"

"Oh no, nothing like that."

"I didn't think so. You two are adorable together. But I thought I'd nip that suspicion in the bud."

Jena squeezed her eyes shut in a tight grimace.

"Well, I really don't want to wait for Travis to tell me. I'd like to hear it from you. I'm not trying to be nosy. I'm just. . .concerned."

"Oh, Bella, I really shouldn't be the one to tell you."

"But you will tell me, won't you? You're my sister in Christ, and I have a hunch whatever is going on involves me and this contract business."

"Yes, you're right. And that's why Travis needs to speak to you."

A long pause. "Jena, I'll tell you a piece of truth if you tell me a piece of truth. Deal?"

"Okay." She didn't see another option out, other than to hang up on Bella and maybe ruin whatever hope remained of her signing with Travis's law firm.

"I've always thought that Travis was an okay guy. But now I actually like him since I met you and those two darling girls."

At the mention of Mandi and Carly, Jena went up on her tiptoes and glanced out the window to make sure they were all right. Seeing the little ones sitting inside their square wooden sandbox near the fence, she returned her attention to the phone call.

"But I must say, Jena, I trust Craig Duncan about as much as I'd trust a rattlesnake. The man appears harmless enough, but I have a feeling he's got a venomous bite."

"Good analogy."

Bella's laugh was as smooth as expensive chocolate. "Thank you. I take it you agree?"

"Wholeheartedly. But of course it's none of my business."

"What? You're Travis's wife. Of course it's your business."

Jena's heart hammered in her chest. "Okay, my turn for a piece of truth. I'm not Travis's wife. I'm his summer girl."

"His what?"

"Summer girl. He hired me to take care of his kids for the summer."

"You're a nanny?"

"Well, yes, but no. I hate that title. Except I suppose that's what I am. . .for the summer." When there was no reply, Jena continued. "It was all Craig Duncan's doing. He lied, thinking that somehow our being married would impress you, and Travis didn't want to expose his rattlesnake partner in front of guests, so he begged me to go along with it for the night. Trust me, I didn't want to, but. . .well, I felt kind of sorry for Travis, being in that awkward position because of Mr. Duncan."

The silence at the other end was deafening. "Bella, please believe me when I say I'm so sorry for the pretense. My conscience bothered me into the wee hours of this morning."

"So am I correct in assuming that only the part about you and Travis being married is a lie?" Bella asked. "The girls are Travis's and he's a widower?"

"That's true." Jena felt as if a two-ton weight had just been lifted off her shoulders. "And Star is a friend of mine, and she really needs a job for the summer. She's excited about the catering possibilities."

"I see."

"Bella, I'm so, so sorry."

"You're a Christian? That part's true?"

"Yes, but I probably don't seem like much of a testimony for Christ right now."

"On the contrary. I admire your tender spirit. I felt like you and I sort of connected last night." She paused. "Tell me. Is Travis a Christian?"

"I'm not sure."

"Hmm. . . Joe and I wondered."

Jena heard the other woman inhale deeply.

"Tell you what," Bella began, "let's keep our Sunday morning date, shall we? I like you, I forgive you for your part in last night's charade, and I think those two girls are so scrumptious I could eat 'em up."

Jena smiled. "I agree. Mandi and Carly are sweeties. And in Travis's defense, I have to say he's a very loving father. He's also extremely generous. He's given me a car to use, he leaves me money for whatever the girls and I might need, he's polite, and he doesn't talk down to me—which is pretty amazing considering he's a lawyer. . . ."

Bella chuckled, sounding genuinely amused.

"I mean, I know all attorneys aren't arrogant," Jena promptly amended, "but I thought Travis was at first. I've learned he's really not."

"Okay, you sold me on his attributes." Bella laughed again. "I forgive Travis, too."

"But I don't know if he'll want to come on Sunday."

"Hmm. Well, if he doesn't, then you can't very well bring him kicking and screaming. But I'd like you to come—and bring Mandi and Carly."

"Okay."

Jena nibbled her lower lip in consternation. Sunday was technically her day off. However, she didn't think Travis would mind her borrowing his daughters—

Unless, after he heard she'd blabbed the truth to Bella, he fired her first!

Chapter 12

Travis loosened his tie as he drove back to that enchanted new world called home. He had called Jena on his cell phone and found she didn't need groceries or anything else. The girls had been fed and bathed and were now watching some Bible story video they had checked out at the library.

Bible story videos—they sure beat the kind of television Glenda used to watch. Pulling into the driveway, Travis parked and decided Meg would be pleased the girls were being introduced to the Bible. In fact, Meg would probably like Jena.

Travis walked through the yard, noting all the toys were put away. When Glenda was here, the place was such a disaster he'd be lucky if he didn't kill himself on the way to the back door. And the house. . . The house always looked as though Hurricanes Mandi and Carly had blown through every room.

What a change, he thought, entering the immaculate kitchen. He paused to inspect the fresh flowers in the center of the table.

"Hi, Daddy!" Mandi pranced into the kitchen, looking like a little princess in her pink nightie.

"Hi, baby," Stooping, Travis hugged and kissed her. "Where's Carly?"

"Sleeping on the couch. She didn't have a nap today 'cuz Miss Jena took us to the beach. On the way back, we bought those," she said, pointing at the colorful bouquet. "Do you like 'em?"

"Yeah, they're pretty." Travis stood. "What'd you eat for supper?"

"The stuff Miss Star made yesterday."

Mandi said the name so fast that Travis didn't catch it. He frowned. "Mister? Mister who?"

"No, Daddy, Miss Star."

"Oh, is she here?"

Mandi shook her head.

Good. Travis had had such a hectic day that he didn't feel like dealing with Mary Star Palmer's antics tonight. All he wanted to do was change into his blue jeans and unwind in a lawn chair outside.

"Hi, Travis, did you have a good day?"

He smiled as Jena entered the room. "It was okay." He'd lost the Baily case, but that had been expected. Now came the appeals process. In two sweeping glances, he scrutinized Jena from head to barefoot toe. "You look about as nk as Mandi's nightgown."

"Yeah, I know." She examined her arms. "I took the girls to the beach today ut didn't bring along enough sunscreen. By Sunday, I'll be one giant freckle."

Travis grinned and stepped closer. "Did you wear that to the beach today?" e asked, noting she wore the same outfit as this morning.

"No, of course not." Confusion pooled in her blue eyes.

He smirked. "I just wondered since I've never seen you wear anything but a ress."

"Oh." She shrugged, still looking baffled.

No wonder Star goads her. Jena's awfully fun to tease.

Travis flashed a charming smile while brushing past her on the way to his ffice. Tossing his attaché case on a nearby chair, he flipped through the mail.

"Hey, Travis?"

"Hmm?" He glanced up to see Jena at the doorway.

"After the girls are sleeping, can I talk to you about something—something nportant?"

The trepidation in her voice put him on guard. Sitting on the corner of his esk, he set the mail down and folded his arms. "What's up?"

"I'd rather wait until Mandi and Carly are asleep to discuss it." She smiled. But I'm not quitting, so don't get your hackles up. Although. . ." A worried little rown suddenly dipped her one eyebrow, ". . .you might not want me working for ou when you hear what I have to say."

Travis wanted to hoot at the comment, but he refrained only because she eemed troubled. "Jena, I highly doubt there's anything you could tell me that vould cause me to let you go. You're doing a great job. You've brought normalcy ack to my home. In fact, after three years it finally feels like a home again."

"That's. . .that's nice to hear," she said with a pleased grin. "But just hold that hought until I get the girls to bed, okay?"

Travis chuckled and picked up the stack of bills and miscellaneous corre- pondence. "Okay."

After reading Mandi a story, Jena turned out the light and proceeded to the first oor, where she scouted around for Travis. She finally found him in the courtyard, tretched out on one of the two padded lounges and reading the newspaper as the un began its nighttime descent.

"The girls are just about asleep."

"Great." Travis folded the paper in two and set it on his lap. He still wore oday's white dress shirt, its sleeves rolled to his elbows. He'd removed his tie and xchanged his classy trousers for faded blue jeans. "So what did you want to talk o me about?"

Jena sat down in one of the plastic lawn chairs. She'd been rehearsing this all day, but now when it came time to tell Travis about her confession, word suddenly escaped her.

"Did you wreck the car?"

Jena's eyes widened. "No!"

A small grin tugged at one corner of his mouth. "Did you nick it, bang it, or dent it, and now you're scared to tell me?"

"No." She couldn't help a chuckle. "That I wouldn't have trouble telling you."

"Oh, okay." He pursed his lips, appearing amused.

But he wouldn't be for long.

"Bella called this morning, right after you left," Jena blurted.

"Oh?" The tone of his voice hung between them like a threat.

With flutters dancing across her midsection, Jena crossed her legs and toyed with a small snag in her jumper. She swallowed hard. "Bella sensed that something was amiss last night, and. . .well, I ended up telling her the entire truth."

Travis swiveled in the lounge chair, and glancing at him from beneath her lashes, Jena saw his navy and white athletic shoes when he set them on the cement ground. He leaned forward, his forearms on his knees, but his expression was indecipherable.

"What did Bella say?"

"She said she doesn't trust Craig Duncan."

"Oh great." Travis ran a hand through his hair.

"But she likes you, and she still wants us to come Sunday. I told her I didn't know if you'd be willing to attend church, and she said in that case I should come without you and bring the girls." Jena cleared the sudden frog in her throat spawned from Travis's penetrating gaze. "Sorry," she croaked.

"Anything else?"

She shook her head, sensing Travis's infuriation. But that's what she'd expected. Nevertheless, she felt the need to explain herself. "If I blew the big contract for your firm, I humbly apologize. On the other hand, I couldn't tell Bella a bald-faced lie. I mean, going along with things last night was one thing—"

Travis held out a forestalling palm. "Say no more. I understand."

"If you want to end my employment here—"

"No, no. I meant what I said earlier."

"Okay." She stood. "Well, it's after eight. . . ."

"Fine. Consider yourself off duty."

He studied his clasped hands as he spoke, and Jena decided he was deep in thought—probably trying to figure out how to tell his pretentious partner that his summer girl had a big mouth.

"Travis, I know it's none of my business, but. . .well, I don't like Craig Duncan. I think Bella has an accurate opinion of the guy."

He glanced up at her, one eyebrow cocked. "You're right, Jena. It's none of your business."

Her breath caught in her throat. She felt as if she'd just been slam-dunked. But in the next moment, she figured she had it coming. She'd been Travis Larson's employee for six days. She was the hired help and hardly entitled to pass judgment on his business partner.

"Sorry."

Jena crossed the courtyard and ran up to her apartment. She felt somehow wounded, she wanted to cry, and yet she believed in her heart she'd done the right thing this morning on the phone with Bella. She'd told the truth.

Deciding to drown her blues in a cup of strong java, she walked to the kitchen and opened the cupboard. Only then did she remember that the coffee was in Travis's kitchen.

With a frustrated groan, she closed the cupboard doors and ambled to her room. By the time she reached it, she'd made up her mind to walk to that little coffee shop she had seen on Oakland Avenue. Since the village of Shorewood was only one square mile, Jena figured she could walk there and back.

Moving to the dresser, she pulled out a pair of black walking shorts and put them on. She winced as they chafed her sunburned legs. Being more careful now, she removed her jumper and hung it in the closet, exchanging it for a short-sleeved black cotton shirt with sprays of tiny yellow, red, white, and lavender flowers. She layered it over the white tee she wore. After threading a belt through her shorts, Jena donned a pair of white sport socks and slid on her white athletic shoes. In the bathroom, she brushed her hair and glided a headband into place. She squirted lotion into the palm of one hand and gently applied it to her face. *I'm so pink I put Star's favorite shade of lipstick to shame.*

With a sigh, she figured there was nothing more she could do in the aftermath of a sunburn, and she slung her small purse over her shoulder and left the apartment. She felt relieved that Travis no longer sat in the courtyard. Taking a deep breath of the evening air, she felt herself begin to relax as she began her trek up Shorewood Boulevard.

∽

Up in his bedroom, Travis sat on the edge of the bed, mourning the framed picture of Meg that he found lying broken on his dresser. He knew just when it had happened, too—this morning when Mandi had playfully jumped on him. He could buy another frame, that wasn't a problem, but somehow the shattered glass above his Meg's smiling face seemed like the final barrier between them. A ridiculous notion, of course, since his wife had been dead over three years now. Nevertheless, he couldn't explain away the sudden sense of permanence that enveloped him.

Meg wasn't coming back.

She was gone forever.

Sniffing back and swallowing the sorrow that crashed down around him every so often, Travis stood and headed for his dresser again. In doing so, something caught his eye, and he glanced out the window.

Jena. . .

An undefined emotion twisted in his chest, and he had to fight the urge to holler out the window, "Wait! Don't go!"

She's not leaving for good, you idiot. She's probably just meeting some friends.

As Travis watched his summer girl walk up the boulevard, her strawberry blond hair swinging just above her shoulders, he regretted being so terse with her earlier. True, he wasn't exactly thrilled that she'd told Bella the truth, but he also cringed at the thought of life without her. In one week's time, Jena had set his skewed world right again.

"That's the Lord, Travis. See what the Lord can do?"

The memory of Meg's voice rang in his ears, and he gazed at her photo again. She'd said those words a thousand times—whenever something good happened. *"That's God,"* or *"That's the Lord."* On the other hand, when hard times hit, Meg said that was God, too. *"We'll rejoice in adversity, and God will see us through."*

Travis shook his head and placed the picture in its damaged frame on his dresser. Meg had been the ultimate Pollyanna if there ever was one. Every cloud had a silver lining, and after every dark storm, there was a bright, beautiful rainbow. Meg had become a Christian shortly after Mandi's birth, and while she'd tried to get Travis to "see the Light," he'd never been interested enough to try to understand.

But there was one thing he now knew for certain: a Christian woman in his home, caring for his girls, was the difference between contentment and catastrophe.

Chapter 13

Jena sat alone at a back table in the coffeehouse, flipping through the bridal magazine she'd purchased at the drugstore across the street. No sooner had she taken a sip of the hazelnut-flavored iced coffee than a young man approached her.

"Excuse me, but don't I know you?"

He stood as tall as a California redwood. After craning her neck to glimpse his face, Jena shook her head. "I don't think so. At least you don't look familiar to me."

"Did you go to Lakeview Bible College in Watertown?"

"Why, yes." Jena smiled. "I still attend, actually. I'll be finishing up my last semester come fall."

"I'm Rusty McKenna," he said, folding his lanky frame into the chair across from her. Jena noted his auburn hair and thought his name was quite fitting.

"Nice to meet you. I'm Jena Calhoun."

He squinted, studying her face, then pointed a tapered finger at her. "You're the one I've seen around Mr. Larson's place."

"Yes, how did you know?"

"Because I live across the street—well, sort of across the street. His place is at the dead end of Shorewood Boulevard, and we're two houses in from the corner."

"Oh." Jena gave him a polite smile.

"Are you a relative taking care of his kids?"

"No, Travis hired me to watch Mandi and Carly for the summer."

Rusty nodded in reply, and Jena considered him. Long and narrow with his nose and jaw jutting outward, there was an equine sort of look to his face. She wouldn't say he was "handsome," but he wasn't unattractive, either. He had fascinating eyes, and an intelligent light shone from their hazel depths.

"What's your major?"

"Home ec," Jena replied. "And yours?"

"Was. . .pastoral studies. I just graduated earlier this month."

"Congratulations!"

He beamed. "Thanks."

"So. . .you're going into the ministry?"

Rusty nodded. "I feel I'm called to preach, but I just don't know where yet."

Hope bubbled up inside of Jena. *Is this the one, Lord?* She'd been praying fo God to send her a husband, and she wasn't being that picky. She wanted a mis sionary. . .or a pastor.

Very discreetly, Jena closed the bridal magazine and set it facedown on th table, beneath her handbag.

"So who's the blond I've seen over at the Larsons'? She drives that older model Cavalier."

"Oh, that's Mary Star. She's become a friend of mine since accepting Chris last December."

"Oh, neat." Rusty bobbed his large head, his wide mouth pursed in thought "You're both single, I take it."

"For the time being," Jena replied with a sassy grin.

Rusty chuckled. "Say, you want a lift back to the Larsons'? I'm leaving in few minutes. I just need to say good-bye to a few of my friends. They're sittin up in front."

"Oh, sure. That'd be great. I'd love the ride home. Thanks."

Rusty stood with a parting smile and walked away while Jena tried to quel her excitement. *Oh God, please let me know if this meeting was ordained by You* Leaning sideways, she lifted the plastic shopping bag containing the analgesi lotion for her sunburned skin that she'd bought along with the magazine. Rollin up the publication, she stuffed it into the bag. Coffee in one hand, she slung he purse over her shoulder, trying not to wince, and gripped her purchases with th other. Then she made her way up the row of tables to where Rusty conversed wit three other young men.

"Hey, guys, this is Jena," he said as she approached.

She sent them each a polite smile, and they nodded back at her.

"She works for Mr. Larson across the street—remember, I prayed abou somehow meeting that woman I told you guys about. Well. . ." He waggled thumb in Jena's direction.

He prayed about meeting me? Jena's pulse quickened.

Meanwhile, grins and exclamations emanated from his buddies. Jena fel her face flush scarlet. She took a sip of her iced coffee in an effort to conceal he chagrin.

"Listen, I've got an idea." Rusty turned to her. "How 'bout we go to the zoc tomorrow? Mark, here, will come with us, and you can ask your friend Mary Sta to come along."

Jena mulled it over. Rusty probably wanted friends to accompany them so he wouldn't feel uncomfortable their first time out together. But there was just one problem.

"I'll have to take Mandi and Carly."

"Oh, sure, that's fine. We don't have anything against kids, do we, Mark?"

"Umm, I have things to do tomorrow."

"You owe me one, buddy."

Mark rolled his blue eyes and glanced across the table at his cronies. "Yeah, okay, but let's go in the morning. I've got stuff to get done in the afternoon."

"Deal." Rusty turned to Jena. "Okay with you?"

"Sure." She was up early and so were the girls. She didn't think Travis would care if they went to the zoo.

"Do you think Mary Star will agree to come along?"

"I can probably persuade her."

"Great." Rusty grinned at his friends. "Mary Star—what do think of that name, huh?"

They all shrugged.

Jena smiled. "She likes to be called Star for short."

One of his pals laughed. "Great. Her name matches the stars in Rus's eyes."

Rusty waved a hand at them, then looked at Jena. "Do you see stars in my eyes?"

Embarrassed, she raised her shoulders in a quick up-and-down motion.

"Listen, you guys, I'll see you later. I'm driving Jena home. Mark, I'll pick you up bright and early—let's say around eight."

"I'll be ready." His tone didn't sound very enthusiastic, but Rusty seemed oblivious to the fact.

"C'mon, Jena."

She followed him out of the coffeehouse and walked beside him up the street until they reached a light blue minivan. Rusty pulled the keys out of his pocket and walked around to the driver's side. Once he'd climbed in behind the wheel, he popped the automatic lock, and Jena, juggling her coffee and drugstore purchases, opened the door.

"Nice night, isn't it?" he asked as she tried to gracefully seat herself in the van without spilling her coffee.

"Yeah, it's. . .nice." She managed to close the door, thinking Rusty should have helped her into the vehicle. Jena had several male acquaintances whom she'd met at school, and they often went out together—girls and guys—as a group. Even in that platonic situation, one of the men would open the car doors for the ladies.

"Do you know Ben Talbot?" Jena asked.

"Yeah, I think so." Rusty started the engine. "Is he short and kind of going bald already?"

"Yeah." Jena hadn't ever heard Ben described in such a negative light before. The guy had a heart of gold. "He's getting married in November to Denise Anderson. Do you know her?"

"No."

"Oh."

It was then that Jena realized Denise had graduated two years ago. She an
Ben were waiting to get married once he'd completed his master's degree.

I'm probably a good three years older than Rusty. Is that going to matter, Lord?

"So how'd you and Mary Star meet? Does she go to Lakeview Bible, too?"

"No. We met last year at my church's Christmas program. . . ."

∽

Travis walked to the front entrance of his home, intending to lock up for th
night. Through the screen door, he spied a blue van as it pulled to the front walk
way. He waited around to see if he could guess the driver's objectives when, to h
surprise, Jena jumped out of the passenger side. As the dim light illuminated th
inside of the minivan, Travis strained to get a look at the driver. It was definitel
a guy.

"Okay. See you tomorrow," he heard Jena say before slamming the door.

"See you tomorrow?" Travis raised a brow, wondering if Jena had forgotten he
responsibilities included Saturdays. Or what if she was planning to move ou
Her male friend had a van. . . .

Making his way through the house with purposeful strides, Travis exited th
back door in time to meet Jena in the courtyard. She startled when she saw hin
and Travis noticed the dark liquid that spilled from the cup in her hand, despi
its white lid.

"Travis, you scared the wits out of me!"

He grinned. "Sorry." Cocking his head, he put his hands on his hips. "Is tha
coffee?"

"Yeah."

"How can you sleep after drinking that stuff so late at night?"

"It's only ten o'clock."

"I'd be awake all night if I drank coffee at this hour."

Beneath the glow of the yard light, Travis watched as she shrugged in reply

"So, Jena," he began, slowing stepping toward her, "I, um, need to apologiz
for being so brusque earlier."

"That's okay. I knew you'd be mad."

"I'm not mad. Never was. Just, oh, maybe disappointed."

"Very understandable."

She took a few paces toward her apartment door, but Travis stepped in fron
of her.

"Jena, if you recall our initial agreement, I said you could have Sundays off."

"Right."

"Well. . ." Travis rubbed his palms together. "I didn't mean to eavesdrop
but I overheard you telling that guy in the van you'd see him tomorrow. Did yo
mean tomorrow night after eight?"

"No. I meant tomorrow during the day. We're going to the zoo, and I planned to take Mandi and Carly with me."

Travis didn't like the sound of it—Jena taking his daughters on a. . .date? No way!

"Look, Jena, I don't know. . ."

"Mary Star is coming, and so is one of Rusty's friends."

"Rusty?"

"Yeah, the guy who drove me home tonight. He just graduated from Lakeview Bible, and he lives just across the street from you."

Travis pursed his lips and mulled over the remark. "What's his last name?"

"McKenna."

Travis recognized the name at once. Jill and Ryan McKenna were nice folks who had been a great help to Meg while she was sick. "I know the McKennas. So you're interested in their son—what's his name? Rusty?"

"I don't know if I'm interested in him or not. I just met him tonight."

Travis folded his arms and regarded her sunburned face. She looked like Rudolph with that red nose. "Not to change the subject, but I think you got cooked at the beach today."

"I sure did. It's starting to smart now. I hope Mandi and Carly aren't sunburned. I doused them with sunscreen."

"And then there wasn't enough left for you, eh?"

"I thought there was. Guess not."

An uncomfortable little laugh escaped her, and she lowered her gaze. Travis, on the other hand, suddenly realized just what kind of woman Jena Calhoun was—a sacrificial one. She had made sure his daughters were spared sunburn even if it meant she got fried.

"Jena, you're a special lady, know that?"

She laughed again. "Uh-oh, sounds like you want another favor."

"Oh, thanks a heap," he retorted, sporting a grin. "I give you a compliment, and you think I'm just trying to butter you up."

"Well, you are a lawyer."

He brought his chin back, and she chuckled at his indignant expression. "I'll have you know I'm an honest lawyer."

She skirted around him and walked the rest of the way to her apartment's outer doorway. Her soft laughter wafted on the gentle breeze and seemed to wrap itself around his heart.

"I think you probably are an honest lawyer. You sure are a good daddy to your girls. They adore you."

"Thanks, but. . ." He frowned. "I don't get the connection."

"Well, maybe there isn't one—a logical one, anyway. It's just that to my way of thinking, if you were a crooked, scheming attorney, it would probably come out somehow in your parenting."

"Hmm, interesting parallel." He couldn't help but think of Craig's son, Josh. At thirty years old, the man still behaved like a spoiled child, and it always made Travis cringe to hear the condescending tone Josh used whenever he talked to his wife.

"Good night, Travis."

Rousing himself from his musings, he saw Jena step inside the door. "Good night. Sleep well."

∽

The next morning, much to Jena's dismay, she felt awful—so bad, in fact, that she phoned Star and canceled their trip to the zoo. Telling Rusty when he came to pick her up at 7:45 had been a major disappointment, as well. But she felt so woozy and sick to her stomach that even the thought of traipsing around the zoo made her want to run for the bathroom. By noon, a drumbeat pounded in her head, and the sound of Travis mowing the lawn out in front of the house didn't help matters.

Sitting in the shady backyard, watching the girls splash in their kiddy pool, Jena held a cold rag to her temples.

"Miss Jena, what's the matter?" Mandi asked, climbing out of her pool and skipping to where Jena sat at the picnic table.

"Oh, nothing. I just have a little headache."

Mandi tipped her head while she contemplated the reply. "Aunty Glenda used to say me 'n' Carly gave her a headache. Did we give you one, too?"

"No, precious. Neither of you gave it to me." Jena figured she probably just had a touch of the flu. She prayed she wouldn't pass the virus on to the girls.

Mandi returned to the pool, and minutes later, Travis rounded the corner of the yard. The girls shrieked with delight when he began splashing and tickling them. The racket made Jena tense.

"Hey, you still not feeling well?" Travis came over and sat down across from her. Beads of perspiration trickled down both sides of his face, getting lost somewhere in his shadowy jaw.

"No, I feel worse. I've got this headache that just won't quit."

"Did you take ibuprofen or something?"

"Yes." She put the wet cloth across her eyes. It felt good. . .for a few seconds.

"Look at me, Jena."

Removing the cloth, she did as he bid her and glanced across the table at him. She suddenly felt as if she'd gotten off one of those spinning rides at the fair.

"You look kind of punky." He tapered his brown eyes in a scrutinizing way. "You're going to the hospital."

"What?" Jena sat up a little straighter and watched him stand and leave the yard. Where was he going? "Travis, wait."

She sighed when he didn't come back, thinking about her rotten health insurance. It only covered big things, like operations, and she couldn't afford a medical bill.

Carly climbed up into her lap. A look of concern pinched her three-year-old features. "How come Daddy said the hosible?"

"I don't know, honey, but I'm going to be just fine." Jena couldn't help wondering if Travis was overreacting because his wife had been so sick.

Within minutes, he returned with Mrs. Barlow in his wake. "I think she's got sunstroke or sun poisoning," he said.

A jab of fear caused Jena's heart to race—which only intensified the brain-twisting pain in her head.

"I'm happy to stay with the children, Travis," Mrs. Barlow said. She stroked Jena's hair back off her forehead. "Oh, you poor dear. You look like a lobster."

"I'll go change." Travis jogged to the back door and disappeared into the house.

Holding Carly on her lap, Jena glanced up into the older woman's kindly face. "Do you really think I have sun poisoning?"

"Perhaps. But we're not going to take any chances one way or the other. You're going to the emergency room, and that's that."

Chapter 14

Travis flipped through an outdated issue of *Time* while a muted baseball game played on the television perched in a corner of the small, sterile exam room. Jena slept in the bed, an IV threaded into her arm. She had been diagnosed with some form of sun sickness, although the doctors were hesitant to label it. She'd become dehydrated, so bags of fluid were being administered. Then Jena was given a narcotic for her headache, and it knocked her out. But the good news was she would be just fine in a day or two.

Travis glanced over at Jena's sleeping form, from her blue-and-white-checked hospital gown to the crisp white sheet that had been neatly tucked around her waist. A déjà vu feeling washed over him. He'd spent countless hours sitting at Meg's bedside during her illness, and while he'd never developed an aversion to hospitals, he didn't particularly care to spend any length of time inside their walls, either. On the other hand, he was grateful medical facilities such as this one existed when he needed them—like now. But in Meg's case, her doctors had done everything possible to spare her life. The cancer had just spread too rapidly.

"Travis, what are you doing here?"

He blinked to see Jena's blue eyes regarding him with what could only be curiosity.

"I thought you would have gone back home by now." Her lids fluttered closed as though the medication wouldn't allow them to do otherwise.

"I'm waiting for you to hurry up and feel better so that we can ditch this place."

A tiny giggle escaped Jena's lips as she floated off to sleep again.

Grinning, Travis checked the score of the baseball game, then returned his attention to the magazine. He'd read two paragraphs into an article when the glass exam room door slid open and Star entered, followed by a very tall young man with auburn hair.

"I got here as fast as I could," Star said. "Mrs. Barlow told me what happened. Is Jena going to be okay?"

Travis stood and put his forefinger to his lips. "She's sleeping," he whispered, "but yes, she's going to be fine."

Star moved to Jena's bedside and stroked her hair. Seeing as he wouldn't get a formal introduction, Travis turned to the young man and stuck out his right hand. "Travis Larson."

"Oh, hi. . .Rusty McKenna."

They clasped hands, and Travis hoped his surprise didn't show on his face. *So this is Rusty.* Could Jena really be interested in this guy? In two sweeping glances, Travis decided Rusty stood about six feet five and had a mug that only a mother could love.

He cleared his throat. "I've, um, met your parents but haven't ever seen you around."

A goofy smile curved his lips. "That's probably 'cause I stayed in the dorms at school, even though the college is only about an hour's drive from here. Plus, during the past few summers I've been away on mission trips."

"Guess that explains it." Travis forced a polite smile, digesting the information. He told himself he shouldn't be shocked that Jena was interested in a man who shared her religious beliefs. But at the same time, it irked him. Then it bothered him that he felt irked.

He glanced at Jena, only to see her sitting up in bed.

"What do you think you're doing?" he asked, walking to the side of the hospital bed. Placing his hand on her shoulder, he gently pushed her back against the pillow. Her curly strawberry blond hair was splayed against the puffy white surface, and in that moment, Jena reminded him of Sleeping Beauty in his daughters' fairy-tale books.

"Travis, I feel better. I want to go home."

Leaning against the guardrails, he gazed down at her, feeling mesmerized.

"Travis. . .did you hear me?"

"What? Oh, yeah. . .I heard you." He forced himself to focus on the situation at hand "Listen, you'll go home when the doctors say you can go home. Which reminds me. . ." He looked over at Star. "Can you spend the night with her? I don't think Jena should be alone up in her apartment tonight."

"Sure. I'll call my parents and let them know." Star glanced down at Jena. "We'll take care of you, honey. You just peep, and we'll be there for you."

"Oh, good grief."

Travis smirked. "Too bad you're so sunburned, Jena. Now we can't see you blush."

With an exasperated moan, she pulled the sheet up over her face, and Travis laughed.

∽

"Are you sure you're okay, Jena? I mean, maybe I should have Travis come up here and take your temperature or something."

"Shut up!" Jena laughed and threw a pillow at Star.

It smacked her shoulder, and Star chuckled. "Well, he's only phoned twice in the past hour and a half to make sure you're all right."

Jena sighed. "Yeah, but that's because Bella Minniati can't take no for an answer. Travis tried to get out of going to church tomorrow morning and lunch afterwards, but Bella won't hear of it. She told him that if I'm too sick, he has to come and bring the girls. Of course, Travis won't argue because he still hopes Bella will sign on with his law firm."

"Oh, what a tangled web we weave. . ."

"Amen!"

Sitting on the opposite end of the couch, Star whipped the pillow back at her, but Jena caught it easily. "So what do you think of Rusty?"

The smile slipped from Star's heart-shaped face. "Do you like him, Jena? I mean. . .romantically speaking?"

At Star's tone, Jena's guard went up. "Why do you ask?"

"Well, because. . .I'm rather attracted to him for some odd reason. He's really not my type at all. I always imagined myself marrying a guy like Travis Larson."

Disappointment swelled in Jena's chest. "What about Tom? You've been dating him on and off for some time now."

"Yeah, well, we're off again. He's got some weird phobia about commitment. But then along comes Rusty. . .and this afternoon he said he'd been asking God if he could meet me, so when he ran into you last night, it was like the Lord answered his prayer." Star shrugged, and two rosy spots suddenly appeared on her cheeks. "I guess I thought that was really romantic. Rusty obviously doesn't have a problem with the idea of lasting relationships."

"That's awesome," Jena replied, even though she felt like sobbing. Rusty had been drawn to Star the entire time, and now Jena felt stupid for thinking it was she who'd sparked his interest. "Well, listen, I'm going to bed. Are you sure you'll be okay here on the sofa?"

"I'm totally fine. I'm just going to read a chapter in my Bible and go to sleep."

"Okay. G'night." Jena walked to her bedroom. Inside, she closed the door and leaned against it as the first of many tears trickled from her eyes.

&

The next morning, the sunshine streamed in through her bedroom window and woke Jena. It was like a hug and a smile from her heavenly Father. Her disappointment had ebbed, and Jena felt more determined than ever to trust God with her future. So what if she ended up husband-less? There were worse fates in life. Jena decided that if she never married, she would simply be a blessing to another family.

After showering, she donned the best outfit she owned, a navy blue coatdress that had white buttons down the front and bold white trim along its V-neck. Her tight, sunburned skin protested her every move, but Jena ignored it. If she ended up a missionary in a third-world country, there would be no concessions for a pampered little rose. She'd have to be as strong as a willow in order to weather the climate and rough conditions. She might as well start now.

Feeling determined, Jena headed over to Travis's, where she prepared a light breakfast. After Mandi and Carly woke up, she gathered their clothes and led them downstairs into the sunny den, where she helped the two little ones into frilly summertime dresses that looked as though they'd never been worn. By the time Travis entered the kitchen, Jena had finished arranging both girls' hair and now encouraged them to eat their cereal and toast.

"Daddy, don't we look pretty?" Mandi asked. She jumped off her chair and twirled around on one heel of her shiny black Mary Janes.

He nodded distractedly and looked at Jena. "You're supposed to be in bed recuperating."

"I'm recuperated."

"No." Travis shook his head. "The doctor made it clear you're to rest for at least forty-eight hours. Now scoot."

Jena knew he was right, but she didn't think going to church would put that much of a strain on her body. "I can rest this afternoon. I'm not a docile little thing. I'm an able-bodied woman."

"Yeah, and I aim to keep you that way so I won't have to miss work tomorrow." He inclined his head toward the back door.

"Travis, I—"

"Don't argue with me, Jena."

His tone and stern expression left no room for debate, although she glimpsed a compassionate light in his cocoa brown eyes as he finished knotting his tie.

Returning a small smile, she stood and pushed in the kitchen chair under the table. "All right, you win," she said, making her way to the back door.

"Thanks for dressing the girls and fixing their hair," he called after her. "I appreciate it."

She glanced at him from over her shoulder. "You're welcome."

"And get some rest, you hear?"

Unable to help herself, Jena saluted.

He narrowed his gaze at her as if warning her not to be so sassy, and she chuckled all the way back to her apartment. Entering the living room, she heard Star singing in the shower. She, too, would be leaving for church soon. Jena glanced around her apartment and wondered what she'd do with her time. She was accustomed to staying busy, barely having a moment to think, let alone hours of idleness.

She walked into her bedroom, where she undressed and hung up her good clothes. She slipped off her stockings, stuffing them in her top dresser drawer. Next she pulled on a yellow printed cotton skirt with a loose elastic waistband and a matching yellow T-shirt. The material felt so soft against her damaged skin that a small sigh of relief escaped Jena's lips. Perhaps Travis had been right in ordering her to rest. She wasn't quite up to par yet.

An hour later, after Star left, Jena pulled out her Bible and proceeded to have some personal devotion time. She praised God for all her blessings, including her summer job. Sunburn aside, the first week had gone extremely well, and at the hospital, the admitting registrar had taken a charity application designed for those like Jena who didn't have quality health insurance. Jena asked forgiveness for envying Star and Rusty and prayed for the Lord to lead in that relationship. She continued to pray, pleading with God to help her feel content as a single woman and to use her to further His heavenly kingdom.

It was then that Jena felt a special burden for Travis's soul. *Oh, please, dear Lord Jesus, let him hear the good news loud and clear this morning. Open his heart so he understands why You left Your ivory palace to live as a man of little means and die a cruel death for our sins. I also pray for Mandi and Carly. Whet their appetite for Your Word, and. . .help them behave. . . .*

After finishing her petition, the heaviness in her spirit for Travis didn't abate. She prayed again. Then once more. At long last she gave the matter over to God, trusting that the outcome would be to His glory.

Chapter 15

Travis tried to stifle another yawn as he sat to Joe Minniati's left. He forced a complacent expression while he listened to the pastor drone on about some such thing. Glancing at Joe, who appeared attentive, occasionally scribbling down a few notes, Travis decided he'd best pay attention in case the Minnatis wanted to discuss the message over lunch.

"The Bible was written as proof and testimony of the deity of Jesus Christ," said the bald-headed African-American man at the pulpit. He had a kind-sounding voice despite the austere look on his face. "There is no way anyone can dispute the fact that Jesus Christ is God, sent from God, and is the second person of the Trinity after reading this Book."

Travis glanced at the Bible in his lap. It had belonged to Meg, and the passage in Colossians from which the pastor's message was derived had been underlined with a purple fine-point pen. Meg had believed this Book. She'd been a devoted Christian.

"And why anyone wouldn't come to Christ after reading John chapter 3 and 'You must be born again' is a mystery to me," the pastor continued. "If Jesus said it, we'd better do it."

That phrase—"come to Christ"—triggered the memory of a promise Travis had made to Meg on her deathbed. Her last wish was that he would "come to Christ" so she would see him in heaven, and Travis vowed he would. Then again, he would have lassoed the moon for Meg at that point just to ease her burden. He'd felt so helpless watching her die.

"Come to Christ"—what did that mean? How did a person go about coming to Christ? Was there a ritual involved? Did he have to join a church? Travis tried to remember how Meg had come to Christ, but he couldn't recall. He thought she might have had some sort of religious experience shortly after Mandi was born, but he didn't know what had brought it about.

Sorry, Meg, I just don't understand.

The congregation suddenly stood to its feet, and Travis realized the sermon had ended. After a short prayer, the pianist began to plunk out a lively melody, and church members vacated their pews and filled the aisles, laughing, talking, and greeting each other.

"What did you think, Travis?" Bella asked. She'd been sitting on the other side of her husband.

"Your pastor is very articulate," he replied lamely.

"He's an educated man," Joe said. "He's got an earned doctorate. He served in the Air Force and has his pilot's license, so he's big on mission aviation."

"What's mission aviation?" Travis couldn't help asking as they left the sanctuary.

"Pastor Richards has flown to third-world countries," Bella answered, "to feed starving people who need the Bread of Life."

"Hmm, I see." Standing in the foyer, he glanced to his left. "This way to pick up my girls?"

Bella shook her head. "No, this way." She motioned to the right. "I hope they had a good time. They're adorable, Travis. I'm just sorry Jena couldn't come today. She's an absolute doll. . .and she fixed the girls' hair so cute."

Travis expelled a long breath and followed a babbling Bella down a crowded corridor and into a large room where the pastor's wife held what the Minniati called "children's church." Inside, Mandi and Carly were having so much fun playing with the toys and the other children that it took Travis a few minutes to get their attention. Once they spotted him, however, they dropped what they were doing and came running, their arms outstretched. The sight warmed Travis's heart.

∽

Jena sat in the shady courtyard, relaxing on the chaise lounge and reading a collection of stories about women who became brides on the Oregon Trail. She enjoyed adventurous, wholesome romances, particularly about brides to be. Jena prayed she would get married someday, but she figured it didn't hurt to read about the thrills and frills surrounding weddings, and she couldn't recall when she'd last been able to enjoy some good fiction. Attending college and working several odd jobs that accommodated her schedule didn't leave much room for relaxation. But her minor debilitation proved to be something of a blessing. Jena had even found time to phone her parents this morning. Of course, the conversations with her mother, father, and brother never got past superficial topics as they each told her about their busy lives. No one asked about Jena, and that hurt. It seemed as if her family couldn't see beyond themselves—but that wasn't new, and she told herself she shouldn't feel surprised. She'd just have to pray harder.

"Hello, dearie."

Glancing up, Jena watched Mrs. Barlow enter the small yard. Dressed in a blue and white dress, the older woman looked to have just come back from church. "What are you doing home? I thought your Sunday afternoons were reserved for your grandchildren."

Smiling, Mrs. Barlow took a seat in a nearby lawn chair. "I was worried about you, so after having lunch with my son and his family, I thought I'd drive back and make sure you're all right."

"I'm fine." Jena felt a tad guilty for worrying her sweet friend.

"Is Travis home? Things sound too quiet around here. Are Mandi and Carly gone?"

"No. . .and yes," Jena replied with a little laugh at the "too quiet" remark. "Nobody's home. Travis took the girls to church with him. He was invited by the Minniatis."

"You don't say? Why, Meg would be ecstatic to hear he took his daughters to hear the preaching of the Word. She tried and tried to get Travis to attend with her. He always said he was too busy."

Jena's heart constricted. "What a shame." She wondered if he regretted those "I'm too busy" decisions now.

The sound of a car pulling into the driveway drew Jena's attention, and she looked up in time to see the front quarter panel of Travis's shining black Lexus. Within no time at all, Mandi skipped into the courtyard.

"Well, hello, darling!" Mrs. Barlow said with a broad grin.

"Hi!" Mandi sat down on the edge of Jena's chair.

Jena smiled. "Did you have fun at church today?"

"Uh-huh. We sang and drew pictures, then Mrs. Smith told us a story about a boy named David who killed a mean giant."

Jena's smile grew just as Travis entered the yard, carrying a sleeping Carly over his shoulder.

"I hope you've been resting," he told Jena before greeting Mrs. Barlow.

"I have, so don't worry. How'd it go this morning?"

"Fine." Travis grinned. "I think Bella's going to sign."

"That's great news!"

"Sure is." Reaching the back door, Travis pulled the keys from his pocket. "Come on, Mandi. Nap time."

"But I'm not tired," she whined.

Travis narrowed his gaze, giving his daughter that sardonic lawyer look for which Jena found him so famous. She bit back a laugh, thinking he might be able to intimidate jurors, but poor Travis had little influence on Mandi.

"I'm too big for a nap, Daddy." The girl turned to Jena, her childish brown eyes pleading for an ally. "Right?"

"Obey your father," Jena prompted on an encouraging note.

Pouting, Mandi rose from the lawn chair and stomped to the back door. Mrs. Barlow put her fingers over her lips in an effort to hide her amusement.

"If I'm not too old for a nap, neither are you," Travis said, following his oldest daughter into the house.

The screen door squeaked on its hinges, closing behind the Larson family.

Jena chuckled at Travis's parting remark and glanced at Mrs. Barlow.

"Travis is such a good father, isn't he?"

"Yes, he is." Jena didn't have to think twice before answering. "Now, tell me what I missed at church this morning. Did Star have a guest?"

"Why, yes. Rusty McKenna, our neighbor right across the street. Do you know him?"

"Just met him." Disappointment gave her a hard jab, but it felt more annoying than painful. "I'm praying for them."

"Well, I was surprised, to say the least. I never would have thought Rusty and Star. . ."

Mrs. Barlow giggled like a girl, causing Jena to laugh, too.

They continued chatting for quite some time before Jena heard the back door open. Glancing off to her right, she half expected to see Mandi sneaking outside and abandoning her naptime. But instead she saw Travis striding toward them. He'd changed from his suit and tie and now wore blue jeans and a short-sleeved T-shirt.

"Hey, can I ask you two something?" Reaching the adjacent lawn chair, he sat down.

"Sure."

"Yes, of course, Travis," Mrs. Barlow reiterated. "What is it?"

Leaning forward, he studied his hands dangling over his knees before meeting Jena's gaze. "What does 'come to Christ' mean?"

Taken by surprise, she blinked. "Isn't the phrase self-explanatory?"

"Not to me. My family attended a myriad of churches when I was growing up and only on special occasions. But my wife had beliefs similar to yours." He glanced across the way. "And yours, too, Mrs. Barlow—and the Minniatis', too. Before she died, Meg said she wanted me to 'come to Christ.' But I just don't know how."

Jena noted the earnest expression on his face and the beseeching look in his dark eyes. Her heart melted with compassion. *Oh Lord, Travis is like that prisoner in the book of Acts who asked, "What must I do to be saved?" Give Mrs. Barlow and me the right words to answer him.*

"Well, Travis, 'coming to Christ' refers to one's salvation experience," the older woman began, "and no two conversions are alike. For instance, I was a young girl when I became a Christian. Jena, what about you?"

"I came to Christ one night when I was in high school. I visited a friend's youth group, and after hearing the pastor's message, I realized I was a sinner and had no hope of eternal life, except by believing in Jesus Christ as the only Way to heaven. Jesus is God and man. He lived a perfect life here on earth and allowed Roman soldiers to crucify Him so that—"

She paused, seeing Travis's confused expression. "Maybe we could explain better if we showed you some verses in the Bible."

"Good idea," said Mrs. Barlow with an approving nod of her head.

Jena swung her legs off the lawn chair and stood. "I'll go get mine. It's upstairs."

"I've got Meg's Bible in the kitchen. Want to use that one?"

"Um, sure." *Oh Lord, he's so open!*

Excitement coursed through Jena as she followed Mrs. Barlow and Travis into the house. But she tried to keep a level head as they took seats at the kitchen table.

Jena watched as Mrs. Barlow reverently opened Meg's Bible to the book of Romans. She noticed verse 23 in chapter 3 had been underlined.

"Look, Travis," Mrs. Barlow said, "God's Word tells us that all have sinned and come short of the glory of God. None of us is perfect. We've all done things wrong. Do you agree with that?"

"Sure."

"Okay, then." The kindly neighbor lady flipped to verse 23 of chapter 6. It, too, had been underlined with blue ink. "God says, 'For the wages of sin is death.' See, because we've done wrong, there are consequences. Just like when your daughters act up. You have to discipline them. Because we've sinned, we deserve eternal punishment since God cannot allow sin into heaven. But look what the latter part of this passage says, 'but the gift of God is eternal life through Christ Jesus our Lord.'"

Jena sent up prayer after prayer while Mrs. Barlow paged back to the book of John and found verse 16 in chapter 3. It had been highlighted in yellow marker. *"For God so loved the world, that he gave his only begotten Son, that whosoever believeth in him should not perish, but have everlasting life."*

"God gave us His Son, Jesus Christ, to take our punishment," Mrs. Barlow explained. "Our heavenly Father sacrificed for us, just like you would sacrifice for Mandi and Carly."

Pursing his lips and looking thoughtful, Travis nodded.

Mrs. Barlow returned to the book of Romans and found chapter 5, verse 8. It, like the others, had been underlined. "'But God commendeth his love toward us, in that, while we were yet sinners, Christ died for us.'" She glanced up from the Bible. "Travis, do you understand about sin and its consequences?"

"Yep. That's one thing I do understand." He sat back in his chair. "The courts prosecute sinners everyday. When people break the law, they have to pay the price."

"Exactly." Mrs. Barlow smiled, and Jena felt elated that the truth of the gospel was getting through to him. "But in this case, Jesus stepped up and told the judge that He would pay for our crimes. He died on the cross for us. But on the third day, God raised Him from the dead. Jesus is alive today—and those who believe will live forever with Him."

"Except we have to die first," Travis interjected.

Jena noted the faraway look in his eyes. She sensed Travis was thinking of his deceased wife. "That's the sin-cursed part of this life," she said. "It'll end in death. The cold, hard fact is everybody is going to die sometime. But where we'll spend our eternity is the decision we make while we're living."

"That's right. Here, look. . ." Mrs. Barlow turned to Romans 10:9. "And this is how a person 'comes to Christ,' Travis." She showed him the verse. *"That if thou shalt confess with thy mouth the Lord Jesus, and shalt believe in thine heart that God hath raised him from the dead, thou shalt be saved."*

"Do you believe that, Travis?"

A pensive expression crossed his face as his soul hung in the balance. Jena prayed as hard as she knew how. *Please, God, let him understand all this. . . .*

"You know what?" he answered at last, "I do believe it. I'll tell you why. I saw something different in my wife after she came to Christ when Mandi was a baby. Over the years, I watched Meg devote herself to our daughter and me. She was so different from my friends' wives. I felt like the luckiest guy on earth. Meg didn't care about material things or push me up the corporate ladder or flirt at dinner parties. When she found out she was pregnant again, she put Carly's life before her own after she learned she had cancer." Travis drew in a deep breath, then shook his head. "Scores of people advised Meg to terminate her pregnancy so she could get chemotherapy, but she refused—for Carly's sake."

Tears sprang into Jena's eyes, and she pressed her lips together in an effort to stave off her emotions.

Travis tapped a finger on the open Bible. "And I believe this is true, Mrs. Barlow, because I've seen it in you over the years. . .and now I've seen it in Jena, too." He looked across the table at her, and their gazes met. "For a single lady, you're really different—and I mean that as a compliment. After one week, I've seen how hard you work, the kind way in which you take care of my girls. You don't swear or watch smut on TV, and you don't have men coming and going all hours of the day and night." He paused, his dark gaze penetrating hers. "I know there's a God in heaven, Jena, because you brought Him back into my house."

She swatted at her tears. "Oh, Travis, I've got plenty of faults. But I'm so blessed to hear that you've seen Jesus in me."

"I have. Know what else? I think Meg would really like you."

Jena could barely find her voice. "I think I would have liked Meg, too."

"She was a lovely person," Mrs. Barlow said wistfully. But then her age-lined face broke into a grin. "But it was definitely no accident that Jena came to work for you, Travis. Somehow I knew she was the one for the summer girl job."

"You were right."

He chuckled and sent Jena a wink that made her cheeks flame with embarrassment. *Good thing I'm already pink from my sunburn.*

"Well, young man, you have a decision to make."

"I do?" He glanced at Mrs. Barlow with questions pooling in his eyes.

"Do you want to get saved?" she asked in a caring tone. "Do you want to come to Christ?"

"Umm. . .that depends. What do I have to do? Walk over hot coals or something?"

Jena couldn't suppress the laugh that bubbled up inside her.

"No, silly," Mrs. Barlow said with a smile. "Here, look." She pointed to verse 13 and read, " 'For whosoever shall call upon the name of the Lord shall be saved.' You just pray, Travis. Confess your sins to Christ, ask for forgiveness, then ask Him to save you. You come to Christ in prayer."

"That's it?" He brought his chin back in surprise.

"That's it."

"Okay. . ." But suddenly he looked so lost. "Uh, praying is sort of unfamiliar territory for me."

"Would you like Jena and me to pray with you?"

He nodded a silent reply.

Jena gave him a smile and stretched her arm across the table, offering him her hand. Travis took it, then clasped Mrs. Barlow's hand, as well.

"Just repeat after me, all right?"

"All right."

Trying to squelch her anticipation, Jena forced herself to concentrate as Mrs. Barlow led Travis in prayer.

"Dear God, I confess to You my sinfulness. . . ." She paused to let Travis echo her. "I'm sorry for all the wrong things I've said and done, and I understand that it was because of me and my sin that Jesus went to the cross and died. . . . I ask You to forgive me, and I ask Jesus to come into my heart and live forever. . . . I ask You to save me. . . . Thank You for this most precious gift of eternal life that I now accept. . . . In Jesus' name, amen."

When Travis finished, Jena lifted her gaze and searched his face. "Did you mean it?"

"Every word."

"Well then. . ." She squeezed his hand and smiled. "You came to Christ and were saved."

"Congratulations, Travis," Mrs. Barlow said as tears of joy filled her rheumy eyes. "The angels are now rejoicing in heaven!"

Chapter 16

The following morning, Jena helped the girls dress, then after baking a pan of brownies, she took them to her church's Memorial Day picnic. The sky was overcast in the beginning, but the humidity thickened once the sun appeared. While Jena expected to have a fun time at the outing, despite the clammy weather, everything that could go wrong did. Mandi whined and complained because she wanted pizza for lunch, not a grilled hamburger. Next she thoughtlessly tossed a ball in the air and it landed on another little girl's head, bringing an aggravated father to the picnic table at which Jena was sitting. Carly wet her pants, and Jena had forgotten to pack extra clothes, so she gathered up their things and walked the girls to the car—only to realize she'd locked the keys inside the Volvo. Three men tried to open the hatch but were unsuccessful, so Jena had to use Star's cell phone and call Travis, who had planned to take the day to catch up on some paperwork. From the tone of his voice, Jena could tell that he was not thrilled to be summoned across town to a picnic because his summer girl had left her brain at home that morning.

"So much for my glowing attributes," Jena said, handing the phone back to Star.

"You're human. So what? Besides, this is probably some satanic attack because you led Travis to Christ. You rocked the Evil One's kingdom, so he's striking back." She grinned. "But you're on the winning side, and Travis is a Christian now. How cool is that?"

"Very cool." Jena smiled, marveling at her friend's perception. Star was a relatively new Christian, too. "But salvation is only the beginning. How do I get Travis interested in a Bible study?"

"That's God's department."

"Right." Jena felt properly chastened.

At that moment, Tammy Bissell approached them. A heavyset, well-intentioned woman, Tammy offered Jena the use of her daughter's spare outfit so Carly could get out of her wet things.

"You're a godsend, Mrs. Bissell. Thanks." Leaving Mandi under Star's supervision, Jena took Carly to the rustic park restrooms, where she washed and changed the little girl. But Carly didn't like the shorts set and pitched a fit. Jena felt her nerves begin to fray.

Deciding there was no point in arguing with the three-year-old, Jena put the wet clothes back on, only to have Carly change her mind and want to wear the other outfit after all. On the way back to the car, Jena felt like a hypocrite. She'd been tempted to throttle Carly in the bathroom for having a hissy fit, and yet she'd given Travis the impression that she was great with kids. Guess she wasn't so great with them after all. Did that mean she'd selected the wrong major in college? Jena sighed. Maybe she wasn't cut out to manage a daycare center, which meant the last eight years of her life had been a complete waste of time.

Or maybe I'm still in the stages of recuperation. An instant later, she realized that was exactly her problem. After all, she'd had sun poisoning this weekend. Anyone would feel less than patient and loving under those conditions. *Thank You, Father, for helping me understand myself.*

Up ahead in the parking lot, Jena saw that Travis had arrived. Star, Rusty, and Mandi stood nearby while he opened the Volvo wagon's hatch and retrieved the car keys.

"Sorry to have inconvenienced you," Jena said to Travis when she reached him.

He tossed the keys at her, accompanied by a long look. But whether it stemmed from exasperation or amusement, Jena couldn't tell.

"Travis Larson! What in the world are you doing here?"

The deep voice of Derek Ryan drew Jena's gaze. He was a man of medium height and build, and she didn't know him well, but suddenly she remembered what little she did know about him: Mr. Ryan was an attorney. Like Travis!

"Hey, man, good to see you again." Travis stuck out his right hand, and Derek clasped it before balling his other fist and giving Travis a friendly sock in the arm.

"I didn't know you were here at the picnic."

"I'm not. My summer girl needed my, um, assistance." Travis glanced Jena's way and cleared his throat loudly. She shrugged, but in that moment, she knew Travis wasn't miffed at her.

"Your. . .who? Summer girl?" A blank expression crossed Derek's face.

"I work for Travis, taking care of his daughters," Jena explained. "For the summer."

"Oh, I get it." He grinned. Raking a hand through his light brown hair, he turned back to Travis. "You up for a ball game?"

"Naw, I've got tons of work to do."

"Okay." A goading gleam brightened Ryan's eyes. "You're probably too out of shape anyway, you old man."

"Yeah, right. I'm no older than you are, and I could take you on in sports any day—just like I do in the courtroom."

Oh, brother! In Jena's opinion, guys were all ego and appetite—and out of the two, they were mostly ego.

"Prove it, Larson. Join our game this afternoon. Let's see what you're made of."

Travis stared off in the distance; his eyes narrowed and seemed to weigh the options. He glanced at Jena, and she decided to get out of the line of scrimmage by walking over to where Star and Rusty stood. Mandi had left for the swings and seemed to be getting along with the other kids. A teenage girl pushed them one at a time, higher, higher, causing the children to squeal with delight.

Folding her arms, Jena returned her attention to Travis, who had tossed Carly over his shoulder like a sack of potatoes.

"You're on, Derek."

"Great. We play with a softball, so you ought to be able to get a few hits in."

With one hand on Carly, Travis chuckled and pointed a warning forefinger at his challenger. "Just keep that pretty head of yours low."

Derek laughed. "C'mon. Follow me to yonder baseball field."

∞

Two days later, Travis sat in his office at Duncan, Duncan, and Larson and massaged his right arm. He must have been nuts to think he could play softball without warming up. What did he think, that he was still seventeen? The only consolation was that Derek had admitted to being just as sore. They had shared a good laugh over it before court this morning.

"Travis?"

Looking up, he saw Marci, his firm's secretary, standing in the doorway. A dark-haired woman in her fifties, Marci had a nervous demeanor, and she flitted around the office like a crazed hummingbird.

"Bella Minniati is here to see you."

"Great. Send her in."

Travis cleared off his desk in time to greet Bella as she entered his office and closed the door.

"Travis, how are you?"

"Terrific. How 'bout yourself?"

"I still get morning sickness, but at least the nausea doesn't linger throughout the day anymore."

Nodding, he offered Bella one of the maroon leather chairs in front of his desk. "Meg was sick a lot at first, too."

Bella replied with an empathetic grin. "I've got the contract here." She reached into her briefcase and pulled out the document. "I rewrote a section before signing it. Here. Take a look."

Travis read it through, noting it stated that he was to act as the exclusive attorney for the Milwaukee Mavericks team. If he ever left Duncan, Duncan, and Larson, the team would remain his client and could not be handed off to either of his partners.

"Craig'll never go for this," Travis said, tossing the contract onto his desk.

"Then I don't sign." Bella sat forward. "Personally, Trav, I think you should get rid of Duncan and Duncan. I don't trust Craig, and I've heard from a reputable source that his son is a chip off the ol' block."

"Look, Bella, that topic isn't open for discussion. I'll have Craig read over the contract, but I can guarantee he won't approve it."

She sat back, and her eyes sparked with something akin to mischief. "Come to work for the Mavericks. The team has enough issues to keep any lawyer busy, and we'll pay you a handsome salary."

Travis chewed the corner of his lip in contemplation. "Hmm. . . It's tempting."

"Think about it."

"I will."

Their meeting lasted awhile longer, then Travis escorted Bella into the lobby.

"Tell Jena hello for me."

"Will do."

Bella paused before exiting the firm's office suites. "You know, Travis, I really should give you fair warning. I plan to steal your summer girl. Joe and I are mulling over the idea of purchasing a daycare center. There are big bucks in daycare these days, and Jena would make an awesome director. I have no doubt that she'd hire the most competent staff." Bella gave her abdomen a loving pat. "And I'm going to need responsible, caring people to watch Junior. . . ."

Travis did his best to act nonchalant. "Jena's a free agent."

"So she is." Bella's red lips curved into a broad smile. "Ta-ta for now, Travis. Get back to me soon about that contract."

He nodded and watched the impeccably dressed woman sashay to the elevators. Then, turning, he made his way back to his office, deciding that Bella Minniati would steal his summer girl over his dead body. Lifting the telephone, Travis called home.

∽

"Hi, Jen, how're things?"

"Fine." Sitting in the yard, holding the cordless phone, Jena smiled. "Mandi and Carly are watering the flowers we planted. It's so cute the way they carry around their toy watering cans."

A chuckle came forth from the other end of the line. "You're staying out of the sun, I hope."

"Yes."

"Say, listen. I've been thinking. You're working out great, the girls adore you—"

"I adore them, too." Jena meant every word. Sure, Mandi had her whiny moments and Carly had her three-year-old meltdowns, but Jena was rapidly learning how to deal with both girls without feeling frazzled.

"I can tell you're fond of my daughters. That's why I wondered if you would consider staying on in the fall."

"No, I can't. I have one semester left of school, and I've worked too hard and too long not to finish my degree."

"I understand. I'm not asking you to drop out of college. We'll work around your classes."

"That might be difficult since I attend a school that's more than an hour away."

"You'll have a car and a rent-free apartment. Won't those two perks make up for the long commute?"

"Hmm. Maybe."

Jena heard Travis's deep laugh. "I'll draw up a contract and bring it home tonight."

She frowned. "Contract? We don't need a contract."

"Oh yes, we do. With people like Bella Minniati in the world, we need a contract."

"Bella? What's she got to do with my working for you?"

A pause. "Nothing." Travis's tone turned somber. "I'll see you tonight."

"Okay." Jena felt totally confused—and a bit worried. "Travis, did I do something wrong?"

"Not at all. You're the best, Jen."

She rolled her eyes.

"By the way, what are you making for supper?"

"Anything you want," she quipped, figuring she would appeal to the appetite side of him, and maybe he'd snap out of whatever funk he'd gotten into. "Name it."

"I'm not picky," Travis replied. "Just don't make anything. . .Italian."

She frowned. Didn't he like Italian food? "All right."

"See you later."

"Bye." Jena pushed the OFF button on the phone and decided that was the weirdest call she'd had in all of her born days.

Chapter 17

True to his word, Travis had a contract drawn up, and Jena signed it. The terms were obvious. For the next twelve months, she agreed to take care of Mandi and Carly, and in return, he promised to allow her to finish college and pay her the same salary she presently earned, along with providing her room and board and unlimited use of his car. What a deal! How could she go wrong? But Jena knew she would eventually have to begin a career. Working for Travis, however, would enable her to finish school and save some money in the process. Then, during the last few months of her employment, she could do some job hunting. By this time next year, Jena hoped to be working in her field of expertise.

"Are you from around here?" Travis asked as he folded his copy of their signed contract. "I don't recall you mentioning your family."

"No, I'm from California."

"Really?" Travis sat back in his handsome leather desk chair. "You're a long way from home, little girl."

"I'm not so little. I'll be twenty-seven at the end of August."

Travis grinned at her tart reply. "I talk to my parents almost every day, and Meg's folks call from Minnesota at least once a week."

"Consider yourself blessed, Travis. My family isn't close. We never have been. Each of us has always operated independently. I talk to my parents once a month—if I can catch them at home—and I've only gone back to California once since I started college. Wisconsin is my home now."

"That's too bad—about your family, I mean."

"Yes, but I can't change them. I can only determine to do things differently when I get married and have kids."

"When?" Travis lifted one dark brow. "Is there something I should know?"

Jena laughed. "I just signed a one-year contract to work for you. What do you think?"

"Just checking." He smirked and sat forward. Pursing his lips, he regarded her in a thoughtful manner. "Hey, I'm curious. . .and I mean no offense by this, but it seems to be taking you an unusually long time to finish college. Did you change your major a couple of times?"

"No. I just didn't want to take out any loans." Jena had become accustomed to people questioning her lengthy college stint. Where once she felt embarrassed about it, she now held her head up with dignity. "I've paid my entire way through school, with the exception of grant and scholarship money. God provided me with the job opportunities and the classes to fit my budget each semester."

"Quite commendable."

"I think so. I read somewhere that the average grad ends his college career more than thirty thousand dollars in debt. I decided long ago that if I ever married a man in the ministry, I wouldn't want to burden him financially with my school loans. So I made up my mind to pay my own way."

"I'm impressed, Jena." Travis tipped his head. "A man in the ministry—is that what you're looking for in a husband? You want a guy like Rusty?"

Jena lowered her gaze and deliberately skirted his question. For some odd reason, she didn't want to discuss boyfriends—or lack thereof—with Travis. "Rusty is interested in Star."

"Yeah, I kind of wondered after seeing them together yesterday. Are you upset?"

"Not at all." She meant that, too. Sure, she had been disappointed at first. But she'd soon gotten over it. Now she felt happy for her friends.

Jena glanced at her wristwatch and realized Star would be knocking at her door any minute. Tuesday nights were reserved for their discipleship lesson, although last week they hadn't met because Jena was still settling into her apartment and adjusting to her new job.

She stood. "I should get going. Star's coming over tonight."

"All right." Travis stood also. "I'll see you in the morning."

"Good night."

His expression couldn't be easily defined, although a soft light appeared in his brown eyes. " 'Night, Jena."

⤜⤐

As the week advanced, Travis found himself easing into a comfortable routine. The girls were happy, and Jena proved to be a master at organization. She even clipped coupons before grocery shopping. The cupboards were stocked, the refrigerator full, and each bathroom had a convenient supply of toilet paper beneath its vanity. Oddly, those common necessities had often fueled veritable crises while his sister Glenda was in charge. But since he no longer had to fret about his home situation, Travis put more effort into his career. He won a long-shot lawsuit, and with that victory came the praise of his colleague Craig Duncan.

"Trav, I think you're back to your old self. I'll admit I was worried for a while."

Placing his attaché case on his desk, Travis glanced over his shoulder and grinned at the older man. "I was worried for a while, too. But now that I have a summer girl. . ."

"Oh yes, Susie Homemaker herself."

"Hey, don't knock it."

"I won't, I won't. If it works for you, great." Clearing his throat, Craig took a seat in a nearby armchair. "Now, correct me if I'm wrong, but did I hear you talking to someone on the phone about attending a. . .a Bible study?"

"You're a seasoned eavesdropper." Travis laughed. "But yes, to answer your question. Derek Ryan leads the study once a week in his home."

"Derek Ryan—do I know him?"

"Yep, he works for Liberty International."

"Oh, that's right. He's one of those guys obsessed with religious freedoms."

"Somebody's got to do it."

"I suppose." Craig yawned.

Travis placed his hands on his hips. "Not to change the subject, but did you read the contract Bella dropped off last week?"

Craig snapped his fingers. "Yes, and I signed both copies. So did Josh. I'll go get the paperwork. I meant to give it to you yesterday."

He signed it? Travis felt himself gape as he watched his business partner stride to his own office and return with the contract.

"Here you go." He tossed the papers onto Travis's briefcase.

"And you, um, read the whole thing?"

"Sure. If Bella wants you to act exclusively on behalf of the Mavericks, that's fine by me."

Travis rubbed his jaw. Craig had obviously stopped there and hadn't read the rest of the contract's terms. "You want to read it over once more—just to be sure everything's in order?"

"What for? Now, look, Travis. I might be pushing sixty-five, but I've got my wits about me. Do you doubt that?"

"Nope."

"Well, okay then. Give Bella her copy. . .and I'm glad it's you who has to deal with that woman and not me. How 'bout we celebrate your recent successes by stopping at the Black Tie and having a few drinks before going home?"

Travis shrugged. "Okay. Sure."

"Great. I'll let Josh and Yolanda know. . .and maybe Marci will even want to tag along." Smiling, Craig walked out of the office.

Travis lowered himself into his chair and loosened his tie. He felt more concerned than ever about his affiliation with Duncan and Duncan. It bothered him that Craig had skimmed through the Mavericks' contract. Craig's lackadaisical attitude could cost the firm everything.

So what do I do now? Part of Travis wanted to keep his mouth shut and toast to the hard-earned signed contract, while another part of him didn't think that would be right. Still another fraction of his being urged him to accept Bella's offer and get out of this partnership before things got ugly.

"Okay, God," he said, reclining in his chair and gazing at the ceiling. "Derek said we're supposed to come to You with everything. So. . .what do You think?"

Inhaling deeply, Travis wondered how long he'd have to wait for a divine reply.

He glanced at his watch. Just after four. His stomach moaned in protest at eating only a chef's salad at lunchtime. Picking up the phone, Travis called his home number. Jena answered, and he could hear some kind of uproar in the background.

"Hi, Travis."

"Hi. What's going on over there?"

"Oh, your parents stopped by to see the kids, and Star came over just to say hello. She's got an important catering job tonight, and Rusty is going to help her."

"Good. Speaking of food, what's on the menu for tonight in the way of our dinner?"

"Well, fish, I think. Your dad brought over some rainbow trout that he caught this morning. Now he's attempting to teach me how to clean the things, but it's totally grossing me out, and Star thinks it's hilarious."

Travis chuckled, imagining the scenario. "Listen, you happen to be speaking to the master chef of fried trout. I'll cook the fish; you make everything else."

"It's a deal."

"Great." Travis grinned. "Put my dad on the phone, okay?"

"Okay."

Several moments lapsed, then Travis heard the gravelly voice of his father. At seventy years old, retired from a local foundry where he'd sweated away forty-plus years of his life, Reuben Larson now enjoyed his well-deserved free time. "Hello, son."

"Hi. I understand you're traumatizing my summer girl."

A jolly guffaw filled the phone line. "Oh, a little fish guts won't scare her off. She works for you, doesn't she?"

"Touché." Amusement tugged at the corners of his mouth, and suddenly Travis longed to be there, visiting with his parents and teasing Jena. He wanted to tickle his daughters and laugh along with them. "Stay put, will you, Dad? I'm leaving the office right now."

"Okay, Mother and I will hang around and pester Jena a little while longer."

Disconnecting the call, Travis grabbed his suit coat and attaché case, locking his door on the way out.

"Hey, where are you running off to?" Craig asked as Travis passed his office. "I thought we had plans to go to the Black Tie."

"Another time."

"Well. . .all right. Josh, Yolanda, and I will be there if you change your mind."

"I won't, but have fun."

After a parting nod to the firm's secretary, Travis left the office suites of Duncan, Duncan, and Larson for that haven called home.

∞

The month of June sped by, and on the morning of July third, as she made a pot of coffee, Jena mulled over the comment Travis's mother had made only yesterday. *"I haven't seen my son this happy since before Meg got sick. . .and it's all because of you."* While Jena knew she should feel flattered, she felt oddly unsettled. But maybe she was reading too much into Carol Larson's remark—and perhaps she was imagining those long looks that Travis often sent her way. Time and time again, Jena found him watching her, and it was all she could do not to feel nervous and self-conscious. What in the world could he be staring at?

Star, of course, had the answer. "He's crazy about you. Can't you tell? I can. . . and so can Rusty."

But Jena had trouble accepting that piece of logic, largely because she'd never known any man to be "crazy" about her. Except she prayed for that very thing—a man to love her and one she could love right back.

Giggles and heavy footfalls on the steps signaled the Larson family's descent from the second floor. Within moments, Travis, wearing blue jeans and a red polo shirt, strode into the kitchen with Carly perched on his shoulders. Mandi skipped in behind him.

"Good morning."

She smiled. "Good morning, Travis." Grabbing Carly's foot, she gave it a gentle tug, and the three-year-old blew her a soupy kiss that drizzled into her daddy's dark hair.

He groaned, lifting her off his shoulders, and Jena laughed.

Mandi hugged her around the waist. "Know what, Miss Jena?"

"What?" She kissed the top of the girl's head.

"My daddy's face is very scratchy when he wakes up."

"Oh." Jena tried not to react, but embarrassment soon engulfed her.

"Get over here and sit down, Mandi. Miss Jena doesn't want to hear about my face."

Her own face was flaming at the present. She turned around and pressed the button on the coffeemaker so Travis wouldn't see.

"And my face is not that scratchy."

"Yes it is, Daddy."

Mandi's matter-of-fact tone struck Jena's funny bone, and she was hard-pressed to contain her mirth. Hearing Travis's approach only made things worse.

"I see you laughing." He gave her a playful nudge.

Jena swallowed the rest of her amusement. "Sorry, Mandi cracked me up."

"Yeah, she's been known to crack me up, too." Leaning his back against the counter, Travis folded his arms, and while she put away the bag of coffee, Jena could feel the weight of his stare, although she couldn't get herself to meet his gaze. A heartbeat later, he reached over her and pulled down a box of cereal from the cupboard, giving Jena a generous whiff of his spicy aftershave. If she didn't know better, she could almost swear that he purposely tried to get her attention—just like when Jeff Sawyer used to pull her hair in the fifth grade because he had a crush on her. Maybe men weren't all that different from boys.

"So what's the plan for today?"

"The plan?"

His arm brushed against hers for the briefest of moments as he retrieved three bowls. "You mentioned something about a parade and a block party. . . ."

Well, if my brain hadn't just turned to mush, I could tell you.

"Bella invited us to the top of her penthouse for the fireworks tonight. I told you about that, didn't I?"

"Um, yeah."

Jena suddenly felt as though they were playing house. Travis was the daddy and she was the mommy. . . .

Oh Lord, help! My thoughts are in a jumble.

"Everything okay, Jen?"

Travis stood beside her again, and this time he touched her shoulder. Jena didn't even try to avert her line of vision and looked full into his face. She allowed her gaze to roam over his clean-shaven jaw and nicely shaped mouth before her eyes met his. She thought she could drown in their deep brown depths. But then she became aware of the tiny mar of concern that indented his dark brow. She forced a smile, and his frown disappeared.

"I'm fine," she reassured him. "I think I just need my morning cup of coffee."

Chapter 18

Jena glanced around the Minniatis' crowded penthouse. Bella really knew how to throw a bash. The kitchen, dining room, living room, and outdoor patio had been decorated in reds, whites, and blues, complete with streamers and balloons. Bella herself resembled an American flag as she mingled with her guests, most of whom were strapping young men. Jena presumed they represented the Mavericks indoor football team, and it appeared many had brought their wives and children along. In addition to a myriad of hors d'oeuvres and relish trays, the caterers served grilled tenderloin finger sandwiches. Jena thought it a shame that Star had already been booked for tonight, although she might not have been able to accommodate this crowd.

"When are the fireworks gonna start?" Mandi wanted to know.

Jena looked at her wristwatch. Eight o'clock. "In about an hour."

Carly heaved a sigh. "That's a long time."

"Not that long," Mandi argued. "Besides, it has to be dark out first before we can see the fireworks, so Daddy said we get to stay up late."

Carly ceased her complaining.

Jena coaxed the girls out onto the rooftop patio. A panoramic view of Lake Michigan spread out before them. A few miles away, a summer festival drew throngs of people to the lakefront, and Jena pointed out the Ferris wheel and other brightly lit attractions.

"Can we go there?" Carly asked. "To the fair?"

"Maybe. But not tonight." Jena thought a weekday afternoon might be a good time to attend, and if she recalled correctly, the festival ran for the next five days.

"There you are!"

Glancing over her shoulder, Jena saw Bella Minniati heading their way, wearing a navy skirt and a red and white silk top. Travis followed close behind her.

"I've been looking everywhere for you! Great news." Bella paused just inches away, and Jena got a whiff of her expensive perfume. "Travis is coming to work for the Mavericks. Isn't that awesome? It's about time he ditched those crooks, Duncan and Duncan. Don't you agree?"

Jena swallowed a laugh. "No comment. I'm only the summer girl."

Travis let his head drop back and hooted. "Since when did that ever stop you from voicing your opinions?"

She gave him an indignant glare before looking at Bella and rolling her eyes.

"You know, you two are really cute together. But. . ." Bella waved a hand. ". . .don't count on me to play matchmaker. I initiated a relationship between a couple of my best friends, and once they got married, they never forgave me."

Jena laughed.

"Listen, Bella, the last thing Jena and I need is you playing matchmaker."

"Whatever you say, Travis." She turned to Jena. "Now then, let's you and I talk some business."

"Bella, this is a party. You're supposed to relax and enjoy yourself."

"You hush."

He expelled an audible breath.

"Joe and I are purchasing a daycare center," Bella said, "and we'd like you to head it up—be its director."

"Me?" Jena could scarcely contain herself. Bella was offering her a dream come true! "When?"

"As soon as possible."

"Well, I, um, have to finish my last semester of college."

"Fine. Can you start January second?"

"Oh, well. . ."

Jena recalled her contract with Travis and what he'd said the afternoon before she'd signed it. *With people like Bella Minniati in the world, we need a contract.* Sliding her gaze to the right, Jena found him rocking on the soles of his feet as he stared out over the lake with an ever-so-innocent expression plastered on his handsome face. That snake! He'd known what he was doing the entire time. But in rethinking the matter, Jena realized she couldn't feel angry with him. He paid her a great salary, and she lived rent-free.

"Actually, Bella, I wouldn't be able to start until June first of next year."

"Oh?" Bella looked at Travis. "And why is that?"

"I signed a contract promising to watch Mandi and Carly for the next year."

"You traitor!" Bella exclaimed with a toss of her blond head. "How could you?"

"I'm not a traitor. You gave me fair warning."

Jena couldn't help feeling rather flattered that Bella and Travis were fighting over her services. "Maybe we can come to some sort of compromise."

Travis gave her a terse look that said he wouldn't budge on the matter.

"On second thought, Bella, I think you're going to have to find yourself another director."

The slim blond woman's face contorted in sheer aggravation. "Don't let him cow you, Jena. I'm sure there's a loophole in that contract somewhere."

"I doubt it, but it doesn't matter. Travis isn't cowing me. He's doing me a huge favor. I'm the one making out in this deal."

"Yeah, see, Bella?" Travis slipped an arm around Jena's shoulders. "I'm actually helping Jena out."

While that much was true, Jena couldn't help but wish she understood her boss. He didn't want Bella to play matchmaker, yet here he stood with his arm around her. Furthermore, he looked at her hard enough to make her knees weak. Was it just his way of being kind? She hadn't thought so this morning. . . .

"I can't believe you went behind my back and did this, Travis, knowing I wanted to hire Jena. I don't suppose you told her about my offer before you convinced her to sign your contract."

"I didn't go behind your back. You said you were giving me fair warning about stealing my summer girl." Travis shrugged. "So I did something about it."

Travis's hand slipped from Jena's shoulder to the back of her neck, where it felt like a branding iron against her skin. She held perfectly still, thinking he should remove it for propriety's sake but wishing he'd hold on to her forever.

"Listen, Bella, if you're looking to hire a spineless attorney, I'm not the guy. But I'm not a crook, either."

Bella pursed her lips and regarded him with a raised eyebrow. "Oh, you're right, Travis. I hate to admit it, but you're absolutely right. You played fair and square." She sighed and glanced at Jena. "Take a lesson from me. Keep your wits about you, or else you might find yourself working for Travis Larson for the rest of your natural-born days!"

"There are worse things in life, you know, Bella."

That's the truth, Jena thought with a grin. But before she could utter a syllable, her attention was captured by two little girls who couldn't wait for the sun to set.

Much later, on the way home after a spectacular display of fireworks, Jena noted that Travis seemed unusually quiet. She didn't question him and instead listened as Mandi sang an interesting rendition of "America the Beautiful." ". . .the land of the Braves and the home of the free."

Jena giggled inwardly. Travis was more influential on his daughters than she gave him credit. But since he was a very sports-minded male, she figured he'd do well as the Mavericks' lawyer.

They reached Travis's white stucco home, and while he carried Carly's sleeping form upstairs, Jena tended to Mandi. Before long, the girls were tucked into bed and on their way to a peaceful night's sleep.

"Hey, Jena. . ." Travis turned on the stairway, his right foot planted on the same step on which she stood, his other one step down. "I've been thinking. . . maybe I did bamboozle you into signing that contract. If you'd like, I'll let you out of it. The last thing I want is for you to be unhappy."

"I'm not unhappy. Not in the least."

"But you might be, come graduation time when that director's position looks a lot more rewarding than watching my daughters."

It occurred to Jena that Travis must have been brooding over this very issue since the show of fireworks began.

"Travis, the contract I signed with you works for me and my schedule. If Bella still needs a director in the spring, then. . .I'll let you negotiate that contract for me." She laughed.

He smiled. "You're sure?"

"Positive."

"Last chance."

She let it go. God showed her she'd done the right thing in agreeing to stay here for the next year. "Travis, did you hear what Mandi said to me tonight just before you turned off her bedroom lamp?"

"She said she loved you. She always says that. Carly, too. That's why I hate the thought of you getting another job."

"And that's why I'm not ready to go. I don't mean to overstate my position here, but I believe the girls need me right now."

"Hardly an overstatement. They do need you. . .and so do I."

Jena's heart seemed to stop at his admission, although she reasoned that he could be referring to the stability factor in his life and in the lives of his girls. But when Travis reached out and brushed several strands of hair off her cheek, Jena had a hunch stability wasn't what he meant. His eyes darkened with emotion, and her mouth went dry. *He's going to kiss me!*

But in the next moment, the telephone rang and jangled them both back to their senses.

"I should go home."

Travis nodded before bounding up the stairs to get the call. "G'night, Jen."

"Good night."

～

As the days progressed, Travis became engrossed with wrapping up his job at his law firm. Jena saw him for only minutes in the morning, and he rarely came home for dinner. She told herself she should feel relieved. No more long looks and emotionally charged interludes in the stairwell to deal with, but the truth was, Jena rather missed Travis. What's more, Mandi and Carly missed their daddy. But he phoned a couple of times each day, and the girls got a chance to chat with him.

Then the month of August arrived, bringing with it a week's worth of thunderstorms. Jena took the girls everywhere she could think of just to keep from getting shack happy. They visited the museum and the art center, saw a silly movie with Star and Rusty, went roller-skating—after which Jena could barely walk. By the end of the week, all she wanted to do was relax at home and read a good book. However, Jena made one more trip—to the library, where she checked out several videos for Mandi and Carly and a novel for herself. Back home, she carried the television and VCR unit up from the basement playroom, rearranged the furniture in the living room, and made a tent for the girls with every blanket she could find upstairs. Finally, she lit a cozy fire in the fireplace and flopped onto the sofa with her story, *A Bride for the Pirate*. All was going well as the storm lit up the gloomy sky outside—

But then Travis came home unexpectedly at two in the afternoon.

"Hi, Daddy!"

Uh-oh. At Mandi's exclamation, Jena froze. She'd been so engrossed in her book that she hadn't heard him come in. Lying on her back, she had her stocking feet up on the arm of the sofa, and she hoped Travis wouldn't mind that she was lounging on the job and that his formal living room had been turned upside down. Slowly she righted herself, combed her fingers through her hair, and stood.

"Hi, Travis." Jena thought he looked shocked as he surveyed the dismantled room. "I had planned to have this all cleaned up by the time you got home tonight."

He pursed his lips and nodded but didn't say a word.

"We've got a tent, Daddy."

"So I see." Looking away from Mandi, he met Jena's gaze. "Something wrong with the TV room or the playroom downstairs?"

She grimaced. "No fireplace."

"Ah. . ."

Carly ran to him, and Travis scooped her up into his arms. "Wanna come inside our tent and watch *Mary Poppins* with us?"

"I won't fit in your tent, baby." After hugging and kissing his youngest, he set her feet on the off-white carpet, straightened, and regarded Jena again. "But I'll tell you what I will do."

She gave him an expectant look and a tentative smile.

He loosened his tie. "I'm going to cancel my three thirty appointment and pop some corn. I mean, Jena, really, how could you have forgotten the popcorn?"

He walked off before she could reply.

Jena gaped in his wake. Sitting back down on the couch, she tried to convince herself of how glad she felt that Travis wasn't miffed at her, but all the while, anticipation surged through her being at the thought of his joining their rainy day diversion.

Minutes later, the smell of hot buttery popcorn filled the house, and Travis reentered the living room carrying a large bowl of the salty snack. He'd shed his tie and rolled the sleeves of his starched white dress shirt to his elbows. Pausing by the tent, he scooped out a portion for Mandi and Carly to share, then he headed for the other side of the sofa. . .or so Jena presumed. But instead Travis planted himself right beside her.

She couldn't curb the nervous laugh that escaped her.

"Popcorn?"

"No, thanks." She'd probably choke on it. Was he being overly friendly again or was he trying to make a point?

He tossed a handful of popcorn into his mouth. "What are you reading?"

Before she could stop him, he'd reached across her and snatched the novel.

He raised an eyebrow. "*A Bride for the Pirate*? Jena! What kind of junk is this?"

With her cheeks flaming from embarrassment, she grabbed back her book. "It's not smut. It's an inspirational romance. The sardonic pirate realizes the error of his ways and gives all his ill-gotten gains to charity."

"And here I thought you were watching *Mary Poppins*."

Jena laughed. She'd missed Travis's teasing. Then he stretched his arm out around the back of her shoulders, and she knew he wasn't just being overly friendly anymore.

She closed her eyes. "Travis, what are you doing?" When no reply came forth, she turned to look at him.

He met her questioning stare. "I'm falling for my summer girl, that's what I'm doing."

Jena glanced down at her hands, gripping the novel in her lap. She could scarcely believe the words Travis spoke—like something out of a beautiful love story.

"The truth is," he said, leaning closer, "I've been falling for you for months."

Her heart seemed to swell in her chest.

"Jena, say something, will you?"

"I can't. I think I just forgot how to breathe."

Hearing his laugh, she looked up at him.

"You're cute, know that?"

Moving his hand behind her head, Travis pulled her toward him and placed a gentle kiss on her lips. Jena's head began to swim in a pool of sheer pleasure that sent delicious tingles to her toes. She didn't want it to stop. As if sensing it, Travis kissed her again.

"Daddy. . . ?"

At the sound of Mandi's voice, Jena pulled back. She noted the stunned expression that crossed the little girl's face. But Travis didn't seem the least bit troubled and kept his arm around Jena.

"What is it, honey?"

Mandi inched her way forward before breaking out in a huge grin. "You were kissing Miss Jena!"

"Yes, I was."

Mandi's steps quickened until she reached her father and climbed up into his lap. Travis handed the popcorn to Jena, and she set it on the floor.

"Do you like Miss Jena, Daddy?" The six-year-old glanced from one to the other.

"Yeah, I like her a lot."

"Do you like my daddy, Miss Jena?"

"Sure I do. I wouldn't have let him kiss me if I didn't like him."

"Satisfied?" Travis poked his finger into Mandi's ribs, and she wiggled and giggled. This brought Carly over to join the fun.

After a tickle-fest, the front doorbell chimed. Both girls jumped off the couch and ran to answer it.

"Expecting someone?"

Jena shook her head. But it wasn't long before Bella Minniati's voice wafted through the foyer and into the living room.

"I suppose we should greet her."

"She'll find us. Don't worry." Travis sent Jena a sheepish grin. "She was the three thirty appointment I canceled."

"Nice going."

Travis laughed.

"Well, well, well," Bella said, entering the living room seconds later, "aren't you two a cozy sight."

"Look at our tent!" Carly cried as she dove inside.

"How fun!" Bella smiled, surveying the blankets suspended from the two armchairs.

"And my daddy was kissing Miss Jena," Mandi blurted before she, too, ducked into the tent.

"Kissing Miss Jena?" Bella raised a brow. "In the tent?"

Jena felt a blush creep up her cheeks and go straight to her hairline.

"No, he kissed her on the couch," Mandi informed their guest.

Bella chuckled. "Was that in your contract, too, Travis?"

He snapped his fingers as if to say he'd forgotten to add that small benefit to their agreement.

Unable to stand the embarrassment a moment longer, Jena stood. "Bella, would you like a cup of coffee?"

"I'd love one."

"Travis?"

"No, thanks."

Walking into the kitchen, Jena took her time preparing the rich-smelling brew. The scene with Travis played over and over in her mind. She felt his kiss on her lips and heard the words he'd said: *"I think I'm falling for my summer girl."*

Oh Lord, she silently prayed, *help me out here. I think I'm falling for Travis, too!*

Chapter 19

Bella stayed for dinner since Joe had to work late that night. She chattered on about her pregnancy and the daycare center. "We're closing on the building next Friday," she said. "I'll be interviewing for a director sometime after that. I think most of the staff can stay, but I really want someone with Christian values running the place."

Jena felt the weight of Bella's stare. But she occupied herself with tending to Carly and making sure the little one got more food inside of her than on the floor. As tempting as the director's position sounded, Jena had made her decision. However, she couldn't help wondering if or how things would change since she and Travis had admitted their fondness for each other.

Once they'd finished their meal, Bella helped Jena clear the table. Shortly thereafter, Star and Rusty stopped by to say hello. The rain had dissipated and the dark clouds broke, allowing slivers of sunshine through. When seven thirty rolled around, the girls kicked up a fuss and didn't want to go to bed, so Jena opted to take them for a walk. After all, the children had been cooped up practically all week. Everyone went along—Bella, Star, Rusty, and Travis.

Ambling along on the sidewalk, heading for Lake Drive, Travis sat Carly on his shoulders while, up ahead, Mandi rode her bike. Jena strolled in between Bella and Star, but the two carried on like magpies, so she stepped back and listened to Travis and Rusty discuss sports scores. The group stopped at the top of Atwater Beach to let the girls climb on the play equipment. Then they began their trek back by way of Capitol Drive.

Arriving home, Jena realized the girls needed baths. They had somehow managed to rove over mud puddles. One by one, the guests bid their adieus and went their separate ways. Jena had just gotten Carly into her nightie when Travis came upstairs. The girls soon talked him into reading them a book, so Jena took advantage of the time and cleaned up the kitchen—even though she was technically done for the day. But oddly, the lines of duty now blurred. That kiss this afternoon had changed everything as far as Jena was concerned. She only wished Travis would come downstairs so they could talk about it. About them. Had it meant more to her than to him? What was he thinking?

What was she thinking?

Oh Lord, I haven't had time to pray about this situation.

With the kitchen cleaned and still no sign of Travis, Jena meandered across the yard and up to her apartment. She kicked off her shoes, turned on the lights, and checked the phone's answering machine for messages. She picked through her mail, opening an envelope with her college's emblem on the upper left-hand corner. To her delight, it was her final class schedule. School began in just three short weeks. . . .

The phone rang, and Jena picked up the call.

"Hey, what about this living room? It's a disaster."

Jena winced. "Oh, sorry, Travis. I forgot all about it. I'll be right over."

She hung up the phone and raced downstairs and across the courtyard. All the while, she thought Travis sounded like her employer again.

Lord, You know I'm naïve when it comes to men. If Travis is falling for me, what's my position here? How do I define it, and when do I act like his employee and when do I act like his friend? Are we even friends?

Jena sighed, feeling baffled. Entering the living room, she pulled a blanket off one of the armchairs and began folding it when Travis caught her around the midsection. A startled gasp escaped her lips, and she dropped the blanket.

"Forget about cleaning up." His warm breath sent shivers down her spine. "I've got other things on my mind."

"Um, Travis. . ."

He began to kiss her neck, and while Jena enjoyed reading about handsome heroes sweeping women off their feet, she suddenly panicked, thinking she might have walked into a situation she couldn't handle.

She turned in his arms, and he kissed the protest from her lips. She felt like giving up and drowning in his ardor but knew she could not. At last she came up for air and managed to mutter, "Stop!" as he trailed kisses across her cheek and down her neck.

"Travis, please stop. Please!"

He brought his chin back, and Jena noted the surprise in his dark brown eyes. With her hands on his chest, she tried in vain to create some distance between them. She felt like sobbing. She felt cheap.

"You're going way too fast for me," she managed.

He looked full into her face and seemed to wrestle with his emotions. "My apologies. I thought the feeling was mutual."

"It is, but you're going to have to take things slowly with me. I'm. . .well, I'm really stupid when it comes to. . .you know, this kind of stuff."

He narrowed his gaze as an expression of disbelief crossed his features. "What are you telling me, Jena? That you're twenty-six and you've never—"

"No, I've never! My chastity belongs to the Lord until I get married!"

Travis appeared all the more shocked. "I didn't mean it that way. I wasn't about to. . .well, you know. . ."

She pressed her lips together, trying to stave off the threatening tears, but they leaked from her eyes despite her best efforts.

She lowered her chin. "I. . .I'm sorry. . . ."

He exhaled, and his breath was like a whisper across her cheek. "Don't cry, Jena, and there's nothing to be sorry about." He gathered her in his arms but held her in a much different way. "I'm the one behaving like a. . .pirate."

She laughed through her tears. "Not at all." Resting her chin against his shoulder, she wiped the moisture from her eyes. Had Travis been less than the gentleman he was, she might have gotten into some serious trouble. "But I really didn't mean to lead you on."

"You didn't lead me on. I mean, I know you're not that kind of woman. But at the same time, I didn't think a little fooling around would hurt anything."

Jena suddenly longed to make Travis understand her views—God's views. "I don't believe a man should touch a woman like that unless she belongs to him in marriage. I should have said something earlier this afternoon. But the truth is, I was sort of in shock when you kissed me on the couch, and I. . .well, I liked it."

A hint of a grin curled one side of Travis's mouth.

"But that doesn't mean it was right. I understand that physical intimacy between two people who are attracted to each other is just expected in this world. But, Travis, you and I aren't of the world anymore. We're Christians."

He narrowed his gaze, thinking over her reply. "Okay. Point taken," he said, allowing his arms to fall from around her waist. "I see what you mean."

"I'm so glad." Jena took a step back.

"I promise to behave myself from here on in."

She regarded him askance. "As my employer?"

Travis blinked, looking confused. "Well, yes. . .although I would like to be more than just your employer." He cocked his head. "What do you want?"

Jena smiled. "I want what God wants. If He has ordained a union between you and me, He'll show us as we walk with Him day by day and step by step."

Travis pursed his lips in his habitual manner. She knew right then that he'd taken her comments to heart.

"I think you're very charming." Jena felt her face warm as she spoke, but she couldn't seem to help what she said. The words glided off her tongue in all honesty.

His face brightened. "Why, thank you. That's the nicest thing anyone's said to me all day."

She laughed, and he pulled another fuzzy throw off the chair. "What do you say we clean up this living room?"

After a nod, she followed his lead and picked up the blanket she'd discarded only minutes before.

∽

Weeks later, Travis stared out the window of his new office. He had a decent

view from this downtown high-rise, unlike the one he'd occupied at DD&L—
make that DD&T now that Yolanda Timmerman had moved into a partnership
there. The career move had proven to be a good one for him. Travis felt he'd
made the right decision. But if it hadn't been for Jena, he probably wouldn't have
had the courage or confidence to leave the firm. God had brought her into his
life at just the perfect time.

Grinning to himself, Travis thought over the candlelit dinner they'd shared
last night in celebration of her birthday. Star prepared their meal and Rusty waited on them as he and Jena sat at his formally set dining room table. Forget any
romance; Travis had never laughed so hard in his life. He was only too glad he
didn't have to pay the wisecracking cook or tip their clumsy waiter.

Chuckling at the memory, he never imagined he'd have so much fun courting
a woman with old-fashioned values—or as Derek Ryan put it, "biblical standards."
Travis found it refreshing. What a relief to know Jena didn't adhere to the popular
culture. She reminded Travis of Meg—but that, and their faith, was as far as the
similarities went. Jena was her own person, and the more Travis got to know her,
the more he grew to love her. Mandi and Carly adored her. His parents liked and
respected her. . . .

*What am I waiting for? Why don't I ask her to marry me? She'd say yes. I can see
it in her eyes. . . .*

"Travis Larson?"

"Hmm?" He whirled around to find a broad-shouldered young man standing
in his doorway.

"I'm Bernie Thomas. Isabella Minniati sent me over to discuss some of the
terms in my contract. My agent will be here in a few minutes."

"Great." Travis smiled and stuck out his right hand. The other man shook it.
"Nice to meet you. Have a seat, Bernie."

∽

Jena looked up at the sky and decided she'd never seen so many stars. They
sparkled like diamonds against black velvet.

"Jen?"

She turned to Travis, who sat in an adjacent lawn chair, his feet up on the
white wrought-iron table.

"It's ninety degrees out at ten o'clock at night. How can you be drinking hot
coffee?"

She laughed and glanced down at the cup in her hand. "It's a terrible habit.
I should quit it. But after all the years of going to school during the day and
working at night—or vice versa—then doing homework in the wee hours of the
morning, I got used to living on caffeine."

"This semester ought to be easier for you."

"It's going to be a piece of cake, and I have you to thank for that."

"It works both ways, Jen."

She smiled. He sure was handsome, sitting there in the courtyard under the moonlight.

"So are you still praying about marrying a man in the ministry?"

Jena frowned. "What?"

Travis chuckled. "Never mind. I guess there's my answer."

She rolled her eyes and looked back up into the sky. *I'm praying about marrying you, silly,* she wanted to say. But she couldn't bring herself to be quite so audacious. Having seen Travis interact with Star and Bella, she sensed that he didn't care for bold and overconfident women, although he could hold his own around them. Jena had seen that, too.

She heard him slap at a mosquito. "Got any special plans for Saturday?"

Jena thought it over. Two days from now. . .

"No, not that I can recall right off the top of my head."

"Well, pencil me into your agenda. We're going to do something special. I don't know what yet, but you, me, and the girls will have a great time."

"Okay."

Travis stood. "I hate to do this, but I'm going in. The bugs are almost as bad as the humidity. You're welcome to join me. We can watch a movie or something."

Jena was tempted—very tempted. She knew Travis would behave like a complete gentleman, and she'd like nothing more than to spend extra time with him. But she had been trying to find a couple of hours all day to sit down and pay her bills and fold her clean laundry. "Oh, I guess I'll call it a night. I have things I should probably accomplish by tomorrow."

"Okay, then I'll walk you home."

She laughed. The distance was probably twenty feet or less.

Travis held out his hand. Jena took it, and he pulled her to her feet. At her apartment door, he placed a chaste kiss on her cheek.

" 'Night, Jen."

"Good night, Travis."

She walked inside, latched the door behind her, then climbed the narrow staircase to her apartment. She turned on the television and listened to the tail end of the nightly newscast as she began her chores.

By midnight, she crawled into bed, and just when she began to doze, she thought she heard the downstairs door open and slam shut. She sat up in bed, her heart racing in fear as she heard footfalls ascending the steps. They sounded too light and quick to belong to Travis or any other man. Next she heard keys jangle as the top door was unlocked and opened. It, too, was forcefully closed as if pushed with a foot.

Curiosity replaced her panic, and Jena slipped out of bed. She grabbed her robe and slipped it on. A thunk sounded, once, twice, as if someone had dropped a heavy box or luggage—or both—on the living room floor. From the doorway of her bedroom, she saw a light go on. With slow, measured steps, Jena made her way toward the intruder. Pausing in the dining room, she thought she recognized the slender woman whose sandy-brown hair was swept up off her neck. She'd seen her photograph around Travis's house.

The woman turned and shrieked when she spotted Jena. "Oh!" she exclaimed, covering the left side of her chest. "Oh, you nearly gave me a heart attack."

"You scared me half to death, too."

The woman narrowed her gaze, a trait Jena knew so well. "Who are you, and what are you doing here?"

"My name is Jena Calhoun. Travis hired me to take care of Mandi and Carly this summer." She smiled. "You must be his sister, Glenda."

"You're very astute, aren't you? Well, that's good. You'll be able to find another job in no time." Glenda collapsed onto the couch. "My flight at O'Hare got canceled, and I was forced to take the bus from Chicago to Milwaukee. But I'm back now, so first thing tomorrow morning you can pack your things and leave."

Jena didn't reply as questions flitted through her mind. Hadn't Glenda left to get married? Where was her husband? Did Travis know his sister had come back? Probably not!

Padding back to the bedroom, Jena closed the door without a sound. Next she picked up the phone and pressed speed dial.

"Yeah, hello."

"Travis, it's Jena. Sorry to wake you, but, um. . .we've got a little problem here."

Chapter 20

"I can't believe you're taking her side over mine."

Travis turned from his office window, where he'd been watching Jena and the girls walk up Shorewood Boulevard, heading to the high school for Mandi's morning swimming lesson. He glared at his sister. "You've got a lot of nerve showing up and making demands."

"Travis, I'm your sister."

"Doesn't matter. You happen to be interrupting a very delightful romance between Jena and me."

Glenda expelled a sigh of disgust. "Oh, Travis, she is so totally not your type."

"That just proves how little you know of the situation. . .and of Jena and me."

Glenda stepped toward him. "Travis, I have nowhere else to go."

"Then you'll have to move in with Mom and Dad."

"Are you out of your mind? I can't call them!" Glenda's face contorted with indignation. "They haven't forgiven me for eloping with Tony."

"Months ago, I would have said I hadn't forgiven you, either. But the truth is, your leaving was the best thing that happened to me."

"Oh, thanks a lot."

He grinned at the quip. "So what happened with Tony?"

"He's a loser, that's what happened."

Travis chewed the corner of his lower lip and folded his arms as he contemplated Glenda's remark. Tony Jenkins had never appeared to be a "loser" while he'd been Travis's assistant for eighteen months at DD&L. "What constitutes a loser?"

"A man who can't even bring in a salary that'll support his. . .family. That's a loser."

"What, did Tony tell you to get a job or something?"

"Or something," came her vague reply.

Travis digested the news. The situation didn't seem so bad after all. Glenda would come to her senses and go back to Tony in a day or two. In the meantime, she could continue to sleep in Mandi's room while his daughters shared Carly's bed.

"Travis, I think our arrangement worked out great, and that's why I want things to be the way they used to be."

"That was another lifetime ago. Our arrangement doesn't exist anymore. I don't know how to explain it exactly, but I feel like a completely different person." He paused and wondered about divulging his secret, then decided Glenda might as well know. "I'm also planning to ask Jena to marry me tomorrow." Travis rubbed his palms together. "I'm going to take her to the mall and stop in front of Rush's House of Diamonds, propose, and let her pick out her own engagement ring. Of course, I'll have to tease her a little bit first. That'll be half the fun."

"Travis, you're off your rocker."

"Yeah, but I'm happy, the girls are happy, Jena's happy. . .so who cares?"

Glenda rolled her brown eyes. "Take it from your little sister. Stay single. Play the field."

"I don't want to play the field. I want Jena. Besides, I've been married before, and I was happy then, too."

"Which raises another question. How can you disregard Meg's memory by remarrying someone like that. . .that. . ."

"Watch it." He pointed a finger at her. "You're treading on very dangerous ground right now. As for my remarrying, Meg would want me to be happy, and she'd like Jena."

Travis walked out of his office and into the kitchen, where he poured himself a cup of coffee. Glancing at the clock above the kitchen sink, he realized he had to leave soon in order to make his ten o'clock appointment. He had a full day ahead and no time for his sister's antics. But one thing seemed sure: Glenda couldn't stay here and harass Jena all day.

She came up behind him as he twisted on the top of his travel mug.

"Travis, I helped you out when you were in a bind. I practically raised Mandi and Carly. They're like my own children. Carly was a newborn when Meg died, and—"

"And I appreciate everything you did for me and the girls, okay? But things are different now." He expelled a weary breath. "Look, Jena said she didn't need the Volvo today. Take the car and go visit Mom and Dad. Tonight you can sleep in Mandi's room again."

"Travis, that's only temporary. I need a residence that's. . .well, more permanent."

He raised a brow. "Why?"

Glenda tore her gaze away from him, and tears filled her eyes. "Because Tony's already filed for divorce, and I'm going to have a baby."

"What?" He felt his jaw go slack before he shook his head. "Oh man."

"I have nowhere else to go, Trav."

"Okay, okay." He held up a hand to forestall the giant pity party he sensed was coming. Leave it to his sister to dump a crisis on him just as he had to take off for work. "Glenda, I want you to go visit Mom today. The two of you need to talk. I'll try to get home early this afternoon, and we can discuss your situation further, all right?"

She shrugged and swatted at an errant tear.

Moving forward, Travis kissed his sister's cheek and gave her a quick hug. "Relax. Everything'll be okay. Try not to worry, all right?"

Again she merely shrugged, and as he left the house, Travis prayed he'd be able to take his own advice.

∽

Jena arrived back home at noon to find Travis's sister talking on the phone and watching a daytime drama in the den. Jena kept the girls in the kitchen while she put together one of their favorite lunches—peanut butter and jelly sandwiches and sliced apples. But even keeping her distance, Jena couldn't help overhearing snippets of Glenda's conversation—mainly because the woman hollered every other word. Soon Jena put the facts together: Glenda's marriage didn't work out, she was pregnant, and her parents didn't want her moving in with them.

Oh Lord, this woman needs to know You so desperately. . . .

When Glenda sauntered into the kitchen, looking as though she'd been crying, Jena tried to reach out to her.

"Can I make you some lunch?"

"No. Thanks."

"I'm available if you need somebody to talk to."

"I don't." She knelt down in between her nieces' chairs. "How about we go to the movies this afternoon? You two and me—just like old times."

Both girls smiled.

"Can Miss Jena come, too?" Mandi asked.

"No, this is just for Aunty Glenda and her girls. I haven't seen you in so long, and I've missed you. That's why I came back."

Mandi glanced over her shoulder and gave Jena a worried look. "But Miss Jena takes care of us now."

"Don't you want me taking care of you anymore? Remember how much fun we used to have?"

Jena suddenly felt like a lioness who wanted to defend her cubs. "Glenda, that's unfair to put Mandi and Carly in such a terrible position. They're children. They don't want to decide between you and me. Besides, it's not their decision to make. Let Travis handle it."

If the glare that Glenda hurled her way had been a stone, Jena would have dropped dead from the impact. "Stay out of it. This is a family affair." She turned back to the girls. "Come on. Let's go see a movie."

Glenda took hold of the girls' forearms and practically dragged them off their seats.

"My samich!" Carly cried, stomping her feet.

Jena put a hand over her mouth to keep from saying something she'd regret. Carly was tired. She needed a nap.

Glenda grabbed the food off the plate and handed it to the three-year-old.

"Here. Eat it on the way."

Mandi glanced at Jena with uncertainty pooling in her eyes.

Jena tamped down her own disquiet and smiled at Mandi. "It'll be okay, precious." Gazing over the girl's head, she saw Glenda heading for the back door. "Hey, wait a sec!"

The woman turned around. "Now what?"

"Do you think it might be wise to call Travis and let him know you're taking the girls?"

Glenda laughed. "I don't have to pester my brother at work for such a trivial matter. I practically raised these children. But you've been here, what—three months?" A little sneer curved her perfectly shaped lips. "If you feel you need to call, go ahead. Travis knows my cell phone number. If there's some problem, he can call me. But there won't be."

Jena didn't have a reply. She didn't know enough about the situation to give one. Moreover, she had no idea what Travis had told his sister this morning. Maybe he'd consented to the movie.

With every muscle in her body tense with protest, Jena watched Glenda leave with the girls. Next she walked to the phone. She didn't care if the matter was "trivial"; she wanted Travis to know about it. Besides, he never cared when she phoned him at work.

Her hands trembled as she punched in his number. But her heart sank when the receptionist said he was out of the office. Jena tried his mobile phone but got his voice mail. She decided to leave a message. "Travis, it's Jena. I just thought I'd let you know your sister. . ." She paused to clear the emotion from her throat. "Your sister took the girls to a movie this afternoon. She said if there was a problem, you could call her cell phone. She said you knew the number. See you later."

Jena hung up and found that she felt so upset she shook like a leaf in an autumn wind. It occurred to her then that she hadn't just fallen in love with Travis—she'd fallen in love with his daughters, too.

A hard knocking at the back door caused her to jump.

"Jena? Jena, are you there?"

"Yes, come in, Mrs. Barlow."

The white-haired lady stepped inside the house and smiled. She wore a navy floral housedress, and on her feet were canvas slip-ons. "I don't mean to be nosy, dear, but was that Glenda Larson pulling away with the girls in the car?"

Jena nodded. . .and then she just couldn't help it. She burst into tears and blurted out the whole sordid mess.

"And now she wants her apartment and her job back. . . ."

Mrs. Barlow pulled Jena into her capable tanned arms. "There, there. You know as well as I do that Travis isn't about to let that happen. He loves you, Jena."

"I love him, too."

"I can tell. It's been so exciting to watch your relationship bloom like my gladiolas!"

Jena had to laugh at the analogy, then stepped back and wiped away her tears. "Mrs. Barlow, it's amazing—my mother is so excited. She called me twice this week to ask if Travis popped the question yet."

The older woman chuckled. "That's what God can do. He can repair and restore."

Jena agreed, but then a cloud of gloom overshadowed her burst of joy. "But what about Glenda? What about this situation? I feel like she hates me."

"Well, I do have a suggestion. I don't know if you'll like it, but. . ."

"Let's hear it." Jena peered into the woman's age-lined face. "You're the one who got me the job here. Maybe God will use you in this predicament with Travis's sister, too."

⁓

Travis listened to Jena's message. Hearing the strained tone in her voice, he knew she was upset. He tried to call her back, but there wasn't any answer at home. When he got ahold of Glenda, he gave her a tongue-lashing, not that it made a difference to his selfish sister. Then, all afternoon, he tried to wrap things up and get home, but the more he attempted to speed things along, the more complications arose. But at last he pulled into his driveway shortly after five o'clock. By phone, he had discovered Glenda and the girls were home, but Jena was still unaccounted for, much to Travis's dismay. He made a mental note to buy her a cell phone at the mall tomorrow—along with an engagement ring.

He walked into the small courtyard and immediately knew things were wrong. Toys had been thrown everywhere. Through an open window upstairs, he heard Carly bawling at the top of her lungs. It was a wonder the neighbors hadn't summoned the cops; the kid sounded like she was being tortured.

Entering the house, Travis made his way into the kitchen and saw the sink of cups and plastic plates. He placed his attaché case on the table and realized too late that he'd set it in a glob of ketchup. A curse surfaced, but Travis gulped it back down.

Lord, I can't handle this. You know I can't handle this. I lived like this for three years, and I cannot—will not—go back.

Mandi ran into the kitchen, her face red and blotchy, tears streaming from her brown eyes. "Daddy," she sobbed, "Miss. . . Jena's. . .gone."

At that moment, Travis didn't know if he should panic over the words his daughter said or the fact that she was about to hyperventilate.

"Mandi, calm down." He lifted her into his arms, and she clung to him, crying in a way that made melodramatics seem calm and rational. "Shh, Mandi, it's okay. Don't cry."

Glenda appeared in the doorway. "You know, Travis, these girls are out of control. I mean, I'm gone for just three months and look what that summer girl has done to them."

Travis felt his blood pressure hit the ceiling. "Glenda, it's a good thing I've got Mandi in my arms right now, or I might be tempted to—"

"Oh, please! Spare me your idle threats." Her face scrunched up into a mask of resentment. "And after all I've done for you!"

"Where's Jena?"

"Don't ask me. She was gone when we came home from the movies."

"See. . .Daddy? Sh—she's gone," Mandi whimpered.

Travis shook his head. "She's not really gone. She's probably just at the store or something."

"Sorry to be the one to tell you this, Trav, but she packed up her stuff in the apartment, bedding and everything. She's gone."

"What were you doing in Jena's apartment?"

"Don't yell at me! The girls were looking for her." Glenda threw her hands in the air. "I'm always the bad guy. Mom does the same thing. Everything that goes wrong in life gets blamed on me."

Travis watched his sister stomp off, and he felt as though his life was spinning out of control. But somehow his common sense managed to surface through the tumult. He knew Jena as well as he knew anyone. She wouldn't just pack up and move out without saying something to him.

"Mandi, stop crying," he said, setting his daughter down. "Miss Jena is not gone. I promise you she isn't. I don't know where she is right now, but she'll be back, okay? I promise."

The little girl nodded, and her sobs began to subside.

Travis stood and placed his hands on his hips, squeezing back his shoulder blades in an effort to ease his stress. He became aware of Carly's temper fit, still in progress, and debated whether he should go up there and see if he could settle her down or let her scream it out. But at that very instant, Jena came strolling into the courtyard carrying an overfilled laundry basket.

"Mandi." He grinned. "Miss Jena's back."

His daughter's eyes widened, and she ran for the back door. Travis followed her outside. Seeing him, Jena smiled, but then her eyebrows dipped into a frown as she glanced at the second floor.

"Oh, poor Carly. I knew she needed a nap today."

Mandi threw her arms around Jena's waist, nearly knocking her backward. Travis caught Jena's elbow, steadied her, and then took the basket.

"Want to tell me what's going on?"

She gave Mandi a little hug and kissed the top of her head. "Let me take care of Carly, and then. . .Travis, I have to talk to you about something."

His eyes widened. "Yeah, I'd say so."

"Will you take the clean laundry up to the apartment for me?"

He nodded as Jena ran into the house. Looking at Mandi, Travis inclined his head toward the apartment door. "C'mon, you can help me."

For the first time since he'd come home that day, he saw his daughter smile.

~

After rocking Carly to sleep, Jena made her way across the yard to the apartment she once called home. She couldn't wait to tell Travis about Mrs. Barlow's wonderful idea. It solved everything. What's more, as the afternoon progressed, Jena had become more and more burdened for Glenda. The woman obviously had emotional wounds that ran deep, and Jena prayed for the chance to tell Glenda about the Great Physician.

She climbed the stairs and entered the living room, where she found Travis and Mandi sitting on the couch, the six-year-old nestled against her daddy's chest.

Jena smiled. "What a sweet picture. I wish I had my camera handy."

"Hmm. . . I'm anxious to hear why it isn't handy. From the looks of this place, you've moved out."

Jena lost her grin. "That's what I wanted to talk to you about."

"I figured." He sat up and plucked Mandi from his lap. "Go play while I talk to Miss Jena, okay?"

"Okay."

Mandi strode toward the door but paused beside Jena and gave her another hug. Jena returned the show of affection, and the child continued on her way.

Travis stepped forward and gathered Jena into his arms. He held her as if she'd been away for six months and they were just now reunited. When he pulled back, she saw that his brown eyes had grown misty. "You're moving right back in here, Jena. I'm not letting you go."

"I don't want you to let me go—and I'm not going, except to Mrs. Barlow's house. I moved in with her. Temporarily."

Travis raised his brows. "You moved in with Mrs. Barlow?"

Jena nodded. "I want to win your sister over. I want to be her friend. I want to show her the love of Christ. She needs to know His love. That's why I think Glenda should have her apartment back."

"Great sentiments, Jen, but this place will be too small once her baby arrives."

"But that's six months from now, and by then she and her husband could be back together, and you and I—"

Jena halted in midsentence. She couldn't believe her blunder.

"And you and I. . .what?" Travis had the nerve to smirk.

She felt her face begin to flame. "I think I, um, forgot what I was going to say."

"Oh, sure you did. Know what I think?"

She didn't reply, but the heat of her embarrassment spread to her neck and ears.

"I think you've been reading too many of those bride stories and wedding magazines."

Chagrined, she looked away and stared at an imaginary spot on the wall until Travis took hold of her chin and urged her gaze back to his. All traces of humor disappeared from his face.

"I love you, Jena."

"I love you, too."

"Know what else I think?" He touched her lips with his and murmured, "I think you're going to make a beautiful bride. . . ."

Epilogue

Emerald green and white silk flowers, arranged in graceful swags, lined the end of each pew all the way to the altar. After earning her degree and graduating from college only two weeks ago, Jena now stood in the back of the church in preparation to meet her groom.

She watched Star glide down the center aisle. Mandi and Carly, dressed in frilly white dresses, seemed to float just behind her. Jena still couldn't believe she had put this wedding together in less than four months. Then again, it wouldn't have been possible without Mrs. Barlow and Glenda's help. It had taken awhile for her future sister-in-law to warm up, but by the time the leaves had turned to their autumn colors, Jena and Glenda had become friends. Shortly thereafter, Bella Minniati offered her a part-time job at her daycare center, which Glenda accepted. Under Bella's influence, her attitude improved, and Jena suspected it wouldn't be long before Glenda came to Christ. Glenda's husband, Tony, noticed a positive difference in her and halted divorce proceedings. He even showed up today to see Travis get married.

Suddenly Mr. Zuttle, the organist, began to play the "Bridal March," and Jena experienced a sudden attack of nerves. As if sensing it, her father gave her hand a reassuring squeeze before threading it around his elbow. Their procession began.

Up ahead, Jena glimpsed Travis, decked out in his black tuxedo. He looked so handsome that she could scarcely take her eyes off him. With cameras flashing on each side, she was only vaguely aware of passing her friends, relatives, and church family.

Reaching the altar, Jena's father handed her to Travis. He smiled into her eyes before looking at the pastor, who stood poised and ready to perform the ceremony. Star, the maid of honor, adjusted Jena's lacy veil and the gown's elegant train, while Jena's brother, acting as the best man, grinned nearby. Jena had wanted more bridesmaids, including Glenda and Bella, but both women were great with child. Then, with the time constraint, it had seemed much simpler to coordinate two people rather than an entire wedding party.

Thank You, Lord, that my family made the time to be with me here today. Maybe this wedding will bring us closer together. . . .

"Who gives this woman to this man?" the pastor asked.

"I do, her father," Jena heard her dad say, just as he'd rehearsed the night before.

Smiling, she clung to Travis as her heart swelled with love. She'd never felt so happy in all her life. Who ever would have thought that an interim summer job would become her lifelong career?

A Letter to Our Readers

Dear Readers:

In order that we might better contribute to your reading enjoyment, we would appreciate your taking a few minutes to respond to the following questions. When completed, please return to the following: Fiction Editor, Barbour Publishing, Inc., P.O. Box 719, Uhrichsville, OH 44683.

1. Did you enjoy reading *Wisconsin Weddings* by Andrea Boeshaar?
   ❏ Very much—I would like to see more books like this.
   ❏ Moderately—I would have enjoyed it more if _____
   _____
   _____

2. What influenced your decision to purchase this book?
   (Check those that apply.)
   ❏ Cover   ❏ Back cover copy   ❏ Title   ❏ Price
   ❏ Friends   ❏ Publicity   ❏ Other

3. Which story was your favorite?
   ❏ *Always a Bridesmaid*   ❏ *The Summer Girl*
   ❏ *The Long Ride Home*

4. Please check your age range:
   ❏ Under 18   ❏ 18–24   ❏ 25–34
   ❏ 35–45   ❏ 46–55   ❏ Over 55

5. How many hours per week do you read? _____

Name _____

Occupation _____

Address _____

City _____ State _____ Zip _____

E-mail _____

If you enjoyed

Wisconsin
WEDDINGS

then read

Louisiana
BRIDES

by Kathleen Y'Barbo

Three Young Women's Hearts

Are Rooted in the Bayou

Bayou Fever
Bayou Beginnings
Bayou Secrets

If you enjoyed

Wisconsin WEDDINGS

then read

LOVE LETTERS

*Four Generations of Couples
Changed by Expressions of the Heart*

Love Notes by Mary Davis
Cookie Schemes by Kathleen E. Kovach
Posted Dreams by Sally Laity
eBay Encounter by Jeri Odell

If you enjoyed

Wisconsin WEDDINGS

then read

The Spinster Brides OF CACTUS CORNER

Four Women Make Orphans a Priority and Finally Open Doors to Romance

The Spinster and the Cowboy by Lena Nelson Dooley
The Spinster and the Lawyer by Jeri Odell
The Spinster and the Doctor by Frances Devine
The Spinster and the Tycoon by Vickie McDonough
